THE WITCH OF TOPHET COUNTY

THE
WITCH
OF
TOPHET
COUNTY

J. H. SCHILLER

Podium

For Mike, who never doubted.

Cover design by Lisa Marie Pompilio
Organization Chart by Sandro Fazlinovic

ISBN: 978-1-0394-5225-1

Published in 2023 by Podium Publishing
www.podiumaudio.com

Podium

THE WITCH OF TOPHET COUNTY

COUNTY CLERK
MICANA'GOS
QUEEN OF PUS & BLOOD

HUMAN MAYOR
HEATHER CHADWICK
#LADYBOSS

SHERIFF
LOMELZAR
DEVOURER OF HOPES & PEOPLE

HIGH LORD OF
RECREATION & CULTURE
ELLIE DAWSON
SHE WHO WON THE GOLD

HIGH LORD OF
PUBLIC SAFETY
ACHARTHO
THE WINGED HORROR

HIGH LORD OF
PUBLIC WORKS
YI'DANAG
THE UNSEEN CREEPING HORROR

DREAD LIBRARIAN
CHLOGHA
KEEPER OF ARCANE KNOWLEDGE

CHIEF MEDICAL EXAMINER
XAY CHANTHAVONG

DREAD LORD OF
ANIMAL CONTROL
MEG'ATHATH
MOTHER OF NIGHTMARES

DREAD CULTURE CZAR
STHOTHUGUA
BANE OF THE UNCLEAN REALMS

DREAD LORD OF CORRECTIONS
ZSTHAOR
SPILLER OF THE LIFEBLOOD
OF THE ANCIENTS

DREAD LORD OF
SOLID WASTE MANAGEMENT
YI'DANAG
THE UNSEEN CREEPING HORRO

DREAD LORD OF
FIRE & RESCUE
E'STHACT
THE LIVING FLOOD

DREAD LORD OF
WATER & SEWER
FRANCISCO SANTOS

DREAD LORD OF
ENERGY & INFRASTRUCTURE
TIFFANY CLARK

TOPHET COUNTY ORGANIZATION CHART

HIGH LORD OF
ECONOMIC DEVELOPMENT
Y'GGARLOS
MISTRESS OF DESPAIR

HIGH LORD OF
HEALTH & HUMAN SERVICES
N'EITHAMIQUG
THE SPINNER OF SORROW

HIGH LORD OF
ADMINISTATION
NOMMAQUTH
BUBBLES

LIAISON TO
CATACHTHONIC UNIVERSITY
DR. CHRISTIAN CARCOSA

DIRECTOR
HEALTH DEPARTMENT
MH'ADRASH
THE JEWELED MONSTROSITY

DREAD LORD OF
HUMAN RESOURCES
SATHACH
LOATHSOME OF LOATHSOMES

DREAD LORD OF ZONING
NAGHACTHOSHA
LORD OF FESTERING SORES

DREAD HEALTH INSPECTOR
MY'YGGDESS
THE ELDRITCH EARWORM

DREAD LORD OF
INFORMATION TECHNOLOGY
ICHAGNO
DOOM OF WORLDS

DIRECTOR
SMALL BUSINESS ADMINISTATION
PATRICIA JONES

DIRECTOR
MANAGEMENT & BUDGET
RONNIE COFFMAN

COUNTY WITCH

CONNIE LINGUS*
GODSFORSAKEN CHAOS GNOME

*PSEUDONYM

DREAD LORD OF
INTERNAL AFFAIRS
STAAR'LAT
SHE WHO LURKS IN DARKNESS

CHAPTER ONE

Read at Your Own Risk

The witch of Tophet County traced her index finger along a line of arcane runes as she read the final words of *The Necronomicon*. She slammed the heavy human-skin-bound piece of shit closed. It shuddered and sailed to an empty stretch of shelving in the Read at Your Own Risk room.

Cthulhu's scaly tea bags. She'd wasted eight months of her life translating eye-screwing squiggles into human words only to find out the entire 666-page turd contained not one freaking word about magical contracts. She glared up at the book, which ruffled its pages in a taunting flutter.

The witch braced her hands on the table and stood, preparing to summon a swarm of silverfish, but a ripple of motion on the shelf above *The Necronomicon* drew her gaze. The corner of a slim volume now protruded from an otherwise-flat row of spines. It would've been difficult to spot in the flickering light of wall-mounted torches, but its jaunty angle bared a flash of white pages. After suffering through an infestation of sentient spores a few years back, the witch knew better than to handle unfamiliar Nomicons. She picked up her barbecue tongs, grabbed the book, and deposited it on the table.

The Necronomicon exploded in a frenzy of eat-shit page flapping, obviously trying to distract the witch from her discovery. She ignored it.

The new book's cover was that blacker-than-black shade known in occult circles as fuligin. It looked like a window into the lightless void of deep space. She sat down and eyed it with growing excitement. In contrast to *The Necronomicon*'s tantrums, this book fell open invitingly, displaying the title page: *The Archonomicon.*

Now, *that* was interesting. She'd slogged through dozens of Nomicons over the years. Not this one. With growing excitement, she turned the page and began to read.

Za'gathoth, the Mindless Mother, matriarch of the Archons of the Nether Realms, lies dreaming in her profane temple beneath the Catachthonic River. To reveal hidden truths, seekers may call upon the Mother by standing on the Bridge of Sighs and speaking her name. Za'gathoth will emerge from the waters and take the seeker to her lair, where she will either divulge esoteric knowledge or consume the one who dared summon her, rending mind, body, and soul until not even the phantom of a memory remains. Depends on her mood. It's a crapshoot, really.

A loud tone chimed through the library's intercom. "Attention, patrons," gargled a wet-sounding voice. "Derleth Memorial Library will close in five minutes. Please collect your belongings and proceed to an open kiosk to check out your materials."

By all hell's devils, the books in the Nomicon section were for in-library use only, and the Dread Librarian's bibliophasic sorcery prevented them from being copied or photographed. The witch scowled up at the shelves. She'd never seen *The Archonomicon* before. If she didn't take it now, she might never find it again, and time was running out. The probationary triskaidecade of her County employment contract ended on the winter solstice, giving her less than two months to sever the bond that held her in thrall. She'd tried everything she could think of over the past thirteen years, but her contract still had her in a magical chokehold. This book might be her only shot at freedom.

The witch bent her head and whispered, "Will you come with me?"

The last thing she needed was to abscond with it, only to have the damn thing screech like a banshee or shoot her with poisoned darts. *The Archonomicon* flipped itself closed and assumed an air of readiness. She'd take that as a yes. She stood and circled around the table to block *The Necronomicon*'s view, then shrugged out of her hoodie and used it to swaddle the book.

Soft, rasping snores emanated from her oversized backpack, which was propped against one leg of the table. She eased the bundle inside and wedged it under the sleeping body of her familiar, then slid her notebook and pocket dictionary of barbarous tongues in as well. *The Necronomicon* thrashed on its shelf as she pushed through the iron-barred door, stepping out of what looked like a medieval wizard's study—complete with meticulously scattered artificial dust—into the fluorescent multimedia nightmare of a modern library.

Sprinting for the exit would only draw attention, so she forced herself to cross the lobby in a nonchalant stroll. The door was a mere ten feet away when someone grabbed her arm and tugged her to a halt. A burly man in a security guard's uniform glared up at her.

Perfect. Todd the Incredible Asshole.

"I'm going to need to search your bag."

The witch crossed her arms, looking down her nose at his freckled bald spot. "Is that so?"

"Something triggered the RAYOR room alarm," he said, hitching up his belt. "You were the only one in there."

That godsdamned *Necronomicon*. . .more like Narc*onomicon*.

"Suit yourself." She jostled her bag as she slid it off her shoulders, startling its occupant into surly wakefulness, and held it out to the uniformed man.

Todd hefted the backpack by its padded straps. "Awfully heavy." Then he loosened the drawstring and peered into the bag. "Gee, I wonder what you've got in—"

Twenty-one pounds of snarling rage catapulted out of the shadowed depths and latched on to Todd's face with all three paws. He shrieked and dropped the bag. The witch snatched it, held it open, and whistled to Keyser Söze, who hissed and leaped inside. They'd have to make a run for it.

A bubbling, phlegmy voice called, "Halt, Witch!"

The witch plastered a vapid smile on her face and turned to greet the Dread Librarian. "Is there a problem?"

Chlogha, Keeper of Arcane Knowledge, glowered at her. Even for an Archon, she had an impressive glower—the kind that turned hair white and loosed bowels. Then again, as a nine-foot-tall toad with a single bloodshot eye, an insectile proboscis bracketed by pincers, and corpse-green skin that shimmered like an oil slick, she didn't need to do much to strike terror in the heart of man. Or witch.

A tentacle unfurled from the wriggling nest under Chlogha's mouth. "The book, please."

"Book?" The witch bit her lip, as though struggling to remember something that had slipped her mind. "Oh, the book. I've got it right—"

She spun and darted toward the door. With a moist roar, Chlogha lunged after her. The witch had just touched the push bar when a tentacle tore the backpack from her shoulders. A razor-sharp pincer the length of her forearm held her at bay as the Dread Librarian's disturbingly human hands rifled through her bag. A clawed fist of fear clenched in her gut. She didn't think the Archon would damage her—at least, not permanently—but Keyser was another matter. She closed her eyes and silently begged him to be still.

The Dread Librarian unfolded the witch's hoodie, revealing the purloined book. *The Archonomicon* seemed to wear an aura of regret.

"This is your third strike, Witch." Chlogha's dinner-plate-size eye fixed her with a baleful glare. "I hereby invoke Rule 42 of the Archonic Library System," she croaked. "May Azathoth have mercy on your soul."

The great toad handed her the backpack and lurched away, shaking the floor with each hop. Keyser's worried face appeared in the circle of the open drawstring, and the witch released a shaky breath. She picked up the bag and cradled it to her chest. Thank Discordia, that eldritch nightmare hadn't hurt him. She closed her eyes to whisper a prayer of gratitude. When she opened them, she was standing on the sidewalk in front of the library.

What the tentacled fuck. . .

The witch shouldered her backpack and turned to head back toward the library, but Keyser issued a low growl of warning. She froze and opened her third eye. An astral bubble surrounded the building, adorned with shimmering script that read *System-wide ban in effect. Forty-one days, twenty-three hours, and fifty-nine minutes remaining.*

A ban?

First Starbucks, now the squidsucking library.

Just when she'd found a promising lead, that frigging frog exiled her for six weeks. She'd only have nine days to find *The Archonomicon* after her banishment ended. But under the smothering weight of disappointment, a seed of hope took root. This book was different. It had *wanted* her to read it. The witch rode a wave of growing excitement as she walked through the crisp autumn air to the motorcycle spot where she'd parked her broom. There was more than one way to skin an octopus. She'd find a way back in tomorrow, rules be damned.

What were the Archons going to do—fire her?

CHAPTER TWO

The Dread Lord of Human Resources

A baddon County Library System interlibrary loan request denied. This patron's Rule 42 ban extends through December 10.

Nice try.

The witch deleted the email with a disgusted sigh. That amphibian asshole had banned her from *all* libraries—not just the Tophet County branches. Even Starbucks hadn't been that harsh.

She was out of ideas. After Monday evening's disaster, she'd used her last three sick days trying to storm the library. Brute force, always her tactic of choice, had been a spectacular failure, leaving her to sleep off a magical migraine. Sneaking in disguised by an illusion hadn't worked, nor had riding shotgun in the body of another patron, astrally projecting into Keyser Söze, and wriggling through the book-return drawer, nor coming up through the sewers. The force field around the library recognized her etheric signature no matter what she tried. It was enough to make her borderline homicidal.

Adding insult to injury, a new email from Tophet County's Online Services Department appeared in her inbox. The subject line read *Mandatory upgrade for scheduling software.*

Not happening, *Chad.*

She tried to delete the message unread, but a dialog box popped up saying she had to install a security patch first. Considering the amount of entropic energy she invested in her daily hex of the scheduling system, she wasn't about to comply.

The witch glared at the only bit of decoration in her office—a photograph taped to the wall facing her desk. She met the haunted eyes of the photo's subject and exhaled a plume of icy breath. A rime of frost covered the image.

The desk phone rang.

The witch smiled.

"County Witch," she said in her sweetest voice. "How can I help you?"

"I see you got my email," Chad said. "Look, I know you're upset about the software update, but—"

"Whyever would you think that?"

"Could you just make it stop snowing in my office? It's not good for the electronics."

The witch lit a Swisher Sweet cigarillo and puffed smoke into the handset.

Chad coughed theatrically. "Did you know the County curse breaker bills upward of ninety percent of his time undoing your temper tantrums?"

"Is that so?" She'd have to up her game.

"I ought to file a complaint with HR," he said. "Especially after what you did to my. . .to Heather."

"I didn't do a godsdamned thing to her."

Wait. . .*had* she cursed Mrs. Chad?

"'May your wife find an amazing opportunity in direct sales,'" Chad said. "Ring any bells?"

Ah, yes—retaliation for mandatory cybersecurity training, if memory served. "That was ages ago. Why complain now?"

"First, she spent four thousand dollars on leggings inventory and turned the garage into a pop-up boutique. Now she's selling It Hurts!™ weight-loss wraps on Instagram." Chad sighed. "She says she's found her why, whatever *that* means."

"You're going to bother the Dread Lord of Human Resources about a prank I pulled last year?" The witch whistled. "That's bold, Chad. He isn't exactly a patient entity."

"He's been way more chill lately, but it doesn't matter," he said with another long-suffering sigh. "Not anymore."

Jeez, Heather was just hocking leggings. No need to be so dramatic.

But an uncharacteristic pang of conscience pricked her soul. She snapped her fingers, putting an end to the indoor blizzard.

"Thanks," Chad said.

"Whatever, just tell me how to make the computer skip this stupid update."

"Turn it off and turn it back on again."

"I swear by the many limbs of the County Clerk, if you ever say that to me again, I'll—"

The witch froze. A pinprick of octarine netherlight appeared, hovering in midair on the other side of her desk.

"Chad, you worthless shitweasel," she hissed. "You already sicced HR on me, didn't you?"

The pinprick grew. This was bad. Her usual protocol before a one-on-one with a senior Archon required a seventy-two-hour period of intense preparation. Worse, Keyser Söze was home sleeping off a hangover. Without her familiar, she was limited to her body's natural reserve of magic-powering entropine.

"No!" Chad cleared his throat. "I mean, I may have made a few tiny complaints over the years, but nothing recent."

The pinprick continued to dilate. Whipping tentacles lashed through the opening, catching the edges and pulling the hole wider. The witch's stomach lurched. She slammed the phone down and looked around her office, fighting a growing panic. She needed to find a fitting receptacle for her most priceless possession. Her eyes landed on a half-empty bottle of Diet Dr Pepper, the champagne of soft drinks. Any port in a storm. . .

Keeping one eye on the growing hole in reality, the witch lunged for the soda and unscrewed the cap. She poured the contents on the floor and shook the bottle, dislodging the remaining droplets. The hole was about two feet in diameter now. Tentacles grasped the edges of her desk, pulling a large, heavy body that stretched and thinned the edges of the opening. The Dread Lord of Human Resources appeared to be crowning.

She put her lips to the mouth of the bottle and whispered, then replaced the cap and dropped it in the trash. A wet, tearing sound rent the air. She looked up to see the Dread Lord folding his nine-dimensional form—gape-mawed and liberally tentacled—into the suited human skin of a mustachioed bureaucrat. She gagged and vomited into her wastebasket. That would be fun later.

"Good morning."

The witch sat up and looked at her unwelcomed visitor. His eyes bulged a few centimeters past normal human tolerance and roamed in different directions. One of them landed on the puddle of soda seeping out from under her desk.

"Oh, dear." The eye swiveled until it found her face. "Have you soiled yourself in terror? I do apologize," he said. "I should have called first."

Apologize? An *Archon*?

"I'm, uh. . .I'm unsoiled." The witch rocked back in her chair, relaxing into an insouciant slouch. "What do you want?"

"The old me would insist on cringing obedience, but I'll settle for common courtesy," the Dread Lord said, misting her desk with a spray of what she dearly hoped was saliva. He had a mass of tiny tentacles instead of a tongue, producing a significant lisp.

"That's not really my thing." Her head was pounding with the effort of keeping her thoughts neutral and innocuous. She needed to get this mind-flaying ass clown out of here. "Look, if you're here about Chad—"

"I've always found your persecution of the technomancer entertaining." The Dread Lord's face shifted in a disconcerting attempt at a smile. "A fine Archonic tradition—the strong tormenting the weak."

Well, shit. That put a damper on Operation Bedevil Chad.

"But that was the old me. I just returned from an intensive course on team-building—two weeks in the Mountains of Madness." He sat across from her and leaned forward earnestly. "Did you know bullying creates a hostile work environment and damages group dynamics?"

Discordia, take the wheel. If he started spouting corporate bullshit—

"It hampers our ability to leverage the synergies of our workforce."

Her eye twitched. "Noted."

"This training was a revelation." The Dread Lord's lips spread in a grin that revealed an appalling collection of mismatched fangs. "My new mission is to put the 'human' back in 'Human Resources.' I've got so many ideas—employee engagement surveys, a new performance review process, interdepartmental retreats." He rubbed his hands together in gleeful anticipation. "I've created a library of icebreaker activities."

The witch broke out in a cold sweat. "Sounds. . ." Horrifying. Loathsome. Torturous. ". . . interesting. Is there a problem with my time card or something?"

"Your time card has indeed been tardy, lo these many pay periods, but that's not why I'm here." A tiny tentacle emerged from his right ear, and she swallowed a hysterical giggle. "The reason I stopped by is to discuss your participation in the Emergence Day celebration."

Oh, gods, no.

"Sorry to disappoint, but I have plans."

The Dread Lord stared at her, incredulous. Well, one eye did. "What could possibly take precedence over commemorating the day we Archons liberated humanity?"

Liberated? What a load of reeking bullshit.

But. . .to be fair, perhaps not entirely off the mark.

Thirty years ago, a bunch of racist assholes at a Unite the White rally got evil enough to tip the cosmic balance, unleashing a menagerie of chthonic dung lords and dooming the human race to eternal servitude under the tentacles of the usurpers. Sure, a couple hundred idiots waving tiki torches wasn't the most despicable act the world had ever seen, but they'd held their hatefest on the bridge over the Fathomless Abyss in Asphodel's town square—which was, unfortunately for them, situated atop the subterranean lair where the Archons had slept since the Earth was young.

One minute, a herd of douchebags was chanting "white power"; the next, boom! Tentacles everywhere.

The witch derived a small measure of satisfaction from the fact that they weren't around to witness the fruits of their fuckery. The writhing knot of razored tendrils and glowing orbs who was now the Tophet County Sheriff had liquefied them and slurped them up through a straw-like appendage. Karma's a bitch.

But that was ancient history. The more pressing issue was that defying the Dread Lord might cost her a few pints of blood or a nonessential limb. It'd taken months to regrow her middle finger the last time she pissed him off. Fortunately, she had an excuse no self-respecting HR professional could deny.

"This year, Emergence Day coincides with the high holy day of my faith," the witch said. "As a devout Discordian, I must spend the day in worship."

"What is this holy day?"

"The Colossal Clusterfuck." She bowed her head in faux reverence.

"This is fortuitous," he lisped, viscous drool dripping from the waxed tips of his mustache. "It's our thirtieth anniversary, and we'd like you to perform the opening ritual. What better homage could there be to the Goddess of Discord than invoking the Formless Darkness that lurks in the heart of the multiverse, waiting eagerly to devour us all?"

"But—"

"The County Clerk herself. . ." He paused for dramatic effect. Everyone knew the Clerk was the real power in Tophet County. ". . . commands you to deliver the opening invocation."

"Oh, I just *love* being commanded."

"Take it as a compliment," he said. "The people of Tophet County expect a little pizzazz at these ceremonies. One of us could deliver the invocation, but part of my rebranding effort is putting a human face on Emergence Day."

"The High Lord of Health and Human Services has a human face. Let her do it."

"But that face is attached to the body of a giant spider. I'm told people find her disconcerting."

"Yeah, but—"

"This is not a request," the Dread Lord said. "You *will* perform the opening invocation, and there will be no shenanigans. I haven't forgotten what you did at the Whacking Day parade."

The witch smirked. Amphibian rain. She'd been quite proud of that.

"If so much as a tadpole turns up at the Emergence Day celebration, I will relieve you of the burden of your arms."

"Wouldn't that create a hostile work environment?"

"Witch, I consider it my sacred duty to teach you the nobility of serving the greater good." He stood, planted his hands on her desk, and leaned toward her. The skin of his face rippled with agitation. "Do you understand me?"

Perhaps a tactical retreat was in order. She was rather attached to her arms, and she'd look like a T. rex regrowing them. She opened her mouth to agree, but the Dread Lord preempted her.

"Besides, you're a contracted employee of the Tophet County government," he said, his voice almost gentle, "and I'm a senior Archon." He offered a pained smile that practically oozed pity. "You don't have a choice."

How dare he feel sorry for her when he was the one who'd trapped her in this godsdamned contract? The pilot light of rage that always smoldered in her chest blazed into an inferno, burning away all traces of tongue-holding self-preservation.

"You can make me show up, but without my name, you can't—"

He unleashed a roar of outrage. His arms flailed in the liquid motion of an inflatable-tube man.

Now she'd gone and done it. Besides the fact that omitting her name had weakened her contract's magical hold, giving her the leeway to attempt breaking it, the Dread Lord had a pathological obsession with maintaining accurate employee records. He'd been apoplectic when he discovered she was using a pseudonym.

"I demand to know your true name, Witch!"

"It's Connie—"

"Don't you dare," he shrieked.

"Lingus!"

His human skin split down the middle like an overripe banana. For a moment, his monstrous form quivered behind a gelatinous caul. Then that tore as well, and his body unfolded into nine repugnant dimensions. The witch, being afflicted with the Sight, could see all of them. His cavern of a mouth, ringed with serrated teeth and lined with squirming tentacles, stretched open as he wailed. She burned through almost all her entropine in seconds fending off his enraged attempt to search her mind. With a final bellow of fury, the Dread Lord telescoped in on himself, folding smaller and smaller until he vanished in a flash of netherlight.

The witch fell to her knees and groped for the trash can. She fished out the bottle, shuddering at the touch of tepid vomit. With shaking hands, she unscrewed the cap and breathed in her true name. Her vision darkened as she tried to push up from all fours. She needed to get to the psychic surgery for auric replenishment before she passed out—otherwise, she'd sleep until her body naturally restored her entropine reserves. That would take at least three days, and Keyser was home alone with no one to keep him from murdering the neighbor's Chihuahua.

She looked around for something—anything—she could use to call for help. Her gaze landed on the picture of Chad tacked to her bulletin board. With the last vestiges of her strength, she sent a desperate plea.

CHAPTER THREE

Nerdomancer

T he strident rings of the witch's BlackBerry tore through the veil of unconsciousness like a chain saw. She opened her eyes to a room flooded with harsh fluorescent light and squeezed them shut again. Where the hell was she? This wasn't her comfortable cave of an apartment, and by the wrinkled dugs of Baba Yaga, her head was throbbing.

She picked up the device and squinted at the screen. *Nerdomancer.*

"Hey, Chad."

"How are you feeling?"

"Like hammered dammit." She looked around the room. Hospital bed. Wall-mounted TV/VCR. Auric dialysis machine. Yep, she was in a psychic surgery suite. Chad must've heard her call. "I suppose a heartfelt thank you is in order."

"Happy to help." He paused, managing to project social awkwardness through the phone connection. "So I, um. . ."

When it became clear that Chad had entered sleep mode, the witch said, "Okay, then. I should go. I need to get home."

"That's why I called," he said. "I'm out front. Thought you might want a ride."

"You came to pick me up?"

"Yeah. I mean, it's pouring rain, and you usually take your broom to work."

The witch blinked, at a loss for words.

He must want something—probably a spell or a charm. People *always* wanted something from the Earth's sole surviving witch. She clenched her teeth, bracing for the inevitable request.

"Never mind," he said hurriedly. "I'm sure you've got a friend coming. I just didn't want to leave you—"

She cleared her throat, forcing away the small smile that had formed of its own accord. "I'll be down in a minute."

Following a spirited argument with the supervising nurse, who refused to punch her Frequent Patient Loyalty Card until she made a follow-up appointment with the etheric med techs, the witch pushed through the double doors that led outside and found Chad waiting in a cobalt Chevy Spark. She opened the passenger door and slid inside. Droplets of water stood in his hair and streaked his brown skin, and his polo shirt clung to his chest.

She forced her eyes back to his face and said, "You're soaked."

He ran a hand through his short locs, producing a fine spray of water. "Torrential rain will do that. How are you still dry?"

"It's a witch thing," she said. "You know, phenomenal cosmic powers."

"Must be nice." He put the car in gear. "Where to?"

"94 Innsmouth Drive."

Chad tapped her address into his phone, and they were off. Considering his nerd prowess, the witch expected the drive to be a master class in stilted silences, but to her surprise, he launched into a series of entertaining anecdotes about his boss, the Dread Lord of Information Technology. The ten-minute drive flew by, and before she knew it, he was parking in front of her squat brick apartment building.

"Any fun plans tonight?"

"Oh yeah," the witch said. "Big plans."

Her current and only plan was to cancel on her Tinder hookup and spend the evening with a three-legged raccoon and a bottle of Chicken Cock Kentucky bourbon. No need to bore Chad with the details.

His smile faded. "Bummer," he said. "The Whovians need a fourth."

"The Whovians? What's that, like a band or something?"

"My trivia team. I was gonna see if you'd be interested in—"

The *Super Mario Bros.* theme blared from Chad's phone on its dashboard mount. The witch glanced at the screen, which displayed the smiling face of a perky blonde helpfully labeled *Heather.*

His wife.

"I should go," she said.

"Hold up—"

"Thanks for. . .for, you know. . ." She opened the car door and slid out, then leaned down and said, "Just thanks."

"But do you want to—"

"See you Monday."

A veritable cornucopia of smells greeted the witch when she opened the door to her apartment. The pungent tang of Keyser's unscooped litter box. The sickly sweet aroma of rotting food from the garbage bag he'd ripped open in the kitchen. The earthy smell of coffee grounds. Ugh. She needed to clean, but she was fresh out of the psychic surgery and still recovering from full entropic depletion. Her usual *Fantasia*-esque bewitching of cleaning implements was beyond her capabilities at the moment. With a heavy sigh, she trudged inside, closed the door, and commenced a half-assed cleaning job, which was still one cheek more than she felt like doing.

An hour later, the reek of trash and raccoon scat had been replaced by the far more pleasant odor of lemon-scented Mr. Clean. She heaved a sigh and flopped down in a creaky papasan chair to catch her breath. Next door, she could hear the neighbors kicking off their weekly game night. Peals of laughter punctuated bursts of animated conversation. Sounded like they were playing Pictionary this week. The witch snorted. What kind of losers spent Friday night playing a children's board game?

As if in answer, an image of herself—a disheveled mess of a woman watching a curmudgeonly raccoon ride the Roomba around the living room—appeared in her mind's eye.

Maybe she wasn't going out or getting laid, but she didn't have to have a lame-ass Friday night. She'd throw her own party and invite her. . .

She could invite. . .

Screw it. So it would just be her and Keyser. Nothing wrong with that. This party was *exclusive*.

The witch pushed up with a groan and stumbled to the kitchen. She examined the contents of the fridge: an ancient Styrofoam takeout container holding Goddess only knew what horrors, a jar of Death by Salsa, and a geriatric carrot. Not a great menu. But the freezer yielded better results—an unopened box of Beef Taco Hot Pockets.

Now it was a real fiesta.

Three minutes and forty-five seconds later, she and Keyser were sitting down to dinner. She poured a slug of Chicken Cock into a dusty margarita glass, stuck a birthday candle to a paper plate with melted wax, and lit it. Martha Stewart, eat your heart out. Then she bit into her Hot Pocket, sustaining third-degree burns to the roof of her mouth, and Keyser Söze ate the godsdamned birthday candle.

TGI-freaking-F.

CHAPTER FOUR

The Sockrifice

The witch dropped her offering into the bubbling cauldron—an early sacrifice in honor of tomorrow's Colossal Clusterfuck. Tendrils of steam rose from the vessel, caressing her face as she chanted. The heat felt good. Her office had marinated in the miasma from her vomit-filled trash can all weekend, and she'd had to open the windows to air it out. Now it was colder than a witch's tit in a brass bra. She paused mid-chant to crank up the dial on her hot plate.

Just as she resumed the ritual, the phone rang, shattering her concentration. If she had to start over, she'd find the unlucky bastard on the other end of the line and make them suffer. She peered over the lip of the cauldron. It was empty save for a few wisps of steam. Her offering had been accepted.

Hail Discordia!

The phone rang again, and she snatched it from its cradle. "What?"

"Could you please give it back?"

The witch smiled. "Give what back?"

"You know what I'm talking about."

She lit a Swisher Sweet and waited.

"My sock," he said. "I was in the middle of a meeting when my left sock just vanished. You know, I thought we turned a corner on Friday."

"I needed it."

"Why on earth—"

"Tomorrow is a holy day in my faith."

"What does that have to do with my sock?"

"Did not the Prophet say, 'And lo, on the first Tuesday following the first

Monday in November, you shall observe the grand workings of Discordia upon the so-called systems of the secular world. Or not. You do you'?"

"I don't—"

"And does not the Mother of Chaos deserve an offering in honor of that most holy of days?"

"I just want—"

"And is there any more fitting gift for Our Lady than a single sock?" The witch lowered her voice to a dramatic whisper. "A sockrifice."

A resounding silence echoed from the phone. The witch drew on her cigarillo and blew a smoke ring.

"I need my sock," Chad said. "Come on, it's a limited edition *Doctor Who*—"

"Nerd much?"

"They're custom compression socks. My physical therapist told me to wear them after long runs."

The witch choked, smoke puffing from her nose and mouth. "You have prescription socks?" She slapped her knee, sprinkling ashes on her leather pants. An impatient quiet wafted from the other end of the line. She wiped tears from her eyes. "You're going to need to refill that Rx, Chad," she said. "The sockrifice—"

"Stop staying that!"

"—has been accepted."

"But I have sensitive skin," Chad protested. "I'll have blisters by lunchtime!"

The witch snapped her fingers.

He squawked. "What the. . ."

She waited, grinning.

"Why is there a. . .a sanitary product in my shoe?"

She listened with satisfaction to a symphony of male mortification. Good old menstrual humor—generating delicious discomfort among the Y-chromosome crowd since humanity crawled out of the primordial soup.

"Oh, stop clutching your pearls," she said. "You're a married man. You know what kind of cyclical mischief vaginas get up to." Fifteen seconds ticked by with no reply. "You there?"

"I'm not a married man," he said. "Not for long, anyway. I, um. . .Heather left me."

The witch dropped her Swisher Sweet in her lap, then panicked and invoked a small waterspout to extinguish it. "What?" she asked, dabbing at the puddle in her lap. "When?"

"About a month ago. She asked for a divorce, then ran off to an It Hurts!™ leadership conference. Things had been strained, but. . ." His long sigh encompassed fifty shades of Eeyore. "She moved the last of her stuff out over the weekend."

The witch dropped her soggy cigarillo in the trash can and burned through some entropine to dry her clothes. "Was it the leggings?"

"She *did* say having her own businesses freed her to be the boss babe she truly is, but no," he said. "It wasn't the leggings. If you want the truth, I think she met somebody else, but she won't talk about it." He heaved another deep sigh. "That's what bugs me most—not knowing why she left."

"Want me to give her boils?" the witch asked. "Parking tickets? An ingrown toenail?"

"You don't have to do that."

"If you change your mind—"

"Maybe a pimple?" he whispered.

She closed her eyes, whispered a quick curse, and sprayed a hail of pustular entropic energy in the general direction of the former Mrs. Chad's leggings-clad derriere. "Done."

"Thanks." After a brief, companionable pause, he said, "You going to the Emergence Day ceremony tomorrow night?"

"Don't have a choice."

"That's right, you're giving the opening invocation, aren't you?"

"Against my will and better judgment."

"Did you tell HR it's your holy day?"

"The Dread Lord of Human Resources is the one who roped me into it. I thought after what I did on Whacking Day, they wouldn't ask me to do this shit again."

"The rain of fanged toads," Chad said. "That was you?"

"Who else?"

"I'll bring an umbrella."

"The Dread Lord made it clear that, if any frogs fall from the sky, I should expect to lose a limb or two. So no toads," she said. "Probably."

A trio of knocks sounded from her office door, which then swung open. An unfamiliar woman stood in the doorway. She was dressed in white, from the tips of her Toms-clad toes to the top of her turban-wrapped head.

What in all the seven hells. . .

"Gotta go, Chad." The witch slammed the phone down, crossed her arms, and glared at the intruder. "You'd better be lost."

The woman approached and stood in front of the witch's desk, extending her hand. "My name is Mitsuki Carcosa. I'm your ten thirty."

The witch ignored the proffered extremity. "My ten thirty?"

She tapped the screen of her BlackBerry and opened her traitorous calendar. Yep, there it was—a confirmed client, marked paid in full.

Dagon's wrinkled balls. Some enterprising asshat must've undone her hex of the scheduling software. That meant any citizen could book magical services online. The County Witch's office functioned on a similar model to Animal Control in that either private citizens or the County itself could request her services. Unlike Animal Control, citizens paid a fee, the proceeds of which went toward Medicare for All. (She had legit beef with Archonic rule, but the health-care plan was excellent. The squigglies might be vicious monsters intent on world domination, but unlike the pre-Emergence ruling class, they weren't totally mor-ally bankrupt.)

The scheduling system was supposed to let her approve or decline appoint-ments before payment, but that feature had never worked, hence, her campaign of terror. As much as she hated phone calls, she wanted the chance to decline requests she couldn't—or wouldn't—fulfill. These technomancers didn't under-stand magical client contracts. Once money changed hands, the witch had an ironclad obligation. That should be *her* decision to make. On top of that, the Dread Lord of IT just added a teleportation feature. Now Archons could pull people to meetings whether they wanted to be there or not. The whole system was—

The woman cleared her throat.

Well, Chad's geek squad had copulated with the proverbial canine once again. She'd just have to take care of whatever dumb bullshit Snow White wanted. . .as long as it wasn't love magic.

The witch looked up and met her client's eyes, and her heart sank. The woman had that telltale, pinched quality typical of the lovelorn.

She'd go old school on Chad over this. Boils or locusts. Maybe telemarketers.

"Park it," the witch said, gesturing to the intentionally uncomfortable chair she kept for clients she couldn't scare off. "How'd you find my office? I keep an illusion over the door."

"It looks like a janitor's closet, yes?"

"Yeah."

"I teach kundalini yoga." She tapped her forehead. "My third eye is wide open. The third eye sees only truth, and truth dispels illusion." The woman gracefully lowered herself onto the wooden chair, then folded her legs up in lotus position. "A new student of mine recommended your services."

The witch perked up. To incentivize her out of rampant misanthropy, the Dread Lord of HR gave her a bonus for each client that came by way of refer-ral—the assumption being she must not have been a total dick if a client recom-mended her.

"Who?"

"She never told me her name," the woman said, frowning. "All I know is she's some kind of heiress."

"Heiress to what?"

"I'm afraid I haven't a clue."

So much for her bonus.

The witch waved a hand impatiently. "What do you want?"

"It's my husband. We haven't been connecting—you know, on a *soul* level."

"Ain't that a punch to the heart chakra."

"Work has consumed his life," she said. "It's all he talks about, all he thinks about. He even dreams about—"

"Let me stop you right there, lady."

"My name is Mitsuki."

"Whatever," the witch said. "The Archons make me keep love magic on my service menu because it's tradition, but let me tell you, it never works out. If Mr. Snow White sucks, ditch him and move on."

"I can't do that. We're twin flames, two halves of the same whole."

The witch's eyes rolled so hard it hurt. "You're sure you don't want something else? I could do a twenty-four-hour beauty spell, a single-use illusion, or. . .hey, do you have any warts?" Mitsuki shook her head. "Too bad. I'm a frigging genius with warts."

"I want to reconnect with my husband," she said, her voice steely with determination. "If you don't fulfill your contract, I *will* file a complaint."

A complaint. Great. That would go right up to the Board of Examiners and that scaly monstrosity of an adjudicator.

Oh, Chad, may the chocolate chips in your cookie ever be raisins. May fungus smite your worthless groin. May your captchas be indecipherable.

But despite her annoyance, she kept her hexes in the realm of thought rather than juicing them up with entropine. It was only Monday, and the poor bastard was having a rough week.

"Fine." The witch chugged what remained of her cooling coffee and stood, gazing at Mitsuki's serene face. "But know this: Love magic only works where there's already love. I can strengthen it, but I can't create it."

"I understand."

Shaking her head, the witch strode to her supply cabinet. Of all the lies people told, love was the stupidest. In the age of social media, that was really saying something. She returned to her desk with a jar, a squeeze bear of honey, a small apple, a magnet, and a lancet.

"What's all—"

The witch flicked her wrist, and Mitsuki's voice cut off midsentence. Her mouth continued to move for a moment before she realized she'd been struck dumb—or, in the witch's estimation, rendered bearable. Most people flailed around like blood-drunk nightgaunts when she pulled something like this, but Mitsuki just met her eyes and raised an eyebrow.

Ovaries of steel, this one.

She rolled the apple across the desk to her client, who caught it with a questioning look. The witch opened a desk drawer and withdrew a capped X-Acto knife, which she also handed to Mitsuki.

"Carve his name on the apple."

After a few minutes of meticulous bladework, Mitsuki looked up and nodded.

"Make a slit through the stem and slide the magnet in. Once you've done that, drop it in the jar and cover it with honey."

Again, she looked up and nodded once she'd completed the steps.

"You brought a personal focus?"

Mitsuki furrowed her brows and shook her head.

"A lock of his hair, nail clippings, something like that?"

She reached into her white macramé bag and withdrew a tiny manila envelope.

"Dump it in," the witch said. "I'll need something from you, too. Hair, nails, saliva—pick your poison."

To her surprise, Mitsuki spit into the jar after she'd added her husband's fingernails.

Now the actual magic began. The witch picked up the lancet, pricked her finger, and squeezed three drops of blood into the jar. All she needed for a spell like this was a clear intention and a few drops of her own blood, but the rubes wouldn't buy into magic that simple. They wanted something witchier, and if they didn't get it, they'd convince themselves the spell hadn't worked—even if it did exactly what they wanted. It was the damnedest thing.

Typically, the witch would've come up with something ludicrous involving a full moon and the whiskers of a lactating cat, but Emergence Day and Chad's wrecked marriage had left her in a shittier mood than her usual low-grade Monday-morning rage. This would have to do. She screwed the lid on the jar and swirled it around, whispering arcane-sounding nonsense, then passed it back to her client.

"Put the jar under your bed and shake it every morning to, um, activate the magic."

Mitsuki took the jar and nestled it in her bag. She stood and opened her mouth to speak, then hesitated and tapped her throat. The witch sighed and returned her voice.

"Thank you so much. I appreciate—"

"I've got shit to do." She pointed at the door. "Bye, now."

Once Mitsuki left, the witch snapped her fingers, locking her office door. She kicked back in her chair and propped her booted feet on the corner of her desk. The lingering aura of a wounded heart dragged Chad's situation back to the forefront of her mind.

His wife had left him.

Dammit, she hadn't meant for that to happen. The direct-sales thing was supposed to be a harmless prank. Heather should've started selling essential oils and annoying her Facebook friends—not become an athleisure mogul and asked for a divorce. Chad didn't deserve that. He was a decent guy. Annoying. Dorky. But decent.

Speaking of Chad, he'd raised the specter of tomorrow's unwanted obligation. Godsdamned Emergence Day. There was no way out of it. She could ignore the Dread Lord and live to tell the tale, but the County Clerk was a different kettle of entrails. The witch shuddered. She couldn't even look at the Clerk without dry heaving. It was embarrassing but, given that the mere sight of her reduced most mortals to shrieks, mindless gibbers, and spontaneous urination, dry heaving had a certain dignity. The other senior Archons insisted she wear a shroud around humans so the County offices wouldn't smell like a diaper pail.

The Clerk. . .

Through the tangled web of guilt, resentment, and simmering rage, the building blocks of a plan began to emerge.

Point the first: The Clerk supervised County elections.

Point the second: Elections were the centerpiece of the sacred Colossal Clusterfuck, and this year, the Clusterfuck landed on Emergence Day.

Point the third: Chad's ex was a direct-sales queenpin with thousands of loyal customers.

Maybe she could kill two birds with one sock—simultaneously avenging Chad and honoring Discordia by injecting a little sacred entropy into the Archons' rigged election. Those noodly bastards *loved* the pomp and circumstance of their precious celebrations. The witch's interference wouldn't change the outcome of the election, but she might be able to smear a little shit on the shoe of the oppressor.

She cracked her knuckles. Time to get to work.

CHAPTER FIVE

A Coven of She-Devils

By the beard of Rasputin, why are you calling me at the ass crack of dawn?"

"I just voted," Chad said.

The witch sat up in bed and rubbed her eyes.

"Heather was on the ballot."

It'd taken three hours of sustained magical effort, but the witch had gotten the job done. Score one for the good guys.

The well-intentioned but ill-tempered and ethically murky guys.

Guy.

Witch.

"Did you do this?" She opened her mouth to reply, but he cut her off. "Never mind. Wrong question. *Why* did you do this?"

Wait a minute. He actually sounded pissed.

"To get back at your ex and stick it to the squidwards," she said. "Why do you think?"

"There are never two names on the ballot, Witch."

"There are now."

"I know," Chad said, with an air of exaggerated patience. "And what do you think the County Clerk will do to the innocent woman she'll suspect of interfering with this travesty of democracy?"

"I don't—"

"I have a few guesses," he said. "And they involve words like 'rend' and 'maim' and 'dis-ensoul.'"

"Calm down, Chad."

"I didn't want Heather dead, for gods' sake—all I asked for was a zit!"

"I won't let anything happen to her," the witch said. "I put her on the ballot to screw up the County Clerk's sham election. No one will actually *vote* for her."

Quiet chagrin leaked from the phone.

"I voted for her."

"Great Bieber's ghost, why the hell. . ." She shook her head. "It doesn't matter. She won't win."

"Are you sure?"

"Of course I'm sure. She's not a politician," the witch said. "She's a member of a suburban leggings cult."

"Are you sure?" he repeated.

"I'm like ninety percent sure." A frosty silence chilled her ear. "Look, she'll be fine. I give you my—"

He hung up.

It was a shitty start to what should've been a day of revelry and mischief. Unfortunately, it only got worse from there. Keyser Söze had gotten into her stash of special brownies and was higher than a giraffe's ass. While she appreciated his enthusiasm for celebrating the Clusterfuck, it left her unpleasantly muzzy. To make things worse, he'd gotten the munchies and eaten all the straw off her broom. Since her bank account balance was in the realm of imaginary numbers, she'd have to take the bus until she could re-bristle it.

As the number ten jounced to a halt in front of the County office building, the witch noticed a few knots of people in front of the Rec Center, one of Tophet County's ceremonial polling locations. When the bus pulled away, she stood on the sidewalk, peering through the early morning gloom.

Oh, gods. . .

They were holding signs.

The witch crunched across frosty grass toward a group of women dressed in garish prints. They marched around a folding table just outside the "No Petitioning" zone as a zaftig woman with a Darth Vader helmet and a megaphone led a rousing chant: "The fempire strikes back!" A hot pink banner hanging from the table read *Heather Chadwick for Human Mayor*.

What the political fuck was going on? She hadn't added Heather to the ballot until yesterday afternoon. Polling places opened less than an hour ago, and Heather's supporters were already here with signs and swag?

One of the marching women noticed her staring and headed toward her, button in hand. "Good morning," she chirped. "I'd like to talk to you about your vote." She handed the witch a button emblazoned with the smiling face of the erstwhile Mrs. Chad. "Heather Chadwick is a former homemaker who launched a wildly successful home-based business. She's smart. She's determined. And she's ready to fight for—"

"She'll be fighting the Clerk if you don't knock this off," the witch said.

"Heather is not afraid of confrontation."

"Is she afraid of being separated, molecule by molecule, into her constituent parts?"

"The only thing that scares her is the status quo." The woman flashed a toothpaste-commercial grin. "Can we count on your support?"

The witch whirled, cloak flaring, and stalked toward the County building. When she reached her office, she flopped down in her chair and dug her fingertips into her temples.

Heather's friends were campaigning. So what? That didn't mean anyone would vote for her.

Well, other than Chad.

The witch's eyes landed on her cauldron, still sitting atop the hot plate and still, by the unnumbered teats of Ut'Ulls-Hr'Her, cranked up on high. She unplugged it and looked into the empty vessel. Discordia had accepted her sockrifice, which she'd offered—as was proper for all gifts to the Mother of Chaos—with a sincere prayer to stir some shit. Whatever else this nonsense was, it was holy Discordian work, which made it her solemn duty to throw in with Heather and stick it to the man.

Er, roughly man-shaped (plus or minus a couple dozen limbs) entity.

She fired up her laptop and clicked her way to the County elections page. Who had the good ol' eldritch horrors chosen as their next marionette? The image of a smiling, mustachioed man loaded on the screen—excruciatingly slowly, thank you, *Chad*.

Karl Lester. The witch's heart sank. He was a favorite of that suppurating freak show, the County Clerk. In fact, Karl was her deputy. He led the Vital Records Department, which archived documents related to births and deaths, marriages and divorces, and dis-ensoulments, existential erasures, and banishings to the depths of the Fathomless Abyss.

Shit on a biscuit.

The polls were closing early—no doubt, so the Clerk could attend the Emergence Day ceremony and gloat as her selected stooge assumed the proverbial throne. Swearing in the new human mayor would be the centerpiece of the festivities, evidence that humans and their benevolent overlords could peacefully coexist.

A tiny sphere of netherlight blossomed in midair across from the witch's desk. It slowly dilated, and an exploratory tentacle snaked its way out. At least she was ready. She'd known she'd be surrounded by Archons at the ceremony, so she'd followed a three-day regimen of preparation, fasting, and mild exsanguination. All she'd ingested since Friday night's Mexican feast was water, black coffee, and Chicken Cock, and she'd chanted barbarous epithets until she was hoarse.

The Dread Lord emerged from the quantum tunnel with a squishy *plop*. She looked away as he accordioned himself into the human skin of what appeared to be an octogenarian mob boss. The wrinkles of the liver-spotted flesh were stretched taut, creating the unpleasant image of an overstuffed sausage. He straightened his lapels and looked at her gravely, the effect somewhat spoiled by the jaunty tentacle waving from his right nostril.

"Witch, I bring dire news," he said. "The sacred rite of the County election has been most cruelly befouled. A coven of she-devils has put forth one of their own for the office of human mayor."

"That's. . ." She paused, struggling to erase incriminating thoughts from her mind. "Wow, what a—"

"Do you wish to be governed by a demoness who swathes her limbs in whimsical knitwear?" The Dread Lord planted his hands on her desk and leaned toward her. Tentacles writhed beneath his skin. "She has found her why," he said in an ominous whisper.

The witch leaned away from the Dread Lord's undulating face. "That *is* alarming."

"Your assistance is required, Witch." The Dread Lord straightened and looked at her. "I just informed the County Clerk of this calamity, and she asks— nay, she demands—"

"As you may have noticed, I don't do demands." The witch hated herself a little, even as she spoke the words. Her life would be so much easier if she didn't provoke him, but she'd spent almost thirteen years chafing at the bonds of a magical contract. She just couldn't make herself kowtow to this bureau-twat. "I barely take suggestions."

The Dread Lord's form swelled inside his double-breasted suit. "Do not test me. You will use your magic to remove this powerful creature from the ballot."

Use your magic.

If she ground her teeth any harder, she'd be paying for another crown.

"You don't need me for that," the witch said. "You can do it yourself."

"Of course, but that would give the, um. . .appearance of interfering with the democratic process."

"Wouldn't want that, eh?"

The Dread Lord examined his fingernails. Well, eight of them. Two of the fingers were tentacles. "Anyhoo, the Clerk wants this woman out of the election forthwith. She has no business in County government. It's too dangerous."

"Dangerous?" The witch raised her eyebrows. "So you consider her a threat?"

"A threat? Ha!" He squared his shoulders in a transparent attempt at manly ruggedness, and a tentacle burst from the center of his chest. The human suit tore like moldy cloth, followed shortly by the squelchy destruction of the glistening membrane underneath. The Dread Lord's unnatural form exploded into the room, pushing the witch's desk back two feet and pinning her against the wall. "Dammit, that's the third time this month."

"Can't. . .breathe," she wheezed, struggling to push the desk away from her rib cage.

"My apologies. I've always been rather generously proportioned, but. . .it's the damned birthdays. Always another cake." The Dread Lord scooted his enormous bulk back a foot or two, relieving the pressure on her torso.

"If you want her off the ballot that badly, I'll take her off." The witch shrugged. "Who cares if humans think you're scared of her?"

"Why would they think that?"

"Why else would you care if she runs for office?" She forced herself to look at him, ignoring her roiling stomach.

"Hmmm. . ." The Dread Lord looked pensive, to the extent a tangled collection of tentacles and teeth can have an expression. "Do nothing. I shall consult the Clerk."

"Doing nothing is my specialty."

"One more thing, Witch," he said. "I apologize for my. . .outburst last week. We Archons settle our differences in combat, but I'm striving to humanize my leadership style." He wriggled self-consciously. "I don't know what came over me. I've been so moody since I got back from my training."

He had no apparent visual organs, but she could sense the weight of his expectant attention.

"Okay?"

"I've sworn off mind-flaying, and I'm in anger-management therapy," he said proudly. "We use the FUCK method—forgiveness, understanding, concern, and kindness. Quite effective, I'm told."

A good FUCK cured most anything, in her book.

A pinprick of netherlight appeared, and with a sound like vomiting in reverse, the Dread Lord of Human Resources slurped himself out of her office.

The witch had her work cut out for her. It would take real magical muscle to give Heather a snowball's chance of surviving this thing—let alone winning. She closed her eyes and began to chant.

And the godsdamned phone rang.

She glanced at the caller ID, heaved an exasperated sigh, and picked up the handset. "What do you want, Chad? I'm working here."

"She's winning," he said. "God help us, Heather is winning."

CHAPTER SIX

I'm with H(eath)er

B y three o'clock, the human mayoral race was a dead heat. The Clerk ordered all County employees to take the rest of the day off and hit the polls. Though she didn't order them to vote for Karl Lester, the spontaneous liquefaction of an accounts manager wearing an *I'm with H(eath)er* button sent a clear message. The witch followed the rest of the sheeple to the polls, where she voted for Chad's ex. Twice. Then she snuck home and spent a miserable hour enchanting straw and lashing it to her broomstick.

Back in her office, she opened the live update page for voting returns. The penultimate update, posted at 4:39 p.m., stated that polling locations were closed and vote counting was underway. According to the most recent entry, Heather Chadwick had a 137-vote lead.

Praise Discordia, she was pulling ahead!

This could change everything. If the Archons' hand-picked patsy didn't win the election, Tophet County might actually—

The page refreshed with a new post, logged at 5:14: *All ballots destroyed in purely accidental fire.*

Those underhanded, squiggly bastards. The witch closed her laptop and rubbed her hands together, building entropic energy.

The door to her office flew open, and a three-man squad of Spectral Forces officers charged in sporting black riot gear and helmets with full-face mirrored visors. She noted with satisfaction that they were cowering behind anti-entropic shields. Although the shields rendered her magic mostly useless, she was more bewildered than concerned. The Archons might torture her or snip off a stray limb here or there, but they wouldn't kill the only witch to survive the post-Emergence wars.

Probably.

Anyway, if these hulked-up minions wanted to fight, they'd have to lower their shields, at which point she'd do something creatively unpleasant.

She folded her arms, cocked her head, and looked at the one in front. "Men's room is down the hall."

He raised his visor, and the witch suppressed a gasp. He looked like a freaking Ken doll. Square jaw. Perfect teeth. A by-Our-Lady dimple in his chin.

"The County Clerk sent us to escort you to the ceremony," said Deputy Eye Candy. "The scheduling software is down again, and she thought you might. . .forget."

"Is that so?" The witch looked at their gear and raised an eyebrow. "Expecting a fight?"

She stood and strode toward the men. They scattered, shields raised, and watched warily as she opened her closet door and retrieved her freshly re-strawed broom. (The Archons loved the traditional trappings of the Craft. When she'd asked for transit benefits, they'd given her a wizardly, handcrafted besom with a gnarled oaken staff. Sadistic assholes. The witch's undercarriage had been sore for a week after her first test drive. Zooming along sidesaddle was a nonstarter, so she'd installed a bicycle seat and stirrups.)

She swung a leg over the staff and winked at Deputy Eye Candy. "Race you."

With a snap of her fingers, the exterior wall of her office misted into permeability. She streaked through it on her broom, leaving a trail of fire just for show. The wall re-formed behind her. She heard a series of thuds and muttered curses as she flew away.

The witch landed on the roof of the high school and left her broom propped against a chimney with instructions to incinerate anyone who gave it a second glance. She diffused the ceiling and drifted down into the gymnasium, landing three feet away from the unshrouded County Clerk. She squeezed her eyes shut and, with a herculean effort of will, suppressed a dry heave.

"Witch," the Clerk said in her fluting, singsong voice. "How lovely to *see* you."

That power-mad mass of oozing sores knew the effect she had on humans, and she reveled in it.

The witch flung a desperate prayer in the general direction of her divine patroness. *Mother of Chaos, please help me not to piss myself.* After a moment's consideration, she added, *Or puke.*

She cracked one eyelid, bracing herself for the sight, but her caution was no longer needed. The Clerk's gruesome visage had been replaced by a giant chicken nugget. Discordia had gifted her with a filter for reality.

"Are you not sickened?" the nugget cooed. "Are you not disturbed?"

The witch bit the insides of her cheeks to keep from smiling. "I'm fine." She eyed the nugget appraisingly. "A bit peckish."

All six of the nugget's eyes widened, waving on their stalks. It turned its crispy head and looked at the Dread Lord of Human Resources, who had procured a new human suit with an unfortunate soul patch.

"Sister, the witch is no doubt using her magic to defend against your overpowering—"

"Silence!" The nugget's face grew petulant. "Sathach tells me it was you who instructed him not to remove this interloper from the ballot."

"Instructed?" The witch assumed an expression of abject humility. "Never, O Pustulant One, would I presume to instruct an Archon of the Nether Realms—"

"Yes, yes," the nugget said, waving one of its many tentacles dismissively. "You tremble before me, et cetera. But did you foresee that this Heather would prevail against my pet?"

The Dread Lord literally said, "Ahem." As a mass of tentacles and teeth stuffed into a human skin, he couldn't quite pull off clearing his throat.

"Against the other candidate?" the Clerk clarified.

"Seeing the future is not among my many gifts."

The nugget pursed its lips, thinking. "How do you propose to resolve this? The Emergence Day celebration begins at six o'clock, and Tophet County must have a new human mayor."

The Sheriff had eaten the last one. Unpaid parking tickets.

"Just spitballing here, but couldn't you let the Formless Darkness decide?" The witch shrugged. "I mean, you've got me invoking it to kick off the ceremony. I could just add a 'Care to weigh in on this mayor thing?' bit at the end."

"Ask the Terror Who Stalks the Sun to choose our mayor?" The Dread Lord shook his head. "That's—"

"Brilliant," the nugget mused. "Azathoth is impossible to please. No doubt he will choose as we would ourselves."

"Which we would not," the Dread Lord said hastily. "Because democracy."

"Ah, yes," the Clerk said. "We Archons of the Nether Realms have a great. . .respect for democracy."

Typical politicians.

The witch peered into the crowded gymnasium of Asphodel High School. (*Go, Hunting Horrors!*) A large *Happy Emergence Day!* banner hung over the stage, and the entire space was bedecked with balloons and streamers—the latter attached to the former to simulate the tentacles of the so-called liberators.

Yet again, the witch cursed the memory of the fucktangular shit-gibbons who'd summoned these devils. On the whole, though, she had to admit she'd prefer to be ground under the tentacles of the Archons than the jackboots of neo-Nazis. The jellyfish brigade might be ancient beings with a penchant for remorseless violence, but at least they terrorized all humans equally.

That said, the witch didn't care to be ground under *anyone's* appendage.

"Witch," the County Clerk said. "The time draws. . ." The nugget eyeballed her from tip to toe. "Is that what you're wearing?"

Scuffed leather pants. Motorcycle boots. A muscle tee that said *Witches Get Shit Done*. The very definition of business casual. . .but something was missing.

Ah, yes.

She snapped her fingers, and a pointy black hat appeared on her head.

A short, curvy blonde wedged herself in front of the witch. She extended a hand to the as-yet-unshrouded County Clerk, who reflexively extruded a tentacle in an approximation of human greeting.

"Heather Chadwick," the woman said, wincing at the Clerk's acidic secretions. "I'm honored to meet you."

Her eyestalks thrashed in outrage as she dropped the hand like a hot potato. "You dare to. . ." She examined Heather's composed face. "Why aren't you screaming and wetting yourself?"

Heather flashed a perfectly lipsticked smile. "I took a Xanax and wore an adult diaper. Didn't want to detract from the solemnity of the occasion."

Damn. Heather was smuggling a pair of brass balls under those #LadyBoss leggings. The witch might actually like her.

"Mortal," the Clerk snapped, "I demand to know how you mobilized your minions to steal this election from my. . .from the other candidate."

"The credit goes to my campaign manager, Vee." Heather looked around the crowded auditorium. "I don't know where she's run off to. I'd love to introduce you. Anyway, before this election, I never dreamed I could have a role in County government. Seeing a strong, um, female being like you in a position of power has been *such* an inspiration."

The nugget preened. "Why, thank you."

"And I've heard great things about you," Heather said, turning to the witch. "If I win, I definitely want you on my team."

The witch recoiled. "I'm busy that day."

One of the lesser Archons approached—a female with a humanoid face, arms, and torso but tentacles instead of legs. A bulging forehead protruded from underneath a beach-waved wig. She extended a disconcertingly human hand holding a steaming coffee cup to Heather and said, "Caramel latte, extra hot."

"Thanks, girl."

The witch—who prided herself on maintaining a don't-give-a-shit deadpan expression, no matter the occasion—gaped in shock. It wasn't that one of *them* was bringing coffee to a human, and it wasn't that Heather called her "girl."

Every one of this creature's tentacles was wrapped in leggings.

Heather took a sip and sighed in satisfaction. "Dee's has the best coffee, and their sticky 'nuts are to die for."

"Sticky nuts?" The witch tore her eyes away from llamacorn print. "Sounds like a personal problem."

"It's a donut crossed with a sticky bun," Heather said. "You've gotta try—"

"Lu-kthu's crawling entrails," the County Clerk said. "You look ridiculous, Thugha."

The junior Archon's face fell. "My name is—"

"Ridiculous!"

"But you permit some of the Dread Lords and High Lords to dress as humans."

"They are afforded that accommodation to facilitate their work—not for. . .for *fashion*." One of the Clerk's tentacles snaked around a knit-clad limb. "I've told you before, leave the human clothes to. . ." She froze, caressing the cloth. "Oh, that's soft." Two of her eyes looked at each other in surprise. "And my excretions are not damaging the fabric."

"Our knits are like butter." Heather leaned closer to the County Clerk and lowered her voice. "I've developed a special material just for Archons—resistant to ridged spines, barbed tentacles, and oozing pustules. I tested it out myself. Would you believe it cleared up a rash of pimples on my—"

"Shroud yourself, sister!" The Dread Lord of Human Resources bustled into view, rubbing his hands together like a Bond villain. "The hour is at hand."

Heather raised a fist in the air. "Time to smash the patriarchy!"

It tested the limits of the human mind to read the facial expression of a multi-eyed piece of fried chicken, but if the witch had to guess, she'd say the Clerk was feeling conflicted.

The Dread Lord helped the Clerk don her shroud and herded the witch and the two mayoral candidates into a line behind her. He opened the locker room door, and they began walking toward the stage accompanied by "The Imperial March." The Clerk took center stage, raised a tentacle, and began the traditional retelling of the Emergence Day liberation.

"Long before humanity's first ancestor walked upright," she warbled, "we Archons were here—dreaming away the eons in our chthonic sanctuary. . ."

"I don't know who you think you are, Ms. Chadwick," Karl Lester said, sotto voce, "but the Clerk promised this position to me. I'll be damned if I'll let a plump little housewife take my job."

Heather leaned back and looked at Karl's suit-clad ass.

"What are you doing?" he whispered. "Stop that!"

Without losing her Barbie-doll grin, Heather said, "I know you're a puppet, Karl. I'm just looking for the tentacle."

Yep, the witch *definitely* liked her.

He opened his mouth to spit an angry retort, but the witch snapped her fingers and he produced a thunderous belch instead. The Clerk, who was just getting to the part where the Sheriff sucked down a few dozen skinheads like lemonade on a hot day, glared at him. He bowed his head in apology, and she continued, finishing her recitation with the customary phrase: "The humans of Tophet County rejoiced, and the peaceful reign of the Archons spread over the Earth."

That was the witch's cue. Showtime.

She stepped to the center of the stage and raised her arms. The crowd fell silent as she wreathed herself in flames and levitated. Unnecessary, but the audience appreciated a little showmanship.

"We call to Azathoth," she intoned, "the dreamer, the devourer, the Formless Darkness at the center of the multiverse!"

At least, that's what her mouth said. Her auric self—the part that counted—called quite vehemently to Discordia. She wasn't sure who'd win in a head-to-head between the Baroness of Bedlam and Archons' so-called Idiot God, but her money was on Chaos.

"We ask your blessing on this Emergence Day celebration." The witch twitched her nose, and the crepe paper tentacles hanging from the ceiling writhed to a chorus of oohs and aahs. "Today, Tophet County chooses a new mortal leader. We ask you to—"

A ropy appendage grabbed the witch's boot-clad ankle and yanked her down to the stage. The leather steamed from the Clerk's corrosive ooze.

"We ask you," the Clerk trilled, "to bless our new human mayor, Heather Chadwick."

As the town cheered, the witch—with a sidelong glance at the Dread Lord of Human Resources—waggled her fingers.

A gentle rain of fanged toads began to fall.

CHAPTER SEVEN

Lightly Fettered Access

She should've let him take her godsdamned arms.

The smell of rotten eggs, decaying vegetables, and interspecies excrement punched the witch in the nose like an olfactory fist. She hovered on her broom, looking out over the Tophet County landfill. The Unseen Creeping Horror, a devouring fog who served as the Dread Lord of Solid Waste Management, dwelt in its depths, slowly feasting on the county's garbage. A lot more slowly than usual, in point of fact. The UCH typically kept the refuse to a grotesque skim of filth, but today, the landfill sported towering piles of trash. That bloody-minded asshole *would* choose this week to slack off.

The landfill sat at the top of a rise, which was—to prevent the inadvertent consumption of citizens—not accessible to the public. A chain-link fence sprinkled with danger signs stretched across the foot of the hill, and dumpsters lined the parking lot side of the barrier. Residents deposited their garbage in the dumpsters, and County workers used forklifts to move the dumpsters.

At least, that was how it usually worked.

After her froggy fanfare on Emergence Day, the Dread Lord of Human Resources—having determined that maiming and rending wasn't consistent with his kinder, gentler HR office—sentenced her to spend Friday's lunch hour hauling trash. Since her contract allowed for "disciplinary measures," she had no choice but to comply.

And *she* didn't get a forklift.

The witch sighed and spiraled down to the parking lot. Might as well get started. She parked her broom and dismounted. Her backpack twitched and grumbled irritably. Even Keyser Söze, king of the trash pandas, found the landfill damn near unbearable. She hated to subject him to it, but as her familiar, his presence substantially increased her entropic capacity.

"Sorry, buddy," she said. "Let's get through this, and we'll knock off early today. I've got a pan of brownies with your name on it."

She unlocked the fence, dragged the gate open, and beckoned to the closest dumpster. It wobbled into the air, and she escorted it up the steep rise to the top.

The witch just had to get through this odoriferous hour, and then she could enjoy a lazy afternoon with *The Thrill of the Chaste*, the latest novel in her favorite series. She scorned the very idea of love, but she was hopelessly addicted to Amish romance novels (though she'd tie herself to a stake and self-immolate before she'd admit it). As a precautionary measure, she ordered her shameful reading material under a false name and hexed each book so it appeared she owned several dozen copies of *The Lazy Gourmand's Calamari Cookbook*.

As she neared the top of the hill, a tortured cry distracted her from day-dreaming about the puritanical passions of Amos and Sarah. Ba'al's balls, some half-witted human must have wandered into the landfill. Grunting with effort, she jogged the rest of the way with the dumpster bobbing erratically behind her.

A woman stood on the concrete pad at the top of the hill, her desperate eyes fixed on the reeking vista. The witch dropped her burden with a resounding *clang* and followed the woman's horrified stare to a tentacled miasma of sparkling fog, which was how her Sight rendered the Unseen Creeping Horror. Most normal humans couldn't see the UCH at all, which meant the woman was probably looking for something else.

Something that was now inside the fog.

Something. . .or some*one*.

"What happened?" the witch asked.

The woman spun toward her in a swirl of crimson curls. "Help him!" She pressed her hands to her ears. "Can't you hear him screaming?"

The only sound the witch heard was the faint crunch of Keyser demolishing a bag of trail mix. Whatever had happened, the poor bastard wasn't screaming anymore.

"You need to get away from here. It's dangerous."

"But we have to—"

The witch reached for the woman's arm, but instead of gripping the sleeve of a down parka, her fingers disappeared into a rapidly expanding quantum asshole.

The squidsucking scheduling software.

She closed her eyes as her physical body swirled into subatomic mist. The witch solidified, stomach roiling, in the lobby of City Hall.

The tentacled beastie who'd dragged her here would have to wait. If she headed to the roof, she could summon her broom and hightail it to the dump.

That spectacular idiot of a woman might decide to try a rescue mission, and the witch had a soft spot for dumbasses. She whirled, looking for the closest exit, but a trio of Spectral Forces goons blocked the door. Deputy Eye Candy grinned like an idiot and waved hello.

"Move," she said. "Now."

"Can't do that, ma'am." He puffed out his chest and assumed a Captain America–esque heroic stance. "The County Clerk sent us to escort you to the mayor's office."

"I don't have time for this," the witch snapped. "I need to—"

"Witch," trilled a familiar voice. "We're ready for you."

She turned to see a shrouded figure standing in the open door to the mayoral suite. So much for her hope that the election would change things. The County Clerk had already burrowed in like a tick.

"I have to go back to the landfill."

The Clerk ignored her and oozed back into the office. The witch followed, trailed by the Sheriff's finest.

A man in an immaculate three-piece suit bustled over to intercept her. The officious little twit sniffed the air and waved his hand, casting a disapproving eye at her T-shirt—which was perfectly respectable, save for the profanity and the hole. Sensing the witch's mood, Keyser growled.

The mayor's aide glowered at her backpack. "You can't bring an *animal* into the mayor's office!"

She shoved past him and brought her animal into the mayor's office.

Heather glanced up at her from behind a minimalist white desk. The Dread Lord of Human Resources, still sporting his snazzy soul-patched human skin, sat at one end of a love seat, and the Clerk sat at the other. Three Spectral Forces minions and one disgruntled administrative assistant crowded in behind her.

"Send me back to the dump," the witch said. "The Unseen Creeping Horror ate someone, and there's another human inside the fence."

The Dread Lord huffed. "Oh, bother."

"Oh, *bother?*" she repeated. "Listen, Winnie the Pooh, you may not give a shit about human lives—"

"I give multiple shits!"

"Deputy O'Brien, take your squad to the landfill," the Clerk said, "and render whatever aid you can."

"Yes, ma'am."

With a vengeful glare at the witch, the mayor's aide escorted the men out. Heather gestured to a white leather chair opposite the love seat. The witch slid out of her backpack and lowered it to the floor, then plopped down and slung a leg over the arm of the chair.

"Sticky 'nut?" Heather pointed to a box centered on the coffee table. "You should try one. Dee only makes them once a day. If you're not there when she opens at ten, you miss out." She leaned forward and said, in a confidential whisper, "Now that I'm the mayor, Dee lets me in early. One of the perks of—"

The Clerk cleared her throat.

"Anyway," Heather said, "there's something we'd like to discuss with you, Witch." She paused and cocked her head. "It's awkward calling you 'Witch.' What's your actual name?"

The Dread Lord's lips spread in an eager grin, skin rippling as the tentacles beneath writhed in anticipation.

"'Witch' will do." A rasping snore emanated from her backpack, and the Clerk's eyestalks whipped toward it. She didn't want that slimy freak show taking notice of Keyser. "Is this about the fanged toads?"

"I understand you owe the County a pair of arms," the Clerk said.

The Dread Lord squirmed. "I made that statement in anger. I'm told removing limbs lowers employee morale."

All six of the Clerk's eyes rolled. She tugged irritably at her shroud, revealing a vivid flash of patterned fabric. Hot-air balloons, if the witch wasn't mistaken.

Heather flashed a blinding smile. "Effective immediately, I'm promoting you to acting High Lord of Public Works."

The witch sat up so fast she almost fell out of her chair. "What?"

"Consider it an expression of my gratitude," Heather said. "My campaign manager tells me your efforts on my behalf were instrumental in the election."

What the hell? Unless this campaign manager had a sit-down with Discordia Herself, there was no way—

"So it was *you*." The Dread Lord narrowed his crossed eyes at the witch.

"I don't want gratitude," she said, desperate to avoid that particular conversational landmine. "And I damn sure don't want a promotion."

Heather rested her chin on her clasped hands. "Then tell me, what *do* you want out of your career?"

"I want out of my career."

"That option is not on the table," the Clerk said.

"Then we have nothing to discuss."

Heather arched an eyebrow. "It comes with a raise."

"I don't want a. . .Wait, how much?"

The mayor consulted a paper on her desk and opened her mouth to reply.

"Never mind." No amount of money was worth having to do actual work. "I don't want a raise. I want to be left alone to serve out my sentence in peace!"

"It's not a sentence," the Dread Lord lisped. "It's just a contract."

It was just a contract in the same way a tornado was just wind.

The day she'd reached the age of reason—six years, six months, and six days old—the witch had signed a statement of intent agreeing to a century-long term of service. (Technically, the duration was one hundred years and a day. That extra day made her madder than a puffed toad.) After the completion of a thirteen-year probationary period that had commenced on her seventeenth birthday, her contract would become permanent and bind her tighter than a gnat's ass. Her Archonic nanny had offered her six-year-old self a cookie to sign WITCH on the dotted line, and now, here she was—trapped for the rest of her unnatural life. She'd barely been able to read *See Rat-Things Run* at the time!

"What you want is irrelevant." The Clerk's shroud fluttered as the grotesque form it concealed shifted in frustration. "You are a public servant."

"I'm a prisoner."

"Not yet," the Clerk said. "But that can be arranged."

"But this Public Works bullshit isn't even *in* my contract!"

"Ahem," the Dread Lord said. "A contractual provision allows the County to assign temporary duties for up to two weeks."

"To hell with your provision. I'm not doing it."

A tentacle slithered out from under the Clerk's shroud and wound around the witch's ankle, then yanked her up into the air. Her boot sizzled as acidic slime ate into the leather.

"You are." The Clerk shook the witch hard, producing a rain of keys, BlackBerry, and Tic Tacs.

The witch shrunk her foot just enough to slide free of her shoe, then flipped in midair like a cat on her ninth life and landed standing on her chair. She snapped her fingers, and the scattered contents of her pockets swarmed back to their original position.

The Clerk dropped the boot, and the tentacle retreated. "You are powerful, Witch," she said, smoothing her shroud. "I like power, and your perversity and casual sadism amuse me. But I will not tolerate disrespect."

The witch sat down and opened her mouth to reply, but the Clerk wasn't finished.

Three of her eyes flicked toward the Dread Lord of Human Resources. "Test my patience again, and he *will* take your arms. You can get by without them for a few days."

"He can try." She'd mop the floor with that squidular shit stain.

"Indeed. His battle form is most"—the Clerk's eyes blinked in unison—"interesting."

Battle form? What was he, a frigging Pokémon?

"Ahem," the Dread Lord said, practically writhing in discomfort. "As Mayor Chadwick said, you'll be the *acting* High Lord of Public Works. The truth of the matter is that we have a personnel crisis."

So this wasn't a reward for getting Spandex Barbie elected. She should've known.

"Not my circus," the witch said, "not my nightgaunts."

"Your nightgaunts are whatever I say—"

"If I may," the Dread Lord said, raising his hand. The Clerk waved a gooey limb, and he continued. "For years, the Unseen Creeping Horror has served both as the High Lord of Public Works and the Dread Lord of Solid Waste Management. Over the past few weeks, his mental state has deteriorated. He should still be able to perform his landfill-related duties, but he is no longer able to lead the Department of Public Works. The mayor proposed you as a temporary replacement while we recruit a more. . .suitable candidate."

"Look," the witch said, "you've been dealing with my shit for years. I'm anti-social. Defiant. Lazy."

"Rude," the Dread Lord said. "Malicious. Scary."

"Exactly!"

Wait. . .*scary*?

"When Heather first suggested you take the position, I was appalled," he said. "But as I learned at my team-building retreat—"

"Oh, here we go," the Clerk muttered.

"—giving an employee the opportunity to lead often results in improved performance. This position will give you unfettered access—"

The Clerk coughed.

"Lightly fettered access," the Dread Lord said, "to the inner workings of the Tophet County government. You'll be rubbing articulated limbs with the Archonic elite. This might be just the thing to reinvigorate your commitment to public service."

The witch opened her mouth, a snappy retort on the tip of her tongue, but something he'd said hovered in the forefront of her mind.

"What kind of access are we talking about here?"

Heather leaned forward with the self-important air of someone about to dish next-level gossip. "The County has a top secret digital archive," she said in a theatrical whisper. "You wouldn't believe what's in there. Roswell, JFK, the moon landing. . ."

Maybe magical contracts?

Forget the public library system. The answer the witch had been looking for could finally be within reach. Her probationary triskaidecade expired when the new fiscal year began at the winter solstice. During probation, the contract bound her body. The permanent version would bind her immortal soul. She didn't have much of a use for the damned thing, but she didn't want these bastards getting their grimy tentacles on it.

Forty days until the solstice. It was worth a try.

"I'll do it."

"Great!" Heather clapped her hands. "I'm so excited to—"

"But don't expect me to go full office bitch and start planning baby showers and birthday parties."

The Dread Lord looked around the room and nodded. "That's settled, then. I'll get you set up with the Dread Lord of IT to upgrade your account privileges. I'll also send a list of your duties and a meeting schedule—"

"There are *meetings*?"

"Isn't it thrilling?" Heather asked. "Before this election, I'd never even attended a County meeting. Now I'm in four or five every day!"

The witch's blood ran cold.

"You'll start first thing Monday morning," the Dread Lord said.

"Thank you for your time, everyone." Heather stood. "If you don't mind, I have a personnel matter to review with the Dread Lord."

The Clerk nodded. "Witch, I shall see you out."

The witch stood and picked up her fallen boot, which was still smoking. Dammit, this was her favorite pair of Docs. She snapped her fingers, restoring the boot to pristine condition, slid her foot inside, and strode out of the mayor's office, followed by the squelchy steps of the County Clerk.

The Clerk sighed. "I'm worried about Yi'danag."

Damn these unending Archonic appellations. "The Unseen Creeping Horror?" the witch guessed.

"Yes, he's been spread too thin of late."

"He's an invisible fog monster. Spread thin is his natural state."

"Truth be told," the Clerk said, lowering her voice, "I suspect it's the change."

"The change?"

"When a male Archon transitions from one stage of life to the next, he undergoes a period of. . .turbulence. He becomes irrational. Bloodthirsty. Unpredictable."

The witch snorted. The Dread Lord of HR had eaten her middle finger the last time she flipped him the bird, and the Sheriff routinely drank people. "I can't imagine." But that got her thinking about what she knew of the Tophet County org chart. "Hold up a minute. I'm going to be supervising Archons?"

"You are not the only human High Lord." The Clerk began walking—well, locomoting—down the hall, forcing the witch to trot along after her. "Ellie Dawson is the High Lord of Recreation and Culture." The Clerk paused and touched a tentacle to the general vicinity of her several hearts, a sign of great respect. "She supervises the Dread Librarian and the Dread Culture Czar with no issues."

Of all the inexplicable bullshit that came with Archonic rule, their superstitious awe of nineteen-year-old Ellie Dawson was one of the greatest mysteries. After earning her Girl Scout Gold Award a few years ago, the Clerk had hand-picked her for High Lordship. Tophet County didn't have many Girl Scouts these days. Enrollment dropped off after a kayak trip on Tehom Lake ended with all but one Girl Scout—Ellie—being dragged off to the Deep Ones' underwater city of Sog'teggothol.

The rest of them might still be Scouts, but they definitely weren't girls anymore.

"She earned the Gold Award," the Clerk said in a reverent whisper. "The *Gold*."

"I'm aware."

"I expect you to give this position your best effort, Witch."

"But—"

"To put it in terms you'll understand," the Clerk said, "don't fuck this up."

She watched the shrouded figure ooze away, leaving a trail of smoking floor tiles under the bare tips of her tentacles. This whole farcical nightmare made no sense. The witch had, at every turn, done her best to demonstrate her unreliability, recalcitrance, and penchant for rebellion. Now her former vocational aspirations—*do as little as possible without being eaten* and *avoid contact with others*—were no longer achievable.

Fine. Screw those tentacled assholes.

She was an acting High Lord with lightly fettered access to a treasure trove of secret information. Her new mission was to find out as much as she could before this assignment ended.

Preferably without being dis-armed.

CHAPTER EIGHT

The Murder Machine

The witch gulped the last of her coffee, still shivering from the broom ride in, and tossed the cup into the Unquenchable Flame (aka City Hall's Archonic Head of Security).

"Hey!" he snapped. "I'm not a garbage fire; I'm an all-consuming inferno of cosmic rage."

She dodged around him, but he spitefully flared up and singed the hem of her cloak with a blaze of blue fire.

Asshole.

The witch picked up her pace and jogged toward the Executive Hearing Room. She was cutting it close. Her first General Session as the acting High Lord of Public Works started at nine—unspeakably early for a nocturnal creature such as herself. For once, she didn't want to be late. Who knew what manner of occult esoterica the High Lords discussed in their super-secret. . .

She stopped in front of the door, panting from exertion, and read the sign. *Tophet County General Session: Open to the Public.*

Lovecraft's withered wiener. If any jackass could attend, she wasn't going to learn anything useful. Might as well head back to her office and take a nap. She spun on her heel and ran smack-dab into the mayor's assistant.

"Good morning, Witch," he chirped, stepping past her to open the door. "Allow me."

"Is *that* how you operate this arcane mechanism?" she asked, all wide-eyed innocence. "The strain of learning something new is too much for me. I must retire to my chamber and—"

"The Clerk asked me to keep the minutes today." He bared his teeth. "I will, of course, be noting who is present, and who is—"

The witch muted him. The iron-barred door fell shut with a thud as he thrashed like a moon-beast in a mating frenzy. He reached for her but recovered his senses before he made contact.

"Simmer down, sweetheart. I'll undo it later." Ignoring his frantic gestures, she snapped her fingers and summoned the last of her Swisher Sweets. "Probably." She lit the cigarillo, winked, and went inside.

A horseshoe of chairs behind a mahogany barrier occupied a raised platform at the far end of the room, and a wildly optimistic number of folding chairs filled the rest of the space. The witch recognized most of the dozen attendees as lower-level County officials. She headed for the last row, slid into a seat, and looked around.

At the center of the wooden arc, Heather sat on a baroque throne upholstered in tufted red velvet. A brass nameplate on the wood paneling read *Human Mayor*. She was chatting with the Archon to her left, a four-eyed winged octopus—Y'ggarlos, the High Lord of Economic Development. Ellie Dawson was next to the cephalopod, seated in her wheelchair. As ever, she wore a white blouse and her tan Girl Scouts sash. Nommaquth, the High Lord of Administration, occupied the final spot on the left. As a cloud of mutagenic glowing bubbles, his "seat" was a large wheeled aquarium.

To the mayor's right, Achartho, the High Lord of Public Safety, perched on a backless stool to accommodate his wings and barbed scorpion tail. The next throne was empty. At the end of the row, suspended between the wall and the horseshoe of chairs, a silvery web glimmered in the fluorescent light. At its center crouched the Spinner—N'eithamiqug, High Lord of Health and Human Services. A matronly, pink-cheeked human face with a beehive hairstyle crowned her bloated spider's body. Besides the standard human pair, the Spinner had six additional eyes—three atop each cheekbone.

The witch shuddered. She hated spiders.

A tentacle snaked out of her peripheral vision, wrapped around her cigarillo, and broke it in two.

"Smoking is not permitted in County buildings," said the Dread Lord of Human Resources. "Don't you know these things cause cancer?"

The witch spent a moment scrambling to clear her mind of her true name before she remembered it wasn't there. Over the weekend, she'd whispered it into an expired jar of Hellmann's and hidden it in her freezer for the duration of this ill-advised occupational adventure.

She shrugged. "So does Bubbles, but you're not harassing him."

"Nommaquth does not cause cancer," the Dread Lord said. "He mutates living creatures as he consumes their life force. It's totally different." The tentacle, which originated from the Dread Lord's left ear, deposited her Swisher Sweet in his open mouth. He chewed and swallowed. "And *he* has the social graces to contain his essence in a sealed receptacle."

A plume of steam rose over the Dread Lord's shoulder. The witch leaned forward and caught sight of Ronnie Coffman, Director of the Office of Management and Budget. Long gray hair and an impressive beard cascaded over a tie-dyed T-shirt. He raised a silver Canna Blast to his lips. The Dread Lord's eyes followed her gaze, and he turned toward Ronnie, hands on his hips.

"Mr. Coffman, I've told you repeatedly, you can't vape marijuana during General Sessions."

"Sorry, man." Ronnie took a final puff and slid the vape pen into his pocket.

The witch stood, intending to sit by her new best friend, but the clammy hand of the Dread Lord's human skin wrapped around her wrist. She tugged her arm free, and he pointed at the vacant throne next to N'eithamiqug.

"*That's* your seat."

Mother of dragons. No way.

"Unless sitting next to the Spinner makes you uncomfortable."

The witch cocked her head and gave him a considering once-over. With his recent team-building bullshit, she couldn't tell if he was messing with her or being sincere. Either way, she didn't really have a choice. She could sit next to that corpulent arachnid horror, or she could reveal a weakness to a senior Archon.

"Uncomfortable?" The witch snorted. "Not likely. I was just hoping to take a nap."

"You are a High Lord of Tophet County. You do not nap during public meetings." His eyes flicked down to today's statement T-shirt: *Resting Witch Face*. "And you should dress more professionally now that you're—"

The crack of a gavel startled him into silence.

"Good morning, everyone," Heather said. Her assistant hovered behind her, pointing from his soundless mouth to the witch. "Yes, I see her."

He threw up his hands and skulked to his chair.

Heather pasted on a smile and surveyed the sparse audience. "I now call to order this General Session of the Tophet County Executives." Her eyes settled on the witch. "Come on up and take your seat, and we'll get started."

The witch sighed and trudged up a carpeted ramp to the raised platform. She eased into her ridiculous throne, and a stiff, hairy spider's leg slid a sheet of paper across the wooden desktop.

An agenda.

A very *long* agenda.

Heather launched into an opening monologue detailing all the shit she intended to do for Tophet County during her first term as human mayor—and

THE WITCH OF TOPHET COUNTY   47

yes, she said *first* term. The witch slouched in her chair. Screw it. She'd take a nap anyway. She closed her eyes and slowed her breathing, but before she was even close to blessed oblivion, something poked her left shoulder. Her eyes flew open in time to see one of the Spinner's oddly jointed legs retreating. The leg was crawling with tiny spiders.

Behind cat's-eye glasses, the High Lord of Health and Human Services winked and whispered, "You drifted off, dear."

The witch felt a tickling sensation on her upper arm. One of the little fuckers had disembarked. "You lost one of your. . .um. . ."

"My children!" N'eithamiqug extended a leg and made a metallic chittering sound. The little spider jumped from the witch's arm back to his mother's horrifying embrace. "Would you believe the County doesn't provide childcare for employees? I'm so excited to have a female mayor."

Heather wrapped up her opening remarks and said, "First on the agenda, we'll be hearing from the Department of Recreation and Culture." She switched off her microphone and nodded to Ellie Dawson.

Every Archon present touched wing, bubble, tentacle, or insectile limb to whatever served as a thorax. The witch eyed the teenage girl who sat serenely, taking it all in. Ellie swept her long, pale blonde hair over her shoulder to display a trio of metallic pins—gold, silver, and bronze—glinting on her sash.

"Thank you, Mayor Chadwick," Ellie said. "Good morning, everyone. R&C only has a few announcements today. First, on behalf of the Dread Librarian, we request the return of *The Get-It-On-Onomicon* to Derleth Memorial Library."

Holy hopping horny hell. Someone had successfully stolen a book from the Read at Your Own Risk room!

"The Nomicons are for in-library use only." Ellie shook her head in disapproval. "Come on, people—this is why we have the internet."

The witch glanced around at the Archons hanging on Ellie's every word. The favor of She Who Earned the Gold was a coveted prize. The tall, dark, and squigglies would turn Tophet County inside out to find that missing book. Bad news for some sticky-fingered horndog, but overall, good news for the witch. This proved it could be done. She just had to wait out her ban and figure out how.

"The Dread Culture Czar thanks everyone who attended last quarter's community workshop, Evil Cults: A Tophet County Tradition. The local branches of both the Illuminati and the Reptilians have revived their plans for world domination, and a small group of citizens formed a new cult. Interested parties can learn more on the R&C website."

"Thank you, Ellie," Heather said. "Next on the agenda, we'll hear from the High Lord of Public Safety."

The witch suppressed a groan as Achartho's buzzing voice droned on in a stream of updates on the County's emergency services and correctional system. Then he passed the oratorial baton to the Spinner for a long-winded report from Health and Human Services.

She might not be able to leave, but they couldn't make her pay attention.

She extended a tendril of auric energy to Keyser Söze, who was at home napping in her clean laundry, and prodded him until he grumpily trundled into her bedroom and opened *The Thrill of the Chaste*. Looking through his eyes, the witch lost herself in the unfolding romance between Amos, the rakish farmhand, and Sarah, the devout farmer's daughter—who'd better, if a certain author knew what was good for her, take a page from *The Get-It-On-Onomicon* and enjoy a long-overdue bonefest before the end of this book. She'd just reached the scene where Amos and Sarah were, after five books of flirtation, lawfully wed and preparing to consummate their love, when a leathery wing nudged her.

"You're up," Achartho said.

"What?" The witch frantically tried to reorganize her circulation so blood was flowing to her brain instead of her McMuffin. She glanced over at Heather, who glared at her with pursed lips. The mayor's aide smirked from his desk at the end of the horseshoe. His lips moved, and the witch wrinkled her nose to unmute him.

"—serves you right, you vicious hag!"

Heather's laser eyes left the witch and burned into the shocked man. "Tim, what has gotten into you today?"

"That's a, um, traditional witch greeting." As much as the witch disliked the little twit, she was always on the side of those in trouble with the boss. She bit the insides of her cheeks to keep from smiling, then said, "And may it serve you right, you scrotal horse's ass."

His cheeks glowed, but he nodded gravely.

Heather cleared her throat. "Okay, then. Any updates from the Department of Public Works?"

Updates? How the hell was she supposed to know? "Uh. . .no?"

A tight smile formed on Heather's face—the kind that meant *I'll deal with you later*. "Very well." She craned her neck to look at the large glass aquarium. "Administration?"

The green light on the microphone in front of Nommaquth lit up as bubbles roiled inside the tank. After several furious bursts of soapy communication, the light went out.

Ellie Dawson shook her head. "That's just chilling."

Heather opened her mouth, closed it again, and finally said, "Thank you, High Lord." She turned to the giant winged octopus on her left. "We'll wrap up with the Department of Economic Development."

After providing a near-fatally boring account of last week's Zoning Board meeting, Y'ggarlos said, "The last item from my department comes from our liaison at Catachthonic University, Dr. Christian Carcosa."

The witch's ears pricked up. She knew that name.

A disheveled man with a unibrow thicker than a caterpillar made his way to the speaker's podium carrying a folded easel under one arm and a tube of rolled paper under the other. He unrolled the paper and secured it to the easel with giant clips.

"On behalf of the Dimensional Physics Department," Dr. Carcosa said, blinking up at the High Lords through Coke-bottle glasses, "I want to thank you for supporting the cutie project."

The cutie? Weird, but it was better than mixed-use zoning designations.

"As you know, we've hit a few snags along the way, but—"

"Yeah, man, I've got a couple questions." Ronnie Coffman now stood at the freestanding microphone reserved for members of the community.

Dr. Carcosa attempted to straighten his bow tie, which was cocked at a forty-five-degree angle. "Sure. But first, if I could just—"

"Go ahead, Mr. Coffman," Heather said.

"So, like, this project has cost almost a million dollars," Ronnie said, "and what you've got so far is a murder machine."

"It's not a murder machine," Dr. Carcosa said. "It's a quantum tunneling device."

Ah, *QT*. That made much more sense.

"Everything that goes in comes out dead, man."

"That's not true," Dr. Carcosa protested. "The subjects didn't come out dead."

"They're definitely not alive. They were like, marble statues, man." Ronnie consulted his notes. "So far, I count eleven lab rats, two rabbits, and a custodian."

"I asked Janitorial not to clean my lab during testing!" Dr. Carcosa ran his hand through a brown mop of Einsteinian dimensions. "No one actually saw what happened, so we can't—"

"There's some wild stuff in here." He waved a stack of documents in Carcosa's direction. "Like, in the section where you're supposed to describe the project's basis, you wrote 'Oneiric inspiration.' What does that even mean?"

"It means the theoretical concept came to me in dreams."

Dreams. That was it—the mopey yogini with the workaholic husband.

"Lovecraft sensed our presence in his dreams," Achartho buzzed, "so there *is* some precedent."

"Fair enough." Ronnie sighed and lowered his papers. "But I'm the money guy. I gotta make sure this thing is legit, you dig?"

"I. . .dig." Dr. Carcosa smoothed his rumpled sport coat and peered over his glasses at Ronnie. "As you know, the County Clerk endowed the Dimensional

Physics Department for the express purpose of studying Archonic teleportation. This project seeks to prove my hypothesis that the ability relies on manipulating random quantum interactions. I assure you, Mr. Coffman, the theoretical foundations of this work are sound—are they not, High Lord Dawson?"

Ellie nodded, sparking a flurry of animated whispers from the audience. The witch rolled her eyes. As if the endorsement of a teenage Girl Scout would—

"If Ellie's good with your science, so am I," Ronnie said. "Just doing my job. Fiduciary duty and all that jazz. We're cool."

As Ronnie shambled back to his seat, the good doctor returned his attention to the row of High Lords. "As requested by the High Lord of Public Safety, I've relocated my laboratory to an abandoned military bunker several miles outside of town," he said. "I'm testing my device at seven o'clock tonight. As stipulated in Section III, Part D, of the Statement of Work, I need an official County observer."

This pronouncement was met with resounding silence.

"My new lab is thirty feet underground, which reduces background entropy and should prevent repeating our past. . .mishaps." Dr. Carcosa glanced hopefully from face to face.

"Not it," Heather said, touching her nose.

A ripple of motion washed over the horseshoe of thrones as fingers met probosides, accompanied by a chorus of murmured negations. Nommaquth's green light flared as his bubbles churned.

Heather banged her gavel. "The acting High Lord of Public Works will attend."

"No way," the witch said. "I'm not—"

"Dr. Carcosa will send you the details," Heather said. "One more announcement before we adjourn. The County is seeking to hire a senior curse breaker. Please refer any qualified candidates to—"

"What happened to Doug?" the witch asked. He'd only been with the government for three or four years. His contractual term couldn't be up already. The only way out of an active contract involved a body bag. . .if, that is, there was enough left to need one.

"He resigned. I understand he's moving to the private sector." Heather banged the gavel again. "This meeting is adjourned."

The Spinner inched toward the witch, a faint gleam of menace in all eight eyes. "I heard Doug lost it after the fanged toads returned last week—invasive species, you know. Difficult to eradicate. He quit the night of the election." Then she shot a jet of web into an expanding sphere of octarine netherlight and vanished in a tangle of legs.

Well, shit. The witch had certainly given the poor bastard a run for his money. She almost felt—

Hold up.

Doug *quit?*

How in the contractual hell had he managed that? Every County employee was under contract with the Archons. Of course, the normies' contracts were measured in years rather than centuries, but still. . .

No one could just quit.

The witch scanned the chamber, but the curse breaker wasn't there. A flash of color caught her eye as Ronnie rose and started making his way toward the rear of the room—vape pen in one hand, blueprints in the other. Ronnie knew everybody, and he'd worked for the County since before the Emergence. She pushed back her throne and hurried after him. He was surprisingly fast for a perpetually stoned bureaucrat. The witch caught up just as he banged through the door leading outside.

"That was about as much fun as a punch to the cumberbatch," she said, falling into step beside him.

"Those things are always a drag."

Ronnie hit the vape pen and offered it to her. She drew on it and passed it back. Good ol' Ronnie.

He sat on a bench in the smoking area, waving a hand for the witch to join him. "At least Vera wasn't there."

"Who's Vera?"

"You know, Vera Vásquez." When she shook her head, he said, "She's always tweeting these wacky conspiracies, and she pops up at meetings to rant about her theories. Last week, she was on about a Dorito that looked like Cthulhu. Said it was a sign that Frito-Lay was a tool of Archonic oppression."

"Were the tentacled beasties pissed?"

"Nah," he said. "They loved it."

She took the proffered vape pen and hit it again. "Big news about Doug, huh?"

"Yeah, man," Ronnie croaked. He exhaled a plume of steam. "Doug's a good dude."

"How'd he manage to quit?" The witch fought to keep her tone casual. The weed helped. "Did his contract have a special clause?"

"Good one." Ronnie elbowed her and chuckled. "Man, it just burns the Clerk up that curse breakers are immune to contracts."

Immune.

The witch forced a smile. "I'm sure it does."

Howard Phillips fucking Lovecraft, curse breakers were *immune* to contracts.

CHAPTER NINE

Dr. Unibrow

O nline Services, this is Chad."

The witch squeezed the phone until the plastic creaked. "Are we still doing this?"

"Are you calling to report a system outage?"

"No, I—"

"Do you require the acquisition or in-house development of new operational functionalities?"

"Gods dammit, would you knock it off? It's been a whole week—"

"Or perhaps you're calling with a proposal for a potentially deadly prank?"

"How long are you planning to stay pissed? For the love of. . ." She paused and took a deep breath. "Look, it worked out, didn't it? Heather's fine. She's freaking *loving* this mayor gig. And anyway, I already said. . ."

"Said what?"

"That I, um, regretted my actions."

"I regret eating that second sticky 'nut," he said, "but it didn't endanger any lives."

Screw this. She wasn't going to grovel. She'd apologized—just, you know, silently.

The witch's eyes drifted to the page of incomprehensible equations she'd copied from *The Quantumnomicon* a few years ago. She'd have to dive face-first into a bowlful of calculus to make sense of this gibberish, and she didn't have that kind of time.

"Thank you for calling Online Services," Chad said. "Have a nice—"

"I'm sorry!" She braced herself for him to exact his punishment, to rub her nose in the proverbial puddle of her own wrongdoing.

"I forgive you."

"What?"

"So, what's up?"

"That's it? I say I'm sorry, and you're just. . .over it?"

"Did you mean it?"

The witch smirked and opened her mouth to say she hadn't when she realized to her growing horror that she kind of had. "I. . .I, uh. . ."

"I thought so."

She could hear the smile in his voice. Against her will, her own stupid face grinned in return.

"That's how it works, Witch. You mess up. You apologize. You move on."

Most of the sentient beings she interacted with hated her, feared her, or wanted to use her. Chad was the only person in her life who'd ever treated her like an actual person. It felt weird. . .but good.

"We're cool."

"Uh, cool," she said. "I'm glad."

"I'm guessing this is about the scheduling software. I've already had like a dozen complaints about the teleportation feature," he said, with an Eeyore-ish sigh. "Apparently, it doesn't transport prosthetic limbs, dental work, or implanted medical devices. We're working on it."

"It's not that." The witch hesitated. If Chad was going to be any help at all, she needed to tell him she was trying to break a magical contract. But if the Archons got wind of her plan. . .Well, she wasn't sure what they'd do, but it would most likely be some combination of excruciating, revolting, and fatal.

"Okay," he said when the pause stretched on. "What is it, then?"

Chad was a good guy. As evidenced by his reaction to her endangering his ex-wife (a service her more vindictive clients had attempted to purchase on multiple occasions), his bizarre code of honor probably wouldn't let him turn her in.

"It's best if I explain in person," she said, "but first, how are you with the Greek-alphabet sort of math?"

"I minored in math at Cat U. I freaking love it."

"Can you help me make sense of some equations from *The Quantumnomicon*?"

"*The Q!*" he exclaimed with a borderline insane level of enthusiasm. "I helped the Dread Lord of IT proof that beast."

"Your boss wrote it?"

"Not alone," he said. "His human co-author covered the higher-level physics—but yeah."

"Then, you'll help me?"

"Sure, sweep on over and I'll take a look."

"*Sweep* on over?"

"You know, because you ride a broom."

The witch rolled her eyes and hung up, shaking her head. She couldn't quite keep the smile off her face as she straddled her broom and kicked off through the wall.

After an afternoon of Chad's enthusiastic mathematical tutelage, the witch had reached her academic limit and headed home. Tragically, that heaping helping of quantum nerdistry didn't end the day's educational torment. Dr. Carcosa paused at minute forty-two of a criminally verbose physics lesson to glance at his watch. If he'd had two eyebrows, they would've drawn together, but as it was, the single brow humped in the center like an inchworm.

"Any questions before we get started?"

The witch opened her mouth to reply, but he kept going.

"I hate to rush off, but I must begin precisely at seven. I've been mapping the entropic tides. Did you know background entropy ebbs and flows on a predictable schedule? It's a fascinating phenomenon! Today's low point occurs six seconds past seven o'clock." He pushed his glasses up the bridge of his nose. "The device functions best with the lowest possible entropy. Being underground helps, but—"

"Just go," she said, desperate to end his monologue. The witch had an experiment of her own to perform, and she needed Dr. Unibrow elsewhere. "I'll be—"

"You'll be perfectly safe."

That was the fifth time he'd made that statement. Not exactly a confidence builder.

"I've shielded the lab against radiation and entropic bursts. Nothing's getting through this," he said, tapping the six-inch-thick glass of the viewing window. He frowned at his reflection. "Nothing I can think of, anyway."

It took her grabbing his elbow and escorting him to the reinforced steel door, but he left. Once she was alone, the witch eased her backpack to the floor and opened the drawstring. Keyser Söze waddled out, emitted a thunderous and eye-watering fart, and curled up on her feet. She retrieved the three-inch-thick binder containing her notes from thirteen years of Nomiconical research, turned to the tab labeled *Quantumnomicon*, and flipped to the heavily annotated section titled *The Quantum Effects of Entropine and Syntropine*.

The potential cure for her contractual ills was obvious. As a witch, she produced a high quantity of magic-fueling entropine. Curse breakers, in contrast, churned out magic-neutralizing syntropine. Magical contracts were, well. . .*magical*. It stood to reason that—unlike normal humans, who were neutral, or the witch, who was staggeringly entropic—a syntropic curse breaker could not be placed under a magical contract. The answer had been staring her in the face and undoing all her best pranks for the past twelve-plus years. If she made herself as syntropic as a curse breaker, her contractual bond should dissolve.

With Chad's patient assistance, she'd deciphered the convoluted equations in *The Quantumnomicon*, then woven in concepts from *The Hexonomicon*. The result was a spell to convert her body's entire reserve of entropine to syntropine. Unfortunately, the converted energy was about as stable as a trailer in a tornado. If the spell didn't hold, it would revert to its original form, releasing a massive burst of energy. She loathed the Archons, and her feelings about her fellow humans ranged from indifference to borderline murderous, but she wasn't quite at the "magical mushroom cloud" level of antagonism.

Then Dr. Unibrow's email arrived. A three-page list of the safety measures protecting the observation chamber convinced her his underground lab was the safest possible place for her experiment.

The witch kept her eyes glued to the digital countdown. She'd trigger her spell at the same time the good doctor activated the QT, which would happen in exactly eleven seconds.

Ten. . .nine. . .eight. . .

She positioned the tip of her sickle-shaped knife blade at the top of her palm. This spell required more than just a few drops of blood.

Seven. . .six. . .five. . .

Keyser stirred uneasily and sat up, gripping her jeans with the nimble fingers of his single front paw. She patted his head, refusing to meet his worried gaze.

Four. . .three. . .two. . .

Discordia, protect us.

One.

The witch drew the blade along her skin, and a rivulet of blood welled. She closed her eyes and whispered the incantation, doing her best not to trip over the consonant-heavy Ouranian-Barbaric tongue. When she pronounced the final syllable, she emptied her entropic reservoir into an astral cauldron. Fully depleted, she'd only have a few seconds of consciousness before she passed out, but Keyser stood ready to top her off once the spell was done. A jagged blaze of light streaked up from the cauldron like reverse lightning. The syntropic bolt lanced into her crown chakra, forming a sphere of energy that descended to her third eye. The psychic tentacles of her Archonic contract stiffened and writhed, and her spirit soared with exultant joy.

But the bolt didn't stop there. It descended the central channel and continued toward her chest. As the sphere drifted below her collarbones, the twining rope of energy that extended from her heart to Keyser's, binding them together as witch and familiar, began to fray.

Oh, gods, no. . .

She'd been so blind, so focused on attaining her freedom that she hadn't stopped to consider the fact that her contract wasn't the only thing bound to her by magic.

If she had no entropine, she was no longer a witch, and if she wasn't a witch, she'd have no familiar.

A hoarse scream tore free of her throat. Her astral hands reached into her chest, grabbed the sphere of syntropic energy, and hurled it away with all her strength. A brilliant white flash blinded her, closing even her third eye. Then the harsh glow faded into inky blackness, and the witch saw no more.

CHAPTER TEN

The Unseen Creeping Horror

Deputy Eye Candy raised his hands and backed away from the witch. "I come in peace!"

She was in no mood for bullshit. After last night's disaster, Keyser Söze had awakened her from a dead faint by biting her earlobe hard enough to draw blood. The damn thing was *still* throbbing. Though he'd immediately re-upped her entropine, the failed spell left her as limp as a Proud Boy's priapus. Worse, her contract with the Archons still bound her tighter than a trussed-up Shantak.

She'd tried to find Carcosa and make sure he was okay, but the lab was empty and the scarlet strobe of warning lights sent her sprinting for the surface. In a fun demonstration of Murphy's law, the godsdamned power was out, so she'd had to carry a pissed off raccoon up eleven flights of stairs in pitch darkness. They'd flown home low and slow through stinging, frigid sleet.

"You're lurking outside the restroom," she snapped. "How do I know you're not about to whip out your Weinstein?"

"My what?" He lowered his hands, displaying a forehead wrinkled under the unaccustomed strain of cogitation. "I'm here to bring you to the landfill."

"I already did my time."

"What?"

"What?"

Then it hit her—the *landfill*. The last time she'd seen the dapper deputy, the Clerk was sending him out on a rescue mission. "Did you save her?"

"Who?"

"The woman I saw at the dump on Friday," she said. "The Unseen Creeping Horror ate her friend. You were supposed to help her."

He stared at his boots, which had been polished to a shine glossy enough to reflect his aggressively masculine jawline. "She was gone when we got there."

Gone.

Discordia, have mercy on her soul.

"Well, her blood's on the Clerk's tentacles," the witch said. "If she hadn't called me away—"

"The Clerk's the one who sent me to get you."

"Why?"

"You're the High Lord of Public Works—"

"*Acting* High Lord."

"—and the Dread Lord of Solid Waste Management is one of your direct reports. He's. . .Well, you'll just have to see for yourself."

That would be Yi'danag, the Unseen Creeping Horror—that vaporous cloud of whinery who'd been *spread too thin* lately.

"He can fuck all the way off," the witch said. "His only job is to hang out in the landfill and eat. He pushed the rest of it off on me."

"Look, ma'am—"

"Ma'am?"

"The Clerk is waiting. If we don't show up soon. . ."

The witch considered her options. She'd planned to bully her way into the psychic surgery later to get topped off, but as of now, she was practically defenseless—especially with Keyser holed up under her bed at home. The poor thing slept like a baby last night, as in he'd shat himself and woken up screaming. After what she'd put him through, it was no wonder.

"Fine." She pushed past the uniformed man and stalked toward her office. "But you're driving."

Deputy Eye Candy, who now insisted she call him Hank, talked nonstop for the whole drive. When they reached the landfill, the witch hopped out before the Hummer had rolled to a complete stop. Slogging up the hill left her with what promised to be a jackhammering bastard of a headache, but all thoughts of her discomfort faded when she looked out over the Tophet County landfill. What had once been a reeking garbage pit was now a featureless snowy plain. The mountain of refuse was gone, and the Unseen Creeping Horror with it. She walked out onto the pristine plateau. The place couldn't have been whiter if it claimed to be colorblind.

A Spectral Forces officer approached what looked like a dumpster-size trapdoor. The witch watched as he bent and grabbed the handle, straining to lift the hatch. When nothing happened, he changed tactics and tried sliding the door. This attempt succeeded, and he crouched to look into the opening. He jerked upright, gibbering like the County Clerk had goosed his undercarriage, and jumped into the hole. The door slid shut behind him.

Huh. That took a sinister turn.

"If you ask me, it's an improvement." The witch looked up to find Heather standing next to her, surveying the alabaster hellscape. Today's leggings were flamingo print and the precise color of Pepto-Bismol.

"Oh yeah?" the witch asked. "Well, I think it broke that cop's brain."

"Deputy Woods?" Heather waved a hand in dismissal. "Oh, we'll fish him out later. You know, I've been meaning to make an appointment with you."

The witch sighed. "Let me guess, you need a favor of the magical persuasion."

"I do," Heather said. "I've been having awful nightmares. Sleeping pills don't help, so I was hoping you might give me a potion or something. I'm exhausted."

Now that she mentioned it, the witch noticed shadowed half-moons beneath her eyes. "No need for a potion," she said. "Chicken Cock'll fix you up."

Heather arched an eyebrow. "Seriously?"

"It's nature's multivitamin."

"How much do I—"

"As much as it takes."

"Well, I'll try anything at this point." Heather returned her attention to the glossy expanse. She twirled, arms extended. "Aaaah, it's like someone came along and Marie Kondo'd the landfill." She closed her eyes and took a deep breath. "Even the smell is better—like clean laundry."

"The scent is not the only thing amiss."

The Clerk had oozed up behind Heather, who whirled and pressed a hand to her chest. Her shroud looked positively dingy against the pristine plateau. As ever, she'd left a slimy trail, but her excretions had no effect on the immaculate surface.

"Yi'danag has. . ." The Clerk's voice thickened, almost like she was getting choked up.

When she didn't continue, the witch said, "I haven't seen him. He must've taken off when whatever caused this went down."

The shroud flared as the Clerk turned on her. "Your Sight fails you," she said. "This *is* Yi'danag."

The witch shaded her eyes and squinted at the empty vista. It was hard to see with the afternoon sun shining against a field of blinding white. Now that she focused, she could make out a faint sparkly sheen.

"Holy shit."

"Sacred excrement, indeed." The Clerk bowed her. . .head? "Poor Yi'danag. He does not deserve such a fate."

Heather's lips pursed like she was sucking on a lemon. "Before you gave him this job, he ate three neighborhoods, an RV park, and two hundred head of cattle."

"He is a being of large appetites," the Clerk said. "We must know what happened here. No human could have done this to Yi'danag, and no Archon would dare."

Heather frowned. "What else is there?"

"Mother told stories. . ." The Clerk's shroud fluttered as if it were caught in a breeze, but the air was still. "Whatever force is behind this attack is a threat to all of us." She turned six watery eyes on the witch. "You will perform a reading."

The witch bit her lip. She was awfully low on entropine, but saying no to the Clerk in her current mood was a suicidal impulse. In normal circumstances, she'd need a personal artifact to identify the UCH's spacetime spoor but given that she was standing on top of him, it shouldn't be necessary. She reached out for his temporal trail. A flash of light seared her third eye, spiking a lance of pain into her pounding head.

"Gods dammit! I can't—"

A keening wail sliced through the air. The witch turned to see the Dread Lord of Human Resources restraining a red-haired woman holding a picnic basket.

That red-haired woman. Her stupidity hadn't been terminal after all.

"Behold!" The Clerk raised a dripping tentacle. "Even humans grieve the tragic fate of the Unseen Creeping Horror."

"Poor Lorelei," Heather whispered.

The Clerk's eyestalks swiveled at the sound of her voice. "By the way, Mayor Chadwick, an anonymous citizen called my office to report this calamity, and I sent for the Sheriff and the witch." She glided a few feet closer to Heather, who instinctively retreated. "How did *you* know to come?"

"I came with Sathach."

The witch winced. Humans simply did not address the Archons by their names. By job titles? Yes. By descriptive appellations like the Unseen Creeping Horror? Sure. But not by their names.

Not more than once, anyway.

"Sathach?" The Clerk advanced another couple of inches.

"The. . .the Dread Lord of Human—"

"I damn well know who he is, don't I?" the Clerk snapped. "What are you two doing here?"

"The UCH. . .he hasn't been. . .himself," Heather stammered, "so the Dread Lord sometimes visits during his lunch hour. I ran into him on my way out and offered to come along."

"How *kind* of you."

"You know, I have to be getting back." Heather glanced at her arm, which sported a large Fitbit. "Yep, almost time for my next meeting, so I'll just. . .uh, skedaddle, shall I?" She backed away from the Clerk. "Lovely to see you, Madam, um, Clerk, and you, Witch." She speedwalked away, her pink leggings a lurid blotch of color against the white backdrop.

"Yeah, I should skedaddle too."

"What about Yi'danag?"

The witch surveyed the glittery haze permeating the white surface. "It's a crying shame."

"I mean, what do you intend to do?" the Clerk demanded. "As the High Lord of Public Works, it is your responsibility to ensure the well-being of your employees. Yi'danag has been harmed on your watch."

"That's ri-godsdamned-diculous!" the witch said. "I had nothing to do with this!"

"As evidenced by the fact that you still live, I'm sure you did not." The Clerk leaned closer and lowered her voice. "Given the nature of the crime, I think it's best if a neutral party investigates."

The witch shrugged. "Sounds reasonable."

"I'm glad we agree."

The Clerk emitted a shrill whistle. The ground shook as the giant nest of thrashing tentacles and glowing spheres that was the Sheriff approached, answering the Clerk's call. "Lomelzar, please provide any evidence collected at the scene to the witch."

Her eyes widened in alarm. Evidence?

The Sheriff responded with an indignant and incomprehensible speech that sounded like a cross between screaming brakes and a donkey in heat. He lunged at the Clerk, whose body swelled, ripping through the shroud. Shreds of taco print fabric drifted on the autumn breeze as her expanding bulk shredded her leggings, revealing tentacles dappled with festering sores, gaping mouths, and blinking eyes. The two titans clashed with a meaty smack. Lomelzar's razored tentacles lacerated the Clerk's body, spattering the white plain with a stunning variety of gruesome fluids.

The witch pulled on her magic to generate a protective shield, but nothing happened. Impossible. She hadn't been *entirely* out of entropine.

An unearthly shriek split the air, followed by the sound of tearing flesh. She turned and ran.

A twitching tentacle thudded to the ground in front of the witch. She hurdled it like an Olympian and sprinted toward the edge of the landfill, dry heaving all the way. The pressure in her aching head eased when her boots crunched on leaf-strewn gravel, enabling her to put on a burst of speed. She raced to the bottom of the hill and banged through the chain-link fence, searching the parking lot for Deputy Eye Candy.

"Hank!"

Where was that muscle-bound moron? They needed to get the hell out of here. If the Clerk came out on the wrong end of this little disagreement, the Sheriff was liable to vent any remaining frustration by spraying a certain witch with acid and drinking her liquefied remains. With her magic not responding, she might as well be a freaking Capri Sun.

The sounds of battle ceased, and the witch glanced up the hill. An enormous figure stood silhouetted at the top against the dazzling sun, tentacles lashing.

Shit, shit, *shit.*

She rattled the door handles.

Locked.

This was it, then. She turned to face what would certainly be an ugly and unpleasant death.

As the approaching figure shrank from full Archonic size to human-equivalent proportions, the witch realized it wasn't the Sheriff. A torn tentacle attached to a luminescent orb dangled from the largest of the County Clerk's mouths. She chewed and the orb burst, spattering glowing ichor.

The witch turned and vomited down the side of Hank's Hummer. She sagged against the vehicle, shaking with weakness and adrenaline. To avoid another pukefest, she kept her eyes fixed on the pavement—dignity be damned.

"Lomelzar harbors rather dated views about the place of females in the Archonic hierarchy," the Clerk trilled. "He's been trying to displace me for years." She dropped a crumpled, gore-specked paper bag at the witch's feet. "This is the only item found at the scene. That idiot Sheriff picked it up himself, which means he's destroyed any physical trace evidence."

Why in all the worlds would the Clerk drag her into this? The witch was neither a detective nor a forensic curse breaker. Mentioning that now, however, could have disastrous consequences for her health. Best to nod and go along with this insanity, at least until she could replenish her entropine. She picked up the bag with trembling hands.

"I expect an update after the General Session on Tuesday," the Clerk said.

"I'll get right on it."

Drops of the Sheriff's neon slime dribbled from the Clerk's tentacles to the asphalt. The witch choked back a queasy surge of bile.

"See that you do."

CHAPTER ELEVEN

May Cause Permanent Madness

The witch glared at the vividly stained paper bag on her desk. She'd ignored her predicament during the Sour Diesel–induced haze of the weekend. Then, courtesy of the thrice-cursed scheduling software, yesterday had been consumed by back-to-back meetings, leaving her in a homicidal temper. Her mood was not improved by the fact that Keyser Söze continued to be plagued by night terrors. She'd given up on sleep at four thirty this morning and come to work blasphemously early.

The Clerk expected an update today, and the witch had nothing. She shivered, remembering the sight of that monstress consuming part of the Sheriff. Best to avoid disappointing someone who used cannibalism for conflict resolution. The Clerk probably wouldn't kill her, but there was a lot of unpleasant real estate between "totally unharmed" and "permanently disembodied."

Maybe she could call off sick. There was that thing going around that caused haunted warts.

No one would buy it. Her wart-destroying prowess was legendary.

Shag a Shoggoth sideways.

Grimacing in disgust, the witch unrolled the top of the gore-specked bag and tipped it over. A white sphere the size of a large grapefruit rolled off her desk and came to rest on the floor under her window. A fat dimple marked one end of the shiny ball, and a mustard-yellow splotch—courtesy, no doubt, of the Sheriff's neon fluids—discolored the surface. She beckoned to the sphere. It should've rolled its happy ass right back to her, but nothing happened.

The witch snapped her fingers. Nothing. She couldn't be low on entropine. After the horror of the landfill scene, Hank had dropped her at the psychic surgery for a full auric replenishment.

With a heavy sigh, she pushed back from her desk and walked to the window to retrieve the godsdamned thing. The witch felt an odd prickling pressure as she drew closer. When she picked up the sphere, it stung her with a tingling zap. It fell to the floor with a clatter as she shook her hand to dispel the sensation.

"You pasty little shit!"

A melodic ringtone chimed from her laptop. The witch inched toward her desk, regarding the device with suspicion. What fresh hell was this?

Incoming video call from Chad Chadwick, Online Services.

She sat down and clicked accept.

Chad's image appeared in a new window on her screen. "Have you seen the Dread Lord of IT?"

"Hello to you too, asshole." She peered at his face. His hair was styled in the same short, freeform locs, but something was different.

"He was acting weird last week, and now he's missing."

The witch examined his formerly clean-shaven brown skin. "Are you growing a divorce beard?"

"What?"

"You are!"

"What do you think?" He ran a self-conscious hand over his chin.

Not bad at all. "You don't look like a truant teenager anymore."

"Thanks." His smile faded, and he said, "I'm worried, Witch. I can't find the Dread Lord, and our systems are acting up."

"The scheduling software?"

"Yeah, but not the usual witch-induced outage." He chewed his lip, staring at something off-screen. "This time, we're seeing a new functionality. Humans can add the teleportation feature to their meeting invitations."

"So, any jack-off can pull me to a meeting?" It was bad enough that Archons could do it, but. . .

A vision of beaming Chad to the Dread Lord of HR's primal-scream therapy circle formed in her mind's eye.

"Not exactly," he said. "For humans, the recipient has to *accept* the invitation."

Oh well.

"People have been using it to hop all over Asphodel. It's a huge drain on the network."

The witch shrugged. "Turn it off."

"I can't," he said. "When the Dread Lord of IT created the system, he injected a bit of himself into the network. It's his. . .essence that powers electronic teleportation. This human-to-human thing is a bug." He flashed a cheesy grin. "A *bug*. Get it?"

"Yes, Chad, I get it. Ichagno, Dread Lord of Information Technology, is an animate swarm of metallic insects animated by an invisible field of malevolent intelligence."

His face fell. "*I* thought it was funny."

"I didn't screw with your software"—this time—"and I don't know where your boss is. Not my circus, not my nightgaunts."

Except the Dread Lord of IT's disappearance actually *was* her nightgaunt, wasn't it?

The witch was supposed to meet with him this afternoon to set up her account for the County's secret archive. After coming so close to freedom last week, she'd planned to pick his. . .Well, "brain" was the wrong word, but he might have insight on *The Quantumnomicon*'s convoluted equations. And who knew what she might find in the archive?

"Can you use your magic to look for him?" Chad asked.

The witch stiffened.

Use your magic.

She'd thought Chad was different. She'd thought he might actually. . .

But he was just like everyone else.

The witch closed her laptop. She should've known better.

"The last update from the Department of Economic Development comes from our liaison at Catachthonic University, Dr. Christian Carcosa."

With the tip of her wing, Y'ggarlos muted her mic. A debonair man in a three-piece suit approached the podium. It took the witch a minute to realize this nattily dressed individual was Dr. Carcosa. His previously wild mop of brown hair was neatly combed, he had two distinct eyebrows, and contacts had replaced the Coke-bottle glasses. He looked a little washed-out, but otherwise, it was quite the glow-up.

"I am here to provide an update on the QT project," he said with razor-sharp diction.

Hell's bells, he even *sounded* different.

"The device was damaged by a. . .power surge during last week's experiment." His eyes scanned the row of High Lords and locked onto the witch. "Entirely random, I am sure."

Uh-oh.

"The project is on hold pending repairs." Carcosa's gaze slid to Heather. "I have a remediation plan, but I do not wish to monopolize this meeting. Madam Mayor, if you have a few moments after the session. . ."

"Of course," Heather said.

Godsdamn him, he was going to rat her out.

"Thank you, Dr. Carcosa." Heather turned to the witch and nodded. "Public Works?"

She examined the index card she'd prepared ninety seconds before the start of the meeting. "The Dread Lord—"

The microphone interrupted her with a squeal of feedback. By the dangling dong of the Demon Sultan, she *hated* public speaking.

"The Dread Lord of Animal Control has issued a safety advisory," the witch said. "A Shoggoth is living in the dugout of the Dunwich Park softball field. The park is off-limits to the public until further notice. That's all I've got." With a sigh of relief, she crumpled the card.

"Nothing from Energy and Infrastructure?" Heather asked. "Solid Waste Management?"

"Nope."

Heather skewered her with a withering glare. "You're sure?"

"I'm looking into the whole landfill thing," the witch said. "In the meantime, steer clear of the dump. That garbage chute ate a Spectral Forces officer."

"Deputy Woods is as good as new, Witch."

Considering the reputation of Spectral Forces, that wasn't saying much.

Heather glanced at her agenda. "To wrap up, we'll hear from the High Lord of Recreation and Culture."

"Good morning, Mayor Chadwick, distinguished colleagues, and members of the public." Ellie Dawson paused as every Archon practically genuflected. "The annual Thanksgiving pie-eating contest is coming up this Thursday. Come and dethrone the Devourer in the Mist, if you dare."

Not likely. He'd taken home the trophy twenty-nine of the past thirty years. The other year he ate two parade floats, the panel of judges, *and* the freaking trophy.

"The Dread Librarian requests that the individual who's been breaking in after hours to re-catalog the books please cease and desist. Also, *The Get-It-On-Onomicon* is still missing." Ellie shook her head and consulted her notes. "Finally, the Dread Culture Czar is proud to announce the Tophet County Players' annual production of *The King in Yellow* on Saturday, December ninth—directed, of course, by the Yellow King himself."

That would be Hastur, an anthropoid Archon who swanned around town in yellow rags and a featureless mask pretending to be a big-time director. Total douchebag.

"As a reminder," Ellie said, "the play may cause permanent madness."

"Thank you, High Lord Dawson." Heather turned toward the half-filled audience chamber. "The mic is open for community feedback."

A Rubenesque woman with glossy black hair styled in a victory roll stood and walked to the podium carrying a poster.

Next to the witch, N'eithamiqug groaned. "Not her."

"Who is she?"

"Vera Vásquez," the Spinner hissed. "She's always raving about the most ludicrous theories."

Ah. . .the woman Ronnie'd mentioned, something about Doritos and conspiracies.

"What a pleasant surprise," Heather said. "I'd like to introduce my campaign manager, Vee. I entered the mayoral race late—"

Entered? Credit-hogging oligarch.

"—but she organized a successful social media campaign, and—"

"Wake up, citizens!"

The witch's gaze snapped back to Vera. Her tawny skin shone under the fluorescent lights. She wore a polka-dot circle skirt and a hot pink T-shirt featuring a cube-shaped Earth and a slogan that read *All You Assholes Were Wrong.* The black cords of a bolo tie hung from a golden enamel slide loosely clasped below her neck.

Heather frowned at her. "Vee, what are you—"

"Invaders from another dimension have infiltrated Tophet County." The barest hint of an accent gave her words a slight lilt. "And I've got proof."

The witch cackled. Heather's vaunted campaign manager was a tinfoil-hat-wearing crackpot.

Vera gestured toward the poster she'd placed on the easel in front of the podium. It portrayed a squat, human-shaped shadow against a white background. "Behold!"

"What am I looking at?" Heather asked.

"One of *them.*" Vera's voice was an urgent whisper. "I saw it at the landfill just after the Unseen Creeping Horror was attacked."

"We don't know that it was an attack. It could've been—"

"*They* did it. It's part of their plan to take over the world, and they've started in Tophet County."

"Last month, it was Slender Man," said the Spinner. "Now it's sentient shadows."

"Don't look at the shadow," Vera said. "Look at what's casting it."

Heather scrutinized the image. "There's nothing there."

"Open your eyes!" Vera slammed her palms on the podium for emphasis.

The rear doors banged open, and three Spectral Forces officers charged in. Deputy Eye Candy brought up the rear of the group. He caught sight of the witch and waved.

"Wake up before it's too late!" Vera shouted as an officer barreled toward her. "Question everything! Trust no one! And beware of the little—"

A gloved hand covered Vera's mouth, and a pair of officers carried their wriggling captive toward the back of the room. The snatch-and-grab crew departed, leaving only the obnoxiously gorgeous Hank. The audience devolved into a cacophony of individual conversations.

"Quick announcement," Heather called over the din. "We're remodeling the Executive Hearing Room, so next week's General Session will be virtual. The link is on our website." She banged her gavel three times. "This meeting is adjourned."

Hank wound through a sea of jostling bodies and flailing tentacles and approached the dais.

"The Clerk wants to see you in her office, Witch."

As she turned to leave, the witch saw Dr. Carcosa stride up the carpeted ramp and sit down on the empty throne next to Heather.

Oh, *wonderful.*

The witch followed Hank through the labyrinthine subbasement to an unmarked door. As he raised his hand to knock, a blood-chilling shriek echoed from an air vent.

"Sweet infant Horus," she said. "What's down here?"

"Most of the subbasements belong to the Department of Corrections."

She shuddered and juiced up her magical shield. Rumor had it the Dread Lord of Corrections' appearance was so gruesome it turned anyone who beheld him into a living mummy.

Hank knocked, and the Clerk's fluting voice invited them in.

Her office was aggressively decorated in a Disney theme. A quartet of framed cels from *Fantasia* hung above a large desk, which was cluttered with figurines of Dalmatians and lions and spotted fawns. A larger-than-life cardboard cut-out of Maleficent—the green-skinned, animated version rather than its razor-cheekboned, live-action successor—loomed in one corner.

"Greetings, Witch." The shrouded Clerk sat at one end of a large conference table. She gestured toward the empty chair at the other end. "Have a seat."

The witch, for lack of a better plan, complied. Hank posted himself next to her chair at parade rest. The Clerk poured a cup of tea from an Alice in Wonderland teapot, and a black-robed human servitor carried it to the witch.

"Milk and sugar?" he asked. "Perhaps a squeeze of lemon?"

A sharp zap sounded as he brushed against her shield. He convulsed and fell to the floor in a heap of black velvet.

The witch winced. "My bad."

"Don't give it another thought." The Clerk waved a tentacle dismissively. "I have dozens of them." One eye swiveled toward Hank. "Deputy O'Brien, please take him to the infirmary. I believe he needs a jump start."

"Yes, ma'am." Hank heaved the unconscious man over his shoulder and hauled him out.

Well, she'd best get out in front of this. "About that evidence you gave me—"

"We'll get to that." The Clerk lifted a flap in the thoracic region of her shroud and took a sip of tea. "There's something I need to ask you first." A tentacle carefully returned the teacup to its saucer. "Will you take over as the permanent High Lord of Public Works?"

"Hell no!" Her two weeks of torture expired this Friday, and she was counting down the hours. But she thought better of her tone and added, "All due respect."

Half a dozen eyes locked on the witch. There were no other facial features to read, but the emotion was clear. It wasn't murderous outrage.

It was desperation.

Her stomach roiled uneasily, and not just from the Clerk's proximity.

"I will not beg, Witch," the Archon said, "nor will I cajole or threaten. As you know, I need your willing cooperation to alter the terms of your contract." The shroud fluttered as the Clerk exhaled. "Per Archonic protocol, I may only ask three times. Will you accept the position?"

For the love of Lovecraft, what should she say? Gods knew what the Clerk would do if the witch delivered three consecutive no-way-in-hells.

Discordia, send your daughter a sign.

"Why me?" The witch's eyes roamed the room looking for an omen. A poster of a flying elephant. A statue of a mouse wrestling a demonic broom. A stack of punch card ballots. Nothing felt right. Then her gaze landed on her teacup. A drift of golden tea leaves had settled under the amber liquid. Perfect. "Can't you get someone else?"

"I don't want someone else," the Clerk said. "According to my. . .to one of my senior advisors, our current predicament calls for your particular gift."

"My particular gift is being the County Witch." She picked up the teacup and drained it. "And what predicament?"

"The Dread Lord of IT is missing."

"I heard about that. One of the technomancers asked me to find him." Though she'd refused Chad's request, the witch had attempted her locator spell right after she hung up on him. As much as she hated to admit it, she needed that irritable horde of titanium locusts. "I tried, but all I got was the same thing I saw at the landfill."

"Which was?"

"White light bright enough to burn out my optic nerves."

"White light," the Clerk repeated, her eyestalks trembling. "Impossible. . ."

"What's impossible?"

The Clerk shook herself as though dispelling a chill. "The Sheriff just sent over a stack of reports on bizarre sightings and unusual crimes." She slid a folder down the length of the table. "Several of our principal software platforms have been compromised. My. . .advisor insists you are the only one who can get to the

bottom of this. Formalizing your promotion grants you the powers and protec-
tions of a permanent High Lord, which will facilitate your investigation."

"It's not *my* investigation." She pushed the folder back toward the Clerk.
"Not my circus—"

"If you value your life, you will not complete that sentence."

The witch closed her mouth and returned her attention to her teacup. She
spun it three times widdershins, hoping to pass it off as nervous fidgeting, and
upended it over the saucer.

The Clerk said, "You chafe at the bonds of your contract."

"You could say that." Again, she turned the cup thrice.

"Then I have a proposition for you."

"Oh yeah?"

The witch lifted her cup and gazed at the contents. The tea leaves formed the
shape of an apple—not just any apple, the golden apple of the Original Snub.
Once upon a time, Zeus had excluded Discordia, better known in Greek circles
as Eris, from attending a wedding fearing She'd cause chaos. In retaliation, She'd
inscribed *For the Fairest* on a golden apple and tossed it into the reception, sparking a divine catfight between Aphrodite, Hera, and Athena.

Oh, and kicking off the Trojan War.

"Agree to this position," the Clerk said, "and I will subtract ten years from
your term."

The witch blinked, tearing her eyes away from the Apple of Discord. She still
hoped to escape her contract before the winter solstice, but for that, she needed
the Dread Lord of IT. The Clerk was practically begging her to find him. Throw
in a thumbs-up from Discordia and the worst-case scenario of time off for good
behavior, and it was a no-brainer.

Best not to seem too eager.

"Under those terms, will you accept the position of High Lord of Public
Works and lead this investigation?"

"Knock twenty years off, and you've got a deal."

"Fifteen."

"Fifteen and a day," the witch said. "Final offer. And I get my normal job
back after this shit's sorted out."

After a moment's consideration, the Clerk nodded. "Agreed."

A glistening tentacle snaked down the table to the witch. She extended a
hand and gripped the oozing rope, grimacing as her skin blistered. The second
they made physical contact, she felt the terms of her contract change. The witch
withdrew her hand, smiling as her magic healed the smoking ruin of her palm.

"Let's assemble your team, shall we?" the Clerk said.

Her smile faltered.

"Team?"

CHAPTER TWELVE

Necessary Cruelty

The Clerk whispered an ear-assaulting word, and the cardboard cutout of Maleficent transformed into a shimmering pool of netherlight. A robed servitor appeared in the opening. He had to turn sideways to squish his paunch through the narrow portal. Then he tripped as he was stepping through, toppling both himself and the standee.

The man scrambled to his feet and uprighted the Mistress of Evil. "Sorry, ma'am. Rolled my ankle." He pointed at the door. "Shall I. . ."

"Please do."

The cowled figure attempted an ominous glide, but a pronounced limp ruined the effect. He opened the door and intoned, "You may enter."

The Dread Lord of Human Resources trooped in and took the seat to the witch's right. "Isn't this exciting?"

Not the word she would've chosen.

A female Archon sat between the Dread Lord and the Clerk. Her bulbous forehead and Real Housewives wig looked vaguely familiar. After a few seconds of blatant staring, the witch's sleep-deprived brain finally made the connection. This was the leggings-wearing squiggly who'd brought Heather a coffee on Emergence Day.

The final guest entered and sat on the other side of the Clerk. Vera Vásquez— campaign manager, get-out-the-vote expert, and conspiracy whacko extraordinaire. As the witch goggled at her, Vera kicked off with a squeal of delight and set her chair spinning.

Sweet crawling chaos.

"Hell no." The witch shook her head. "There's no way you're sticking me with this bunch of—"

"I'm sure you all know the County Witch," the Clerk said.

"We're old friends." The crossed eyes of the Dread Lord of Human Resources met her gaze. He dipped his chin and said, "May it serve you right, you. . .you angry"—he lowered his voice to a scandalized whisper—"*a-hole*."

"Sathach!"

"It's a traditional greeting in her culture."

"She's making fun of you," the Clerk said.

The witch disguised her surprised laugh as a coughing fit. "Nice alliteration, but it needs more spite. For example. . ." She cleared her throat. "May it serve you right, you moronic monkey's man-dangler."

"I see the diff—"

"Enough!" The Clerk's shroud drifted on the winds of a grievous sigh. "The witch is our new High Lord of Public Works."

The Dread Lord raised a finger. "*Acting* High Lord."

"Actually, Sathach, she just accepted the permanent position."

His mouth fell open, revealing a writhing nest of tiny tentacles. "But I was planning to apply!"

"Aw, cheer up," the witch said. "My probationary triskaidecade doesn't end until the solstice. I might screw up and get fired."

"Don't be ridiculous," he snapped. "The only cause for terminating a probationary contract is collusion with our ancient enemy."

"Who's your ancient enemy?" Maybe she could find them and collude.

"Probably each other," the Dread Lord said, glaring sullenly at the Clerk. "It's just standard boilerplate." His soul patch trembled, and a greasy film coated his eyes. "I'll start the paperwork."

"As I was saying," the Clerk said, "our new High Lord—"

"I want Chad."

Vera stopped spinning and arched an eyebrow. "Oooh, who's Chad, and what do we want to do with him?"

The witch burned through a bit of entropine to dispel a furious blush.

Chad worked for the Dread Lord of IT, and he knew computer shit. Yeah, he'd asked her to use her magic, but it was the first time in all the years she'd known him, and it hadn't even been for himself. Over the past few weeks, he'd proven she could count on him in a pinch.

"Look, Clerk," the witch said, "you've saddled me with these three ass clowns."

"Inappropriate," the Dread Lord muttered.

She pointed at him. "*He* once ate my middle finger."

"I said I was sorry!"

"As for her," the witch said, gesturing toward Vera, "let's just say the wheel is spinning, but the hamster's not home." She jerked her chin at the bewigged female Archon. "According to you, this one's a spandex fashionista. At least Chad has relevant skills."

"Very well." The Clerk opened her laptop and gripped the joystick that served as a keyboard for the tentacularly-inclined. After a burst of sticky-sounding manipulation, she said, "Invitation sent."

Before she'd finished speaking, the image of Maleficent rippled and a khaki-clad leg emerged, followed in short order by the rest of a bewildered Chad. His hands dripped water onto the scarred tile floor.

"I was in the bathroom, for God's sake! What if I'd been—" Chad's mouth snapped shut when he caught sight of the Clerk.

"Good morning, Mr. Chadwick," she said. "You've been appointed to the witch's task force, where you will support her investigation into recent attacks on senior Archons and other troubling events."

"Attacks on senior. . ." His eyes widened. "This is about the Dread Lord of IT." Chad beamed a grateful smile at the witch. "You *are* going to help me. Did you find the Dread Lord?" he asked, taking the empty chair next to her. "What happened to him?"

"That's what you're here to find out." The Clerk closed her laptop and fixed one eye on each face at the table. The witch got two. "This is a *secret* task force. Never discuss it with anyone not present in this room—especially the Sheriff's office. The exception to that rule is Deputy O'Brien, head of my personal Spectral Forces detail. He and I have. . .an arrangement."

So, the Clerk had a spy in Spectral Forces? Good to know.

The Dread Lord raised his hand. "What 'other troubling events' are we investigating?"

"Glitches in several County software platforms, a spate of unusual crimes over the past week, and sightings of. . ." Two of the Clerk's eyes flicked to Vera. "Sightings of little—"

"Little white men!" Vera crowed. With a witch-worthy cackle, she set her chair spinning again.

"Ms. Vásquez," the Clerk said, "if that chair isn't still by the time I finish this sentence. . ."

Vera's stilettos threw up a shower of sparks as she ground to a halt on the tile.

"Little *green* men?" Chad asked. "Like aliens?"

"No, they all left when the Archons woke up." Vera leaned toward him. "I mean little *white* men."

The Archon with the fivehead gasped. Her green skin looked significantly paler. "You can't mean—"

"Of course she doesn't," the Dread Lord said. "She means short Caucasian—"

"I mean little white men."

He recoiled as though she'd slapped him. "But they aren't real!"

"Certainly not," the Clerk said, "but someone wants us to think so. And after last time. . ."

The emerald eyes of Heather's coffee minion filled with tears, and she pressed a hand to her quivering lips. The Dread Lord patted her shoulder, but his attention was glued to the Clerk.

"You're right, sister," he said. "This investigation must remain top secret."

"What the little white fuck is going on?" The Archons flinched in unison at the witch's choice of profanity. Good gods, they looked scared. And the only thing on earth that could scare an Archon would be. . .a bigger, badder Archon. "You think one of *you* is involved."

"That's what I need you to find out," the Clerk said. "Each member of your team brings a particular talent to the table." She flicked a tentacle toward Chad. "As you suggested, Mr. Chadwick is best suited to look into the software issues. The Dread Lord of Human Resources can serve as your interface with the Archons. Ms. Vásquez has a gift for identifying suspicious happenings in the community. Thugha, whom you may address as Night Walker—"

The she-Archon raised a French-manicured hand. "I prefer Magnolia."

"That is a human name," the Clerk said frostily.

"Ahem," the Dread Lord said. "Tophet County policy is to use the name an individual prefers."

Unless it's Connie Lingus.

"To do otherwise is needlessly cruel, and HR only permits necessary cruelty."

The Clerk huffed and adjusted her shroud. "*Magnolia* will serve as the witch's assistant. She will coordinate meetings, draft reports, and perform other tasks to support this effort at the direction of the witch."

An Archonic assistant? This was getting out of hand.

"Quite the team." The witch forced a smile, then allowed her face to fall. "But I gotta say, I'm out of my element here. I couldn't do a damn thing with that evidence you gave me. Probably best if someone else takes the lead."

The Dread Lord raised his hand. "Ooh, ooh!"

"Leading this task force is a requirement of your new position, Witch," the Clerk said. "And as I told you before, this situation calls for your particular gifts."

The witch leaned back in her chair and crossed her arms. She'd show that pus-filled horror her particular gifts. According to Mother Mayhem, her childhood guardian at the Witchery, she had unique talents for undermining authority and avoiding responsibility. If she couldn't make any headway with this bullshit, she'd apply *those* gifts.

"I'll attend your meetings as I'm able. Magnolia"—the Clerk pronounced the name as if it were contagious—"will keep me updated." She stood, sweeping her sextuplicate gaze around the table. "Good luck."

CHAPTER THIRTEEN

WTF

A second desk now occupied a corner of the witch's office previously inhabited by a tribe of semi-sentient dust balls. In the time it took to fly home and check on Keyser (asleep, the little shit), an interloper had moved in. Magnolia hastily minimized the open window on her laptop, but not before the witch saw what was on the screen.

"No need to hide your shoe shopping from me," she said, shrugging out of her backpack. "I'm all for misusing County resources."

A ruddy blush tinted pale green skin. "I can't wear them, so I collect them." She opened the browser and gazed longingly at a pair of Brother Vellies. "My, um. . .significant other thinks it's silly, but a girl can dream."

Magnolia stood, and the witch did a double take. Mistaking astonishment for interest, the Archon twirled to showcase her outfit. The witch tried not to gape at tentacles swathed in turkeys, pumpkins, and fall leaves.

"I'm a certified knitwear consultant," she said. "If you're interested in stocking up on our holiday prints or, better yet, joining Mayor Chadwick's sales team—"

"Sorry, I'm allergic to multilevel marketing."

The witch sat down and massaged her temples. She was running on three hours of sleep and feeling meaner than a wet panther.

"Coffee?" Magnolia held out a Dee's to-go cup in a hand that had, the witch would swear on a stack of Necronomicons, been empty the previous second. "Black, extra hot, extra strong."

She accepted the cup and took a scalding sip of coffee so strong it roused Keyser Söze from his nap in the dryer back at her apartment. Perfect.

The witch narrowed her eyes. "How did you know I drink my coffee black?"

"I used my melon," Magnolia said, tapping her domed forehead. "It creates a field of quantum resonance that—"

"Give me the kindergarten version."

"Sometimes I can pick up what's on a person's mind."

"You're a telepath?" The witch's panicked thoughts darted to the Amish romance she'd planned to read over lunch. This was going to get real awkward real fast.

"Nothing like that," Magnolia said. "I see the intersection of what someone desires and what's most likely to happen. You wanted a coffee, and you were probably going to get one." The skin of her bulbous forehead wrinkled in concern. "I used the Public Works meeting budget to pay for it. Is that okay?"

The meeting part sucked, but the witch was all for having a budget. "Hell yeah."

"Great. Shall we review your schedule?" Magnolia grabbed a sheet of paper from her desk and handed it to the witch. "Your expertise with warts is legendary, so I offered your services to the Health Department. They're wrestling with an outbreak of—"

"Haunted warts." The witch rocked back in her chair. "I heard."

"I thought if we filled your calendar with wart removals, we could keep you from getting roped into services you don't want to provide."

Apparently, the witch's reputation preceded her. . .but it wasn't a bad idea. No one could book a love spell if her schedule was full.

"You have a few appointments this afternoon," Magnolia said. "And it's the third Wednesday of the month, so we have a Planning Commission meeting."

"Hard pass."

"If you don't show up, the scheduling software will pull you over." Magnolia sat in the chair opposite the witch's desk, tapping a pen against disturbingly human teeth as she thought.

"Let's reply that I'll attend in your place," Magnolia said. "I'll update you later."

The witch raised her coffee cup in salute. "I like your style." This whole having an assistant thing wasn't half bad.

"At four, we've got our first WTF meeting—"

"What the fuck?"

"The. . .the task force. . ."

"Oooh. Witch's Task Force."

"I can change the acronym if you—"

"Don't you dare," the witch said. "Speaking of which, I'd like to pick your melon."

"Sure," Magnolia said, glancing at her watch, "but we might not have—"

"Hello?"

Magnolia rose and turned to greet the invader. "Good afternoon. You must be—"

"Dr. Carcosa," the witch said. Creator of the murder machine and probably the work-obsessed husband of her lovelorn client. Thanks to the nondisclosure clause of her client contracts, she couldn't come out and ask, but Carcosa wasn't exactly a common name. "That's one hell of a makeover."

He glanced at his perfectly pressed suit. "Ah, yes. I've been inspired to make a few changes."

The love spell must be kicking in. "You know what they say—happy wife, happy life."

He frowned. "Wife?"

The witch was getting perilously close to a contractual oopsie. "She teaches yoga, right?"

"Indeed," he said. "Are you one of her students?"

"We've met." She rubbed her hands together. "All right, let's see those warts." When Carcosa didn't move, she said, "Look, I know the nasty bastards like to pop up on the old beanbag, so—"

"I should go and. . .I should just go." Magnolia fled the office, slamming the door behind her.

"Don't be shy." The witch waved an impatient hand. "I'm the freaking wart whisperer."

"I have a confession."

She sighed. "You don't have any warts."

"I do not."

If he wasn't here about the wife or the warts. . .

"You sabotaged my quantum tunneler."

The witch considered denying it, but he sounded awfully damned certain. "It was an accident."

Carcosa's immaculate eyebrows rose. "An accident?"

"I was testing a new spell, and things went sideways."

"What kind of spell?"

"That's not important."

Carcosa leaned toward her. "I have an R&D contract with the Clerk. Until this project succeeds, I cannot pursue other areas of research." His pale blue eyes flashed under the fluorescent lights. "Someone with your power simply cannot understand the torture of such bondage."

Cannot *understand*? When it came to magical covenants with the Archons, she was patient fucking zero.

"I was trying to break my employment contract." The words flew out before the witch consciously decided to say them. "As evidenced by my continued presence in this hellhole, it didn't work." She laughed bitterly, shaking her head. "You think I don't understand torture? Those shitbirds have me locked in for a century."

"Yet you dare to defy them?"

"Frequently, and with enthusiasm."

He scooted the chair closer and rested his elbows on the edge of her desk. "Witch, I am part of a group that seeks to free humanity," he said in a conspiratorial whisper. "We plan to use the QT to end the Archons' reign."

"How?"

"Are you familiar with the higher-level mathematics of dimensional physics?"

"Like. . ." The witch racked her brain for any vestiges of the single semester of calculus forced upon her by Catachthonic University. "Like integrals?"

"Like eigenvectors, Hilbert spaces, and spectral theory."

"Not my wheelhouse."

"Then let's focus not on the *how* but on the *what*," he said.

"Which is?"

"Liberating the human race."

The witch leaned back and propped her booted feet on the corner of the desk. This conversation was getting dicey. The first, last, and only rebellion against the Archons ended with the death of all witches, save one scrawny newborn. She wanted to buy what Dr. Two Brows was selling, but what if the Clerk had sent him to test her loyalty? She didn't know this dude from Dagon, and he was trying to suck up to her and—

"I do not like you," he said.

"What?"

"You are crude and inconsiderate, and your hygiene is reprehensible." He wrinkled his nose and looked around her cluttered office. "But I respect you. You do not accept these monstrosities as your masters, and neither do I."

"Yeah, well, we're shit out of luck, aren't we?"

"Not necessarily," Carcosa said. "They are strong, but they are also fallible." He gestured toward the witch. "Take you, for example. You are the only surviving witch, a being of immeasurable power, but do they have you curing diseases? Developing hybrid technologies? Making the world a better place?" Carcosa let his hand fall into his lap. "No, you spend your days removing warts and crafting beauty charms."

"I don't give a single solitary shit about making this world better." Why should she? Discordia knew the world had never done a damn thing for *her*. "All I want is my freedom."

"Then our goals are aligned." His eyes held hers with magnetic force. "Tell me about your spell."

Gods, what to do. . .

This guy was a physicist. Maybe he could troubleshoot her magical jailbreak. On the other hand, he might be a spy for the Clerk or the Sheriff or, hell, the godsdamned Dread Lord of Human Resources.

The witch wanted his help, but she couldn't trust him.

But perhaps with a little risk mitigation. . .

"Sure." She bared her teeth in a smile-adjacent expression. "But first, you have to promise you won't sell me out to the eldritch horrors."

"You have my word."

The witch spit into her hand and held it out. Saliva wasn't a requirement for magical oaths, but she couldn't resist messing with the fastidious prick. "Shake on it?"

His lips pursed in a moue of disgust. "I. . .This is not necessary, Witch."

"Suit yourself." She withdrew her hand. "I'll see you around."

"Fine." Carcosa paled even further, but he clasped her hand, and. . .

And nothing. No tingle of binding. No sparkle of magic. No surge of entropine.

"Fuck me!"

Carcosa dropped her hand like a horny heat-lizard. "What?"

"My magic's on the fritz."

"Has this happened before?"

"Yeah," she said. "Once at the landfill the day after I tried that spell and again this morning." The witch bit her lip. "I don't get it. I was fine all weekend."

"This began after you damaged the QT." His expression grew pensive. "There must be a connection. Are you"—Carcosa's eyes flicked to her wrinkled T-shirt, which read *Big Witch Energy*—"wearing the same clothing?"

"Am I *that* gross?"

"Did you do similar magic?" he asked.

"Nope."

"Strange. I would have linked this to your thaumaturgical experiment, but with no evidence to—"

"Evidence!"

"Yes, Witch," Dr. Carcosa said. "Evidence is how scientists prove or disprove—"

"Stop mansplaining." The witch pointed an accusing finger at the white sphere from the crime scene. "That thing was found at the landfill after the Unseen Creeping Horror was attacked. The Clerk pawned it off on me, stuck me with this High Lord gig, and put me in charge of the investigation. I'm supposed to figure out what it is, but I can't even touch it."

He rose and approached the sphere. "May I?"

The witch nodded. Carcosa picked up the glossy object—no painful zap for him—and turned it in his hands, running slender fingers over the dimpled depression.

"What is it?"

He tore his eyes away from the device and looked at her. "It appears to be an apparatus of some kind—a field generator, if I had to guess."

"You can tell just from looking?"

"Call me the technology whisperer."

She snorted. "Fair enough."

"We could help each other," he said. "I could take this artifact back to my lab, run a few tests, and produce a report for your investigation. All I want in return is—"

"My magic?"

"No," he said, with a grimace of pure disgust.

He was one of *those*. In her experience, eight out of ten normies coveted her magic, one didn't give a shit about it, and one viewed it as a crime against nature.

"All I want is information," he continued. "The details of your spell. Updates on the investigation. It sounds like the Archons are in crisis. My associates and I could take advantage of that."

"Can't do it. The Clerk wants this whole thing kept hush-hush."

"Do you not find it remarkable that you were promoted to High Lordship just prior to these events? And that the Clerk gave you an artifact"—Carcosa raised the sphere—"that impairs your abilities?"

"It's not like that."

"Perhaps not," he said. "Well, I am sure your minder will help you."

"Minder?"

His eyes darted to Magnolia's desk.

"She's my *assistant*."

"An Archonic assistant," he said. "How. . .progressive."

An oily ball of unease formed in the pit of her stomach. A sudden, unde-served promotion. An investigation she was unqualified to lead. A tentacled, mind-reading secretary. It didn't pass the smell test.

"I hope she will be more helpful than my assistant," Carcosa said. "Lorelei has been useless of late."

The name banged a gong in the witch's memory. "Red hair? Prone to hysterics?"

"You know her?"

"I've seen her around," the witch said. "Seems like she's a few peanuts short of a Snickers. No offense."

"None taken." Carcosa placed the sphere atop a pile of coffee-ringed papers on her desk. "Well, I must be going. Best of luck with your—"

"I converted entropine to syntropine," she said. "That part of the spell worked." The witch squeezed her eyes shut against the unwelcome memory. "But then I almost got severed from Keyser Söze, so I—"

"What is Kai-zer So-zay?"

"Who, not what." She picked up her BlackBerry and showed Carcosa her wallpaper—a photo of Keyser asleep in her bathroom sink.

"A pet?"

"My familiar," she said. "He's kind of like a magical battery."

"Ah. How did you make the conversion?"

"Why does that matter? You're not a witch."

"True," he said, "but for most magical operations, there is a mundane counterpart." Carcosa gestured at the cup on her desk. "You could warm your coffee by using magic to agitate the molecules and produce heat. I could use the same principles to accomplish the same goal with technology."

The witch's eyes drifted to the sphere. This was either a lucky break or an opportunity for a spectacular cock-up. There was definitely more to this than the Clerk was saying, and the only halfway-competent ally she had was a freshly separated nerdomancer who wore prescription socks.

She took a deep breath and said, "Have you read *The Quantumnomicon*?"

"How was your afternoon?"

"Warts were a cakewalk," the witch said around a mouthful of corned beef.

Magnolia had returned after the last of the appointments bearing the welcome gift of a Reuben from Mile High Clubs, the witch's favorite deli. Though she hated the idea of being spied on, having a personal flunky who could low-key read her mind was kinda nice on the catering front. The witch's previous lunch plans had centered on her hip flask and a handful of Tic Tacs—though she'd prefer that to Magnolia's distressingly small salad. She must be a member of that vegan cult, the Seitanic Temple.

On second thought, probably not. Who ever heard of an Archon joining a cult?

"Before I left," Magnolia said, rising to retrieve a notepad, "you said you wanted to pick my melon."

"No need. I'm on a roll."

"Walk me through what you've got, and I'll draft an update for the WTF meeting."

Oops. She should've kept her godsdamned mouth shut.

But she couldn't, could she? The Clerk expected a progress report.

"I think the sphere from the landfill is a. . .a field generator."

Magnolia's green eyes remained glued to the witch as her hand flew over her notepad. "Did you conduct magical testing?"

"Something like that."

"Can you be more specific?"

"Nope."

Magnolia stared at her notepad, chewing her lip with perfect Chiclet teeth. "You don't trust me."

Play it cool, Witch.

If Magnolia *was* spying for the Clerk, the best strategy was to keep her close and make her think they were on the same team. No good would come of revealing her suspicions.

"Not as far as I can throw you."

The major downside of being an anarchist was that no one could tell the witch what to do, up to and including herself.

"Look, I'm not trying to be a dick, but you're an Archon and I'm a witch. Actually, I'm *the* witch—as in the only one left." She paused to let the historical ramifications sink in. "So yeah, I have trust issues."

Magnolia's seafoam complexion grew mottled and her eyes shone, but she held the witch's gaze. "I don't blame you." They sat in uncomfortable silence. Just as the witch was considering melting through the floor to escape, Magnolia said, "I'm truly sorry for what the Archons did after the Emergence. You must think we're monsters."

The witch shifted uncomfortably. The Archons didn't have a monopoly on monstrous behavior. Mother Mayhem had designed her homeschool curriculum, and the Emergence had been the first lesson in the history unit. From there, it was a greatest-hits list of humanity's most horrifying deeds. The decimation of Native peoples by American colonists. The abduction and enslavement of millions of African men, women, and children, and the sadistic barbarism of chattel slavery. The unspeakable atrocities of the Holocaust. Centuries of witch hunts.

In fact, given witches' low birth rate, humans had probably killed more of her people over the years than Archons.

"I know it will take time," Magnolia said, "but I'll do everything I can to earn your trust. I won't let you down."

The witch wanted to believe her—gods knew she needed allies—but she couldn't risk exposing Carcosa. What she *could* do was dole out a few crumbs of info and use them to test Magnolia's loyalty.

"I'll share what I've got." Some of it, anyway. "When I'm near the sphere, my power's about as useful as a screen door on a submarine. I think it produces an anti-magical field, but for obvious reasons, I can't test it myself. So I, um. . .handed it off to an expert. And now that it's gone, I've got my mojo back." She held up a hand, shooting jets of flame from her fingertips. "Once I hear from my source, we'll have something solid to give the Clerk."

Magnolia looked pained. "But she told us not to speak to anyone outside the WTF."

"She also told us to investigate." The witch shrugged. "This is me investigating. Spectral Forces does shit like this all the time. It's like using a CI to set up a drug bust."

"Doesn't the Sheriff ceremonially consume the CIs at the end of an investigation?"

"We'll cross that abyss when we come to it. For now, let's keep this little detail just between us."

"What will we tell the WTF?"

"We'll just say I'm handling the sphere."

"And if anyone asks questions?"

The witch smiled, showing her teeth. "I'll take a page from the Sheriff and eat them."

CHAPTER FOURTEEN

Children and Fools

Thunderous techno music assaulted the witch's ears the second she pushed through the door of Larry's Lazertag Emporium. A growl of displeasure rumbled from her backpack. She double-checked the address on the sticky note Magnolia'd given her before she left to pick up Keyser. Sadly, she was in the right place.

A poster glowed under the black lights: *Welcome, WTF! Party Room #4.*

The witch followed luminous arrows painted on the floor until she encountered Magnolia greeting the Dread Lord of Human Resources.

"Help yourself to coffee and pastries," Magnolia said.

"Pastries?" The Dread Lord shot through the open door.

"Lovecraft's leaking lizard," the witch said, watching him unhinge his jaw to admit three donuts. "Why are we meeting in this neon nightmare?"

Magnolia's eyes darted from left to right like a cartoon spy. "This is a *secret* task force. In County buildings, the walls have ears."

"That's just Conference Room B."

"I upgraded our party package," the Dread Lord said around a mouthful of what was presumably a jelly donut, judging by the lurid slime pooled in his soul patch.

The witch shuddered. In her book, jelly-donut consumption was equivalent to serial murder.

"We're doing a Slay the Sandworm team-building mission." He licked crimson preserves from his fingers. "I could use the exercise. I just came from a retirement party. *Giant* cake." The Dread Lord held his hands three feet apart, and the buttons of his suit jacket strained over a growing gut.

Keyser grumbled irritably, and the witch knelt and released him from her bag. He hissed and scurried under the table. She eyed the Dread Lord, who was hovering over the donut tray. Better grab something for Keyser before it was too late. She damn near lost a finger—*again*—snagging a chocolate glazed.

Chad approached the coffee station, looking tired and preoccupied. The witch opened her mouth to say something devastatingly clever, but instead watched in silent astonishment as he dumped packet after packet of sugar into his mug. She lost count at twelve.

"Wow. Sweet tooth much?"

"I was up late going through code." Chad covered his mouth, stifling a yawn. "Caffeine and sugar are the only things keeping me vertical." He took a sip of his coffee, wincing at either the scalding temperature or near-fatal sweetness. "Still no sign of the Dread Lord of IT."

"We'll find him."

They had to. That sentient swarm held the key to the secret archives.

"Thanks, Witch." Chad squeezed her shoulder and drifted toward the table.

She stared after him, still feeling the heat of his hand. A tug on her jeans drew her attention to Keyser, who'd been captured by the siren scent of Dunkin'. She gave him the donut and scratched behind his ears. "Here, buddy. This shouldn't take—"

The Dread Lord of Human Resources clapped his hands. "Attention, everyone!"

That arrogant cocktapus was trying to take over *her* meeting.

The witch marched to the head of the table. "Okay, people, sit down and shut—"

"I propose we begin with an icebreaker," he said. "Two truths and a lie."

She pasted on a fake smile. "I'll go. One, the Clerk put *me* in charge of this task force. Two, I'm the magical equivalent of a thermonuclear bomb. Three, I have a high tolerance for bullshit and would never use my power to scorch the facial hair off an entity who annoyed me." She looked around the table. "Any guesses?"

Vera Vásquez raised her hand, showcasing a T-shirt that featured Prince Charles with bloody vampire fangs.

The witch ignored her. "We don't have time to screw around. The Clerk—"

"Ahem." The Dread Lord raised his hand. "If we're going to work together, we need to be comfortable with each other. As an entirely random example, I am not acquainted with your assistant."

The witch looked from him to Magnolia. "Of course you are. She's an Archon."

"Magnolia and I are perfect strangers."

"You just said her name."

"I remembered it. From this morning. Which was the first time we met."

Magnolia's pale green cheeks blazed red as she stared at the agenda.

Oh, these two were *totally* tangling tentacles. The Dread Lord must be the significant other she'd mentioned. Not a topic the witch cared to explore further.

"When I was at the landfill," the witch said, "I saw the Clerk rip off one of the Sheriff's glowy orb-things and eat it when he pissed her off." She glared at the Dread Lord. "Do you think she gives a shit about our comfort?"

His skin rippled as he considered the question. He shook his head.

"Let's get to it, then." She sat down and glanced at the agenda. "Speaking of the Sheriff, he found a small, white sphere at the landfill after the UCH was defogged. I'm working on figuring out what it is."

"Could be a baseball," Vera said.

"It's not a godsdamned baseball." The witch blew out a frustrated breath and shook her head. "It's. . .an apparatus."

Chad raised his hand. "My undergrad was in mechanical engineering. I could take a look."

Magnolia caught the witch's eyes, no doubt wanting her to confess that she'd given their one piece of physical evidence to an outsider.

Huh. Didn't sound great when she put it like that.

The witch gave her head a tight shake and said, "No, we need you focused on technomancy. According to the Clerk, some of our systems have shit the bed."

"You could say that," Chad said. "First, there's that teleportation glitch I mentioned."

"You said part of the Dread Lord of IT's in the scheduling software," the witch said. "Maybe it's related to his disappearance."

"Could be," he said, running a hand over his beard, "but I can't do anything about it. Every time I open my laptop, the budgeting program takes over and shows the same series of transactions."

The Dread Lord frowned. "What transactions?"

"Transfers from the mayor's general fund to the university partnership and Energy and Infrastructure."

"Could be the work of the little white men." Vera lowered her voice to a whisper. "They're everywhere."

"Chill, crazytown. We'll get to that." The witch nodded to Chad. "See what you can learn about those transfers and let me know if the Dread Lord of IT turns up. That leads me to our next item—attacks on senior Archons."

"As head of HR, I believe *I* am best suited to lead this effort," the Dread Lord said.

"All Human Resources does is write bullshit policies."

"Human Resources," he said, "is the thin, bright line between anarchy and civility."

More of a squiggly blob, in his case.

"He probably knows everyone in County government," Chad said.

The Dread Lord preened. "I try to keep a tentacle on the pulse."

"Except Magnolia," Vera said, toying with the golden clasp of her bolo tie. "He doesn't know her."

Managing this meeting was worse than herding Ultharian cats.

"Fine," the witch said. "You were tight with the Unseen Creeping Horror, right?" The Dread Lord nodded. "Talk to whoever he was close to and see if they know anything—same for the IT guy. Just keep it low-key."

The Dread Lord scooched closer to Chad and gave him a sidelong glance. "I hear your boss has taken a bunk."

Chad raised his eyebrows. "A bunk?"

"What's the dope?"

"I don't—"

"You will tell me what you know, human!" His soul-patched face tore down the middle, revealing a nest of thrashing tentacles surrounding a fang-rimmed maw.

"*That's* your idea of low-key?" the witch asked. The Dread Lord's tentacles drooped, the very picture of dejection. Gods dammit. She groped for something positive to say. "At least you didn't flay his mind."

He sat up straighter, adjusting a necktie that now encircled a knot of ropy limbs. "My therapist will be so proud!"

"Why don't I help with the interviews?" Magnolia asked. "It would give Sathach and I a chance to. . .get acquainted."

"Sathach the total stranger?" Vera flashed a salacious wink and kicked off, setting her chair spinning.

Magnolia practically glowed.

With a sound like a machine-gun fart, the rest of the Dread Lord's human skin tore down the middle. His expanding bulk propelled his wheeled chair to the coffee station.

"Human suits aren't what they used to be," he said. "Poor quality, that's what it is."

"At least you have the option," Magnolia muttered.

They hadn't even gotten through the first meeting, and the WTF was already a shit show.

A vicious snarl sounded from Pastry Corner, followed by a horrified squeal. Gods below, what *now*?

"Witch, your beast stole the last Boston cream!"

"Maybe you should—"

"When I tried to reclaim it, he defecated on my feeding tentacle!"

A literal shit show.

"There's no reason," the Dread Lord lisped, "you should drag this useless creature—"

"Useless?" The witch whistled for Keyser, who launched toward her at a furious waddle. "He doubles my entropic capacity. You, on the other hand—"

Magnolia cleared her throat. "Perhaps we should move on to the next agenda item?"

"Knock yourself out."

Magnolia traced a finger along the agenda, and her face fell. "That brings us to Ms. Vásquez. Vera, the Clerk. . .invited you—"

"Invited?" Vera said. "She had her squad of bruisers snatch me just because I tweeted about the little—"

"The Clerk is quite interested in your observations," Magnolia said. "Could you share them with us?"

"Sure. I've observed little white men."

The ensuing silence was broken only by the soft whir of a spinning chair.

"Okay. What do they look like?" Magnolia asked. "What were they doing?"

Vera pulled out a plastic bag from Cumming Attractions, the sex shop just outside town. The witch perked up, but to her disappointment, the bag contained only a beat-up technicolor Trapper Keeper covered in unicorns and puffy hearts. Vera opened the binder and held it up to display a sketch. The drawing resembled one of those thick stick figures from a restroom door.

"This," Vera said, tapping the drawing, "is an LWM. And these"—she flipped through four or five pages packed with loopy cursive handwriting—"are my notes. Dates, locations, astrological hours. . .everything you need."

Chad leaned in for a closer look, but Magnolia cringed away.

The witch met her wide eyes. "You're *scared*, aren't you?"

"These entities are our version of boogeymen," the Dread Lord said. "A story to scare the young into eating their entrails. Imagine the Clerk asking a human to investigate monsters under the bed. You'd find it both ridiculous and unsettling."

The witch couldn't relate. She'd been raised by an actual monster, no need for boogeymen. But somebody wanted to frighten the squidwards. Whoever was behind this was either an Archon, or someone who knew a hell of a lot about them. Ever since Lovecraft's dreams—which were prophetic, as it turned out—took tentacles mainstream, there'd been a certain brand of human who was pathologically obsessed with the cosmic sideshow. Pre-Emergence, they'd been all about hastening the return of the Archons. Now they focused on theatrical worship.

"We need to check out the cults," the witch said. "Vera, you're plugged into the more, uh, fringe elements of Tophet County society. Heard anything out of the ordinary from the Illuminati? The Seitanists? SoulCycle?"

The Dread Lord piped up from his den of pastries. "Witch, I assure you, the cults have nothing to do with this."

"Humor me."

"Same old, same old," Vera said. "Blah, blah, virgin sacrifice, blah, blah, world domination. Nothing new."

New. . .

Little Miss Gold Award had said something about a cult that launched just before the attack on the UCH. Suspicious timing.

"How about the new cult?" the witch asked.

"It's very secretive," Vera said. "I don't even know its name. But I'm sure it involves wearing robes and masks and bowing before unfathomable eldritch horrors."

"That's my point," the Dread Lord said. "The cults worship Archons." A disturbingly long and slender tongue snaked out of his mouth to lick frosting from a tentacle. "They'd never act against us."

"Maybe not, but someone might've used them to gather intel on you. As the one who puts the 'Witch' in 'Witch's Task Force,' I want every cult checked out."

He huffed, raising a cloud of powdered sugar. "Waste of time."

"Time is a plaything for children and fools," Vera said.

The witch stared at her. That phrase. . .

Vera winked and grinned. "I'll get right on it."

"Okay, that's it for today," Magnolia said. "I'll send out the minutes, and—"

A siren blared from a wall-mounted speaker, then a male voice said, "Hey, party people, it's go time!" A metallic series of ratcheting clicks sounded as a grate slid down from the ceiling, blocking the door. "Your only chance to escape this building alive is to Slay the Sandworm!" A section of wall dropped into the floor, revealing a strobe-lit expanse of sand dunes. Five black backpacks sat just over the threshold. "Gear up, warriors!"

The voice took a deep breath, then spoke in an auctioneer's rapid-fire patois. "As per our liability waiver, your presence in this facility is a tacit acceptance of dire risks to life, limb, and immortal soul. Larry's Lazertag Emporium is hereby absolved of responsibility for damages to entity or personal property." A blood-chilling shriek echoed across the sandy vista. "Have fun!"

The witch grabbed a backpack, unzipped it, and rifled through the contents. Her hand closed on the grip of a weapon. She picked it up and fired at what should be an exterior wall. It produced a blaze of red light but no visible damage.

"Ahem." The Dread Lord raised a tentacle. "We Archons use this facility for parties and ritual hunts. The walls have been sealed against—"

The witch fired at the appendage. It disintegrated into a cloud of green-black mist.

"Hey!" The Dread Lord cradled the already regenerating limb. "That *hurt*."

Real laser guns.

The witch smiled.

"Saddle up, shitheads. We're going hunting."

A burst of static hissed into the witch's earpiece.

"I've got eyes on the sandworm," Chad said. "The Dread Lord—"

"My laser-tag name is Rambo. Over."

"Rambo's circling around behind it. Vera and I have the flanks. Witch, can you and Magnolia make a frontal assault?"

"We're on it."

She army-crawled up the side of a dune and scanned the shallow valley until she spotted the telltale bulge of the worm's body. After an hour on the hunt, she had sand in every crevice, and her shoulders ached from the weight of a sugar-crashed raccoon in her backpack. But to her surprise, she was. . .

Dammit, she was having fun.

"We'll go on three," the witch whispered. "One, two—"

"Hold your fire!" the Dread Lord screamed. "She's guarding eggs!" The snuffling sounds of a tentacled beastie crying like a baby filled her ears. "It's so beautiful!"

The worm burst out of the sand and surged toward the Dread Lord, who crouched next to a clutch of beach ball–sized eggs. It swallowed him whole, then coiled protectively around its offspring.

"We've got to get him out!" Magnolia's voice was shrill with alarm. "We only have a few minutes before she starts digesting him." She lunged forward, but the witch grabbed her arm.

"Rushing that sandworm is suicide," she said. "I don't want him dead, but it'll be a cold day in hell before I sacrifice myself for—"

"For an Archon?"

"We'll think of something," the witch said. "Just—"

Magnolia tugged her arm free and ran toward the worm.

Mother of Chaos, keep them alive. . .

"For the fairest!" Vera's battle cry roared from the radio as she charged the beast.

Her words hit the witch like a sledgehammer. That phrase had been inscribed in Greek on the golden apple of the Original Snub. And the quip about children and fools came from the unsacred scriptures.

Odin's other eye. Vera was a *Discordian.*

A sphincter-clenching shriek echoed over the dunes. The sandworm's body whipped around, and Vera raced into its open mouth. Magnolia skidded on loose sand, tumbling ass over tentacle. The witch leaped to her feet, but before she could take a step, the segmented length of the sandworm convulsed. Its body lifted like a cobra dancing to a snake charmer's tune. Then it sneezed, and a slime-covered ball of limbs flew out of its mouth. The worm burrowed headfirst into the sand. Its tail lashed the wall, leaving a hole the size of a Mack truck.

The witch sprinted toward the snotty mess, where she met Chad and Magnolia.

Chad braced his hands on his knees, gasping for breath. "We should. . .grab them and. . .make a. . .run for it."

"He's right," Magnolia said. "She'll be back."

The knot of arms, legs, and tentacles writhed on the ground as Vera strained to free herself. "We're all tangled up."

The witch levitated the gooey mess and snagged it with a magical tractor beam. "Let's go." She jogged toward the blown-out wall, followed by one nerd, one assistant, and one messy pile of crazy.

Once they were safely in the parking lot, the witch held Vera and the Dread Lord in midair as she sorted through the mess of appendages. One of the Dread Lord's tentacles had wound around Vera's thigh in a constrictor knot. Even with Keyser's reserves, it took nearly all her entropine to untangle and deslime the pair. She released them and sagged against the brick wall, heaving like a hunted ghast. Between the magic and the unaccustomed physical exertion, her ass was kicked. One of these days, she was going to cook up a fitness spell and sell it for billions to the Dark Lord of Purdue Pharma (a human—the Archons lacked the capacity for that level of cold-blooded evil).

Vera staggered to her feet and started hobbling across the parking lot.

"Wait," the witch called. "I need to talk to you."

"Later," she said. "You asked me to check out the cults. Peloton meets uptown at six." Vera straddled an ancient black Vespa, clapped a helmet on her head, and sped out of the parking lot.

The witch watched until she was out of sight. She'd pin Vera down later. In the meantime, she had a bargain to fulfill.

She fished her BlackBerry out of her pocket and started drafting a text to Carcosa.

CHAPTER FIFTEEN

Witchin' Ain't Easy

T he witch stared at a ketchup-smeared meat loaf decorated with twelve candles. Mother Mayhem tried, but she never got human traditions quite right. The branches of her treelike body rustled as she lit them, a generous gesture for an Archon made of kindling.

"Make a wish, child." The golden lanterns of her eyes glowed as brightly as the tiny flames.

She did, knowing all the while it wouldn't come true. She wished for the same thing every year, something the world's only witchling couldn't have.

After she'd eaten and opened Mother Mayhem's gift (a dagger—edged weapons were, Mother claimed, traditional for one's twelfth year), the witch retired to her room to get ready for bed.

"Meh-eh-eh-any happy returns," brayed an unfamiliar voice.

"Who's there?" The witch whirled, searching for the speaker, but she was alone. Had she eaten too much birthday meat loaf and passed out? She pinched herself.

"You're not asleep, little witch."

She scanned her room, heart thundering, but nothing was there. Well, not nothing nothing—but nothing new. Her dresser. A full-length mirror. A life-size marble statue of a nude goat-headed woman, her crotch concealed by what the witch had recently realized wasn't patchy fur.

All perfectly ordinary.

The statue opened its mouth and said, "Meh-eh-eh-erry meet, daughter of Discordia!"

The witch stumbled backward, bumped into the bed, and sat down.

The statue stepped off its pedestal with the sound of stone grinding on stone. Its hooves kicked up sparks on the obsidian floor tiles. "You're wide-awake, just not in the same dimeh-eh-eh-eh-eh-eh—" It cleared its throat and tried again. "You're on the astral plane."

"The what?"

"The astral plane," it repeated. "This is your palace of meh-eh-eh-emory, where you'll store your witchly knowledge. And this is where I'll train you for your initiation."

"You're. . .you're going to stay here? With me?" Maybe this would be the year her wish came true. "What initiation?"

"Your initiation as a Discordian."

"But who are you? What's a Discordian?"

"We'll get to Discordianism in good time." The statue ponderously turned and sat on the bed beside her. Wood creaked and splintered, then the bed collapsed. The creature took no notice. Its marble legs splayed out stiffly in front of it. "As for who I am, well, you can call me Nanny. A better question would be, who are you?"

"I'm. . .I'm a witchling."

"Indeed, you are, daughter, but you have a name." The statue said, in a conspiratorial tone, "Would you like to know what it is?"

A name. She had a name. Not just "witchling" or "child" or "godsforsaken chaos gnome." An actual name.

"Yes," she breathed.

"You must never reveal your true name to anyone, especially an Archon. If you do, they'll have power over you." Nanny shook her head, producing a cloud of stone dust. "You don't want that."

"Just tell me!"

"Your name," Nanny said, "is—"

"Tamagotchi!"

The witch blinked, drawing her consciousness back to the physical plane. She looked around her office, bleary and confused.

"Tamagotchi!"

Magnolia's all-too-human eyes rolled back in her head, revealing the quivering pinks. The witch stood and walked to her side.

"You okay?"

Magnolia trembled violently, then collapsed onto her desk. Discordia, take the wheel.

The door burst open. Vera Vásquez strode in and rushed to Magnolia's side. She placed her hand on the swell of Magnolia's melon. The warm bronze of her skin glowed against the sickly green dome. When Magnolia groaned and began to stir, Vera removed her hand and stepped back. With a sharp intake of breath,

Magnolia jerked upright. She winced and massaged her visibly throbbing melon. The witch shuddered.

"What happened?" Magnolia's eyes, dilated to wide black circles, darted from the witch to Vera. She flinched. "My head is pounding."

Vera patted the trembling Archon's arm. "You'll be fine." She loosened the drawstring of the purple Crown Royal bag that served as her purse and pulled out a sandwich bag, which she handed to Magnolia. "Something sweet will help."

"Thank you." Magnolia opened the bag and removed a large cookie—the thick, buttery kind that leaves a grease spot on a napkin.

Vera looked up at the witch. "She needs caffeine for that headache."

"Okay."

"Well?" Vera glared at her and crossed her arms, displaying yet another excellent shirt: *Finland Is a Figment of Your Imagination.*

The metal clasp of her ever-present bolo tie caught the witch's eye: a godsdamned golden apple.

"Do you have a coffeepot?" Vera asked. "A can of Coke?"

"I've got bourbon and Tic Tacs."

"You," Vera said, pointing to the witch. "Come with me."

"Where are we—"

The smaller woman spun and stalked out the door, hips switching. The witch stared after her. Seconds later, she returned, muttering in emphatic Spanish. She grabbed the witch's arm and tugged her along.

"Is there a vending machine?" Vera looked up and down the hall. "A cafeteria?"

"There's a snack bar."

"Lead the way."

The witch started walking, trailed by the tapping of her companion's stilettos. Vera was one of those bombshell-type women who made her feel like a tall, gangly bag of coat hangers—wiry angles where there should be curves. Their coloring was similar, and they shared excellent taste in T-shirts (hers read *Witchin' Ain't Easy*), but that was the end of the resemblance. And there was something about her, an aura that gave the witch a low-grade entropine buzz.

Vera was the reason the witch had just visited her palace of memory. She wanted to review everything Nanny taught her about Discordianism over the year and a day of her novitiate. But now that Vera was here, the witch could grill her directly.

"We'll take a large Coke and. . ." Vera scrutinized the snack bar menu, then looked back at the witch. "Want anything?"

"I'm good."

Vera shrugged and flashed a wide smile at the cashier. "And a hot dog."

The woman replaced Vera's cash with a mammoth fountain drink and a paper sleeve containing a doughy bun and an elderly wiener. Vera handed the

Coke to the witch and grabbed the hot dog. She turned and started walking back toward the office.

"A hot dog on Friday," the witch said. "You *are* a Discordian."

The unsacred scriptures encouraged the faithful to eat a hot dog on Fridays to protest the religious strictures of old-school Catholicism (no meat on Fridays), Judaism and Islam (no pork), Hinduism (no beef), Buddhism (no meat), and Discordianism (no hot dog buns).

Vera arched an eyebrow and took a bite but did not reply.

"I'm more of an April-Fools'-and-Clusterfuck devotee," the witch said.

According to Nanny, witches were Discordia's spiritual children. Did that mean Vera was. . .

Impossible.

The woman had been near senior Archons, including the Clerk. The squid-wards could sniff out magic like truffle pigs.

Unless Vera knew how to hide.

The witch grabbed her elbow and tugged her to a halt. "Are you a witch?"

Vera laughed mid-bite and inhaled half-chewed hot dog. "Don't be ridiculous," she croaked. "All the witches but you are—"

A coughing spell cut her short. Eyes streaming, she pointed to the floor.

Six feet under.

"I know." The witch sighed heavily. "Are you a wielder?"

Unlike witches, wielders could fly under the Archonic radar. It was all about hormone balance. A witch's body made a shit ton of entropine, curse breakers produced syntropine, and normal human bodies made neither. Wielders had watered-down witch ancestry. Their bodies produced the barest trace of entropine. They couldn't perform their own magic, but they tended to have uncanny knacks and could sometimes use magical items.

"No. I'm the head priestess of the Ordo Dea Discordia." Vera pressed her palm over the clasp of her string tie and dipped her chin. "As above, so bolo."

"What does the Ordo. . .whatever do?"

"The ODD maintains the Discordian section of the Akashic Library, which houses every thought, event, or idea from time immemorial." She shook her head. "The place is overrun with porn. I had to move our collection up here." Vera tapped her right temple. "We've got a bit of everything—chaos theory, magical techniques, a complete history of Operation Mindfuck. . .you name it."

The entire storehouse of Discordian philosophy and entropic praxis was crammed inside Vera's head?

That explained a lot, actually.

"How big is this Order?" the witch asked.

"It's just me."

Then Vera's tapping stilettos were off and running. The witch jogged after her.

"I thought only witches were Discordians."

"Where'd you hear that?"

"I didn't hear it anywhere," the witch said. "I just assumed—"

"You know what they say about assumptions."

Yet another artifact of her inadequate education. Pre-Emergence, she'd have learned the sorcerous arts and the tenets of Discordianism from senior witches. Instead, she'd learned about the human world from the Archonic equivalent of the Wicker Man and gotten magic lessons from a nude statue. No wonder her knowledge base was lacking.

Vera took another bite of her hot dog and said, around a mouthful of bun, "It's like squares and rectangles. All witches are Discordians, but it doesn't hold the other way around. You should brush up on your *Principia Discordia*."

"I read it prepping for my initiation." It had been no small feat. Its verses were written on a collection of used cocktail napkins, ragged Post-its, graffitied fragments of concrete, and—memorably—a photo of a tattooed ass cheek.

Vera opened a door labeled *Janitorial Staff Only* and walked into the witch's office. She grabbed the soda and handed it to Magnolia. "How are you feeling?"

"Much better after the cookie." Magnolia took a sip and looked up at the witch. "What happened?"

"You shouted something, then your eyes rolled back, and you fainted."

"What did I say?"

"Tamagotchi," the witch said. "What does that mean?"

"I don't know." She looked up at the witch, chin quivering. "I'm sorry."

"It's okay." Vera patted Magnolia's shoulder. "Has this happened before?"

"No." Magnolia ran her fingers through her hair, rearranging the wig's gentle waves. "I mean, I have visions, but I always remember what I see, and I've never passed out."

Vera perched on the corner of her desk and crossed her legs. "I'm just glad you're okay."

The witch sat down and lit a Swisher Sweet. "Well, did your Discordian spidey sense bring you here to help Magnolia, or is the timing just a coincidence?"

"Coincidence is Discordia's way of remaining anonymous," Vera said, with a Sphinx-like smile. "I dropped by to update you on the cults. The Reptilians and the Illuminati are still competing to take over the human world for the glory of Cthulhu. The Luciferians are holding a Black Friday Black Mass tonight. Let's see. . .who else? Oh, CrossFit's opening a new box across town, and the Seitanists are having a vegan chili cook-off."

"What about the Church of the Flying Spaghetti Monster?"

"They've developed a new strain of indica called Beer Volcano." Vera whistled. "That's some potent bud."

"And the new cult?"

"Sketchy as hell," Vera said. "I still don't even know their name." She rubbed her hands together. "Now that we've ruled out the cults—"

"Ruled them out?" the witch asked. "You just said the new one was sketchy."

"It's a cult, Witch. Sketchy is their brand."

"But we still need to—"

Magnolia's desk phone rang. Still massaging her head with one hand, she picked up the receiver. "County Witch's office."

"Looks like you're busy here," Vera said. "I'll keep tracking the little white men and report back at our next meeting."

"Wait—"

"Excuse me, Witch," Magnolia said. "It's Dr. Carcosa."

"That guy creeps me out," Vera said, wrinkling her nose. "I ran into him on my way here."

So, she was cool with black-cockerel-sacrificing cultists, but a priggish scientist gave her the willies?

The witch puffed on her cigarillo, watching the flashing light on her phone. Gods, she hoped Carcosa had good news about the sphere. The Clerk would expect progress on Tuesday. She looked up to ask Vera to stay for further interrogation, but the woman had vanished.

"Are you available," Magnolia said, "or should I tell him you'll call back?"

"I'll talk to him."

"Do you mind if I head to the psychic surgery? I feel. . .weird."

"Have at it."

After Magnolia grabbed her purse and left, the witch stubbed out her cigar and picked up the phone.

"What do you have for me?"

"Good afternoon, Witch," Dr. Carcosa said, "I have completed my initial examination of the item."

"And?"

"I cannot say exactly what it does yet, but I have learned three things," he said. "First, my supposition was correct. It is a field generator."

Not a baseball, then, *Vera*.

"Second, its activation mechanism has been damaged."

Made sense. It'd been in the middle of an epic battle between the Clerk and the Sheriff.

"Third, it is not human technology."

The witch sat up straighter. "You're sure?"

"Quite," Carcosa said. "I suspect the Clerk knows more than she has shared with you. I dare not speculate about her motives, but. . .tread carefully, Witch."

"I'll watch where I stomp," she said. "I've been thinking about what kind of field this apparatus might generate. Whatever it was, it shot my powers to shit. Could it be anti-magical?"

"It is theoretically possible. I am conducting further testing, but it will take more time than I anticipated. My research assistant is out of the office yet again." Carcosa heaved an exasperated sigh. "Lorelei barely shows up for work anymore."

"Lay off her a bit, Doc," the witch said, thinking of the incident at the landfill. "I think she lost someone recently."

"Indeed. A member of her club, as I recall."

"Her club?"

"Self-help, I think. They follow a guru called the Evil Angel."

"And what sort of help does this Evil Angel give them?"

"Lorelei will not discuss it," Carcosa said. "She says she has a sacred duty to preserve anonymity."

Sounded like a standard twelve-step program. Gods knew Tophet County was lousy with addictive substances. The toadlets in Tehom Lake produced hallucinogenic slime that would—

"Speaking of anonymity," he said, his voice strained, "you and I are rather recently acquainted. It occurs to me that, with your knowledge of my allegiances, you hold my life in your hands." He cleared his throat. "The Clerk commissioned my research, but she has not involved herself in the daily minutiae. Should she grow suspicious. . ."

"Chill," the witch said. "I haven't said a word."

Well, she'd said a *few* words, but all she'd told Magnolia was that she'd given the sphere to a qualified expert.

Of course Carcosa, the eminent physicist, had visited her office that very day. Time for a subject change.

"About your research," she said. "Why would the Clerk want humans to understand Archonic teleportation?"

"In my line of work, one does not question funding freely given."

Fair enough, but it made about as much sense as Vera's plague of little white men—which reminded her. . .Vera said she'd run into the good doctor on her way in.

"Did you just try to come by my office?"

"I did," he said, "but that deranged Vásquez woman was lurking outside your door."

"Don't come here again. We shouldn't be seen together." The witch shivered, thinking of Magnolia's mind-reading melon.

"Very well," he said. "I must go. I shall be in touch when I have news."

The witch hung up, feeling a queasy sensation that was definitely not guilt.

CHAPTER SIXTEEN

Love Is a Devil

Y ou're muted."
   The beak-like mouth of the cephalopodic High Lord of Economic Development moved soundlessly in her square of the grid. A suckered tentacle smacked against the lefthand side of the screen.

"No, click *here*," Heather said, pointing at the bottom of her own square. "On the picture of the microphone."

A potato replaced Y'ggarlos's image. Its quartet of eyes blinked in succession as the mouth continued to open and close in total silence. The witch snickered. She'd been dreading using the County's videoconferencing system, the aptly named FML (Fios Meeting Lair), but it was the most entertaining thing she'd seen since the Flying Spaghetti Monster apparated at Olive Garden to liberate his noodly brethren.

Heather massaged her temples. "May I suggest using your joystick? Your anatomy isn't compatible with the touchscreen."

One of the potato's stalklike tentacles twitched.

"—YOU HEAR ME NOW?"

Keyser Söze, who'd been sleeping on the witch's keyboard, jerked awake with a yowl of alarm. He leaped to his feet, gifting Tophet County with an intimate view of a raccoon's chocolate starfish. A smattering of disgusted grunts and one disturbingly intrigued aah chorused from the witch's speakers before he made a run for it.

"You don't have to shout, High Lord," Heather said. "We can—"

"WHY AM I A TUBER?"

"Just go ahead with your updates."

"And for the love of Azathoth," buzzed Achartho, framed in the grid by the curve of his scorpion's tail, "stop bellowing."

The potato huffed and said, "The Zoning Board reminds citizens that a permit is required before constructing a subterranean hideout. While we applaud the community's enthusiasm, unauthorized tunneling recently resulted in a sinkhole near Dunwich Park." Four mismatched eyes glanced at her notes. "Several local businesses have lodged complaints with the department regarding acts of corporate vandalism. For example, someone replaced Big Roy's Junkyard and Salvage with an AutoZone. We support hostile takeovers, but the proper forms must be filed."

"Anything else from Economic Development?"

"Not unless anyone knows how to—"

"Oops, looks like you're muted again," the mayor said with a furtive tap of her mouse. "If there's nothing else—"

Dr. Carcosa raised a virtual hand. "Madam Mayor, might I steal a moment of your time after we conclude this meeting? I have an updated project plan to review with you."

"Of course. My assistant will send you a link." Heather glanced at her Fitbit. "That's all the time we have. Renovations of the Executive Hearing Room are still in progress, so we'll be using FML again for next week's session." She shook her head. "God help us all."

The witch reached forward to end the call, but Heather kept talking.

"One last announcement," she said. "My office is throwing a Darkest Night party on the bridge over the Fathomless Abyss to commemorate the winter solstice and celebrate the Archonic New Year. Call my office to volunteer." She banged her gavel. "This meeting is adjourned."

Heather's image vanished, followed by a string of others in rapid succession. Ronnie Coffman pulled a joint from behind his ear and lit it. He stood, displaying Puff the Magic Dragon boxer shorts, scratched his Sandra Bullocks with great enthusiasm, and wandered out of the camera's range.

One shitty meeting down, one to go.

The crack of splintering wood thundered through the witch's apartment, followed by the sounds of booted footsteps.

"Fan out, men! I'll take the—"

The rasping burr of Keyser's snarl interrupted the invader.

"Get it off me! Get it off me!"

The witch slammed her laptop shut and revved her auric engines. Someone's morning was about to get apocalyptically bad.

"Witch," a man called, his voice just audible over the shrieks of Keyser's prey. "It's Hank. Hold your fire!"

Deputy Eye Candy led the Clerk's personal Spectral Forces detail. She might get pissy if Keyser slaughtered one of her minions. The witch willed him to execute a tactical retreat. After a brief scuffle, his victim's desperate shrieks faded to snivels and sniffs.

"You guys were supposed to *knock*," Hank said.

"But we wanted to try the new battering ram—"

"Wait outside."

A pair of raised hands appeared at the door of her bedroom, hovering over an inordinately attractive face.

"Let me guess," the witch said, "the Clerk sent you to escort me to my own damned meeting."

Hank furrowed his immaculate brows. "The Clerk?" He shook his head. "No, I'm, uh. . .helping the Sheriff out today."

Code, no doubt, for doing a little spying.

"He asked us to bring you in for a. . .friendly interview. He wants to see that thing he found at the landfill."

Shit, shit, *shit*.

The witch lifted a shoulder in what she hoped came off as a careless shrug. "Can't make it. I'm running late for a meeting with the Clerk." She stepped toward him and lowered her voice. "This tug-of-war is above our paygrade, Hank. Tell the Sheriff to take it up with *her*." She looked around her room, searching the mounds of clothes for something cleanish. Leather motorcycle pants and her *Hex the Patriarchy* shirt. Perfect. "I'm stripping on the count of three. If you're still here. . ."

"I'm going!" He backed out of her bedroom, pulling the door closed behind him. "Want a ride?"

The witch wriggled into her pants and cracked the blinds. It was pissing frozen rain outside, which would make for a miserable trip via broom. Even with an entropic bubble, sleet always found a way in. She zipped her boots and jerked the door open, startling a squeak of alarm from Hank. "That'd be great."

She caught his eyes wandering around her shithole of an apartment as she hunted for her bag. Piles of laundry. Empty bottles of Chicken Cock. Stacks of books. He peered at the spines of one such pillar, all of which read *The Lazy Gourmand's Calamari Cookbook*, and picked up the topmost volume. The witch suppressed the urge to tear the book out of his hand and beat him with it.

"You're really into seafood, huh?"

"Something like that." She caught sight of the nylon strap of her backpack trailing out from under a sagging futon and yanked it free. Keyser, responding to her mental nudge, appeared and climbed inside. "Let's go."

Hank watched with a pained expression as she magically cinder-blocked over her destroyed door, then they climbed into his Hummer. "Where to?"

The witch consulted Magnolia's email invitation. "67 Arkham Street." She frowned and looked up at Hank. "Any idea what's there?"

"Probably some sort of primordial evil."

Always a good guess in downtown Asphodel.

They drove in blessed silence for a few moments before Hank started fidgeting. "So. . .um, have you read any good books lately?"

Oh, gods. He'd handled one of her Amish romances. What if the illusion hadn't held?

"What's *that* supposed to mean?" She scowled at him with such ferocity that his eyebrows crisped to cinders. "Whatever you think you saw—"

"I was just making conversation!" One hand maintained a death grip on the wheel as the other drifted to the streaks of stubble above his eyes. They rolled to a stop at a traffic light, and he fixed her with a wounded gaze. "I want to get to know you better—you know, since we work together."

"Oh. My bad." The witch fished a Sharpie from her bag. "Come here." She batted Hank's hands away and drew a mostly matching set of downward slashes over his eyes. It was, admittedly, not her best work.

A horn blared behind them, and he eased off the brakes. He checked out his reflection in the rearview mirror and flinched.

"Was that permanent marker?" Hank flashed an Angry Birds glare in her direction. "It'll take weeks to wear off."

"Perfect timing. Gives your eyebrows a chance to grow back. Until then, you're very. . .intimidating."

By the time his phone announced they'd arrived at their destination, the Hummer's interior was cloaked in a tense silence that was part wounded indignation, part repressed hilarity.

"Thanks for the lift." The witch slid out and shouldered her backpack. "Tell your boss I'll send an invoice for property damage." She watched him peel out, then turned toward the site of her meeting.

A movie theater–style marquee read *Welcome to the Museum of Demonic Dolls*. Heads of all shapes and sizes covered the building's facade. Coquettish kewpies. Sinister ventriloquist dummies. Porcelain nightmare babies.

Nope, not happening. Magnolia would just have to move the meeting.

The glass double doors, painted black to conceal what lay behind them, burst open, and the Clerk oozed out onto the sidewalk. "Witch," she barked, "we need you."

Apparently, it *was* happening.

She followed the Clerk through a shadowed hallway, listening to the eerie childish giggles of the museum's denizens. A sharp pain in her calf drew her attention to a battalion of vintage Barbie-sized G.I. Joes, one of whom had just stabbed her with a bayonet. She punted it down the hall.

The Clerk led her into a windowless meeting room lit by dripping candelabra. Chad and Vera sat at a conference table, their eyes glued to the unfolding spectacle. A portal hung in midair. It emitted a faint nimbus of netherlight, which was mostly blocked by the struggling body of the Dread Lord of Human Resources. Magnolia tugged fruitlessly on a tangle of tentacles wedged into the hole.

"By the weeping teats of the Black Goat," the Clerk said, "what have you been eating, Sathach?"

The eyeless visage of the Dread Lord strained against the edges of the portal. "Witch, thank goodness you're here," he lisped.

One of his tentacles lashed free of the portal. A sinister titter echoed from a dark corner of the room, and a blur of motion streaked in front of the witch. A red-haired doll clad in overalls hacked off the tip of the tentacle with a miniature axe and disappeared under the table. The Dread Lord shrieked.

"I wanna play too," Vera said as she slid under the table.

Well, *that* wasn't creepy.

The witch circled around the portal, examining the problem from all sides as she kept a wary eye out for pernicious poppets.

"Looks like he's stuck."

"Even the Idiot God could see that," the Clerk said. "We need to get him out."

A tentacle snaked around the witch's wrist. "Please," he said. "This is humiliating."

The witch sighed and waggled her fingers. A tub of Vaseline appeared in Magnolia's hands.

Magnolia frowned at the plastic jar.

The Clerk grabbed it, removed the lid, and scooped up a blob of poor-man's lube on the end of one leggings-clad tentacle. "Let's grease him up."

A few minutes' work led to the successful delivery of the Dread Lord. He stuffed himself into a new human skin, slightly broader across the beam than its soul-patched predecessor. Shame-faced, he took his seat at the table.

"Ahem," he said. "I do apologize."

"Nothing wrong with being a little thick." Vera crawled out from under the table holding a swaddled bundle. Muffled obscenities leaked out around a pacifier strapped to plastic cheeks. She patted her wriggling charge and grinned at the Dread Lord. "I'm a curvy girl myself."

"Shall we begin?" The Clerk settled into her seat, gesturing for the members of the WTF to follow suit. "I'm eager to hear what you've learned."

"After exhaustive testing, I can conclusively state that the white sphere found at the landfill is not a baseball." The witch shot a glare at Vera. "It's a field generator, and it's not human technology." She watched the Clerk intently, alert for any reaction that would betray prior knowledge, but a tangle of eyestalks was hard to read.

"That is. . .troubling," the Clerk said. "What kind of field does it produce?"

"I'm still working on that. Should have an answer next week." The witch nodded to the Dread Lord, whose generously freckled human skin sported hair the approximate color of a radioactive carrot. "You're up."

"Magnolia and I interviewed those closest to the Dread Lord of IT and the Unseen Creeping Horror," he said. "According to the UCH's associates, he'd been withdrawn and unsettled for weeks, and. . .ahem." The Dread Lord tugged at his collar. "He'd been dreaming of little white men."

Vera frowned. "That's weird. I didn't see any LWM until after his transmogrification."

"His fog is diffused through time as well as space," Magnolia said. "He could've picked up temporal echoes."

"What of the Dread Lord of IT?" the Clerk asked.

"That's been a bit tougher," Magnolia said. "He's a loner—misanthropic, misarchonic, and generally miserable."

"The only people close to him are his subordinates," the Dread Lord said, glancing at Chad. "Thorough interviews revealed no information about his whereabouts, only that the software problems began after his disappearance."

"The scheduling software was acting up before he vanished," Chad said. "We have frequent issues"—his eyes flicked to the witch—"with that system, but they're usually outages. What we're seeing now is a new functionality. The source code's been altered. We've got a forensic computer scientist combing through it now."

"Thanks, Chad." The witch consulted her notes. "Next up—"

"Sorry," he said. "One more thing. I've been asking around about those transfers from the mayor's General Fund. Ronnie Coffman says he never approved them. Whoever's behind them also put in a few equipment requisitions."

"For what?" the witch asked.

"Anti-entropic shields."

Damn. She didn't like the idea of some asshole making himself witch-proof. "Who ordered them?"

"I can't access the records." Chad ran his fingers through short locs. "I'll keep trying."

"Keep me posted," the witch said. "Last but not least, Vera checked out the cults this week."

"Nothing worth mentioning." The doll whimpered, and Vera jiggled it in a soothing rhythm. "I'm ready to focus on the little white menace."

"We need to know more about the new cult."

"No luck there," Vera said. "You have to register for meetings online. I tried the link on the R&C website, but it didn't work."

"I'm on it." Chad picked up his BlackBerry, fingers flying as he typed.

They needed to get a mole in that cult. The witch didn't trust Vera with an operation this delicate, and Magnolia and the Dread Lord were the wrong species. That left. . .

Her. Of course.

She could hag it up and infiltrate the nutjobs.

"I'm going in," the witch said. "I'll wear a disguise, lie low—"

Chad chuckled, shaking his head. "You? Lie low?"

She looked around the table. No one met her eyes.

"I shall perform this task." The Dread Lord adjusted his tie. "This is a brand new human suit. No one will recognize me."

Magnolia nodded. "That could work."

This time, it was the witch who laughed. "You're joking, right?"

"Humans are my business," he said as a slender, suckered limb crept out of his left ear. "I'll fit right in."

"Sathach," the Clerk said, "I think it's best we leave this task to a human." A tentacle swathed in a Disney Princess print slithered out from under her shroud and pointed at Chad. "This one will do it."

"Me? No, I'm a computer guy." Chad looked around the table, desperation written on his face. "Know how you can tell introverts from extroverts in Online Services?" When no one responded, he said, "The extroverts look at your shoes when they talk to you."

An awkward silence fell.

The Dread Lord leaned toward Chad, scrutinizing his stricken face. "I'm a more convincing human than he is."

"You should've seen the whack jobs I ran into poking around the other cults," Vera said.

Vera's shirt of the day featured a T. rex using his tiny arms to place the capstone on the Great Pyramid of Giza. If *she* thought they were whack jobs. . .

"These cultists don't get out much," Vera said. "All they talk about is video games and world domination."

Social rejects who are way too into video games? The witch eyed Chad speculatively. He was born for this. "Did you find their website?"

"They've got a private Meetup group," Chad said. "It's called the Temple of the Evil Angel."

Gods below. Carcosa's assistant isn't in a twelve-step group. She's in a cult.

Vera peered over Chad's shoulder. "Says here singles are welcome. I bet it's a"—she muffled the ears of the swaddled doll—"*sex cult!*"

Chad glanced from face to face in increasing panic. "I don't even answer the phone if I don't recognize the number. I'd have no idea what to do at. . .at an orgy!"

Vera shrugged. "Dive in and start licking something. If all else fails, try for a sixty-eight."

The witch knew she shouldn't ask, but morbid curiosity compelled her. "What's a sixty-eight?"

"You do me. I'll owe you one."

"For the love of Lythalia, get your minds out of the gutter," Magnolia said. "'Evil Angel' is part of a quote from *Love's Labour's Lost*. 'Love is familiar. Love is a devil. There is no evil angel but Love.' Such a beautiful play."

"First, you take a human name," the Clerk said, "and now you're reading Shakespeare?"

"I study human culture to. . .to better subjugate these cattle."

"I see."

The Clerk did not appear to see.

"I still need you to check it out, Chad," the witch said. "If people start stripping, just bail."

"But—"

"When's their next meeting?"

"This Friday night in the Odious Pit at the Rec Center," Chad said. "BYOB and an app to share."

"How'd you do that?" the Dread Lord asked. "You said it was a private group."

"Dude, I'm a technomancer. It was child's play."

Vera's doll wriggled violently. She pressed it to her ample chest and made shushing sounds.

Chad scrolled down the page. "At least a potluck at the Rec Center's better than their last meeting."

"Oh yeah?" the witch asked. "What was that?"

"A picnic at the landfill. Who'd want to. . ." He looked up and met her eyes. "The Unseen Creeping Horror."

The Clerk leaned forward eagerly. "Excellent work, Mr. Chadwick."

"Can you see who's in the cult?" the witch asked. "Names? Photos?"

"No names, and the only image is their logo." Chad held up his BlackBerry.

The tiny image showed a squat stick figure with both arms wrapped around a pile of pasta. She grabbed the BlackBerry and looked closer.

Those weren't noodles. . .

They were *tentacles*.

"That's a little white man," the witch said. "And it's strangling an Archon."

CHAPTER SEVENTEEN

Tooth by Tentacle

The last vestiges of a dream about a certain farmhand plowing her proverbial fields faded from the witch's mind. She sat up and rubbed her eyes.
Something had roused her. Maybe Keyser was dreaming again. She patted the
foot of the bed where he usually slept curled against her shins, but he wasn't
there.

A flash of white streaked across the room, barely visible in the moonlight.
The witch heard an enraged growl and the click of Keyser Söze's claws on the
wood floor, followed by a loud clatter. She groped for her bedside lamp and
turned it on.

A white sphere lay on the floor next to her bed. Keyser Söze stood on his
hind legs, his front paw gripping the shoulder of an impossible creature. It stood
three feet tall and looked like a 3D gingerbread man made of white porcelain.
Keyser lunged forward and clamped his teeth onto the thing's arm. He shook his
head, snarling.

Holy hells. . .Vera's little white men were *real*.

The LWM wriggled free and darted away, but Keyser—so intent on attack-
ing seconds ago—didn't give chase. Instead, he threw himself on the sphere.

The witch's eyes closed instinctively against a brilliant flash of light. When
she opened them, Keyser Söze was gone. A small flattened oval on a loop of ball
chain lay where he'd been.

"Keyser?" Her voice came out in a strangled whisper.

The LWM slithered out from under her bed and grabbed the white ball. She
launched herself at it with a scream of rage, knocking the sphere from its grasp.

Though she was working no magic, she felt a burst of entropine flare from her body as they made contact. The thing emitted a psychic wail, and strips of it peeled away into flailing ribbons. Shrieking soundlessly, it fled.

"Keyser?"

The witch pushed up to hands and knees and crawled to the object that sat where she'd last seen him. She hooked her finger through the chain and lifted it. The plastic shell of the oval was striped black and gray and bore a single word in bold white letters: *Tamagotchi*.

The word Magnolia yelled during her fit.

A pixelated image of an animal paced the length of a small video screen. Its face sported a black bandit's mask, and one front paw was missing.

It couldn't be. . .

The little creature looked up at her and pressed its paw against the screen. The witch covered Keyser's paw with the tip of her finger as tears streaked down her cheeks. She moaned and pressed the plastic case to her heart.

It couldn't be, but it *was*.

The office door smoked under the weight of the witch's furious glare. She checked the time. Seven thirty. Magnolia should arrive soon.

After the two a.m. attack, the witch made a pot of the blackest, bitterest coffee she could stomach and dug into magical research. She couldn't think straight with the sphere shorting out her magic, so she stuck it in a Styrofoam cooler in her building's basement storage unit. Then she combed through her Nomiconical notes for anything that might help.

When her search proved fruitless, she researched Tamagotchis. The sphere had turned Keyser into a godsdamned digital pet. She figured out how to feed him by pushing a button on the case. True to life, he gulped down his food and immediately fell asleep, leaving her to brood.

The witch was accustomed to futile anger. It was, in fact, her default setting. But the righteous fury she now felt put all previous emotions to shame. Her bones were filled with lava. Her magic was a devouring fire. She was going to dismantle this county tooth by tentacle until she took her vengeance in blood. . .or the equivalent Archonic fluid.

Her mood was not improved by the odor permeating her office. Fresh paint. The formerly water-stained ceiling and smudged walls were now an eye-assaultingly bright white. And that wasn't the only change. Almost thirteen years of accumulated professional detritus—stacks of papers, unread manuals, empty food wrappers, and a long-dead spider plant—had vanished.

More of Magnolia's handiwork, no doubt. The witch was going to kill that wig-wearing werewoman. . .but not until she fixed Keyser.

The metallic click of a key in the office door sent a fresh surge of anger boiling through her veins. Magnolia pushed the door open with her foot, holding her keys in one hand and a cardboard tray in the other.

"You're here early for a Monday morning." Magnolia lifted the tray, which held two Starbucks cups. "I know you like Dee's coffee best, but they don't open for a few hours. Something told me to grab a Venti for you." She smiled and tapped her bulbous forehead. "I'm back in the game. No headaches all weekend!"

"I'm *so* glad."

Magnolia's smile faded. "You don't look glad. You look—"

"Enraged?" The witch bared her teeth. "Oh, I am." She stood. The force of her emotions was so great that her toes barely grazed the floor. With shaking fingers, she removed the Tamagotchi from a carabiner clipped to her belt loop and held it up. "Anything to say for yourself?"

"What's that?"

"This?" She raised her hand higher. "Oh, this is my familiar."

"I thought he was a raccoon."

"He has a name," she said. "And it's Keyser fucking Söze."

"I don't understand."

"Don't you?" The witch glided toward her, booted toes skimming the tile floor. "Last night, a little white man broke into my apartment and planted one of those spheres in my bedroom."

Magnolia's seafoam skin paled, and she dropped the tray. A geyser of what had to be scalding coffee sprayed her tentacled lower half, but she didn't react. "You. . .You *saw* a little white man?"

"Keyser attacked it, but it escaped." The witch drifted closer. "Know what happened next?"

Magnolia shook her head. "I. . .I don't—"

"Keyser dove onto the sphere. When it went off, it turned him into *this*."

"Oh, Witch, I'm so sorry," Magnolia said, her fear-stricken face softening with sympathy.

"And what the hell did you do to my office?"

"What?" Magnolia's eyes swept the room. "I wasn't even in town this weekend!"

"You'd better give your heart to Discordia," the witch said, "because your ass is mine."

"Can we just—"

"Tama-gotcha!"

Magnolia cocked her head. "What?"

"I said Tama-*gotcha*." It sounded much cooler in her mind. "Elvis's throne, Magnolia. . .this"—she shook the plastic oval—"is a Tamagotchi."

"That's the word from the vision I had last week! My melon must have—"

"Bullshit." The witch lowered Keyser's electronic prison. "You said your melon picks up on what I desire. Well, I'd never heard of a Tamagotchi until you said it, and I godsdamned well didn't want Keyser turned into a squidsucking passel of pixels!"

Magnolia flinched at the anti-Archonic slur. The witch felt a momentary pang of guilt, but rage burned it to ash. Entropine flooded into her bloodstream. From the look on Magnolia's face, she sensed the magical tide, but instead of backing away, she stepped closer to the witch and grabbed her hand.

"I swear on my life," Magnolia said, looking deep into the witch's eyes, "I did not do this."

Juiced up as she was, the magical oath took immediate effect. The witch could feel the truth of Magnolia's words in the marrow of her bones. The anger drained from her body, leaving only an empty, exhausted shell.

"I. . .I'm sorry." The witch's voice was a hoarse whisper. "He's the only family I've ever had, and now he's. . ."

As good as gone. She could see him, but she couldn't touch him, couldn't hold him, couldn't pet his silky fur. She was alone, just as she'd been before Nanny came. Just as she'd be for the rest of her stupid, gods-cursed life if she couldn't get him back.

"I know." Magnolia rested a tentative hand on her shoulder. "Witch, you told me Keyser was having night terrors. The UCH dreamed about little white men before he was attacked. I think—"

The phone rang. Magnolia raised her eyebrows in question, and the witch nodded.

"County Witch's office." Her eyes flicked up and caught the witch's gaze. *Chad*, she mouthed.

He was a smart guy. Maybe he could help her figure out how to get Keyser back.

The witch nodded. She walked to her desk and dropped heavily into her chair, weak from the aftereffects of a combined adrenaline and entropine rush.

As she pushed a button to transfer the call, Magnolia said, "The Clerk needs to know there's been another attack on a High Lord of Tophet County."

"Good idea." The Archons took care of their own. Maybe the Clerk could do something. Maybe she could help.

"I'll head to her office." Magnolia grabbed her purse and walked to the door. She paused, her hand on the knob, and looked back at the witch. "I'm so sorry." Then she left, easing the door closed behind her.

The witch gently laid Keyser on her desk. A cloud of *Z*'s surrounded his digital image. Still sleeping. With a shaky sigh, she picked up the phone.

"Hey, Witch," Chad said. "You'll never guess. . ." His voice trailed off. "What, no insult today?"

She opened her mouth, but no words came.

"What's wrong?"

Again, the witch tried to speak, but to her horror, what came out was a choked sob.

Her BlackBerry buzzed.

Chad said, "Accept my meeting request, okay?"

The witch picked it up and tapped accept. She braced herself to disintegrate into elementary particles, but nothing happened. A shimmering spark of netherlight appeared across from her desk. Seconds later, Chad misted in. He must've set the location to her office, not his. He grabbed the wooden visitor's chair, dragged it around to her side of the desk, and sat down, elbows propped on his knees.

Something about seeing his stupid face with its stupid puppy eyes shattered what remained of her self-control. She picked up Keyser Söze and curled forward, her breath hitching. Chad rested a hand on her back. He didn't say anything, didn't ask what was wrong or tell her everything would be okay. He just sat with her. Once the worst of it had passed, he pulled a stack of tissues from one of the dozen pockets on his stupid cargo pants and passed them to her. She mopped her face dry and sat up.

"If you ever say a word about this, I'll—"

"I know," he said. "You'll exact a humiliating revenge. I'd expect no less." He leaned back in the chair and gazed at her. "What's wrong?"

"My. . ." Her voice broke. She took a deep breath and tried again. "Vera's not crazy. Well, she probably *is*, but one of the little white men broke into my apartment last night. I woke up when Keyser Söze attacked it. He's my—"

"Your familiar. The three-legged raccoon," Chad said. "You got him on your thirteenth birthday, right?"

"The day after. How did you—"

"We've known each other for years." He shrugged. "I pay attention."

He actually *listened* to her dumb stories?

"So, he attacked the little white man. . ."

"Yeah," the witch said. "It got away, but it left another of those white spheres in my bedroom." She stared at her hands, shredding the wad of damp tissue. "Keyser dove on top of it. There was this flash of light, and then. . ."

Unwilling to risk further tears, she raised the loop of chain so Chad could see. His hand brushed hers as he slid his finger into the loop and took it.

"A Tamagotchi," he said. "Man, I haven't seen one of these in years."

"You know what it is?"

"Sure," he said. "I love vintage electronics. They're pretty cute. You push buttons to play games with them or feed them or clean up after them."

"Clean up after them?"

"What goes in must come out."

Keyser *would* find a way to make her scoop his shit even as an electronic entity.

"But I don't get it." His eyebrows drew together as he shook his head. "What does a Tamagotchi have to do with your familiar?"

"It *is* my familiar," she said. "When the white ball. . .detonated or whatever, it turned him into this."

Chad sat up, eyes widening. "You mean this"—he pointed to the Tamagotchi's screen—"is Keyser Söze?"

The witch nodded, blinking back more useless tears. "Magnolia had some kind of fit last week." She took Keyser from Chad's open palm and tapped the white letters on the case. "She yelled this word. I thought she must've had something to do with it, but—"

"No." He shook his head. "No way. She'd never do something like this."

"It can't be a coincidence."

What was it Vera had said? *Coincidence is Discordia's way of remaining anonymous.* Could Magnolia's fit have been a warning instead of a threat?

"The Sheriff found a sphere at the landfill, right?"

"Yeah," the witch said. "Exactly like the one in my bedroom."

"Whatever it is, it. . .It digitized Keyser and transformed the Unseen Creeping Horror." He met her eyes, and a bit of color drained from his brown skin. "Witch, someone wanted to do that to *you.*"

CHAPTER EIGHTEEN

Neighborhood Watch

The witch closed her eyes and whispered a prayer as she dropped a stiff rectangle of paper into her cauldron.

Mother of Chaos, help me get Keyser back.

The offering blackened and curled in a bloom of flame. She stared at the rapidly disappearing punch-card ballot—a symbol of discord if ever there was one. She'd magicked it away from the stack on the Clerk's desk. The election had gotten them into this mess. Maybe the election could get them out.

As if on cue, the Tamagotchi vibrated. Keyser Söze glared at her from the small screen. His hungry meter was down to a single heart. She pushed a button to dispense virtual cookies. Knowing Keyser, he'd be in a food coma within seconds. A nap sounded pretty damn good to her, too. But no sooner had her head touched the desk than the office door opened, and a horrifying vision in white appeared.

"Oh gods, what do you want?"

Mitsuki Carcosa said, "I have an appointment."

"No, the hell you don't."

The witch only had one client today, and he'd left an hour ago. Deputy Woods, the cop who'd been temporarily eaten by the UCH, came in wanting a football field–size illusion generator for who knew what kind of fuckery. She chugged her eleventh cup of coffee and opened her calendar.

Mother of monstrosities, there it was.

"Park it."

Mitsuki folded her long legs into Padmasana and said, "Your love spell didn't work."

The witch opened her mouth to protest. Hadn't Carcosa remodeled himself to suit his wife's wishes? What more did the woman want? But mentioning her association with Dr. C was a bad idea. "I warned you."

"You did."

"So, why are you here?"

Mitsuki rested her hands on her knees, thumbs and forefingers touching. "I want to know where my husband was last night."

Knowing Carcosa, he was either playing with the murder machine or meeting up with his Guy Fawkes friends. But Mitsuki must have reason to suspect otherwise, or she wouldn't be asking.

"You think he's after some strange?"

"I don't know what to think." A ripple of discomfort troubled the placid pool of her face. "He's been more distant than ever. He's even sleeping at his office. When I called his cell last night, I heard. . ." She cleared her throat. "I heard a woman."

"Isn't his assistant a woman?"

Mitsuki's sharp eyes skewered the witch. "How do you know that?"

Hump a hunting horror. This was getting tricky. She schooled her features into what she hoped was an enigmatic smile. "I know more than you can imagine."

"It wasn't Lorelei's voice." Mitsuki pressed her trembling lips together. "He said he had the TV on while he was grading papers, but Christian despises television. He doesn't have one in his office."

The witch hissed in a breath. Ouch. "You're sure you wanna know?"

"I am."

Gods dammit. She wanted to stay out of her co-conspirator's marriage, but if Mitsuki was on her calendar, the service contract was in the system.

Curse that cheating choad. She had no choice.

"Suit yourself," the witch said. "I'll need—"

"I have it." Mitsuki reached into her purse and retrieved a small baggie containing a tumbleweed of dark hair.

The witch shook it into her open palm and closed her eyes. She revved up her auric engines and followed the thread of Dr. Carcosa's energy signature through the quantum foam. His etheric spoor was strange. Most people left a sort of vapor trail—a puffy cloud that became more amorphous with time and distance. His tracks were closer to a laser beam. She had no problem tracing him through the underbelly of reality. When she found the right spot, she did the psychic equivalent of pressing play on a video clip.

Carcosa definitely hadn't been in his office. The witch had never seen it, but she'd bet it didn't have two queen beds and a mini-fridge. A curvy blonde stood silhouetted against the window, peering through the curtains. Her generously proportioned lower half was sheathed in banana-print leggings. The woman turned, and the witch barely suppressed a gasp. In her mind's eye, Heather walked toward the bed where Dr. Carcosa waited.

She fled the scene and opened her eyes.

"It's true," Mitsuki whispered. "He was with another woman."

"I'm afraid so."

The witch braced herself for Mitsuki to demand the details. Her top priorities were restoring Keyser and getting out of her contract. Throwing Madam Mayor under a marital bus could stick a dick in the works.

But Mitsuki didn't say a word. She stood and glided toward the door. Just as she grasped the knob, Vera charged in, barreling into her like a wrecking ball on heels. Mitsuki grabbed Vera's arm to keep from falling, and her eyes widened.

"You." Mitsuki took a step back and glanced at the witch. "This is the student who recommended your services."

"The heiress?"

"Guilty as charged." Vera took Mitsuki's hand. "Great class last night—cleared up the astigmatism in my third eye." She tapped her forehead and squinted up at the taller woman. "Speaking of which, are you okay?"

Mitsuki yanked her hand free with a vehemence that belied her preternatural calm. "Not remotely." She gave the door a very un-yogini-like slam on her way out.

Vera stalked toward the witch's desk. "What did you do?"

"Exactly what she—"

The Tamagotchi buzzed. The screen displayed a soft-serve swirl of shit next to a visibly disgruntled Keyser. She pushed a button to clean it up.

Vera snatched the plastic oval and cupped it in her hands. She lowered her head toward the case and whispered, then turned her ear toward it. After a moment, she straightened. "Those little white pendejos. . ."

"You. . .How did you. . ."

"I've been watching the LWM for weeks," Vera said, passing the Tamagotchi back to her. "I recognize their handiwork."

The witch glanced at the tiny screen. Keyser's eyes were throbbing hearts turned adoringly toward Vera. Despite the woman's Discordian pedigree, the witch had been sure the LWM were either a delusion or a scare tactic. Vera clearly knew more than she did. If that was the case. . .

"Do you know how to bring him back?"

Vera shook her head and sat down. "I'm sorry, Witch. I don't."

"Can you check your mental library?"

"It only holds Discordian lore. Whatever did *that*"—she pointed at the Tamagotchi—"was not Discordian. And I wouldn't recommend experimenting. With no body, the Tamagotchi is the only thing tethering him to the physical plane." She stared at Keyser's besotted face. "This is bad, Witch. You said he doubles your strength. Without him, you're vulnerable."

"No shit, Shoggoth."

"The little white men are growing bolder," Vera said. "That's why I came by. I won't be at the WTF meeting tomorrow. I'll be on patrol."

"On patrol?"

"Wake up!" Vera slammed her palms on the desk, and the witch's sleepy senses roared to alertness. "This is the first wave of an invasion! Everywhere the LWM go, they spread"—Vera's lips twisted, and she shuddered—"order."

Order. The witch regarded her newly renovated office through fresh eyes.

"Think about it." Vera stood and paced, her stilettos clicking on the tile floor. "They turned the Unseen Creeping Horror into a giant white garbage chute. They transformed the junkyard into an auto-parts store." She pointed at Keyser. "And look at him. He used to be a living, breathing being that ate and shit and made messes."

The witch squeezed the smooth shell of his case, her eyes burning.

"Now he's a low-entropy collection of pixels." Vera paused in her circuit and stood across the desk from the witch, arms crossed over her *Chemtrails Made Me Do It* shirt. "We must stop them before they do further harm."

"So, you're going to. . .what, roam around Asphodel alone, looking for—"

"Not alone," Vera said. "Do you know the most observant creature in all of Discordia's creation?" The witch shook her head. "If a child starts a lemonade stand without a permit, a Karen will be there. If a strange car is parked on the street, a Karen will take note. If a side of fries is served cold, a Karen will ask to speak to the manager. When I ran Heather's campaign, I met such women in her leggings mafia. I'm using their powers for good."

"How's that?"

"I've formed a neighborhood watch staffed by the ladies of athleisure."

"I've tangled with a Karen or two," the witch said. "Seems like they'd vibe with the little white men. Those bastards spread order."

Vera threw her head back and laughed. "Witch, you misunderstand them. They may look pulled together, but underneath that pristine exterior lurks a seething kettle of repressed primal impulses." She sat and leaned toward the witch. "Take a peek in one of their enormous purses. Attend one of their sex-toy parties. Watch them rosé-all-day at a children's soccer game. You'll see."

Huh. Well, the witch should know better than to judge a cookbook by its cover. "What will you do if your patrol sees little white men?"

"We haven't worked that part out yet," Vera said, frowning. "You should blow off the WTF and come to our kickoff meeting. I tried to move it, but we must work around many brunches and play dates."

Finally. . .something the witch could *do*. She'd hit the streets—maybe find an LWM and exact vengeance. Screw sitting around in a conference room with the godsdamned Clerk.

Shit.

"I can't. The task force is in my new contract."

"So?"

"I'm bound—"

"Bound?" Vera snorted derisively. "You are no such thing. You can leave any-time you want."

"Like hell," the witch said. "I've tried to leave more times than I can count. I get weaker with each step I take away from where I'm supposed to be. I've never even made it across the Tophet County line."

"You don't know much about magical contracts, do you?"

The witch flipped her off.

"Touchy subject," Vera said. "Magical contracts use the true name of each party to bind the signatories to an agreement. Your contract is. . .different."

"How do you know what my contract says?"

"Oh, I know more than you can imagine, brujita."

"I've had enough of your mysterious priestess horseshit," the witch said. "*I'm* the witch. *I'm* the one with dark powers and occult knowledge. You don't know—"

"I know the Archons don't have your name," Vera said. "And for that, you are incredibly fortunate."

"Fortunate?" The witch shook her head. "Gods, you're as nutty as a ghoul-cake. They've still got me trapped."

"No, they don't," Vera said. "Instead of being bound by your name, which is directly linked to your free will, *you* are bound by your magic. You can leave whenever you want—you just can't take your magic with you."

She looked at the Tamagotchi and rubbed her sandy eyes. "Then I can't leave."

"There's one more thing you should know." Vera leaned back and crossed her legs, resting clasped palms on her knee. "All Archons are party to a mutual-aid magical contract. It allows them to share power."

The witch's eyes widened. "That's why I can't use their names against them." She'd always wondered why the Archons were so casual with their true names. She'd tried—repeatedly and unsuccessfully—to use them for mischief. "I'd have to be powerful enough to hex all of them at once."

"Bingo," Vera said. "Can't be done."

"Doesn't that mean an Archon can't be bound by a contract?"

"No, Witch. It means if one is bound, they all are."

CHAPTER NINETEEN

No Rest for the Wicked

The witch muted the unfolding debacle that was this week's virtual General Session. She had too much on her mind to focus on bureaucratic bullshit. Plus, every time she looked at Heather, her traitorous imagination conjured a movie reel of the mayor and Carcosa dancing the devil's tango.

The witch wouldn't have thought he had it in him—or that he'd put it into *her*.

The affair explained a few things, though. Heather's whispered huddles with Dr. C after meetings. His recent and dramatic glow-up. The fact that Heather had known Lorelei's name the day the UCH was defogged. But every answer led to another question. Case in point, Lorelei had been at the landfill for a cult picnic. Could the Unseen Creeping Horror be the cult's Evil Angel? Maybe his transformation was the result of a ritual gone wrong or, stranger yet, an attempted deicide.

Enough mental gymnastics.

What Carcosa did with his gigglestick was none of the witch's business. They weren't friends, for Ghroth's sake. He'd help her with the Baseball of Doom, and she'd pass along WTF intel. That was the sum total of their relationship. She'd called him yesterday morning, told him what happened to Keyser, and asked him to step up the pace. Almost twenty-four hours later, the witch hadn't heard boo. She grabbed her BlackBerry and tapped out a text.

WITCH

Any updates?

She chewed a hangnail, staring at the *I'm typing* dots under her message.

CARCOSA

I am attempting to repair the sphere's damaged activation mechanism. You should give me the sphere left in your home. I can secure it in my lab.

WITCH

I'll get it to you.

When will you have more info?

The Tamagotchi twitched on the bed next to her. Keyser was throwing a digital tantrum, whirling around like a Tasmanian devil. She pushed the food button a few times.

CARCOSA

As soon as the sphere is functioning properly, I can determine what kind of field it generates. I need at least a few days.

A few days?

"Hang in there, buddy," she said, stroking the screen.

WITCH

Well, *I* need to reverse the fx ASAP.

CARCOSA

As I told you, I can make no guarantees, but I will try.

Try? The witch threw her BlackBerry, wincing when it clattered to the floor. He'd better do more than *try*.

She sighed and tapped a button to unmute the General Session meeting.

"—updates from the High Lord of Administration?"

The square of the FML grid occupied by a large glass aquarium lit up. Nommaquth's mutagenic bubbles roiled furiously for a few minutes, then subsided into a lazy drift.

"Thank you, High Lord. Very, um. . .informative." Heather straightened a stack of papers on her desk. "I have three quick announcements before we conclude. First, my office is still looking for volunteers for the Darkest Night party. Many hands make light work! Second, the High Lord of Public Works—"

The witch sat up straighter. That was *her*.

"—shared a report of a Shoggoth at the Dunwich Park softball field. Please be advised that the field is home to an entire abomination of Shoggoths. Dunwich Park is closed to the public until further notice. Third, we'll be back in the Executive Hearing Room next week. I look forward to seeing you in person again." Heather banged her gavel. "This meeting is adjourned."

In the top left square of the FML grid, the Dread Lord of Human Resources removed his headset and stood, revealing that only his upper half wore a human suit. The witch didn't want to think about how that worked. He reached one arm behind him and wriggled. The suit fell away, revealing a writhing mass of ropy appendages contained in a gelatinous membrane.

"Sathach," Heather said, "your camera is still on!"

But his audio must've been transmitting through the headset.

A barbed tentacle slithered under the membrane. It tore open, and his enormous body Ursula'd its way free in a majestic *flop*. The tentacle scratched a bulging midsection, and Dread Lord slithered toward an open door in the background. The witch could see the gleaming porcelain of a toilet.

Y'ggarlos's voice boomed from the speakers. "We can see you!"

The witch snapped her fingers, and a bowl of popcorn appeared in her hands. She tossed a few pieces in her mouth as the Dread Lord settled his bulk on the commode.

A highlighted box appeared around N'eithamiqug's eight-eyed human face. "Is he," she said, spider legs twitching in horror, "*excreting?*"

On the screen, the Dread Lord's tentacles stiffened and curled toward something out of the camera's view. Then the door to the bathroom slammed.

I'M SO SORRY! The words landed in the witch's brain (and—judging by the ripple of winces on the screen—everyone else's) with the force of a pile driver. *I DIDN'T KNOW THE CAMERA WAS STILL ON!*

She closed her laptop, chuckling. Too bad this would be the last week of virtual meetings. Calling in from her bed and watching eldritch monsters get walloped by modern technology was a vast improvement over going in person.

The witch picked up her BlackBerry and checked her calendar. Praise Discordia, she had two precious hours of freedom before the WTF meeting. She needed time to think.

This Heather-Carcosa situation was tricky. On the one hand, why should she care if two pasty bureaucrats were banging outside the marital bond? But Carcosa was her literal PIC, and Heather was in her chain of command. On top of that, Chad was Heather's ex.

That's what bugs me most, he'd said. *Not knowing why she left.*

If he found out the witch knew and didn't tell him, he might be pissed— or worse, hurt. And it seemed likely he'd find out. Those transactions he was obsessed with moved money from the mayor's general fund to the university partnership. Heather was obviously funneling money to her bon ami's pet project. It might not be illegal, but it was shady as hell.

The witch needed to hunt her down and confirm her suspicions. Then she could decide what, if anything, to do about Chad.

The mayor was nowhere to be found. The witch searched Heather's office over the hysterical objections of her infuriatingly tight-lipped receptionist, whom she'd duct-taped to the wall. (Some things were more fun *without* magic.) Then she checked the conference rooms and kicked open the door of every bathroom stall in the building. Nothing.

She had two minutes to make it to the WTF meeting on time. Normally, she wouldn't give a shit about being late, but this meeting was in the Clerk's office at the bottom of the elevator to hell. She took off for the lobby at a sprint.

"Hey, Witch," Hank said, standing at parade rest by the elevator doors.

"Can't talk. I'm late for a meeting."

"That's why I'm here. The Clerk asked me to meet you since you don't have a key card for the subbasement levels."

The doors slid open, and the witch followed him into the elevator. He inserted his card and pushed B15. The car lurched into motion.

"How's your first month as a High Lord going?"

"About as much fun as a root canal."

"Oh." After an excruciating pause, punctuated by periodic dings, he said, "I've been meaning to ask you—"

The elevator jerked to a halt. Hank frowned at the floor indicator, which displayed a skull and crossbones. Several terrified-sounding *dings* chimed as the elevator attempted to close, but a human hand appeared in the crack between the doors. A middle-aged man in a sweater vest and pleated pants stepped inside. The newcomer inserted his card into the panel and pressed B13. They lurched into motion.

Hank stiffened to attention. "Good morning, Dread Lord."

The man pushed half-moon spectacles up the bridge of his nose and glanced up at Hank. "How are you today, Deputy?"

"Very well, sir. Thank you, sir," he said. "And you?"

"Eager to get to work." He smiled, revealing a sharklike array of viciously pointed metal teeth. "No rest for the wicked." The man turned and fixed his eyes—one a faded blue, the other a swirling void of soul-sucking black—on the witch. "And who is this?"

"This is the County Witch, our new High Lord of Public Works."

His sandy-blond eyebrows rose. "Another human High Lord?"

Her mouth—operating independently of her common sense—opened to issue a biting retort, but Hank spoke first.

"Witch, this is the Dread Lord of Corrections."

She closed her mouth. This was Zsthaor, Spiller of the Lifeblood of the Ancients, ruler of the subterranean warren of torture chambers where both human and Archonic evildoers were punished. The elevator slowed to a halt, and the doors opened, saving her from the need to reply. A cacophony of shrieks and gibbers sounded from the impenetrable blackness outside the car. The Dread Lord stepped out and turned to face them.

"Pleasure meeting you," he said with a grin. His lips widened, stretching far beyond the limits of human tolerance. The top of his head tipped back and—

And the door closed.

Hank exhaled a shaky breath, and the witch sagged against the wall. They studiously avoided looking at each other as the elevator completed its descent.

The witch stepped out of the car. "I can take it from here." The doors jerked, but she placed her booted foot across the threshold. "What was it you wanted to ask me?"

"It can wait." Hank pushed a button on the elevator panel. "Have a good meeting."

She wound through the maze of hallways to the Clerk's cartoon nightmare of an office. The members of the WTF—minus Vera—chatted at the conference table while the Clerk had a whispered phone conversation at her desk. The witch sat at the head of the table and massaged her temples. She was getting a gods-damned headache, and the meeting hadn't even started yet.

"May it serve you right," said the Dread Lord of Human Resources, "you cadaverous camel's toe."

She laughed, surprising both of them. "Better."

"Hey, Witch."

She looked up at Chad, who was seated to her left.

"Hey yourself."

Big brown eyes framed by puppy-dog lashes studied her face. She'd cried in front of him. Now he was going to fawn over her. If he pulled out a concerned *How* are *you?*, she was going to lose her everloving—

"You look like hell."

Chad was good people.

The Clerk hung up and took her seat at the far end of the table. Her eye-stalks were stiff, and she ignored the chattering overtures of the sycophantic Dread Lord of Human Resources. Something was definitely on her mind. Her half dozen eyes flitted from seat to seat, coming to rest on the empty chair that should've contained Vera's rampageous rump.

"Where is Ms. Vásquez?" she snapped. "The scheduling software should've grabbed her."

Chad cleared his throat. "The teleportation feature has been. . .temperamental."

The Clerk slammed a tentacle on the table, causing the scarred veneer to blister and smoke. "This is unacceptable! Ichagno needs to. . ." Her voice trailed off as she remembered that the Dread Lord of IT was missing.

"On that note," Chad said, "I have an update."

"Speak, technomancer," commanded the Clerk.

"I was looking through files in the Dread Lord's office." He reached under the table, grabbed a battered Catachthonic University backpack, and pulled out a gallon Ziploc bag. "I found this under his desk."

For a moment, the witch was distracted imagining how a swarm of metallic insects sat at a desk, but once she'd corralled her wandering attention, she registered what the bag contained.

A white sphere.

The plastic shell of the Tamagotchi twitched, and she unclipped it from a carabiner hanging at her belt. Keyser was lunging toward the sphere like a raccoon possessed.

What was it Vera had called his new look? A low-entropy collection of pixels. . .And her entropine-fueled magic didn't work near the spheres.

"I know what those things do," the witch said. "When my familiar dove on the sphere—"

"What happened to your familiar?" The orange caterpillars of the Dread Lord's eyebrows lofted skyward. When no one else reacted, he said, "Does everyone know but me?"

"It turned him into this." She held up the Tamagotchi. "Keyser's alive, but in a very low-entropy form."

If the sphere could pull entropy out, there had to be a way to put it back. Auric dialysis, maybe? She eyed the plastic oval. Maybe not.

"Oh, Witch, I'm so sorry." The Dread Lord's voice broke, and his eyes oozed grayish-yellow slime. "How *are* you?"

She ground her teeth. "I think the spheres generate an anti-entropic field." How hard was *that*, Carcosa?

Chad said, "I could run some tests to confirm your—"

"No!"

The Clerk and the witch, who'd spoken in unison, exchanged a glance. A healthy sense of self-preservation prompted the witch to gesture for her shrouded superior to continue.

"Mr. Chadwick, I need you focused on restoring our software systems."

"I agree." The truth was, the witch didn't want Chad anywhere near one of the spheres. So far, they'd defogged the UCH, digitized Keyser, and disappeared the Dread Lord of IT. It was too godsdamned dangerous. "I'll take it."

Chad handed her the Ziploc bag. Maybe she could use it to appease the Sheriff. Wait. . .*hell* no. She wasn't about to give that murder squid an anti-witch warhead. Carcosa would just have to take this one too, whether he liked it or not.

"Anything else, Chad?" the witch asked.

"I went to that cult meeting."

"And?"

"Just a couple of humans in cloaks and masks chanting barbarous names. They even used these cool voice changers so they sounded like Sith Lords." He brightened. "And my deviled eggs were a big hit!"

"Don't tell me that's all you got," the witch said.

"It was mostly small talk and arcane rituals." He shrugged. "They're going to see *The King in Yellow* on Saturday."

"The cult angle is a waste of time." The Dread Lord leaned back and rested his hands on the rotund belly of his human suit. "We should focus on—"

"What progress do *you* have to report?" the witch asked.

"I. . .Well, I've been conducting interviews."

"And?"

"Yes, Sathach," the Clerk warbled. "I am most eager to hear."

He raised his hands in a gesture of helplessness. "No one saw anything, no one heard anything, and no one knows anything."

"That is disappointing." The Clerk fixed a withering stare on the Dread Lord. "I expected more from a senior Archon."

An awkward silence fell as the Dread Lord sniffled.

"Moving on," the witch said, "Vera's got a team patrolling the—"

"And I expected more from you, Witch." the Clerk added. "I am. . .displeased."

The witch needed something to give her—and fast. She turned desperate eyes on her assistant. "Have you had any more prophetic fits?"

Magnolia paled. "What?"

"A few days before Keyser was transformed," the witch said, meeting a few of the Clerk's eyes, "Magnolia had a. . .a vision, I guess. She yelled 'Tamagotchi.'"

"Which is?"

She pointed to the Keyser's new home. "*This* is a Tamagotchi."

The Clerk's eyestalks waved in excitement, then swiveled toward Magnolia. "Well?"

The witch felt a twinge of remorse, but as an Archon, Magnolia had better odds of surviving the Clerk's *displeasure*.

"I. . ." Magnolia shook her head, sending fake hair cascading over her shoulders. "I'm sorry, I haven't."

"Could you, um. . .have one now?" the witch asked.

"It doesn't work like—"

"Do try, *Magnolia*," the Clerk said, her voice dripping scorn.

"I'll do my best." She closed her eyes and sat in silence, her face pinched with effort.

The witch held her breath. *Discordia, give us something. . .*

"It's no use. I—"

Magnolia's body stiffened and shook, and her eyes rolled back in her head. "Let the storm rage ooooooooooon," she bellowed. "The cold never bothered me anyway." Her body went limp, and she slid bonelessly out of her chair.

"There you go," the witch said. "We just have to figure out—"

"*Frozen.*" The Clerk rose and glided to the wall behind her desk. She extended a glistening tentacle and tapped a framed cel of a blond ice queen. "Lyrics from a Disney musical." She whispered an indecipherable word, and a black-robed servitor appeared from a shadowed corner. "Take her to the psychic surgery." The servitor bowed and backed away. "This has been an utter waste of time. Get out."

The witch stood. No need to ask her twice.

"Not *you*," the Clerk said.

Fucking fuckety fuck.

The Dread Lord and the servitor—who had Magnolia draped over one shoulder—walked to the door. Chad followed them, flashing her a worried look.

"Hello, Dr. Carcosa," the Dread Lord said.

The witch looked up to see her accomplice standing in the doorway. He was visibly alarmed and paler than death.

"Excuse the interruption, ma'am," he said. "I thought we had a meeting."

"I'll be with you in a moment." She waved a tentacle, and the door slammed in his face.

The witch yelped as her rolling chair whipped around the table, launching her at top speed toward the Clerk's desk. She banged into the edge, causing a row of figurines to topple like dominoes.

"I enjoy having the world's only witch." The Clerk set about restoring her toy menagerie. "It's like owning a prize-winning show dog. It conveys a certain prestige, and the creature itself is amusing, so one tolerates the occasional puddle on the carpet."

"I'm doing my best to—"

"Until, that is, the dog stops winning."

The Clerk lifted her shroud, and a tentacle lined with gaping mouths surged toward the witch and wound around her throat. Her skin sizzled, and black spots swam before her eyes.

"Do not make the mistake of urinating on my rug one too many times, Witch." The Clerk squeezed tighter. "You will not enjoy the consequences of failure."

CHAPTER TWENTY

It Hurts!

D o you have an appointment?"

The witch glared at the officious prig seated at a pathologically neat desk. "My assistant booked a meeting under the name 'Witch.' Seeing as I'm the only one, you're asking a question to which you already have the answer."

The door to the mayor's office opened, and the Dread Lord of Human Resources skulked out. When he saw her, he turned to skulk right back in, but the receptionist cut him off at the pass, darted into the office, and closed the door in his face.

"Hello, Witch," he said. "I was just. . .conducting perfectly normal County business."

"Oh yeah?"

"The mayor and I were discussing, ahem. . .amendments to a contract."

She narrowed her eyes. "Whose contract?"

"That's sensitive information."

The witch grabbed his necktie and pulled him close. "If you give me another godsdamned job, Discordia as my witness, I'll—"

"The mayor will see you now."

She glanced at the receptionist. "I'm in the middle of—"

"The mayor," he said, "will see you *now.*"

The witch raised her hands in mock surrender and walked into Heather's office. The mayor sat at her desk, checking her appearance in a small folding mirror. Her asymmetric bob was sharp enough to cut glass. She looked up and flashed a brilliant smile.

"Lovely to see—"

"Why was the Dread Lord here?" The witch plunked down in an overstuffed leather armchair. She snapped, and a lit cigarillo appeared between her fingers.

Heather coughed and waved a hand. "We were formalizing—"

"I swear by Cthulhu's cockleshells, if you try to pile more bullshit on my plate, I'll hex you with intractable flatulence."

"Sathach was here to amend a Spectral Forces contract and increase the size of my security detail." She pursed her perfectly glossed lips. "I've been getting death threats, if you can believe it. Apparently, *some* people don't like progress."

The witch blew a smoke ring. "Or maybe *some* people don't like the mayor screwing one of her subordinates."

Heather's eyebrows shot up. "How dare you insinuate—"

"I'm not insinuating. I'm stating facts." The witch's BlackBerry vibrated with an incoming text. She glanced at the screen. "Ah, here's your boyfriend now."

Carcosa was finally answering her repeated messages. Running into him at the Clerk's office on Tuesday had thrown her for a loop. She'd taken an enormous risk trusting him. At any moment, he could rat her out for sharing WTF intel, which would be extremely bad for her health. And continued existence. She opened the message.

I shall answer your queries in the order in which I received them. (1) I have not lost my f***ing mind. (2) My research contract requires monthly meetings with the project sponsor, hence, my appointment with the Clerk. (3) Your theory about the sphere is plausible. I will know more soon.

Heather craned her neck, trying to see the screen. "What does it say?"

The witch slid her BlackBerry into her back pocket. "I know who you're bumping uglies with."

"You couldn't possibly. . ." Two pink circles bloomed on Heather's pale cheeks. "I don't have to explain my love life to—"

"Gods, please don't. It's bad enough seeing you guys whispering together like horny teenagers, but. . ." She wanted to say that Carcosa's wife was onto them, but the client contract curbed her tongue. "I've been hired by an injured party."

"An injured party?" Heather cocked her head and frowned. "That's over."

"Pretty sure this person would disagree."

"I. . .I didn't think—"

"People with banging on the brain rarely do."

Heather released a shaky breath. "My worst fear was that someone would find out. Now that you have, it's. . .Well, it's not as bad as I thought."

"Some people might pin a scarlet *A* to your chest, but I don't give a shit who you do the no-pants dance with," the witch said. "All I care about is how it affects me."

"How could this possibly affect you?"

"First, there's his. . .The person *you* hurt."

Heather propped her elbows on her desk and cradled her head. "We never meant to hurt anyone." She grabbed a tissue and theatrically dabbed the corners of her eyes. "We didn't plan to fall in love."

Yeah, love was *definitely* what dragged Heather and Dr. C to a no-tell motel.

"Second," the witch said, "you haven't hidden your creative accounting as well as you think." She dunked her cigar in a half-full cup of coffee on Heather's desk. "I know you're moving money to fund the murder machine."

The mayor's mouth opened. Closed. Opened again. "I can explain."

The witch raised a hand to silence her. "Not my circus, not my nightgaunts."

Heather tossed her crumpled tissue in the trashcan. "Then what do you want?"

"I'll tell you what I *don't* want," she said, "and that's your personal shit screwing up my job."

"It won't." Heather crossed her arms and regarded the witch. "You know, I had no plans to run for office when he and I got together."

As the one who'd put her on the godsdamned ballot, the witch was well aware. "How'd you two hook up, anyway?" Carcosa didn't exactly strike her as a ladies' man.

"He was one of my first clients when I started selling It Hurts!™"

"The weight-loss wraps?"

Heather nodded. Her eyes traveled the length of the witch's lanky body. "You don't need them, of course, but they just melt abdominal fat away. There's some scarring, and it hurts like you wouldn't believe, but overall? Great product."

The witch frowned. Carcosa was on the slim side of average, but maybe that hadn't always been the case. Mitsuki must have a thing for skinny dudes. If she'd shamed Dr. C into using flesh-melting diet aids, it made sense that he'd jump ship when the opportunity presented itself.

Heather's eyes went soft and dreamy. "From the moment we met, we've had this incredible connection." She leaned toward the witch and lowered her voice. "And the sex is—"

"Look at the time." The witch glanced at an imaginary watch. "Gotta go."

"Wait," Heather said. "Could you give Chad a message for me?"

"I don't—"

"Tell him I'm sorry."

The witch pulled her broom up to a seventh-floor window and banged on the glass. After a startled squawk, the window opened, and Chad's face appeared.

"Witch, what are you—"

"Hop on, loser," she said. "We're going drinking."

"What?" He goggled at the broom. "I am *not* getting on that thing."

Seventeen seconds later, the witch was plunging toward the sidewalk with a terrified Chad squeezing her torso in a not-entirely-unpleasant fashion. She pulled up at the last minute and zoomed along Main Street, heading for the outskirts of town and her favorite bar, Asenath's Alehouse. Located just past the public boat launch at Tehom Lake, Asenath's was frequented primarily by Deep Ones and their hybrid offspring. The clientele was insular, suspicious, and hostile. Her kind of people.

The witch parked her broom in a motorcycle spot in front of the ramshackle building. Chad staggered around the parking lot getting his land legs back until she gripped his elbow and dragged him inside. She led him to her favorite spot: a corner booth in the back of the bar. A waitress with bulging eyes strolled over to take their order. She wore her hair in a high ponytail, revealing nascent gills on her neck and flat tympanums instead of ears.

"What'll it be?" she croaked.

Chad opened his mouth, but no words came out.

"Two Keystones," the witch said.

The server burbled her assent and headed for the bar, moving in an odd, sidling gait.

"Were those, um. . ." He hooked a thumb toward the departing woman. "Did she have gills?"

"This is a Deep One dive bar, Chad." She pointed at a large hole in the floor that opened to the lake beneath them. Three fishlike humanoids with slippery gray skin and ridged backs lounged in the water. Two of them held longneck beer bottles in their webbed hands, and the third sipped an appletini. "Those are full-fledged Deep Ones. Their females mate with human males to reproduce. Weirds me out a little, but I like it here."

Chad shrugged. "I guess people are people, gills or not."

The waitress reappeared with two cans of beer and two smudged glasses.

"Thanks, Eliza." The witch cracked hers open and took a long swallow straight from the can. "There's something I need to tell you."

Chad's face fell. "I thought you wanted to hang out."

"I do." Gods dammit, she actually *did*. "You're one of the least annoying humans in Tophet County."

"I try." He took a swig from his own can. "Is it about the investigation?"

"Sort of."

"I have a question first." Chad set his beer down a little too hard, and a river of foam bubbled onto the sticky table. "Why don't you want me looking at the, um. . .at our physical evidence? I know you think I'm just some dumb IT guy, but—"

"I don't think that." The witch leaned toward him and lowered her voice to a whisper. "Those things are strong enough to take out a senior Archon, Chad. It's too risky."

"Aw, you were worried about me."

Desperate to hide her blush, she chugged her beer and crushed the can on the table.

"What did you need to tell me?" he asked.

"It's about those transactions." The witch stared at the flattened can, reluctant to meet his eyes. "And it's got to do with your personal shit."

"My personal shit." He ran a hand over his chin, petting his divorce beard like a comfort animal. "Let's hear it."

Should she try to cushion the blow? Come at it sideways? Drop a vague hint?

"Heather cheated on you."

As usual, her mouth got ahead of her brain.

Chad stared down at his hands. "I thought so."

"You did?"

"Yeah." He scanned the room, caught Eliza's eye, and lifted his chin. "When she started selling leggings, she seemed. . .I don't know, more fulfilled? But she completely changed after she joined It Hurts!™ She was distant but also, like, way happier. Is it Deborah, her up-line?"

"No, it's—"

Chad held up his hand. "You know what? I don't want to know."

"I don't want to know either, but it's related to those transactions."

Eliza waddled to their table with another round. Once she'd gone, Chad said, "How is it related?"

"Have you met Dr. Carcosa?"

"Yeah," Chad said. "The murder-machine guy. He was trying to get in to see the Dread Lord of IT last week. I had to tell him. . ." His eyebrows drew together. "You don't mean. . ."

The witch nodded.

"But Heather left me before the election. She didn't even know him yet."

"He was one of her weight-loss customers."

"The transfers," Chad breathed. "She's been funneling money to pay for his project and upgrade the electrical grid to support it."

"She said to tell you she's sorry." He just shook his head. When the witch could bear the silence no longer, she said, "You okay?"

"Huh?" Chad looked up at her and shrugged. "I guess."

"Do you. . .miss her?"

"I miss being with somebody, but. . ." He sighed. "Heather saw me as a fixer-upper. She was a little exhausting."

"You should see what she's done with Carcosa. Poor bastard used to have some personality, but she's got him plucked and combed and stuffed into three-piece suits."

"She tried to take my cargo pants," Chad said, his voice heated. "I had to draw the line somewhere." He sipped his beer. "It's just weird to see her so into another guy that she'd embezzle for him, you know?"

The witch shrugged. "Well, if you need any embezzling done, I'm your girl."

Shit. *I'm your girl?* Her cheeks felt like they were glowing.

The witch's BlackBerry buzzed with a notification. She checked her email, hoping the pause would distract him from her last statement. It was just an update from the author of the Amos and Sarah series. The next novel, *Chaste Makes Waste*, was due to be published in a few months. The witch would have to check the latest gossip on the *Are they ever going to bang?* subreddit. (After five celibate books, the current consensus was that they were not.)

Chad cleared his throat to get her attention. "I'm glad I heard it from you, Witch." He flagged Eliza down. "This round's on me."

CHAPTER TWENTY-ONE

Friggin' in the Riggin'

K eyser Söze glared at the witch from a screen littered with droppings. She squinted at the buttons, trying to force her fuzzy brain to remember how to clean up. He raised a blocky digital paw and pointed.

Nope. He wasn't pointing.

Gods, she was hungover. The last thing she remembered was singing sea shanties with Chad and a couple of barnacled Deep Ones.

Oh, *balls*. . .

That wasn't the last thing.

After the final refrain of "Friggin' in the Riggin'," Chad had grabbed her shoulders and planted an enthusiastic and surprisingly skillful kiss on her lips, a kiss she'd returned with interest. Something that felt a hell of a lot like a butterfly fluttered in her stomach.

The ear-battering jangle of her BlackBerry hit her skull like an ice pick. What kind of monster would call before eight?

A morning-after Chad might.

She lunged for the BlackBerry, trembling from more than just the Keystone flu. Her heart sank when she saw the caller's name. *Cannibal Specter.*

"Hello, Clerk."

"You're needed at the fire station."

"Let me grab coffee and shower, then I'll—"

"If the system cooperates, I'm pulling you over in five minutes."

The witch hung up and rifled through mounds of laundry. She got her hair to start braiding itself and found a pair of not-visibly-dirty jeans, but her only cleanish top was a ratty Cat U sweatshirt. Not consistent with her brand, but it would have to do.

As she dumped her dirty clothes in the washing machine, her BlackBerry emitted an ominous buzz. Shit. She was still barefoot. The witch had just pulled her left sock on when an octarine spark of netherlight blossomed six inches from her nose. She re-formed in an ankle-deep puddle of frigid water. She considered conserving her entropine, but three of the Clerk's eyestalks were fixed on her feet. She snapped her fingers and summoned her boots and her last pair of clean socks.

The Clerk's shroud rustled as her olfactory organ sniffed the air. "You smell like a distillery."

"A brewery, actually. Late night at Asenath's."

Two of her eyes looked at each other, an expression the witch had learned to read as surprise. "*You* drink at Asenath's? But the clientele is. . .unhuman."

"The beer's cold, and the price is right."

"I see," the Clerk said. "Follow me."

She led the witch behind the fire station to the large tank where the Dread Lord of Fire and Rescue, aka the Living Flood, had his humble abode. A row of shrubs encircled the plexiglass enclosure, affording him a modicum of privacy—though what a sentient fountain needed privacy for, she couldn't imagine. But instead of a malevolent wave, a large ice cube occupied the tank. A Spectral Forces team armed with flamethrowers was inside, directing roaring jets of fire at the glacier. It wasn't even breaking a sweat.

The witch frowned. "I didn't know he could freeze. Tehom Lake was solid as a rock last winter, and the Living Flood was still sloshing around."

"He did not freeze."

She stared pointedly at the ice cube.

"He was frozen," the Clerk clarified.

An earsplitting shriek tore through the air as one of the Spectral Forces men accidentally enflamed another.

The Clerk sighed. "It's a good thing I sprayed them with flame retardant."

One of the uniformed men waved his hands and called, "We need you, ma'am!"

"Just put him out!"

"No," he said. "We found something."

An angry female voice snapped a retort the witch couldn't quite make out.

"Some*one*."

"On my way," she trilled.

The Clerk left a smoking trail in the winter-browned grass as they wound around the perimeter of the tank. Two Spectral Forces officers guarded a hand-cuffed woman who was shaking with cold and grinning like an idiot.

Deputy Eye Candy flashed a quick smile at the witch, showcasing the world's hottest dimples. His expression sobered as he shifted his gaze to the Clerk. "Ma'am."

The Clerk ignored him, gazing in horror at the captive. "Abhoth, have mercy!"

The witch stepped closer to the prisoner. Despite the temperature, her feet were bare, and she wore a fabric hula skirt with cotton tendrils dangling from the waist. An animal carcass and a drift of white fingernails littered the grass in front of her.

"Hi, Witch," the woman said.

That voice. . .

Gods below, that limp, hairy pile wasn't an animal. It was a *wig*. The fingernails were veneers, and each of those cotton strands had once encased a tentacle. She mentally added a bulging forehead to the woman's face.

"Magnolia?" The witch walked a wide circle around her no-longer-Archonic assistant. "What happened?"

"I had a—"

"Get those cuffs off of her," the witch said. "Now."

"Leave them on."

Hank winced as the acid-slimed tentacle encircling his wrist ate into his skin. "Yes, ma'am."

"But that's Magnolia."

"Indeed," the Clerk said. "Magnolia, who has wanted a human suit for ages, who wears human clothing and reads human literature, who insists on using a human name." The Clerk oozed closer to the witch. "Don't you find it odd that this. . .*attack* granted her wish?"

"If you're so suspicious of her, why'd choose her as your task force spy?"

"I'm not a spy!"

"She most certainly is not," the Clerk said. "My spies are competent, unlike the two of you. On your watch, yet another senior Archon has been attacked and—"

"Frozen!" Magnolia stepped toward the Clerk, dragging the officers with her. "Don't you remember the vision I had in your office? You said I was picking up lyrics from one of your precious musicals, but it was about the Living Flood," she said, jerking her chin toward the tank. "If I was a traitor, why would I warn you?"

"Perhaps you are as bad at betrayal as you are at—"

"Come on, Clerk," the witch said. "She had nothing to do with this."

"Then why, pray tell, is she here?"

"Uncuff her, and we'll find out."

The officers glanced at the Clerk for confirmation. She nodded, and they removed the cuffs. Magnolia rubbed her wrists, shifting her weight on feet that must be colder than Kris Kringle's keister. The witch summoned a pair of socks from home, and a dripping, foamy wad of fabric appeared in her hands.

Godsdamned laundry day. She tossed them into the shrubs.

The witch gripped Hank's shoulder, slid her right foot free of her boot, and removed her sock. She repeated the process on the left foot and handed the still-warm pair to Magnolia.

"While she tends to her. . .*feet*, I'll tell you what I know," the Clerk said, "One of our EMTs saw Magnolia portal in next to the tank. There was a blaze of white light, then she became human, and the Living Flood froze solid."

Three of her eyes swiveled toward Magnolia, whose struggle to shove her new human appendage into a sock revealed she was bare-ass naked under what remained of her tentacled leggings. Hank slid off his uniform coat and draped it over her shoulders, covering her to mid-thigh.

"What I do *not* know," the Clerk said, "is why she was here in the first place."

The witch arched an eyebrow at Magnolia. "Well?"

"During my first fit, I said 'Tamagotchi.' That foretold what happened to your familiar. At first, I thought the Clerk's explanation for my 'frozen' vision made sense, but. . ." She shook her head. "It didn't feel right. 'Tamagotchi' was a literal prediction. I figured 'frozen' had to refer to water, and the Living Flood *is* water, so I popped over to check on him."

"What did you find?"

"I saw a group of white. . .creatures. One of them was holding a sphere."

"Little white men?" the witch asked.

"They were little and white, but they weren't men. They had extra limbs—almost like. . ."

"Like what?"

"Like tentacles," Magnolia said. "It doesn't make sense, but that's what I saw." She shivered and huddled under Hank's coat. "The Living Flood was asleep when I got here."

How in gods' names could she tell?

"They were next to his tank, and I yelled at them to get away. The one with the sphere did something to it, and then. . ." She looked down at her brand-new human body.

The Clerk oozed closer to her. "You must admit, the timing of your arrival is suspiciously expedient given the. . .outcome."

Magnolia flushed, but she stood her ground. "You've always been comfortable with who you are. I've never felt that way until now. I would never have done this to him," she said, gesturing toward the immense ice cube, "but I won't apologize for how I feel about what's happened to *me*."

"I. . .I didn't realize. . ." The Clerk's shroud fluttered in the chilly breeze. "Ma'am?"

Her eyestalks whipped around to lock onto the approaching Spectral Forces officer.

"The Sheriff's here."

"Wonderful," the Clerk muttered. "Lomelzar and the Dread Lord of Fire and Rescue are old drinking buddies."

The witch eyed the erstwhile Living Flood. Drinking buddies?

"If the Sheriff hears about your presence," the Clerk said to Magnolia, "he'll have your head on a spike." She turned to Hank. "Deputy O'Brien, while I speak with the Sheriff, I need you to make it known among your men that Magnolia came here at my request."

He furrowed his brow, which was still haunted by the ghost of Sharpies past. "But you had us cuff her."

"We had to protect her cover," the witch said, catching on to the plan.

"Come with me, Deputy." The Clerk glided after the retreating officer.

The witch grabbed Hank's arm. "Did you guys find the sphere?"

"We went over the scene with a fine-toothed comb." He shook his head. "Nothing."

Damn. The little bastards must've taken it with them.

Once she and Magnolia were alone, the witch said, "Are you—"

"I had another—"

They stopped and looked at each other. Magnolia gestured to the witch. "You first."

"Are you okay?"

"I'm more than okay," she said. "Being in this body feels like. . .like coming home."

"How's your, um. . .significant other going to feel about all this?" An abrupt change of species might be a dealbreaker—even for a human resources professional.

Magnolia's face softened into a dreamy smile. "She's always known who I am."

"She? Aren't you and the Dread Lord of HR—"

"Ew, no! Sathach's just a friend. We share. . .common interests," she said. "Speaking of my partner, I think she can help us. She's a cleared County employee, and her scientific expertise is legendary. Even the Clerk respects her opinion."

The witch flipped through her mental Rolodex, but seeing as she'd avoided contact with senior squigglies for most of her career, she drew a blank. Couldn't hurt to have an Archonic scientist on standby, though—especially since they weren't dealing with human technology.

"Go ahead and loop her in wherever you think she can help," she said. "So, what were you going to say?"

"I had another fit this morning," Magnolia said, "just before I came."

"Why didn't you tell the Clerk?"

"Five minutes ago, she was ready to hand me over to the Dread Lord of Corrections."

Fair enough.

"Do you remember what you saw?"

"No, but I'd asked my partner to record me if I did anything weird. She missed the beginning of it, but what I said was. . .I said. . ."

"What?"

"I said, 'He's juggling balls.'"

The witch bit her lip. "Juggling balls, you say?"

"My partner asked a few questions before I passed out. I told her I saw a man in a suit juggling five white balls. I think—"

"Those balls are the spheres."

"Exactly. We've seen four so far," she said, ticking them off on her fingers. "The Unseen Creeping Horror, the Dread Lord of IT, the Living Flood, and. . .and Keyser Söze."

"There's one more out there. We need to figure out who the cult will hit next."

"Witch, the cult has nothing to do with this. Like Chad said—"

"They must've seen through his cover." No surprise there. "Think about it, Magnolia. They had a picnic at the landfill the day the UCH was hit. Their godsdamned logo is an LWM throttling an Archon!"

"But—"

"The Yellow King!" Hot damn, it was coming together now. "Chad said the cult is going to that play tomorrow night. Hastur must be their next target." The witch rubbed her hands together. "And I'm gonna be there." Her BlackBerry buzzed, but she ignored it. She was on a roll. "Maybe the Evil Angel is an Archon with a grudge. The spheres aren't human tech or witch magic. The only other power on Earth that could make something like that is Archons."

"The only power on *Earth*."

"What, aliens?" The witch rolled her eyes. "The little green men and the Roswell Grays haven't been seen since you guys woke up."

"What if someone's using the cult to bait you?"

"What if it's actually the cult?"

Magnolia held her gaze. "I know for a fact the Temple of the Evil Angel isn't involved. Can you just take my word for it?"

"Sure."

Magnolia's shoulders sagged as she released a pent-up breath.

"Just tell me how you know."

"I can't do that."

The witch barked a bitter laugh. She'd started to think of Magnolia as a. . .

What was it Mother Mayhem always said? *A friend is just an enemy who hasn't betrayed you yet.*

"Go home," the witch said, her voice colder than the December morning.

"What?"

"I'll see you on Monday."

"But—"

"I'm going to that godsdamned play, Magnolia."

"Take someone with you," she said, "in case it's a trap."

The witch's BlackBerry vibrated again. She pulled it out of her pocket and glanced at the notifications. A text from Nerdomancer. Even through the haze of disappointment, her stomach flip-flopped when she saw his name.

"If you don't have anyone else," Magnolia said, "I'd be happy to—"

The Sheriff shrieked loud enough to rattle the fillings in the witch's teeth. "You should go before he decides to question you."

Magnolia nodded and squeezed her eyes shut. Opened them. "I can't teleport."

"Welcome to the human race," the witch said. "Hope you like walking."

She spotted a Spectral Forces officer heading toward the parking lot, put her fingers to her lips, and whistled. "Hey, you! Get your ass over here." He pointed to his chest. "Yes, you, gods dammit." When he was within normal talking range, the witch said, "Goon, Magnolia. Magnolia, Goon."

"I wish you wouldn't call us that, Witch," he said. "It's hurtful."

"Give her a ride wherever she wants to go, got it?"

"But I was on my way to—"

She released a trickle of entropine, just enough to levitate a few feet in the air and make sparks shoot from her fingertips. "Got it?"

He nodded frantically, then took Magnolia's elbow and escorted her toward his Hummer.

The witch unlocked her BlackBerry and opened Chad's message. Messages, actually.

CHAD

Hey, Witch. You feeling as rough as I am?

CHAD

You there? Your BlackBerry says you're online.

CHAD

So yeah, last night was. . .

Three dots appeared under his message. He was typing. She held out for about ten seconds before she started drafting her own reply.

WITCH

Last night was ducking—

Godsdamned autocorrect. Did anyone *ever* mean "ducking"?

WITCH

—*fucking awesome!*

Let's do it again.

Want to come with me to—

His reply popped up before she'd finished typing.

CHAD

Well, last night got kinda crazy. I'm sorry.

He was. . .sorry?

CHAD

I was pretty tipsy & this divorce thing has me in a weird place.

I shouldn't have kissed you like that. I hope I didn't screw things up.

CHAD

Are you there? Can we talk?

The witch re-read his words and started typing a response. *I shouldn't have kissed you. . .*

She deleted what she'd typed and wrote a new message.

WITCH

Chill. We're cool.

She considered throwing her BlackBerry into the street but settled for powering it off.

"Want a ride home, Witch?"

She looked up to see Deputy Eye Candy strolling toward her. In contrast to the cold day, he was hotter than Vulcan's forge. She could stand to sit next to him for a few hours.

"Hell yeah," she said. "Wanna go see the Yellow King's play with me tomorrow night?"

"Really?" Hank broke into a big stupid grin. "That would be awesome! I've been meaning to ask you to, like, hang out away from work."

"Well, now's your chance."

Fuck a bunch of Chads.

CHAPTER TWENTY-TWO

The Widow and the Devil

What's this?"

The witch frowned at the plastic clamshell box Hank had just handed her. A riot of pink petals was smooshed against the top.

"It's a corsage."

The Tamagotchi vibrated at the witch's hip. She unclipped it and looked at the screen, where Keyser Söze was clutching his midsection in paroxysms of laughter.

"We're not going to the prom, Hank."

"I know." He tugged at the necktie impeccably knotted above a charcoal suit that showcased his athletic build to tasty effect. "I've been wanting to ask you out for weeks, but you beat me to it. I just. . .I wanted to make it special."

Oh no. He thought this was a godsdamned *date*.

The witch opened her mouth to clarify the situation, but she froze—taking in his trembling hands, his over-starched shirt, the cotton-candy flowers. If she told him the truth now, he'd be crushed. Well, an evening alone with her should cure him of any romantic interest.

"That was, uh. . .That was nice of you." She opened the box and removed a ball of pink carnations and roses. A stick pin tipped with a faux pearl was jabbed through the ribbon-wrapped stem. The witch considered her outfit: a T-shirt and her second-best pair of leather pants. Nowhere to pin this heavy-ass flower bomb.

"Which witch?"

"What?" She looked up to find Hank's eyes locked on her chest. "My face is up here, asshole."

Hank's cheeks flamed scarlet. "No, I wasn't. . .I mean, not that I wouldn't like to, but. . ." He gulped and said, "Your shirt."

100% That Witch, one of her newer creations. (It wasn't the first time her shirts had been misinterpreted. She'd been very proud of *Fuck the Tentaclarchy*, but it turned out some humans were into that sort of thing. *Very* into it.)

She shook her head. Deputy Eye Candy was nice to look at and probably fun to get naked with, but he was no scholar.

"It's just a shirt." The witch twitched her nose, and her hair wound itself into a bun. She jammed the stem of the corsage through the center and secured it with the pin. Cocking her head so Hank could see, she said, "There. How's that?"

"You look beauti—"

"You're looking good yourself." She grabbed her bag and slammed the door of her apartment. "The eyebrows are growing back."

His fingers stroked the stubbled ridges. "I just wish they weren't growing in white."

"I've got my Sharpie if you—"

"No!"

"We should get going," the witch said, checking the time. "The play starts at seven."

She climbed into Hank's Spectral Forces Hummer. Next stop, Catachthonic University's Alhazred Hall—Tophet County's finest entertainment venue.

"They didn't have, um. . .Chicken Cock," Hank said, blushing furiously. "I got you a glass of chardonnay."

He handed the witch a carton of popcorn and a plastic goblet of weak-ass fruit water. She turned a withering glare on the pale liquid until it darkened to a bourbony amber. Probably should've saved the entropine, but. . .chardonnay? She might as well complain to the manager and join Vera's neighborhood watch.

Hank slid into the seat next to her, a Coors Banquet in one hand and a program in the other. He leaned toward her and pointed at the disclaimer.

"Will this play actually make me go insane?"

"You're with me, kid." She crunched her way through a handful of popcorn and licked buttery fingers. "The Yellow King can't—"

"Pass up the opportunity to meet a local celebrity." The witch glanced up at the source of the hissing voice, which spoke in a comically bad British accent. A thin figure floated in the aisle next to the witch's seat. He wore a tattered yellow zoot suit and a Dick Tracy hat that cast his face in shadow. "The County Witch, I presume?" Hastur bowed and extended a gloved hand.

The witch ignored it. "Yep." She sent a subtle pulse of entropine to her optic nerves, then leaned toward Hank and whispered, "Close your eyes." He whimpered and gripped her arm.

The King straightened and pushed up the brim of his hat.

Classic Archonic intimidation tactic. *Look upon my face, ye mortals, and despair!*

Through the magical filter she'd applied to her vision, looking at him was like watching the flickering images of a zoetrope—a series of horrific pictures blurring together to create the impression of a corporeal form. Like most entities in the entertainment industry, this jackass was all smoke and mirrors.

The witch squinted at the shadowed blur of his face. She caught sight of a severed limb here, the iconic fanged maw there. "You've got a little something. . ." She touched the corner of her mouth.

The whirring stream of pictures stuttered to a halt, and Hastur dabbed gingerly with a gloved hand. "Did I get it?"

The witch, whose visual cortex had been temporarily rewired to display cat videos, shook her head. "Still there."

"Oh, bugger! Well, if you'll excuse me, I must touch up my makeup before the performance begins."

"Sure. Nice to—"

And he was gone.

She rolled her eyes and elbowed Hank. "The coast is clear."

He released a shaky breath and let go of her arm. "Sorry I freaked out. I just. . .I've heard rumors about him, you know?"

"That poncy twit spreads them himself." The witch patted Hank's knee, surreptitiously wiping butter from her hands. She opened her bag, fished around, and pulled out a pair of Wayfarers. She revved her auric engines and breathed on the lenses, fogging them with steam, then offered the glasses to Hank. "Don't take these off. They'll screen out the freak show he projects on the rubes."

"Thanks." He slid the glasses on and grinned at her. "How do I look?"

Pretty damn good, you square-jawed, dimple-chinned—

"Ladies and gentlemen," boomed a resonant voice, "on behalf of the Yellow King and the Tophet County Players, welcome to the Alhazred Hall Theater!" The lights dimmed. "Tonight, we are honored to present *The King in Yellow*. Be warned—this play may cause permanent madness." The voice trailed off into a high-pitched lunatic titter.

The witch's BlackBerry rang. The speaker broke off mid-laugh and cleared his throat.

"Please silence your mobile devices."

She killed her ringer and glanced at the screen. Vera. Her leggings militia might've found something.

"Gotta take this." The witch handed her popcorn to Hank. "High Lord business."

She jogged up the carpeted aisle and exited into the lobby. Just as she was about to call Vera, the Tamagotchi vibrated and swung erratically from its loop on her belt. She looked at the tiny screen. Keyser was losing his mind, lunging and snarling like a rabid dog. Her eyes followed his frantic motions, and she saw a snow-white blur streak across the lobby.

It was a little white. . .something. The godsdamned thing was lousy with tentacles.

It eased open the door and disappeared into the night.

"Oh no you don't."

The witch sprinted after it, but when she stepped outside, it was gone. She scanned the street in both directions. Nothing.

A furtive noise drew her into the alley next to the theater, but the only animate creatures she saw were rat-things. Scratch that, one costumed member of the Tophet County Players had stepped out for a smoke. He held the backstage door open with his foot. The sounds of melodramatic dialogue interspersed with strains of eerie music echoed in the alley.

"You, sir, should unmask," said an actress's tremulous voice.

The little bastard had gotten away.

"I wear no mask," boomed the King.

And she'd forgotten Vera's call. The witch needed her to send reinforcements stat.

"No mask?" the actress cried. "No mask!"

A blinding burst of white light blazed from the open door. The actor stumbled back, and the door slammed shut.

"Was that part of the show?" the witch asked.

He started at the sound of her voice. "No, the King doesn't like bright lighting. He says it shows his age."

That thing must've detonated a sphere on a time delay. . .and Hank was in there.

The witch shoved the man aside and rattled the door handle.

"It locks automatically," he said. "You'll have to—"

She blew the door off its hinges and stepped across the threshold.

The hallway was dark. Silent. The witch charged up her shields and summoned a flashlight heavy enough to serve as a club if the opportunity arose. She walked past vacant dressing rooms, including one marked with a star wearing a yellow crown. A soft, rhythmic rasp drew her attention to a dark corner just off stage right. She aimed a beam of light toward the source of the sound.

That's when she saw the first body.

The witch prodded the man with a booted toe. The costumed actor flinched, emitted a thunderous snore, and rolled onto his side. She continued on, weaving through a curtained maze until she emerged onto the stage. Three more sleepers lay on the scuffed wooden floor, but there was no sign of the Yellow King. She walked behind the backdrop, tracing the beam of her flashlight over every square inch of space. Nothing there either.

The Tamagotchi twitched in her hand. In the ghostly glow, she saw Keyser's front paw pointing offstage. She followed his gesture, and a flash of color caught her eye.

She picked up what looked like a large magnifying glass with a yellow plastic rim and handle. The witch's face, rendered demonic by the upward angle of the flashlight, stared back at her. Not a magnifying glass—a mirror. A sparkling cloud of fog shimmered over her reflection, and the image of the Yellow King appeared. He pounded on his side of the mirror, lips moving soundlessly.

She set the mirror down and panned her flashlight over the sleeping audience. The sphere had to be here somewhere. Not only had it transformed Mr. Sunshine into a low-entropy version of his essential self (a mirror was perfect for that vainglorious trouser trumpet), it had also changed the effect of his play from lunacy to sleep.

"Oooh, high atop a lonely hill a widow lived alone!"

But not everyone had succumbed.

"An inn she kept, and as she slept, she'd toss and turn and moan. . ."

The witch scanned rows of folding seats, searching for the owner of a rather nice baritone.

"Many a randy traveler has spent the night with me," the voice sang, "but there's no man in all the land who can keep up with me!"

She finally located Hank standing on the railing of one of the private boxes. His suit jacket was unbuttoned, his tie askew. He took a long swig of beer, then raised the bottle and continued.

"Well, some can go a time or two, and some go three or four. Alas, for me, I never see a man who can do more!"

Sweet merciful Mother of Chaos.

Her sunglasses. She'd magicked them to protect him from madness. Instead of falling asleep, he was thoroughly hammered.

"I'd give my soul to find that man, in heaven or in hell," Hank bellowed. "And as she spoke those fateful words, a traveler rang her bell."

The witch levitated and zipped across the theater to grab Deputy Eye Candy before he took a nosedive.

"The widow hastened to the door and threw it open wide, and when she did, the tall and virile devil came—"

He noticed her and stopped mid-verse, grinning crookedly and wobbling on his precarious perch. She glided up to him, slid her shoulder under his, and eased him to the floor.

"Witch. . .'s you." He rested his forehead against hers. "You're so pretty. Mean, but pretty. Almost makes up for it." A beery belch erupted in her face.

She recoiled, waving away the yeasty fumes.

Gods dammit, she'd never catch the trail of that little white asshole babysitting two hundred pounds of inebriated male perfection. She needed to get someone over here to wake the sleepers. Tophet County still didn't have a curse breaker, but they could commandeer one from Gomorrah Township.

Magnolia would know what to do. The witch tapped out a text and clicked send.

"The devil said, 'I've heard your call and come to do you right, but, my love, your soul is mine if I can last the night!'"

Gods, she might have to gag him.

A clatter from the stage drew her eyes. She turned the flashlight to its brightest setting and swept it across the stage. A little white. . .

Holy hell, a little white *Archon* stood highlighted in the beam, clutching a sphere to its thorax with noodly limbs.

"Hey!"

The LWA's head swiveled, then it turned and lurched off stage right—slithering, no doubt, toward the open door. The witch snagged Hank with a tractor beam and raced after it.

"Now, when they tumbled into bed, the devil did her well," Hank sang, bobbing behind her. "And he just knew when they were through, he'd take her back to hell."

Her entropine plummeted from the strain of lugging the big lug. She briefly considered leaving him in the alley, but gods only knew what he'd get up to.

"But when they came to their fifth romp, the widow hollered, 'More!'"

For a harrowing moment, the witch thought she'd lost the little white shitbird. Then she caught the tail end of a snowy tentacle disappearing around a corner.

"And when they'd finished number ten, the widow screamed, 'Encore!'"

The witch charged into a courtyard at the center of campus. The LWA was racing toward the arched bridge spanning the Catachthonic River. She gave it everything she had and closed the distance between them.

"Heiress, I've got eyes on a bogey!" yelled a shrill voice.

The witch slowed to a gasping halt at the river's edge. Her quarry stood at the center of the bridge. At the other end, a woman in candy cane–striped leggings blocked its escape route.

The spandex army was here. Now they had this thing by its little white marbles.

Hank dropped to the ground with a muffled "oof," putting a blessed end to "The Widow and the Devil."

Vera appeared next to the woman at the other end of the bridge. Excellent. The LWA had nowhere to run.

"Do you know who this bridge belongs to?" Vera asked the white figure as she planted a foot on the wooden planks.

A passage from *The Archonomicon* surfaced from the depths of the witch's memory. This was the Bridge of Sighs. If Vera said the Mindless Mother's name, the ancient Archon would appear and drag her to its lair.

"Vera, don't say—"

"Za'gathoth!"

The river roiled, and a dripping tentacle of water whipped up from the surface. Vera leaped backward, and it lassoed the little white Archon and pulled it into the river. The witch jogged to the apex of the bridge.

"Dammit, I wanted that sphere!"

Vera and her lieutenant walked out to join her. "We could send Pumpkin Spice in after it."

The other woman shook her head. "My sitter has to leave at eleven." She pointed at a slender brunette. "What about Uggs? Her kids are with her in-laws this weekend."

"Who's Za'gathoth?" asked a bleary voice.

The witch turned just in time to see a watery tentacle encircle Hank's waist.

"Hey, that tickles! Stop—"

His voice cut off midsentence as he disappeared beneath the surface.

"Hank!" The witch leaned over the railing, searching desperately for any sign of him. "Do you have a rope?" Vera shook her head. "A belt? A. . .a fucking *anything?*"

"Witch, we can't—"

"We have to get him out," she yelled. "He'll drown. . .He won't. . .He's. . ."

"There's nothing we can do." Vera rested her hand on the witch's shoulder, but she shook it off. "I'm sorry."

A gust of wind blew a pink petal free of her bun. It drifted to the now-placid surface of the river. Her reflection shimmered back at her, the petal crowning her hair.

Hank was gone, and it was her fault.

The witch was always primed to be pissed when people used her for her magic, but she'd done the same thing to Hank. She'd used him. She'd known this might be dangerous, but she hadn't given him the chance to opt out. Worse, Magnolia had warned her that the play was a trap, but she hadn't listened.

She *never* listened.

Vera's reflection appeared next to hers. For an instant, she felt a surge of rage. It wasn't her fault; it was Vera's. *She* was the one who'd summoned the river monster.

But the tide of her anger quickly ebbed. She knew who was to blame. . .and who had to save Hank.

What exactly had *The Archonomicon* said?

Za'gathoth will emerge from the waters and take the seeker to her lair, where

she will either divulge esoteric knowledge or consume the one who dared summon her. . .

There was a chance he wasn't dead. He might be experiencing forcible
enlightenment.

The witch met the dark eyes of her rippling reflection. She wouldn't just
leave him.

"Witch," Vera said, "what are you—"

"Run."

The rapid tapping of stilettos on wood was the only reply.

She gripped the railing.

"Za'gathoth."

CHAPTER TWENTY-THREE

The Mindless Mother

A ribbon of frigid water surged up from the river, wound around the witch's waist, and yanked her beneath the icy surface. Her lungs burned as the tentacle whipped her through the water with dizzying speed. After what felt like an eternity, it hurled her onto dry land, where she crash-landed on her bony ass.

The witch squeezed her eyes shut against the sudden brightness and rolled onto her back, sucking in delicious lungfuls of air. She groped for the Tamagotchi. It was still there, but shit. . .Keyser was electronic now. River diving couldn't be good for him. She sat up and squinted at the screen. His face was buried in his food bowl. She ran her hands over her body, her shirt, her hair. Bone-dry.

"Come on in, little sister."

The witch stood and looked around, searching for the owner of the creaky voice. Her jaw dropped. The pool from which she'd emerged occupied one corner of a vast and mystifying chamber.

This was the profane temple of the Mindless Mother?

It looked like a sitcom grandma's living room, only at triple the scale. Pink-and-white-striped wallpaper adorned the walls, topped with a hideous floral border. A massive chintz sofa (the seat cushions hit at eye level) covered in a plastic slipcover dominated one wall. Matching paintings of fruits and flowers hung centered over the couch, crowned by a dusty garland of fake ivy.

"Sit by the fire and warm up." The voice came from an immense glider positioned in front of an electric fireplace, facing away from her.

The witch tried to juice up her shields, but nothing happened. Dragging Mr. Man Candy around campus must have tanked her reserves. Hopefully, Za'gathoth was in an esoteric-knowledge sort of mood.

"I'm looking for my friend," she said. "He should've. . .arrived just before I did."

A massive, insectile leg poked out from the right-hand edge of the chair. "You mean that?"

A man-size birdcage loomed on a half-moon accent table. Inside, the little white Archon flailed and shook the bars. The Tamagotchi buzzed as Keyser lunged toward it, his digital face fixed in a fierce snarl. The sphere sat under a glass cake dome next to the LWA's prison.

That explained her magical whiskey dick.

"No," the witch said, continuing her slow advance. "I'm looking for a human male."

"Oh, him. Such a nice young man."

The witch circled around the glider to see who she was dealing with. A hunched figure wearing a crocheted shawl watched her with a pair of faceted eyes drooping from wilted stalks. The Mindless Mother looked like an enormous stag beetle, complete with serrated mandibles. Her dull carapace was a creamy beige dotted with liver spots and rippled with wrinkles. A quartet of humanish hands protruding from her midsection drew multiple needles through an expanse of fabric stretched across an embroidery hoop the size of a garbage-can lid.

"Where is he now?"

"Ate him," Za'gathoth said. "Let too many seekers live, and they swarm like ants."

Oh gods, no. . .

The witch fell to her knees. She'd gotten Hank killed.

"Oh, for pity's sake. . ." The colossal being convulsed, and a vertical fanged maw opened in her saggy thorax. After a series of nasty clotted-sounding retches, a stream of bile and slime spewed from her mouth, and a human body hit the floor with a squelchy *plop*. A fleshy bear trap of jagged teeth followed. Za'gathoth yelped, grabbed her dentures, and popped them back into her mouth.

"Hank!" The witch knelt next to him and patted his face. "Wake up!" He didn't respond. "Come on, asshole!"

"I'm not. . .an asshole," he croaked.

Za'gathoth extended a trembling leg and tapped the center of his forehead. He collapsed on the damp carpet.

"Hey!"

"He's just sleeping." The Mindless Mother adjusted her shawl and resumed sewing. "We need to talk, and males annoy me." A withered tentacle snaked out from under the shawl, snagged the leg of a tufted ottoman, and dragged it to the witch. "Sit."

She sat.

"The world's going to hell in a handbasket," Za'gathoth said. "These young ones are nothing like the Elder Gods of old, I'll tell you that." She shook her head dolefully and rocked in her chair. "You know, I warned her this would happen."

Warned her. Could Za'gathoth have sent the visions?

"You warned Magnolia?"

"What-nolia?"

"Not what, who. She's—"

"I warned Micana'gos."

The Clerk.

"I don't mind saying she's getting too big for her britches." Za'gathoth rolled her eyes. "Miss La-Dee-Dah, Shadow Leader of the Earth's Archons. Ha!"

"You've lost me," the witch said. "Puny human mind. You warned her about what?"

"The Swarm, of course." She jabbed a jointed leg toward the birdcage and its frantic occupant. "I told Micana'gos they'd found us. I told her they were planning an invasion. I even told her to put you on the case."

"But why?"

"Because it calls for your particular gift."

So *she* was the Clerk's mysterious advisor.

"What gift?"

"Your entropine, you moron!" the elderly Archon said, baring yellowed teeth.

The chair jerked to a sudden halt. Za'gathoth's rheumy eyes narrowed, wavering on their spindly stems. The witch's flight instincts (she was fresh out of fight) were twanging so hard, her legs twitched.

"I know what they call me up there: the Mindless Mother. Ha! They're the ones who are mindless." She heaved a wet sigh. "And the way they treat me is shameful, that's what it is. No one calls. No one visits."

"I'm here," the witch said. "And I'd love to hear about the Swarm."

Za'gathoth examined the horny nails of one arthritic hand. "Well, I suppose if you're interested. . ." One eye flicked up to the witch to confirm her attention. "Now, this all started back in the old country."

"The Fathomless Abyss?"

"No, dummy!"

The witch ground her teeth. *Call me another name, you crusty old—*

"You don't know anything, do you?" Za'gathoth asked.

"I know what everyone knows."

"What's that?"

The witch shrugged. "Those dumbass skinheads held a Unite the White rally on the bridge over the Abyss. Their evil woke you—"

"No, no, no," Za'gathoth snapped. "It wasn't just that they were evil, and I didn't mean the Abyss. I meant *before*."

"Before?" She frowned. "I thought you'd always been there."

"We came from another universe—the same one as *them*." The Mindless Mother's antennae waved at the LWA. "Our species were at war for ages. The final battle lasted longer than the entire history of Homo sapiens."

"Who won?"

"If we'd won, would we be hiding on this blighted rock?" She adjusted her pink shawl, her fingers toying with the faded fringe. "I saw the writing on the obelisk, so I hid with our young—the eggs and larvae, a handful of juveniles. When the war was over, we were the only Archons left. I tried to escape to the Dreamlands, the space between our universe and yours."

"What happened?"

"The Morpheus Gate was closed." Za'gathoth sucked her teeth with a revolting slurp. "But it's the damnedest thing. . .Lovecraft always said he learned about us in dreams. The right sort of human—or the wrong sort, in his case—can visit the Dreamlands during sleep. Seems to me there'd have to be at least one Archon holed up in there." Her antennae rubbed together, an anxious gesture oddly reminiscent of wringing hands. "But when we couldn't get in, I had to tuck my tentacles and portal to this layer of the Sheaf."

"The Sheaf?"

Za'gathoth stomped a slipper-clad. . .foot? "The multiverse, imbecile! An infinity of different universes stacked on top of each other."

"Couldn't the little white men just follow you?"

"If the Swarm could teleport, I wouldn't be sitting here, would I?" She stared into the flickering fake flames as though they were a window to the past. "After the war, I brought the kids to this universe, found a planet with no intelligent life, and burrowed into a pocket dimension."

"Earth *has* intelligent life."

"It was nothing but big lizards back then. Anyway, I'm not so sure humans qualify," she said. "We were content for a while. It was a little cramped, but we were safe. The children didn't remember our home, but I told them stories. When they acted up, I'd say, 'You better be good, or the little white men'll get you!'" The wrinkled abomination shivered and huddled into her shawl. "Then you jackasses got their attention and upset them, and now. . ." She raised her hands, palms up. "Well, here we are."

Hank moaned and stirred. Za'gathoth thumped him with what seemed like more force than was strictly necessary.

"After they emerged, I told Micana'gos—she's the eldest, you know—that if they kept carrying on in temporal reality, they'd eventually attract the Swarm." The glider squeaked as she started rocking again. "But she thought our ancient enemy was just a bedtime story."

If the LWM were the Archons' ancient enemy, and collusion with the ancient enemy was cause for canceling an Archonic contract. . .

"I know what you're thinking." Za'gathoth's slash of a mouth spread in a sly grin. "Why not just let them wipe us out?"

"It might've crossed my mind."

"The Swarm is a hive mind," she said, her eyestalks swiveling toward the bird-cage. "They have one goal: the total destruction of individuality. When they've Borged your universe like they did ours, your lot'll be a couple billion little white men in a little white world." Za'gathoth shifted her focus to the witch. "Is that what you want?"

The witch clutched the Tamagotchi, imagining her life without Keyser, without Chad. "No."

They sat for a moment, the silence broken only by Hank's rasping snores and the creak of the glider.

"One thing I don't get," the witch said. "If it wasn't evil that roused the Archons, what was it?"

"The children were too young to remember, but we came here fleeing an army intent on whitening us," Za'gathoth said. "When those fools stood on the bridge over the Abyss yelling about white power and yearning for a white world, the kids felt it. It was just pure bad luck that the oldest clutch of boys was hitting the change. They were—"

"Irrational. Bloodthirsty. Unpredictable," the witch said, recalling the Clerk's description.

"Just like a male to chalk everything up to hormones, isn't it?" she asked. "Their battle instincts took over, and they tore out of that hole in a tantrum of terror."

"A tantrum of. . ." The witch looked up at Za'gathoth's insectile face. "You're telling me they were *scared*?"

"Scared scatless. By the time they came to their senses, your armies were dropping bombs, and your witches were throwing fireballs, and. . ." Her mandibles quivered with tremulous emotion. "And it was too late."

If Za'gathoth spoke the truth, the vicious monsters who'd taken over the Earth were traumatized orphans, and witches and humans were collateral damage in the aftermath of the war that nearly annihilated them.

"If you don't want everyone you know and love turned into one of those"—the Mindless Mother's eyes flicked toward the LWA—"you'd best stop the Swarm."

"*I'd* best stop them? Why does it have to be me?"

"Because of your—"

"My particular gift."

"Now you're catching on, little sister." She hissed a sibilant word. A bowl of cherry Jell-O and a plastic spoon appeared in her hands, and she deposited a wobbling mouthful in her maw. "You've only got until the stars are right."

"When's that?"

"The winter solstice, when the membrane between layers of the Sheaf grows thin." She pointed at the witch with her spoon. "That's when they'll invade."

The solstice was in eleven days. Not a lot of time to come up with a plan to save the world.

"I convinced Micana'gos to work on a backup plan." Za'gathoth shoveled more Jell-O into her mouth, dribbling red syrup on her shawl. "She's trying to build an escape hatch out of this layer."

"Can't you just leave the way you came in?"

"'Fraid not. The dimensional membrane of our home universe was porous. We could teleport from there to other layers of the Sheaf." She slurped up the last of the Jell-O and set the bowl and spoon on a glass-topped end table. "This layer's different. We could get in, and we can hop around inside it, but we can't get out. I couldn't even scope out our pocket dimension until I found the thin spot in the Abyss."

That explained why the Clerk funded Carcosa's murder machine.

"Time for you to go, little sister," Za'gathoth said. "*WWE SmackDown!* starts in five minutes."

A metallic clatter drew the witch's eyes to the LWA, which was rattling the bars of its cage. "What're you going to do with that thing?" She stood and took a few steps toward the birdcage. "And why has it got. . ." She trailed off and waved her arms in a tentacular motion.

"Your universe leaks entropy like a sieve. I expect our little friend has soaked some of it up. As for what I'll do with it. . ." Za'gathoth chuckled a throaty smoker's laugh. "I suppose I'll introduce it to the glory of Roman Reigns." She waved a hand in a shooing motion. "Go on, now. Jump in the pool, and you'll pop up topside."

The witch's eyes flicked from the cage to the cake dome. She considered asking for the sphere, but hell, it was safer down here than on the surface. "One last question," she said. "Do you know how the spheres work?"

"There's a syntropium crystal in there," the aged creature said. "Hoovers up entropy like a Shop-Vac."

"Can the process be reversed? My familiar. . ."

The Mindless Mother's mandibles flexed, somehow conveying an impression of shared grief and, yes, sympathy.

"I'm. . .I'm sorry, Witch."

CHAPTER TWENTY-FOUR

The Cat Who Ate the Cockatrice

"Are you in there?"

The witch pulled a pillow over her head to block out a barrage of aggressive knocks.

"I brought coffee," sang the voice.

She sighed and levered herself up from the futon. The phantom impression of its wooden slats haunted her spine as she hobbled to the door and yanked it open. Without a word, Magnolia thrust a travel mug into the witch's hand. The witch waved her inside and stumbled toward the kitchen. She checked her BlackBerry, but it was as dead as her dreams. Once she'd plugged it in to charge, she sat at the table and attached the coffee firmly to her face.

Magnolia sank into a chair and crossed her slender human legs. "I was worried to death last night. The Clerk talked to Mother, so I knew you and Hank made it out alive, but. . .are you okay?"

"If I was any better, I'd have to take something for it." A grotesque exaggeration, but the coffee was working its magic. "Hate to say I told you so, but that new cult's definitely involved in this. The Unseen Creeping Horror was attacked after their landfill picnic. Then the same godsdamned thing happened to the Yellow King during their field trip to the theater. They must've teamed up with the little white jack-offs."

"Except the cult never went to that play."

The witch sat up straighter. That couldn't be right. "Where'd you hear that?"

"I thought Chad was going to the play with you," Magnolia said. "But when I saw him Friday afternoon, he, um. . ."

"I changed my mind."

"Well, we were afraid you'd go alone. Chad decided to sneak in with the cult. But when he went to their Meetup page to RSVP, the event had been canceled."

"They're covering their tracks."

"I'm telling you, Witch, the cult is innocent."

"If you want to tell me something, why don't you explain how you can be so sure?"

Magnolia blew out a frustrated sigh and shook her head. "Just walk me through what happened."

The witch considered giving an enigmatic, Vera-esque non-answer, but the truth was, she couldn't save the world alone. As an Archon—well, a *former* Archon—Magnolia might have valuable insights. Plus, she was good at organizing and analyzing and all that crap the witch blew past on her way from idea to impulsive, ill-advised action. So she described her shitty evening, ending with her conversation with Za'gathoth.

When she'd finished, Magnolia sat in silence, a pained expression creasing her forehead. "Witch, I need to—"

The witch's BlackBerry vibrated with a volley of staccato bursts. "Hold that thought." She reached for her phone, telling herself firmly that the texts probably weren't from Chad, that she didn't care either way.

They weren't.

She did.

The messages were from Carcosa. Last night, she'd sent him an update text so long, she'd almost considered calling to prevent grievous phalangeal stress. But what kind of monster called when texting was an option?

"Listen," Magnolia said, "there's something I have to—"

"Just let me read this. It'll only take a minute."

What a harrowing adventure. I am glad you are unharmed. I would also like to speak in person, but I agree we should not be seen together. The Archons have eyes and ears everywhere. Literally. Retrieve the sphere from Za'gathoth's lair and send it to me. I was unable to repair the first sphere's activation mechanism, so I will need it for research. Besides, I worry about an Archon having access to this technology.

It was a reasonable-ish concern, but the witch felt like she'd kind of vibed with the Mindless Mother. Plus, Za'gathoth was really pushing this whole *Help me, Obi-Witch Kenobe, you are my only hope* thing.

The containment field around the sphere's syntropium crystal is unstable. That is why being near the weapon weakens you. I am working on a way to reverse the effects. However, given the amount of stored entropy, the process is extremely delicate and quite dangerous.

Kind of a mixed bag there. No quick fix, but at least Carcosa was making progress toward finding a way to restore Keyser Söze.

And the UCH and the Living Flood and the Yellow King and probably the Dread Lord of IT.

Magnolia cleared her throat. "Witch, can I just—"

"Gods, chill!"

Regarding the Clerk's purpose for funding my research. I should have expected deceit from such a creature. I am sorry the Archons you trusted have deceived you as well. I cannot imagine why they did not share this information with you when they asked you to investigate.

"The Archons you trusted."

The witch had told Magnolia she saw a little white man in her apartment, and she'd run off to inform the Clerk. The two of them had known what threatened Tophet County for most of a week. They could've clued her in, but they'd let her flail around like a moth-man caught in the Spinner's web. Her cheeks burned as she imagined them conspiring, laughing at her.

"The Swarm, the war, your godsdamned ancient enemy," the witch said, her voice trembling with rage. "Everything I just told you. . .you already *knew*."

"That's what I was trying to say. You have to understand—"

"I don't have to understand shit," the witch snapped. "What happened to you earning my trust?"

"Remember what Za'gathoth told you." Magnolia's voice was low and urgent. "Remember what happened the last time Archons even *imagined* the Swarm was here."

"I'm the only witch left, Magnolia. I don't need to be reminded."

"Then you understand why we couldn't risk saying anything," Magnolia said. "What do you think the Sheriff would do if he heard that, not only are the little white men real, they're *here*, and they're on the verge of a full-scale invasion? Do you think he'd agree to sit down with the humans and calmly figure out a plan?"

"That's not the—"

"Because I think he'd freak out and start killing anything human-shaped." Magnolia wiped away the tears streaming from her eyes. "Yes, I've been hiding things from you. Yes, I still am. But so are *you*. My secrets are kept to protect people," she said, pointing at her own chest. "Can you say the same for yours?"

"I think you should—"

"Go?" Magnolia asked. "Gladly." She stood and stormed to the front door. "Why do you make it so hard to be your friend?"

The door slammed, then it banged open again. Magnolia charged into the kitchen, grabbed the travel mug from the witch's limp fingers, and left. The witch stared at her empty hand, unsure who was the injured party.

It *was* her, wasn't it?

A melodic chime rang through the apartment. The witch followed the sound to her bedroom, where her laptop was open on her desk—just the way she'd left it last night when she was googling *syntropium* and *how to stop extra-dimensional invasion* and *last verse of "The Widow and the Devil."*

The screen read: *Incoming video call from Chad Chadwick, Online Services.*

The witch ran a hasty hand through her hair and accepted the call. Chad's image appeared. Annoyingly, her stomach did a now-familiar slow flip. She schooled her features into a nonchalant smirk.

"Hey."

"Man, it's good to see your face," Chad said. "I've been going crazy. Magnolia said you were planning to ask me to go to that play with you, and then you didn't, and I understand why, and I totally respect that, but I tried to call you a bunch of times to make sure you got home safely, and it went right to voicemail, and I was starting to think something had gone very, very—"

"Aw, you were worried about me," she said, failing to suppress her grin.

"I guess I was."

"As you can see, I'm perfectly fine."

"What happened at the play? The cult canceled their outing."

"Magnolia told me," the witch said. "But some weird shit went down." She ran through the whole story.

When she finished, Chad shook his head and said, "That's wild. I'm glad you're okay." He rubbed the back of his neck. "Look, I know we've got more urgent stuff to deal with, but I was wondering if we could talk about what happened at Asenath's."

The witch swallowed as a blush reddened her cheeks. "Yeah. Sure."

"I hope I didn't screw things up between us. I mean, I've been wanting to. . ." He took a deep breath and closed his eyes. "Witch, I really like—"

"Oh, hey, Chad!"

The witch had been so fixated on Chad that she'd completely forgotten why she slept on her shitty futon last night. Between the intoxicating effects of the sphere and repeated KOs by Za'gathoth, Hank had been a hot mess when they crawled out of the river. He'd staggered out of the water, puked down the front of his shirt, and started bellowing another Irish drinking song. The witch patted him down—no funny business; the poor bastard wasn't in his right mind—but his wallet and keys were presumably at the bottom of the Catachthonic River. So she'd taken his drunk ass back to her place, stripped off his nasty shirt, and put him in her bed.

And there he sat, propped up on a mound of pillows. He was shirtless, riddled with flawlessly defined muscles, and grinning like the cat who ate the cockatrice.

"Uh. . .hi, Hank." Chad stared down at his keyboard. "Sorry to wake you, man. I should get going. I'm sure you guys have, um. . .plans."

"Wait, Chad—"

This video call has been ended by the host.

CHAPTER TWENTY-FIVE

The Enemy of My Enemy

You."

The Dread Librarian scowled at the witch. The pincers framing her proboscis twitched in apparent indignation.

"Me," the witch said. "It's been forty-two days."

Chlogha sighed. "What's it going to be today? Planning to flood the conference room again?"

A failed experiment from *The Hexonomicon*.

"Make one of the children's books come to life?"

That caterpillar had been a lot more than very hungry.

"Or perhaps you'll try to steal another book from the Read at Your Own Risk room?"

If only she could. . .

The witch planted her hands on the information desk, staring down at her boots. She couldn't believe she was doing this. "I need your"—she swallowed hard and met the creature's Cyclopean eye—"help."

The Dread Librarian opened her wide mouth, but she uttered neither word nor croak.

"I'm looking for one of the Nomicons." She'd searched the RAYOR room, but as she'd expected, *The Archonomicon* was nowhere to be found. "I've seen it before, but I can't find it on the shelves."

Chlogha regained her composure. "*The Get-It-On-Onomicon* is still missing, but I could pull the *Kama Sutra*."

"I'm looking for *The Archonomicon*."

The Dread Librarian narrowed an eye the size of a soccer ball. "That's the one you tried to smuggle out of the library, isn't it?"

"I won't try to take it." The witch held out her hand. "I give you my word."

One of the wriggling tentacles that bearded Chlogha's rainbow-slicked countenance extended and wound around her wrist. The tingle of a magical oath rippled up the witch's arm, raising goose bumps. To her surprise, she didn't feel the urge to yank her hand free and douse it in hand sanitizer.

"The word of the County Witch," the great toad said thoughtfully. Chlogha retracted the appendage and stared at her. "That will do." She eased her bulky form out from behind the desk. "Let's see what we can find."

The witch followed the Dread Librarian's odd, hopping gait to the RAYOR room. Chlogha closed the door behind them and lowered a bar that looked like an immense femur. Nictitating membranes slid into place over the Dread Librarian's eye, and she scanned the shelves. Her gaze moved from left to right, top to bottom, along the spines. The books shivered and sighed.

At the bottom of the third set of shelves, Chlogha's head froze, and her thin lips curved in a satisfied grin. A long, pink tongue shot out and stuck to what looked like a patch of empty air. With a sound like ripping Velcro, it snapped back toward her. One of her beard-acles wound around an invisible object. She deposited it on the table with a resonant *thump*.

The Dread Librarian whispered a word in the soul-rending language of the Archons. *The Necronomicon* appeared on the table, emitting an air of sulky reproach.

"But that's not the book I'm—"

Chlogha raised a tentacle, silencing the witch. She braced her absurdly small hands on her bloated torso and glared at the quivering tome. "Spit it out." *The Necronomicon*'s covers squeezed together, compressing its pages into a petulant brick. "You spit it out right now, or I'm putting you on the coloring table in Story Corner."

The human skin of the cover paled. After a moment to consider its options, the book ruffled its pages and disgorged *The Archonomicon*.

"Son of a star-spawn," the witch hissed.

"That's Lovecraft for you."

She stepped closer to the table and stared at *The Necronomicon*. "Wait, you're telling me *he's* in there?"

"Oh, yes." The Dread Librarian thumped the cover, and the book cowered. "When he got sick—cancer of the bowel, I think it was—he hired a witch to set it all up for him. She sat the deathwatch and transferred his soul into the book when he passed. Per the provisions of his will, *The Necronomicon* was rebound in his skin."

The witch stared at the cover. A mole with a long, black hair growing out of it stared right back at her. Ugh! What if it was an ass cheek?

"Why has he been hiding *The Archonomicon* from me?"

"It conflicts with the canon of his Cthulhu mythos, so he doesn't want anyone reading it." Chlogha cleared her throat delicately. "And he wouldn't be inclined to help you, as you're neither male nor Caucasian."

"I see," the witch said, her tone so icy that frost formed on the cover of the book. She walked to the shelves and removed a book bound in blue fur. Chlogha watched her closely but said nothing as she *thunk*ed the furry-puppet-themed MahNàMahNàmicon on the table and opened the cover. Cheerful music filled the RAYOR room.

Mah Nà Mah Nà, doo DOO da doo doo.

She picked up *The Necronomicon*, plopped it on top of the singing book, and forced the covers closed. Only then did she meet the Dread Librarian's eye.

"Hope that's cool with you."

Chlogha grinned. "I expect it will do him good." She picked up the furry volume and slid it back into its place on the shelves. "Well, if that's all you need. . ."

The witch opened her mouth to send the toad on her way, but she hesitated. Since the Dread Librarian was here and in a cooperative mood, she might as well seize the opportunity. Nothing ventured, nothing gained.

"Do you have any books on magical contracts?"

Chlogha's shimmering forehead wrinkled in confusion. "You're a contracted County employee. You should've gotten a copy of *The Depectio'nomicon* on your first day of work." A tentacle snaked to the shelves and grabbed a familiar-looking paperback. "All parties to an Archonic contract receive one."

"I remember getting a book that looked a little like this." Same dark red binding. Same symbols on the spine. "But it was the Tophet County Employee Handbook. The Dread Lord of Human Resources demanded I read it, so. . ."

So she'd promptly incinerated it and put it out of her mind.

The Dread Librarian rolled her enormous eye. "Sathach wanted to give the workplace a more human-friendly feel. He rebranded the whole thing. Since the terms of your employment are embedded in your contract, I suppose his new title isn't completely inaccurate. The copy he gave you should have the specifics of your personal contract, along with everything included here." She tapped the cover with a tentacle.

"I've seen it here before," the witch said, "but I thought *depectio* meant something to do with lies or illusions."

"Ah. Deception. *Depectio*. But no." Chlogha shook her head. "*Depectio* is the Latin word for *contract*."

The witch had scanned a Latin primer at some point in her occult education, which meant the language was in her palace of memory. All it would've taken to translate that word was a moment's attention, a mere instant of concentration, but she'd assumed she knew what it meant. Worse, the godsdamned Dread Lord of Human Resources had given her a godsdamned copy of the very godsdamned book she'd been seeking for almost *thirteen godsdamned years*.

"Are you all right?" A milky membrane slid over Chlogha's eye and retracted. "You seem to be. . .steaming."

"I'm fine." The witch forced a smile, hoping the result was more grin than grimace. "Uh, thank you for. . .you know. Helping me."

Chlogha lifted the bone crossbar and opened the door. "That's why I'm here."

Alone in the RAYOR room, the witch considered the books before her. She'd have thought her fingers would be itching to dig into the primer on magical contracts. (Given the provenance of *The Necronomicon*, she might wind up with itchy fingers anyway—courtesy of some Lovecraftian gluteal fungus.) But it was *The Archonomicon* that held her captivated. She wasn't here for herself today.

She was here because the Swarm was planning an invasion.

She was here because they'd attacked Keyser Söze.

Freedom would just have to wait until she'd eradicated the pale menace and restored Keyser to his ill-tempered, poorly litter-trained, garbage-eating self.

She opened *The Archonomicon* and began to read.

The fuligin cover of the book slid from the witch's nerveless hands.

Little sister. That's what the Mindless Mother had called her. Za'gathoth knew the truth of what she was. Maybe all the Archons knew. The witch and her belligerent hatred of the tentacled ruling class were probably a countywide laughingstock. After all, she wouldn't exist without them.

Eons ago, before the earliest human ancestor stood on two legs, the Archons fled their home and came to this universe—or, to borrow the Mindless Mother's term, this layer of the Sheaf. She'd burrowed under the earth and created a pocket dimension in the Fathomless Abyss. The Archons' presence dramatically increased the planet's baseline level of entropy, which made magic possible. Made *witches* possible.

No wonder the post-Emergence rebellion was a miserable failure. A witch fighting an Archon was like using a flamethrower to extinguish a multistate wildfire.

The witch shook her head. Her existential crisis would have to wait. The Swarm planned to launch a full-scale invasion in nine days. Earth's current odds of victory were comparable to a snowman's chance of strolling unharmed through the gates of hell.

Calling in the armed forces wasn't an option. The Archons' first order of business in the chaotic post-Emergence years had been taking over the military. If she even whispered the truth to a man in uniform, the tentacled higher-ups would know. Za'gathoth and Magnolia were justifiably concerned that leaking the news would trigger another "tantrum of terror." It'd be worth the risk if the

Archons could defeat this adversary, but the Swarm had already mopped the frigging floor with them.

According to *The Archonomicon*, during the early days of their war, a colony of Archonic fire vampires attacked a village of little white men in retaliation for the destruction of their nesting grounds—and their nestlings. The ensuing inferno's extreme heat transformed little white bodies into syntropium crystals, much as carbon atoms fused into diamonds. The surviving LWM took those crystals and built the spheres, which absorbed entropine and turned Archons into little white men. Victory by assimilation.

The witch mentally sidestepped into her palace of memory. A stack of index cards appeared in her astral body's right hand, a spool of red thread in her left. Time to review what she'd learned. She flipped through the cards, tacking each to a corkboard as she went.

Your universe leaks entropy like a sieve. [Za'gathoth]

That explained why the spheres' effects were different here than in the Archons' home layer of the Sheaf.

The QT functions best with the lowest possible entropy. [Carcosa]

The entities attacked with spheres were the most entropic in Tophet County: a sentient fog, a swarling swarm of titanium insects, a turbulent wave monster, a stuttering film reel. As for Keyser, if the witch was an entropine generator, he was her battery. Hitting those targets would yield a significant reduction in local background entropy.

I convinced Micana'gos to work on a backup plan. She's trying to build an escape hatch out of this layer. [Za'gathoth]

Which meant the QT's true purpose was to pierce the dimensional membrane so the Archons could flee.

If the Swarm could teleport, I wouldn't be sitting here, would I? [Za'gathoth]

The little white men couldn't teleport to this layer, which meant they'd need to tear a hole in the dimensional membrane to invade.

Carcosa's assistant isn't in a twelve-step group. She's in a cult. [Badass Witch]

. . .A cult whose logo was a little white man strangling an Archon.

If the witch was right about the cult—and she *knew* she was—they could be using Lorelei to gather information and funnel it to the LWM. And when the stars were right at the winter solstice, they'd seize the QT and use it to invade.

She wound red thread from tack to tack, producing a shape that looked an awful lot like a raised middle finger. The implication was clear: They were screwed.

The witch left her palace, picked up her BlackBerry, and dashed off a warning message to Carcosa. While she was at it, she texted Magnolia something in the neighborhood of an apology. Magnolia had made a fair point: the witch was keeping secrets too. And reading the Archons' tortured history had left her feeling. . .well, if not sympathy, at least a greater level of understanding. Being an entropic badass wasn't the only thing she had in common with her tentacled pals. Like her, they were war orphans with psyches poisoned by hatred and fear.

And they shared a common enemy. The witch reached for Keyser's Tamagotchi. Those little white shits came after her because she was an entropy-generating sibling—perish the thought—of the Archons. They'd gotten Keyser instead. For that, the Swarm was her enemy. The Archons, in turn, were *their* enemy.

How did that saying go? The enemy of my enemy is. . .

Oh, *balls*.

CHAPTER TWENTY-SIX

Rhymes with "Witch"

Witch, *I really like—*
        Working together?
Doctor Who?
Tacos?

She'd started and deleted a dozen texts to Chad. The suspense was killing her.

"What's wrong with Nommaquth?"

Y'ggarlos's strident voice cut through the witch's teenage angst–fest. The cephalopod leaned forward, her bulbous mantle wobbling as she peered around Ellie Dawson's wheelchair.

Ellie halted midway through her routine plea for the return of *The Get-It-On-Onomicon*. Nommaquth's bubbles, usually roiling in a somewhat mesmerizing display of aeronautics, lay motionless at the bottom of his aquarium. Ellie's mic picked up a soft, soapy pop as one of the glistening spheres burst.

"It's this damned room." Achartho's giant wings were tucked close to his body, and his barbed scorpion's tail drooped.

"The decorators may have gone overboard." Heather's eyes wandered over the Ikean nightmare of blond wood and glossy white. "I asked them to brighten it up, but this is beyond the pale."

A few more bubbles popped with a sound like pattering raindrops.

Next to her, N'eithamiqug drummed bristling spider legs on the white desktop. "End the meeting."

Heather said, "But we still have two more—"

"I think," the Spinner said, fangs protruding from her lipsticked mouth, "we should adjourn early."

Heather tapped the button on her mic. "Due to, um, unforeseen circumstances, we'll need to stop here for today. Check our website for additional updates, and remember, next week's General Session is on Wednesday rather than Tuesday." She banged her gavel. "This meeting is adjourned."

The witch stood. If she hurried, she could catch Ronnie and hit the old vape pen before the WTF meeting. Her nerves were shot to shit.

"Witch," N'eithamiqug said, "you sense it too, don't you?"

She chose a pair of arachnid eyes and met them. "Sense what?"

"It feels. . .wrong in here."

The Tamagotchi vibrated. Keyser's face scrunched in a moue of pain, and a skull floated above him. She pressed a button to dispense medicine, but his expression didn't change.

Something *did* feel off. The witch's body was heavy and sluggish, and her head was pounding. Granted, she'd drowned her sorrows in Chicken Cock last night in a futile attempt to blot out *The Archonomicon*'s revelations and distract herself from the Mysterious Incomplete Sentence. But this wasn't a normal hangover. It felt like. . .

It felt like being at the landfill after the Unseen Creeping Horror's "renovation." She looked around the room. White tile. White walls. White thrones.

N'eithamiqug nodded. "You *do* feel it," she said. "I'm getting out of here." The great spider trembled but didn't move. "I can't make a portal!"

Increasingly frantic, the Spinner turned toward the open door. A shimmering sphere of netherlight appeared in the hall outside the room. N'eithamiqug sagged with relief. She raised her bloated body, aimed her hindquarters at the glowing orb, and shot a streamer of web into it. Her body telescoped in on itself as the sticky strand receded, drawing her into the shrinking hole.

Heather brushed past the witch, practically sprinting for the door.

"Hey, wait up!"

The mayor checked the time on her Fitbit. "I've got to—"

"You've got nothing. This meeting was supposed to run until ten."

"Can we walk and talk?" Heather asked. "I need to squeeze in a call before my next appointment."

"Fine." The witch followed her into the hall. "Tell me more about this remodeling project."

"The contractor was recommended by a colleague. I asked for a minimalist aesthetic, but they took it a bit too—"

"Witch!" Magnolia skidded to a halt in front of them. "Word got around that the General Session ended early."

Word got around? In two minutes?

"I'm sorry to interrupt," she continued, "but our. . .special guest wants to begin. Now."

"Not a problem," Heather said with obvious relief.

Magnolia grabbed the witch's arm and tugged. "Come on. The Clerk's waiting."

It was worse than the Museum of Demonic Dolls.

"I will not set foot in that godsforsaken hellhole."

Life-and-death laser tag? Sure.

Murderous Barbies? If she must.

But *Starbucks*?

"Anyway, I can't," the witch said. "I've been permanently banned."

"What did you *do*?" Magnolia held up a hand to forestall the witch's reply. "Never mind. Look, the Clerk's in there. If anyone tried to bar one of *her* guests. . ." She arched a perfect caramel eyebrow.

Hmmm. That was an enticing prospect. That hipster twit Dashiell could use a slice of humble pie.

Magnolia held the door as they walked into the proverbial lion's den. It'd been more than a year, but nothing had changed. Same lame-ass decor. Same stale coffee smell. Same douchey barista.

"The Clerk claimed the upstairs seating area," Magnolia said. "She wants you to cast a cone of silence over the second floor. Oh, and we all have to buy a drink. Tell me what you want, and I'll—"

"I wouldn't miss this for the world." The witch strolled to the counter, examining the menu with faux deliberation.

Behind the register, a plaid-shirted bearded man with horn-rimmed glasses crossed his arms and said, "You know you're not allowed in here."

Magnolia sidled in front of her. "She's with. . ." She pointed up the stairs.

The man's lips pursed. "Fine."

"I've got this, Magnolia." The witch stepped around her and bellied up to the counter. "Hello, Dash."

"It's Dashiell."

"Oh, *now* you're interested in getting people's names right. I recall an error on my cup the last time I was here."

He smirked. "It rhymes with 'witch.'"

"By the bearded balls of Black Phillip, I will curse your limp little—"

"She'll have a Venti Sumatra." Magnolia gripped her shoulders and aimed her at the steps. "Clerk. Upstairs."

The witch fixed her eyes on Dashiell's ferrety face. "You're lucky I have a meeting. Make sure he doesn't spit in my coffee, Magnolia."

"Of course he won't. If I thought he'd done any such thing, I'd have no choice but to call the Dread Health Inspector."

Dashiell paled. "There's no need for that."

The witch stalked toward the stairs, suppressing a grin. He was shaking in his Vans now, wasn't he? The Dread Health Inspector was a sentient pile of steaming entrails who communicated by stuffing his barbed tongue in a human's ear and twitching in Morse code. It took most people weeks to recover. Some never did.

Halfway up the staircase, the witch paused and cast an incantation that enveloped the second floor in a soundproof bubble. She staggered as her entropine dropped. The lack of sleep and solid food was catching up with her. When she stepped out of the stairwell into the cone of silence, she was greeted by the grating *screeee* of table legs on tile. The Dread Lord of Human Resources hovered at one end of a long table while Chad strained to lift the other.

"What the heck, man?" Chad lowered the table. "I thought you were going to help."

The freckled hands of the Dread Lord's human suit fluttered ineffectually. "I'm not supposed to lift anything heavy." His eyes rolled in opposite directions as the tentacles beneath his skin roiled. "I was diagnosed with a medical condition yesterday." He caught sight of the witch and bowed his head. "May it serve you right, you cocky cockwomble."

"Dirty," she said admiringly. "I like it."

"It is not," he protested. "A cockwomble is an obnoxious fool."

Huh. All that cock and not a dick in the mix.

She glanced at Chad, but his eyes were fixed on the table. The vibe was so strained, it was almost physically painful.

The witch sighed and curled a finger. The table wobbled into the air, but she didn't have enough juice to keep it there. So she lifted her end and said, "Where to?"

Chad jerked his head toward an open area. "Over there."

The Dread Lord stood by, examining his fingernails, as they lugged the table across the room.

Medical condition, her ass.

Magnolia appeared with a tray of drinks and a dimpled Spectral Forces escort. "Hey, Witch," Hank said. "I, um. . .heard you'd be here."

Chad wore a panicked expression. He clearly yearned to escape, but the table had him hemmed in.

"Thanks for letting me crash at your place," Hank said. "I haven't been that drunk since college. I don't know what happened. One minute, I was fine. The next thing I knew, you were cleaning puke off me. And I'm sorry I took your bed."

"No worries," she said, very carefully not looking to see if Chad was listening. "Did you find your wallet and keys?"

Hank's face brightened. "Yeah, I left them at the theater's concession stand. I'd lose my head if it wasn't attached," he said, tapping one perfect temple. "I gotta go, but. . .well, thanks for being a good friend."

Desperate for something to do with her hands, the witch checked her BlackBerry as Hank walked away. She could feel the weight of Chad's gaze. Her finger hovered over an unread text from Carcosa, but Chad cleared his throat.

"That was cool of you," he said. "You know, I thought you guys might be—"

"Playing Hide the Wand in the Chamber of Secrets?"

He grinned and shook his head. "I was going to say 'dating.'"

"It's a no on both counts."

"That's, uh. . .That's good. So, um—"

"Shall we begin?" the Clerk trilled.

The witch reluctantly tore her focus away from Chad. As he found an open seat, she walked past Vera and Ellie Dawson to the end of the table opposite the Clerk. "Let's get to it. I. . ."

Wait a minute. Ellie Dawson?

She hooked a thumb at the serene teenager and met two of the Clerk's eyes. "What's *she* doing here?"

"After Magnolia updated me on your latest news, I thought it prudent to loop in High Lord Dawson," the Clerk said. "She's been fully briefed, and she has examined the sphere from Mother's chamber."

"You gave an anti-Archonic weapon to a godsdamned Girl Scout?" Any shred of guilt the witch felt about bringing in Carcosa melted in the face of this spectacular bullshit.

"Need I remind you," the Clerk said, "that High Lord Dawson earned the—"

"The Gold Award. I've heard."

"Interrupt me again at your peril, Witch." The room fell silent, save for the faint hum of the cone of silence. "The sphere has been returned to Mother's custody. Now, please," she said, gesturing with an oozing tentacle, "get on with it."

"Fine," the witch said through gritted teeth. "You've all read Magnolia's report on my progress?" Everyone nodded. Good. That saved the witch from having to relive Saturday night and revisit the depressing truths laid bare by *The Archonomicon*. "Any questions?"

The Dread Lord raised his hand. "Is this decaf?" he asked. "Because I have a—"

"Sathach," the Clerk snapped, "if you say the words 'medical' and 'condition' again, I'll lower your performance rating to a 4.5."

The hand retreated.

"Why don't we start with our special guest?" The witch dipped her chin to Ellie. "Madam Girl Scout, the floor is yours."

Magnolia fixed the witch with an outraged glare.

"Thank you," Ellie said. "I must admit, Witch, I would've had no idea what I was looking at if you hadn't learned the core was a syntropium crystal. Until now, syntropium has been purely theoretical. It can't exist in our universe due to entropic leakage."

"What do you mean it can't exist?" the witch asked, still annoyed but somewhat mollified by the hat tip. "You just said you looked at it."

"I saw an image generated by a millimeter wave scanner. The crystal itself is enclosed in a quantum stasis bubble that—"

"If you mean the containment field," the witch said, "don't wanna screw around with that. It's unstable. That's why being near one of those things tanks my magic."

"Yes, Maggie told me—"

"Maggie?"

"Apologies," Ellie said. "Magnolia told me the sphere interferes with your magic, but it's not generating a field of any kind. As I was saying, the crystal is suspended in a quantum stasis bubble."

"Which is?" the Clerk asked.

"A hypersphere of spacetime within which there is no quantum activity," Ellie said. "It impacts your magic because quantum stasis is essentially perfect order, perfect syntropy. The good news is that the energy absorbed still exists. The bad news is that it's trapped in the bubble like an insect in amber."

"You might even say it's *contained*," the witch said. "In a field. A containment field, if you will."

Ellie smiled sweetly. "I would never presume to lecture you about magic, Witch. Please return the courtesy."

"If we were talking about selling cookies or designing a freaking playground—"

"Enough!" Magnolia's voice was sharper than a ghast's talons. "Ellie's Gold Award project earned her a nomination for the Nobel Prize in Physics. If that's not good enough for you—"

"You're shitting me." The witch gaped at Ellie. "Gods, you guys have really been burying the lede. What was the project?"

"A study of the quantum mechanisms of Archon-induced mutagenic transformation," Ellie said. "I came up with it after my troop. . ." Her eyes filled with tears, and Magnolia patted her hand.

"It was groundbreaking work," the Clerk said. "And High Lord Dawson's contributions to *The Quantumnomicon* were superlative."

So *she* was the Dread Lord of IT's human co-author. Damn, Heather had some competition in the #LadyBoss department.

The Clerk waved a tentacle. "Please continue with your analysis, High Lord."

"Of course. Where was I?" Ellie traced her finger down a bulleted list of notes. "The dimple on the sphere is an activation mechanism. There's a time delay after the button is pushed, then it disrupts the quantum stasis bubble so the syntropium crystal can absorb entropy. The stasis bubble reseals, and the apparatus is inert."

"What would happen if we pushed the button again?" Chad asked. "Would that release what's stored in the crystal?"

"No," Ellie said. "It would just absorb more entropy. But the power supply is only designed for a single use, so the stasis bubble couldn't reseal. Theoretically, the hypersphere would sort of. . .melt back into regular spacetime, which would cause systemic, propagating dysregulation at a subatomic level."

"That's bad?" the witch guessed.

"Let's just say there would be a very big boom."

"One last question. . ." The witch clutched Keyser's Tamagotchi under the table. "Is it possible to undo what the spheres did?"

Ellie's ice-blue eyes softened. "I'm running some simulations. I hope to know more soon."

Soon. And in the meantime, Keyser grew less active by the day.

The witch took a sip of coffee to ease the tightness in her throat. She nodded to the Dread Lord of Human Resources. "You're up."

"I'll be out next Tuesday. I have a doctor appointment for my. . ." His crossed eyes darted toward the Clerk. "Ahem. I'm afraid my interviews have yielded no new insights."

The Clerk's answering glare was so fierce the witch almost felt sorry for him.

"Any progress on the IT front, Chad?"

"I don't know if I'd call it progress," he said, "but I've got updates. "A, um. . .source"—his eyes flicked to the witch—"confirmed that the financial trans-actions I've been seeing came from the mayor. She moved money from her general fund to the QT project, and she allocated resources to upgrade the electrical grid. What I *don't* know is why my system displays them every time I log in."

The Dread Lord sniffled and dabbed his eyes. "Ichagno would know, but he's. . .He's. . ." He fanned his face with both hands. "Magnolia, my candy bag!"

Magnolia rummaged in a canvas tote and tossed him a Snickers. He swal-lowed it whole, wrapper and all.

"Believe me, I miss him too," Chad said. "I could use his help. The County network is riddled with malware, but two programs are really *bugging* me." He raised his eyebrows, but no one took the dad-joke bait. "The worst is a program I call Whiteout. It does just what the name says. The screen goes white, and it deletes anything you have open. We've already lost some property records, vote counts from the last election—"

"That may have been. . .unrelated," the Clerk said.

"—and the entire top-secret archive."

"Roswell, JFK, the moon landing," the witch said. Magical contracts. Maybe information on the little white men and their little white weapons. "*That* archive?"

"Yep."

The witch spewed a stream of profanity so vile and thunderous, the belea-guered cone of silence emitted a shower of sparks.

After a respectful pause, the Clerk said, "And the second program?"

"It doesn't respond to commands, and it vanishes when I try to isolate it," Chad said. "It's like it doesn't want to be found."

The Dread Lord whimpered. "That reminds me of Ichagno."

"Sathach, what has gotten into you?" The Clerk's shroud fluttered with an irritated huff. "Lately, you weep at the drop of a—"

Chad's eyes widened. "What if the program *is* the Dread Lord of IT?"

"It certainly sounds like him," the witch said. "Antisocial. Shitty communicator. Never around when you need him."

Not that there's anything wrong with that.

"By the eyeless Idiot God, Mr. Chadwick might be right," the Clerk said. "Our Dread Lord of Solid Waste Management was transformed into a garbage chute. The witch's familiar is now a digital pet. It seems fitting the Dread Lord of IT would become software."

"And perhaps," Ellie said, "he took his attacker with him."

"Whiteout," Chad breathed. He grabbed Magnolia's legal pad and started jotting down notes. "If we're right, I might be able to communicate with him using the terminal."

"I have news too," Vera said.

She'd been so uncharacteristically quiet, the witch had forgotten she was there, but the Tamagotchi vibrated at the sound of her voice. Keyser's digital avatar gazed at Vera with lovestruck heart-shaped eyes. That little horndog. . .

"But first, I have something for each of you." Vera handed the witch a walkie-talkie and a charging cradle. She circled the table with a tote bag, distributing a set to each WTF member. "These are long-range radios. My neighborhood watch has been using them on patrol."

"My call sign is Rambo," the Dread Lord said.

Chad raised his hand. "Time Lord!"

Vera looked from the Clerk's shrouded form to Ellie's wheelchair. "Sorry, I don't have one for either of you."

"Thank all the gods," the Clerk muttered.

She shrugged and returned to her seat. "My team and I have been tracking the LWAs."

"What are LWAs?" Ellie asked.

"Little white Archons," Vera said. "They started out as little white men, but they've been changing. And their behavior has been increasingly bizarre."

The witch couldn't wait to see what counted as "bizarre" in Vera's book.

"Remember that big storm Sunday morning?" Vera asked. "I had a team out afterward, and we saw LWAs clearing trees off the road."

Chad frowned. "Why would they do that?"

"Because they're order incarnate," the witch said. *The Archonomicon* had said as much. "They can't stand a mess. Gods, they've been at it for weeks—reshelving books in the library, painting my office, getting rid of Big Roy's junkyard."

"A pathological obsession with neatness?" Vera rubbed her hands together. Her eyes glinted with a Discordian spark of mischief. "We can work with that."

CHAPTER TWENTY-SEVEN

Home Sweet Hell

N eighborhood Watch Surveillance Report Operative: Pumpkin Spice Heiress dispatched Team #3 to lure LWAs to Zone 6B in search of the enemy's base. Per Heiress's instructions, we tagged the skateboard ramp at Billington's Wood Park with an obscene drawing.

The witch snorted, picturing a group of soccer moms spray-painting a giant johnson.

Two LWAs arrived on the scene within minutes and commenced cleaning. We attempted to trail them, but they disappeared into a drainage tunnel near City Hall (possible underground lair?). Uggs has a mold allergy, so we fell back to Starbucks for lattes and an After-Action Review. Lululemon offered her twins' playroom as a trap for future ops.

She filed the report, propped her booted feet on her desk, and made a phone call.

"You have reached the voicemail of Dr. Christian Carcosa. . ."

The witch hung up. She'd been trying to call him for three days—ever since a shitty text exchange after the last WTF meeting. She read through the mess for the hundredth time.

WITCH
Lock down the QT.
WITCH
LWM might come for it.
CARCOSA
The little white men have harmed no humans.
CARCOSA

You seem to have forgotten who the true enemy of mankind is.

CARCOSA

Why do you continue to fraternize with the monsters who annihilated your people?

WITCH

LWM are the ones who hurt Keyser.

CARCOSA

You still believe that? Even after your assistant's so-called vision?

WITCH

Dude, she didn't do it.

WITCH

She swore a magical oath!

CARCOSA

Do not call me "dude," and OF COURSE SHE DID NOT DO IT.

CARCOSA

You were there. You already knew that.

CARCOSA

It does not mean she is innocent.

WITCH

Fuck off. I want the spheres back.

WITCH

You were wrong, btw.

WITCH

No containment field.

WITCH

Ellie D says it's quantum shit.

WITCH

And she's HUMAN.

CARCOSA

You trust the word of teenager over that of a highly regarded dimensional physicist?

WITCH

Basically.

WITCH

Where's YOUR Nobel nom?

CARCOSA

The Clerk could have put Ms. Dawson up to this, or perhaps it was your precious assistant.

WITCH

Don't be a dick.

WITCH

Humans have legit beef w/ Archons.

WITCH

But rn, they aren't the biggest threat.

WITCH

Hello?

WITCH

Do NOT ignore me.

WITCH

Answer your godsdamned phone!

Et cetera, et cetera. . .with no response.

The witch had to get those spheres back. They held the key to freeing Keyser. Typically, she'd use her power to snatch them, but the frigging things wilted her magical willy. It was more than a little concerning that Carcosa wouldn't give them back. And his tone was freaking her out. She'd never thought to ask what he planned to do with the QT, but if he whipped it out at the wrong time, he might play into the Swarm's hands. Or stubs or shit, whatever they had.

The witch longed to hit back at the Swarm and hurt them the way they'd hurt Keyser. Until the little white bastards discovered syntropium crystals, they and the Archons had been evenly matched. But according to *The Archonomicon*, conventional weapons of the projectile or slash-and-rend sort were useless. If only there were a way to level the playing field. . .

Her only idea was putting an Archon in a blender, which probably wouldn't go over well, and dunking an LWA in the resulting entropic soup. Or maybe they could get a firehose and spray the liquefied entropy—

Oh gods. The answer had been right in front of her all along. In her veins, to be precise.

Her *particular gift*. Za'gathoth had been right. She *was* a moron.

They didn't need a firehose.

They had a witch.

"Any luck with the Akashic records?"

"Yep," Vera said. "It's called the entropic strike."

"Yes!" The witch damn near dropped her BlackBerry doing a victory dance.

"Don't get excited yet. This is battle magic—very advanced, and very dangerous."

"Don't care." She pressed the phone between her ear and her shoulder and lit a celebratory Swisher Sweet. "Can you teach me how to do it?"

"I can try," Vera said, "but we'll need to go somewhere safe, entropically sealed. If you get this wrong, it could be. . ."

"Could be what?"

Vera made an explosion sound.

Not exactly reassuring.

Okay, entropically sealed spaces. . .

Well, Larry's Lazertag Emporium was out of the question. Screwing around near a mother sandworm was just asking to experience digestion from the other side.

Carcosa's lab might work, but he was being so squirrelly. Even if she could reach him to ask, it didn't feel right.

The witch knew of only one other place sealed against stray entropic discharges.

"We can go to the Witchery." The Tamagotchi vibrated, and Keyser pressed his paw against the screen. He knew better than anyone how hard this would be for her. She covered the tiny block with her fingertip. "Any chance you're free now?"

"We're actually waiting for you out front."

"Who's 'we'?"

"See for yourself."

Shaking her head, the witch ended the call. She stubbed out her cigarillo, grabbed her backpack, and locked up the office, wondering all the while who the hell was with Vera.

It'd better not be Pumpkin Spice.

She shaded her eyes with one hand and scanned the first row of parked cars. The strains of "La Cucaracha" echoed from a sleek silver Tesla, and a heavily bangled arm beckoned from the passenger window. As the witch approached, she saw two other figures inside—one in the driver's seat, and one in the back—but she couldn't make out their faces. She turned her attention to the car, the ass end of which was plastered with bumper stickers.

COEXIST, with each letter forming a religious symbol. (The Apple of Discord was notably absent.)

I'M WITH H(EATH)ER!

*PEACE * LOVE * HUMAN RESOURCES.*

The witch stopped dead, six feet from the Tesla. Oh, dear gods.

The freckled face of the Dread Lord's human suit appeared in the passenger window as he leaned over and waved. "Road trip," he sang.

She was hemorrhaging badassness merely standing next to this car. "Maybe this isn't such a—"

The rear window slid down. "Hey, Witch."

"Chad? What are doing here?"

"Vera told us you're working on some heavy magic," Chad said. "We figured a little moral support couldn't hurt. Magnolia said she wishes she could be here, but—"

"Did Vera mention this new technique could literally explode in my face?"

"I'm not worried."

"Seriously, Chad," she said. "You could get hurt."

His forehead creased with worry. "*You* could get hurt." Then his face relaxed, and he grinned. "But you won't. You've got this, Witch."

She opened her mouth, but she couldn't think of a single godsdamned thing to say. So she walked to the driver's side, opened the back door, and got in.

They drove in peaceful silence for all of five seconds.

"Let's do a few icebreakers to pass the time," the Dread Lord said. "How about Favorite Things?"

"I will self-immolate if you even try it."

"Would you rather"—Chad glanced at his phone—"have a mullet or a rattail?"

"Rattail!" Vera and the Dread Lord answered in unison.

Monsters.

"Definitely a mullet," the witch said.

Chad raised an eyebrow. "Really?"

"David Bowie rocked one. Of course, he was an Andromedan. I don't know if an earthling could pull it off."

"I know one who could." He passed his phone to Vera. "Your turn."

Vera read the prompt and waggled her eyebrows. "This is a good one. Would you rather—"

"We're here," the Dread Lord said, putting on his turn signal.

The witch's stomach—which had spent most of the drive fluttering like a punch-drunk butterfly—plummeted when she saw the cheery Crayola-colored sign that marked the gravel drive.

Welcome to the Tophet County Witchery!

The car fell silent as they approached a slate-gray three-story Gothic Revival. The house was tucked against the tree line of an old-growth forest and sprinkled with pinnacles, parapets, and lacy wooden bargeboards.

Home sweet hell.

Chad reached for her hand and gave it a squeeze. "You okay?"

The witch pressed her lips together, returned the squeeze, and got out of the car.

Walking through the front door took every ounce of self-control she had. When she'd left on her seventeenth birthday, she'd sworn never to return. So much for promises.

The enormous chandelier in the entryway provided only dim light, as more than half of its candelabra bulbs had burned out. Vera's heels echoed on the marble floors as she navigated the labyrinthine floor plan. Around every shadowed corner, the witch expected to see the branching limbs of Mother Mayhem's arborescent body or the glowing lamps of her eyes, but the Witchery's halls were deserted.

They stopped at the top of a tight spiral staircase that disappeared into a pitch-black hole. The witch whispered a word, and the lights came on in the chamber below. She took a deep breath and led the way downstairs. Unlike the rest of the house, the basement was entropically sealed. If the witch had lived with her parents, their magic would've counteracted hers until she was old enough to control her power. Given her parents' existential challenges (i.e., their extreme deadness), the Archons had to rely on different methods. They'd used curse breakers to infuse anti-entropic compounds into the foundation and walls so no errant magic could escape.

The Dread Lord hesitated at the bottom of the steps, his nervous eyes darting to cobwebbed corners. "What is this place?"

The witch traced her fingertips over the mahogany cradle where she'd slept as an infant. "This was my nursery," she said, looking up to meet his crossed eyes. "My playroom. My school. I grew up down here."

A trembling hand flew to his mouth. "I had no idea it was so. . ." His gaze traveled over the windowless cinder-block walls. "This is no place for—"

"Let's get to it." The witch walked to the edge of an industrial-strength containment circle chiseled into the rough concrete floor. She crossed her arms and looked at Vera. "Start talking."

Vera nodded and strode to the center of the ring. "We're here to prepare for our last stand." Her hair, which the witch would've sworn was pinned up in a vintage hairdo, flowed over her shoulders. The incandescent bulb dangling over her head cast shadows behind her that looked like great black wings. "Traditional weapons will be of no use in this battle, so we must rely solely on the witch."

"Jeez," Chad said. "No pressure."

Vera clasped her hands behind her back and began to pace. "The witch is also likely to be our enemy's primary target. From what my neighborhood watch has observed, we believe the LWAs' vision is keyed to order and disorder rather than light. Humans blend into the background entropy of this world, and the LWAs mostly ignore them. As long as we—"

"I apologize for interrupting," the Dread Lord said, raising his hand, "but I have a medical condition—"

Oh, here we go. . .

"—and I'm finding this very upsetting." His face rippled queasily. "I want to be supportive, Witch, but perhaps I should wait outside."

She shrugged. "Fine by me."

"No!" Vera stopped in front of the Dread Lord and planted her feet. "In a combat situation, would it not behoove you to have a thorough understanding of the witch's capabilities?"

The Dread Lord blanched. "How did you—" His eyes darted to the witch. "Ahem. I suppose, as the senior Archon on the WTF, I should—"

"We understand each other." Vera resumed pacing. "First, you need a lesson on the true nature of reality." She reached into her bag and pulled out a stone the size of her fist. "This is a solid rock, yes?"

"Looks that way," Chad said.

"But at the smallest level, it's not solid at all." She tossed it to the witch, who caught it with one hand. "That rock is made of unimaginably tiny particles that pop in and out of existence, that travel through time, that could be entangled with atoms on the other side of the galaxy. Disorder underlying seeming order." Vera stepped toward the witch and touched the center of her forehead.

The witch batted her hand away.

"Close your eyes and examine the rock with your third eye."

"Can we just get to the—"

"Look at the rock."

She rolled all three of her eyes but did as Vera asked.

After a minute of straining, the witch said, "It's a freaking rock."

"Try again."

She clenched her jaw and psychically squinted at the stone. Her view zoomed in as though she were falling *into* the damn thing. Solid rock became a grid of gray blobs, which became a murky cloud filled with luminous sparks, which became. . .something else. A kaleidoscope of multicolored light pocked with flecks of. . .of Presence that were there and not there at the same time.

The rock landed on her boot, and she yelped.

"It fell right through your hand!" Chad exclaimed.

"Okay, so the rock's not really solid." The witch kicked it away. "Now what?"

"Can you conjure lightning?" A jagged blaze struck the floor between Vera's feet, singeing a sooty smear on her stockings. "Good. Do it again but freeze it before it vanishes."

She spiked a jagged bolt of lightning from the palm of one hand and froze it in midair.

"Do the same thing you did with the rock."

"But I already know lightning isn't solid."

"Just look," Vera said.

The witch sighed and closed her eyes. With her Sight, she followed the forking branch to a tip and zoomed in. Only the tip wasn't really a tip—it forked again, and then again, and yet again. There was no end to it. No matter how closely she looked, there always another fork, always another branch.

"That pattern," Vera said, "is a fractal. Fractals have a property called self-similarity, which means they have the same shape at different scales."

The witch opened her eyes and looked at Vera. "Whatever you're trying to tell me, I don't get it."

"You're saying there's order within disorder," Chad said, "and disorder within order."

Vera clapped her hands. "That's it! And that dance between opposites. . .*that* is chaos. The LWAs are syntropic, which means they have an affinity for order. Witches and Archons are entropic, which means they have an affinity for disorder. But chaos—"

"I get that you're a priestess and philosophical shit is your jam," the witch said. "But we're five days away from global annihilation. Being here gives me the overwhelming desire to inflict grievous bodily harm. For the love of Lovecraft, could you maybe saunter toward the point?"

"Suit yourself." Vera braced her hands on her hips and looked around, surveying the contents of the basement. "Anything down here we can use for a target?"

The witch shrugged. "Like what?"

"That'll do." Vera strode to the far end of the room and grabbed a horrifyingly familiar object.

"Uh, that's pretty flimsy," the witch said, straining to keep desperation out of her voice. "Why don't I go upstairs and find something else?"

"No need." Vera stood the cardboard cutout up on its stand at the far end of the circle. "This is perfect."

"What *is* that?" The Dread Lord crossed the training ground and walked around the four-foot tall girl-shaped cutout, examining the figure's clumsily drawn face and yellow hair. He squinted at its hand-lettered T-shirt. "What does that say?"

"Vera, I want you to put that thing—"

"'My best friend,'" the Dread Lord read.

His words echoed through the basement, followed by a deafening silence.

"It was a, um. . .an art project," the witch said. "For school."

Glistening goop leaked from the Dread Lord's eyes. "This is the most heart-breaking thing I've ever—"

"All right, Vera, time's a-wasting!" The witch rubbed her hands together. "Let's do it."

The Dread Lord opened his mouth to say more, but Chad grabbed his elbow. "Come on, man," he said. "We should get out of the way."

The witch didn't look at them as they left the circle. She might not be able to look at them ever again.

"The first thing you need to do," Vera said, "is form the sacred K mudra." She raised her right hand, curled her pinky and ring fingers into her palm, and tucked her thumb between her raised index and middle fingers. "Like so."

"What's the sacred K?" the Dread Lord asked between damp sniffles.

"*K* is for 'Kallisti,'" the witch said as she positioned her fingers. "The Greek inscription on the Apple of Discord." She looked up at Vera. "Now what?"

Vera smiled. "Now the fun begins."

* * *

The witch fired a bolt of entropy at the grandfather clock she and Chad had dragged onto the training ground. It disappeared in a glittering cloud of dust. The Dread Lord of Human Resources watched the practice session in uncharacteristic silence, a pensive expression furrowing his baby-carrot eyebrows. She dropped her hands and fell to her knees as a wave of near-debilitating weakness washed over her.

"Entropine depletion," Vera said, rushing to her side. "Without your familiar, your storage capacity is much lower."

The witch groped for the Tamagotchi and looked up at Vera. "If the sphere sucked up Keyser's entropy, could hitting him with an entropic strike put it back?"

"I'm afraid not. You saw what happens when the strike hits home." Vera dug inside her purse and pulled out a Ziploc bag of cookies. She opened it and handed one to the witch. "Eat this. It'll help."

"You gave one of these to Magnolia after her fit, didn't you?"

"Yep." Vera offered a hand and pulled her to her feet. "Holy Chao snickerdoodles," she said. "Old Discordian recipe. They'll restore your entropine like that." She tried to snap but failed miserably. "Eat one now and save the others. You'll need them."

The witch shoved the bag into her coat pocket and took an immense bite. Before she'd even swallowed, she sensed entropine surging in her bloodstream. Gods, that felt good—tasted pretty good, too. The Tamagotchi buzzed. Keyser stretched a digital paw toward her cookie. She pushed the little piglet's food button.

"Make sure you keep them in that bag," Vera said. "It's infused with antientropic shielding. Without it, those cookies will draw LWAs like ghouls to a grave." She propped her hip against the witch's old arts-and-crafts table and crossed her ankles. "Speaking of beacons, when you use the strike, keep in mind that it will always hit the most syntropic target. That can get tricky in a combat situation."

"Seems like a healthy advantage to me."

"Perhaps," Vera said, with an enigmatic smile. "Witch, the time has come for you to join the Ordo Dea Discordia."

"I'm not much of a joiner. Thanks, but—"

"As above, so bolo." She loosened the string tie around her neck, slid it over her head, and handed it to the witch. "When the final battle comes, may the golden apple of this unsacred neckwear remind you that Discordia is always with you."

"Final battle?" she repeated. "Do you know something we—"

"Even when it seems all hope is lost, She is only a prayer away."

"Uh. . .thanks." She looped the bolo tie through the carabiner that held Keyser's Tamagotchi.

Vera nodded and glanced at her watch. "We've done what we came here to do. I'm on patrol in an hour. Ready to get out of here?"

"*Gods*, yes."

Vera nodded and walked toward the stairs, stilettos tapping on the concrete floor. The witch started after her, but a gentle hand on her shoulder stopped her in her tracks. She turned and met Chad's deep brown eyes, bracing herself for a dose of saccharine sympathy.

"Total legend," he said. "I knew you'd kill it."

She brushed imaginary dust from her shoulders. "All in a day's work."

"Look, I'm sure it was weird having us here," he said, stepping closer to her, "but I'm glad I came. I feel like I know you better, like I'm starting to *get* you. And I really want to—"

"Ahem," the Dread Lord said. "May I have a private word, Witch?"

She ground her teeth. "I'm in the middle of—"

"Yeah, man." Chad squeezed her shoulder. "See you outside."

The witch watched him climb the stairs, then turned to the Dread Lord. "What's up?"

"I think. . ." Beads of slime formed in the corner of the Dread Lord's eyes. He paused and tried again. "Ahem. I understand why you've always been so hostile toward me."

"Hostile is my dominant personality trait."

He smoothed the hanky wadded in one fist and dabbed his eyes. "Your childhood. . ." The Dread Lord shook his head. "This was wrong."

A reflexive wave of anger surged in her gut, but she choked it down with the last bite of Vera's magic cookie. "What's done is done. It doesn't matter anymore."

"It *does* matter." He wiped his eyes again. Viscous ooze hung in strings from the hanky. "After the Emergence, after the witches. . ." He took a deep, shuddering breath. "The Clerk said we should make it right, that we should raise you and bring you under our contract. We thought we owed you our protection."

Protection? What the tentacled fuck was he trying to say?

"We thought we were keeping you safe." The Dread Lord looked around the windowless basement. "But we only hurt you more."

He took her hand and opened his mind to her in a complete reversal of his previous mind-flaying attacks. She felt his guilt, his outrage, and by all hell's devils, his deep, sincere empathy.

The witch dropped his hand like a hot potato. She didn't have time for feelings—not when so much was at stake.

Not when invaders were coming to destroy her world.

Not when Keyser was counting on her to save him.

"I'm done with the past," the witch said. "It's time to kick some little white ass."

CHAPTER TWENTY-EIGHT

The Nefarious Agents of Order

The witch was spinning her wheels harder than the High Priestess of Peloton, and she'd gotten exactly nowhere.

Vera's neighborhood watch continued to lure the LWAs out, at which point the witch would roll in and deploy the entropic strike. That was the plan, anyway. But the little white shits weren't cooperating. They wouldn't come out when the witch was present. When she wasn't, they cleaned up messes, but all efforts to track them to their lair failed.

She'd also hit a brick wall investigating the Temple of the Evil Angel. The cult's private Meetup page was gone. Clicking the original link now brought up a group called Cooking with Cannabis, the organizer of which was none other than Ronnie Coffman. (And yes, the witch joined.)

Carcosa had totally ghosted her. In desperation, she attended one of Mitsuki's yoga classes to gather intel. According to his jilted wife, he hadn't been home in a week. Mitsuki suggested she hunt Carcosa down at his underground lab. The witch checked it out, but the doors to the bunker were padlocked shut. (The class hadn't been a total waste of time. Her third-eye Sight was now keener than a godsdamned eagle's.)

Heather was next up on her to-do list. As Dr. C's side piece, she should know how to find him. Naturally, the mayor had been out of the office both yesterday and today for "personal reasons." Based on her lack of response to calls and messages, Heather had joined her lover's anti-witch boycott.

She may as well try the lab one more time. Even if Carcosa wasn't there, she'd bet dollars to sticky 'nuts the spheres were. All she had to do was blow the doors off their hinges and search the place.

It felt good to have a plan.

Just as the witch stood to go, her desk phone rang. She glanced at the caller ID and answered. "Hey, Chad."

"I found the Dread Lord of IT," he said. "He's been in the County network all along. I haven't been able to communicate with him, but I'm getting close."

"Keep me posted."

"Will do. Any luck hunting down the LWAs?"

"Not yet. Oh, hey," she said, careful to keep her tone light, "have you seen Heather this week?"

"Nope. What's up?"

"I just. . .I need to ask her about something. High Lord shit."

Speaking of shit, she was starting to feel like a giant pile of it for hiding Carcosa's involvement from Chad and the WTF, but what else could she do? If the Clerk caught wind of his true aims with the QT project, he was a dead man—or he'd soon wish he was.

"If I hear from her, I'll tell her to give you a call."

"Thanks, Chad," the witch said. "Bye."

She glanced out the window at a perfect winter's day. A thick layer of cloud and not a ray of sun in sight. Her kind of weather.

Screw it, she was taking the broom.

From her bird's-eye view, downtown Asphodel looked. . .different. No nightgaunt nests. No rat-things scattering the contents of a dumpster. The bike path by the Catachthonic River ran in a rigidly straight line instead of forming the soul-eating sigil Tlyuth, and Kingsport Street's carnivorous trees had all been trimmed to uniform dimensions. Off to the west, the glossy white landfill glowed under the overcast sky.

The nefarious agents of order were definitely at work in Tophet County.

A convoy of Spectral Forces Hummers surrounding a covered flatbed truck roared by on I-666, heading back toward town. The witch flipped them the double bird—only slightly regretting it when she remembered Hank might be with them. A few minutes later, she descended upon the abandoned army base that housed Carcosa's bunker. The bunker's doors stood wide-open.

Something was finally going her way.

A troubling trend presented itself as the witch tromped down eleven flights of stairs. The walls shifted from industrial gray to pearly silver to eyeball-assaulting white. The buzz of entropine in her blood gave way to the beginnings of a headache, and the Tamagotchi buzzed as Keyser Söze started losing his everloving mind. As she neared Carcosa's lab, she heard a scuttling sound from inside, and the lights flicked off.

The witch had seen enough horror movies to know this was a bad idea, but. . .well, bad ideas were sort of her thing. She groped for the light switch by the door, flipped it on, and stepped inside.

"Dr. Carcosa?"

The Tamagotchi vibrated as Keyser lunged toward the rear corner of the cavernous space. Several immense pieces of equipment had recently been removed. Disconnected cords and partially disassembled machines dotted the center of the floor, and the walls were lined with. . .plexiglass bubbles?

No. Spectral Forces–issue anti-entropic shields.

Chad's mysterious equipment requisitions. Carcosa must've been using them to lower the background entropy around the QT.

The fluorescent bulb above the witch's head popped, fizzled, and went out as she approached a tall metal storage cabinet. She tried to charge up her shields, but her magic wouldn't respond inside this witch-proof cocoon. If she had any sense, she'd get the hell out of there.

The witch yanked open the cabinet's doors. She caught a flash of white under the bottom shelf and backed away. Her hands formed the sacred K, but no magic meant no entropic strike.

"Get your ass out here," she called. "Where's Dr. Carcosa? What did you do to him?"

Fabric rustled as the figure emerged. Her jaw dropped. Dr. Carcosa's skin was as white as snow. His facial features had been. . .blunted, smoothed, and he'd lost at least a foot of height. His clothes hung on him like a kid playing dress-up in his father's suit.

"The Swarm stormed my lab," he said in a flat, tinny voice. "They are formidable fighters, and they. . .They activated a sphere. I must have passed out." He stepped toward her, and she instinctively recoiled. "Everything was gone when I woke up—my computers, my equipment, the QT. They took it all. And now I am. . ." His eyes grew round in an almost cartoonish expression of bafflement. "What is happening to me?"

The Tamagotchi buzzed in her hand like a magic wand.

Dear gods. This was what happened if no highly entropic target was around to take the brunt of the blast: Dr. C was turning into a little white man.

"Were any Archons with them?" she asked. "Any humans?"

He shook his head, pressing stubby white hands to his temples. "I cannot remember."

Her theory had proven true. The LWAs planned to use the quantum tunneler to bring in their invading army. She had to find that godsdamned device, and she only had a little more than twenty-four hours to do it.

The witch scanned the floor, taking in the size of the QT's footprint. An Archon could teleport something that large, but not from here. Anti-entropic shields weakened them just as much as her. In fact, the reason Spectral Forces had them was for apprehending Archonic miscreants. Whoever took the QT would've had to get it topside the hard way.

She scanned the lab until her eyes landed on a huge metal sliding door marked with black-and-yellow caution tape. A large safety notice posted on the wall read *This elevator is for cargo only.*

A cargo elevator. That would do the trick. But once the LWAs got it to the surface, they'd need. . .

They'd need a freaking flatbed. She'd passed one on the way here, and it'd been traveling with a Spectral Forces escort.

"Someone in the government is working with these assholes," she said. "I just saw a Spectral Forces convoy escorting a truck. I'd bet my last bottle of Chicken Cock they had the QT."

"Someone in the government. . ." Carcosa looked up at her with his odd, flat eyes. "It's him. *Them.* Those metal bugs."

"What are you talking about?"

Carcosa began to pace, sending Keyser into fits of buzzing rage. "The Dread Lord of Information Technology summoned me about a month ago. He said the County needed to install a firewall to protect my data." Dr. C shook his oversized Ping-Pong ball of a head. "Ever since I gave him access to the system, nothing has worked properly."

But Chad had found a sphere in the Dread Lord's office, and it'd transformed Ichagno into software. Why would Ichagno help the very beings who'd attacked him?

Unless. . .

Magnolia had called him a loner. Now he lived in a digital world where he'd never have to deal with humans or Archons again. What if the Dread Lord of IT was behind the whole thing?

She had to warn Chad.

Shit, she had to tell the Clerk.

"I'll take this to the task force. We'll deal with Ichagno," the witch said. "You just. . .Just hang tight, okay?"

Carcosa shook his head, quaking in fear. "Witch, you must not tell them what happened to me. I fear the Clerk would—"

"I won't say anything." The less she said about her involvement with Carcosa, the better for both of them. She'd come clean if they survived the solstice.

The Tamagotchi twitched in her hand. Keyser was going for poor Carcosa like a hound of Tindalos after a tibia. Both his happy and hungry meters were close to bottoming out from the anti-entropic shielding. She had to get him out of the lab, but first. . .

She spun, looking around the ransacked room. "Where are the spheres?"

"They were here," he said. "In this cabinet. The attackers must have taken them."

Gods, could a witch catch a freaking break?

Once they were topside, Keyser ate enough food to restore him to a stable condition, though he still prowled his screen restlessly. The witch pulled out her BlackBerry, but. . .who to call first? The most urgent issue was finding the murder machine. If Za'gathoth was right, the Swarm would invade on the solstice, which was *tomorrow*. And now they had a quantum tunneler to rip open a door for their army.

The Clerk. She had an all-access pass to the County government. She could find out where they'd taken it. The witch called her direct office line. No answer. She tried the Clerk's BlackBerry. Again, no answer.

Who else could track a Spectral Forces convoy?

Hank answered on the first ring.

"Witch, how are you?"

"Screwed six ways from Sunday," she said. "And I need your help. I just saw Spectral Forces Hummers escorting a flatbed truck on I-666. I'm pretty sure they stole Carcosa's murder machine. I need to know who sent them and where they went."

"I'm not supposed to—"

"Hank, this is WTF business. The Clerk will cover for you with the Sheriff."

"Okay, let me see what I can find." She heard the clack of a keyboard, followed by a sharp intake of breath. "Our transport log says the mayor requisitioned that truck from the County fleet a few hours ago and sent her personal security team to pick it up."

"Are you sure it was her?" the witch asked. "Could someone else have used her account?"

"Let me pull up the requisition and take a look."

It couldn't be Heather. She was knocking boots with Carcosa. She wouldn't do anything to hurt him. . .would she?

Besides, the Dread Lord of IT was haunting the network. He was the ghost in the godsdamned machine. Maybe he'd used her credentials to—

"Says here she made the request in person."

The witch sat in stunned silence. She tried to come up with an explanation, but no amount of mental gymnastics produced a scenario that exonerated Heather, which meant. . .

Gods below, Heather was in on it.

"You there?"

"Yeah," the witch said. "Yeah, I'm here. Thanks, Hank."

She hung up and slid her BlackBerry into her pocket.

It looked like Tophet County's queen bee had joined the Swarm.

CHAPTER TWENTY-NINE

Dee's 'Nuts

The witch showed up five minutes early for the General Session, intent on cornering Heather. If necessary (and she kind of hoped it was), she'd beat the truth out of her.

Instead of answers, the witch found a disgruntled knot of humans and Archons milling around outside the hearing room. She scanned the crowd for the Clerk, who still hadn't answered her calls or texts. But no one was pissing or puking, and she saw no sign of a white shroud.

Her eyes followed the curve of Achartho's scorpion tail as he threaded through the press of bodies and read a sign taped to the door. His wings snapped in irritation as he turned and left. The witch pushed her way to the front, already suspecting what she was going to see.

Today's meeting of the Tophet County Executives is canceled. The Executive Hearing Room is currently inhospitable to Archonic personnel. The mayor's office is arranging for remedial action and apologizes for the inconvenience. Per my email this morning, departments may submit updates to MayorChadwick@TophetCounty.gov.

Email. *What* email?

The witch checked her BlackBerry. Sure enough, the most recent of her seventy-two unread messages was from Heather, sent at 8:51. . .and it didn't have that little note at the bottom that read *Sent from my BlackBerry.* That meant Heather was in her office.

Tama-gotcha.

Ninety seconds later, the witch blew open the door to the mayor's suite with a gale-force wind. "Is she in there?"

"You just missed her." Heather's aide whipped out a pocket comb to smooth his mussed hair. "Mayor Chadwick said she had some errands to—"

"Bullshit."

She strode to the office door and rattled the handle. Locked. The entropic strike reduced forty pounds of oak to a swirl of glitter, producing a satisfying gasp from a certain secretary. But Heather wasn't there.

The witch sat down at the mayor's desk and flipped through a planner so aesthetic, it resembled a scrapbook. Yesterday morning was marked with a heart. Inside the heart were the words "three months."

Heather and Carcosa were a thing, so the heart had to be their anniversary. . .unless Heather was cheating on the guy she'd cheated on Chad with, which would be some shady *Real Housewives of Tophet County* shit. Carcosa was hit with a sphere yesterday and turned into a little white man. Surely Heather wouldn't have marked that occasion with a heart on her calendar.

She looked around the mayor's office. Offensively tidy white desk. White leather chairs. White rug. The decor echoed the newly remodeled hearing room, which was *inhospitable to Archonic personnel*. And witches. For reasons she could not fathom, Heather had hitched her wagon to the Swarm's little white star.

Her eyes drifted back to the heart on her planner. But sacrificing her true love to the little white menace would require a deep reservoir of straight-up sociopathic cruelty. As Mother Mayhem said, the one thing you could count on people to do was disappoint you.

The only entry on her calendar for today was the General Session, and that was crossed out with a perfectly straight line. Heather's laptop was gone, and the desk was empty, save for a lamp and the landline phone. She reached under the desk and slid out the trash can, but all it contained was a coffee cup from Dee's.

If you're not there when she opens at ten, you miss out. Now that I'm the mayor, Dee lets me in early.

The witch glanced at her BlackBerry. It was twenty past nine. If she grabbed her broom and left now, she might beat Heather there. It was worth a shot.

The witch ate the last piece of her sticky 'nut and moaned in near-orgasmic pleasure. Keyser Söze watched longingly from the screen of the Tamagotchi. She licked her fingers and checked the time—9:42. Heather should be here any minute. In the meantime, she had a new text from Hank.

I've been thru Dispatch records 3x. No location for that flatbed.

Sorry I couldn't help. Have a super day! :)

Damn. She had only hours to find the QT. . .and the missing spheres.

The bell above the door gave a merry jingle. The witch glanced up just as Heather walked in, sporting a strikingly ugly Christmas sweater and matching leggings.

"I'll have my usual, Dee," Heather said. "A half dozen sticky 'nuts and a large—"

The proprietrix's eyes darted in the witch's direction, and Heather turned.

The witch waggled her fingers. "Morning, Mayor Chadwick."

"Oh. . .hi there, Witch." Heather rummaged in her purse and pulled out her BlackBerry. "So nice to see you. I'm just, um, picking up my 'nuts." She flashed a desperate grin, fingers flying over the tiny keyboard under the device's screen. "I'll settle up with you tomorrow, Dee, if that's okay."

"I know what you're up to, Heather."

Her blue eyes widened, and she ran a reflexive hand over the golden mushroom of her hair. She forced a painfully fake laugh. "I can't imagine what you—"

"Sit."

"I'd love to, but I can't stay."

"I'm trying to conserve entropine in case I need to save the world tonight, but I can spare enough for a creative curse if you insist." The witch snapped her fingers and sparks flew.

Heather grabbed her box, walked to the table, and sat.

The witch gestured toward the front door. The lock snicked closed, and a metal grate rolled down.

"Hey!" Dee said.

"I strongly suggest you wait in the back."

For an entertaining moment, the witch thought she'd get to do some cursing after all. Then Dee shrugged and disappeared through a door marked *Employees Only*.

The witch lifted the lid of Heather's box and grabbed one of the pecan-topped, syrup-soaked rings. She bit into it, and her eyes damn near rolled back in her head. "Gods, these things are fan-freaking-tastic."

Heather watched, lips pursed, as the witch deposited the rest of the pastry on a napkin. "What do you want?" she asked.

"You stole the murder machine."

Heather narrowed her eyes—not the expression of an innocent woman.

"And you're working with the Dread Lord of IT," the witch said. "Or should I call him the Evil Angel?"

Heather's expression morphed from caught-red-handed to confused. "The Dread Lord of IT's not in our cult."

Our cult.

So the cult was involved in all this, and Heather was a member, but the Dread Lord of IT wasn't their leader. . .or Heather didn't *know* he was. Cults didn't always share the full story with their members. Maybe they'd modeled their revelatory system on Scientology's pay-to-play Xenu scam, and she hadn't bought her way to the top yet.

"Tell me, Heather," the witch said. "Why are you helping the Swarm?"

"What swarm? I have no idea what you're—"

"The little white men."

Heather held up a hand, palm out. "Just let me explain."

"Howard Phillips fucking Lovecraft," the witch said. "How could you do this to someone you're supposed to love?"

"*To* him?" Heather said. "I'm not doing anything *to* him." She leaned toward the witch, her expression fierce. "I'm doing this *for* him." To the witch's horror, Heather's eyes filled with tears. "I'm doing it for our child."

"For your. . ."

The stupid puffy heart on that desk calendar. *Three months.*

Heather was pregnant.

"How does this help your baby?" The witch shook her head. "These little white assholes want to—"

"You don't understand." Heather's eyes lit with the spark of religious fervor. "The Archons don't belong here, Witch. They're the embodiment of pure disorder, and our universe is about to shatter under the strain. I've watched it happen over and over in my nightmares. If we don't act now, our world will implode. Every living thing—including the love of my life *and* my baby—will die."

"Heather, the only threat to this universe is the little white men. They want to—"

"They want to save us," she said, "to restore the natural order."

"Order isn't natural!"

"And when they're done, it'll be safe for—"

"Safe?" the witch repeated. "You unleashed these things on the father of your child, and you're talking about *safe?*"

"We should be on the same side." Heather's voice was an ardent whisper. "You despise the Archons. Sathach told me you wanted nothing more than to get out of your contract so you can. . .I don't know, go be hateful somewhere else."

"Yeah, I want out of my contract, but that doesn't mean—"

"He also told me your probationary period ends on the solstice."

The witch's mouth hung open. Suck a sticky 'nut. One way or another, tonight's astronomical event was going to screw her over.

"Nothing to say?" Heather asked. "No clever retorts or snide comments?" She shook her head. "I'd have thought you, of anyone, would understand a strong woman going after what she wants."

"But you're hurting people."

"Hurting people? Oh, you care *so* much about the well-being of others," Heather said with a bitter laugh. "You tortured Chad for years, just for doing his job. Sadistic, spiteful little tricks you pulled just to amuse yourself."

"That's not what I—"

"At least when I hurt people, I do it for a better reason than my own enter-tainment." Heather grabbed her box and stood. "I do it for the greater good."

"You're ending the freaking world," the witch said. "I was just joking around."

"Joking?" Heather snapped. "You gave him jock itch. Hilarious. You melted his favorite *Doctor Who* figurine. Soooo amusing. Oh, and you cursed his wife, triggering the end of his marriage." Bright spots of color burned on the witch's cheeks. "You're not funny, Witch. You're mean."

The front of the store exploded in a shower of glass. A Spectral Forces bat-tering ram protruded from the wreckage. A six-man squad of the Sheriff's finest cleared the door and forced their way in, anti-entropic shields raised.

Heather smiled. "That's my ride."

The witch had a handful of options, none of them good: (1) Attack those jackbooted jackals. . .but with their shields raised, she couldn't do any real dam-age. (2) Take Heather out. . .but gods dammit, she couldn't hurt a pregnant woman. (3) Stand here like a dumbass and watch the villain escape.

She stood there like a dumbass, watching helplessly as the men parted to let the mayor through.

In Heather's shoes, she'd head for the QT and beef up her defenses. If the witch followed them, she could regroup and figure out what to do next. She shouldered her backpack and held out a hand. Her broom zipped across the room, landing in her palm with a satisfying *thwack*. She straddled it and lifted off, but three Spectral Forces shitheads had formed a barricade blocking the door. Tires shrieked outside as the Hummer peeled out.

Up and out, then. She flipped the men an enthusiastic bird, phased the ceil-ing and roof to permeability, and kicked off. She shot up like a Roman candle.

Not one, not two, but *three* identical Hummers roared down Main Street, lights flashing. At the next intersection, one turned right, one veered left, and one continued straight.

The machine was huge. Heather couldn't just take it back to her place. It needed a cargo door and an industrial-strength power supply. Carcosa's original lab, the one he'd had before the underground bunker, was already rigged for the QT, and one of the Hummers was headed toward the Cat U campus. She followed it. The vehicle circumscribed a spiraling path around the Dimensional Physics building before parking in the lot behind the annex. Heart pounding, the witch tipped her broomstick into a dive.

The driver's door flew open, and a Spectral Forces officer climbed out and ran for the building. The witch flew a low, slow circle around the Hummer, peer-ing in the back windows. It was empty.

She'd lost Heather's trail.

CHAPTER THIRTY

Third Base

The witch eased her broom onto the narrow balcony that circled the belly of Tophet County's water tower. She gripped the railing and looked out over downtown Asphodel, considering her options.

Carcosa was becoming that most dreaded and feared of creatures—a little white man. Heather was in on the Swarm's invasion plan, and she had a contractually bound Spectral Forces squad at her beck and call. The Dread Lord of IT was sentient software that could gain access to any online platform and pop up through any networked device. And Chad was trying to chat with him.

Even thinking Chad's name made the witch's face burn with shame. The worst part was that Heather's recitation of pranks was only the tip of a ten-year iceberg. She'd done much worse.

Mother Mayhem always told her there are two kinds of entities in this world: predators and prey. And Mother said she was luckier than other humans because, as a witch, she got to choose her role.

And she had, hadn't she?

Heather was right. She was a bully—a mean-spirited, sadistic jerk. She liked Chad—*really* liked him—and she'd treated him like shit.

The witch knew how to be angry. She knew how to be afraid. She knew how to be cruel. She did not know how to be a friend. She'd grown up in isolation, raised by a monster, and it showed.

Well, she could hate herself tomorrow—if there *was* a tomorrow—but for now, she had to put her self-flagellating bullshit on hold. Heather could call

Chad at any minute, or the Dread Lord of IT could get to him. He was in real danger. For once, she could actually *help*.

The witch pulled out her BlackBerry and called him. He answered on the first ring.

"Witch?"

"Hey, Chad. I've got news."

"So do I."

"Mine's about Heather."

"Is she okay?"

"She's in on it, Chad," the witch said. "She's been working with the Swarm all along. I just came from Carcosa's lab. She sent a bunch of the LWAs over there to attack him, then her Spectral Forces security detail stole his device."

"But you said Heather and Carcosa were—"

"They were. Heather seems to think they still are." The witch paced the circumference of the galvanized steel walkway, staring through the metal grate at the ground more than a hundred feet below. She closed her eyes and forced herself to say the rest. "She told me she's doing this for their. . .their baby."

"Their baby?"

Was she imagining it or did his voice hold a note of wistfulness?

"That doesn't explain why she'd attack him," he said. "Did she try to recruit him and he said no?"

"No clue, but the solstice happens in"—the witch lowered her BlackBerry and checked the time—"twelve hours. That's when the Swarm will make their move, and now they have the QT. Hank tried to find out where her goons took it, but—"

"Was it by chance under a tarp on a flatbed truck?"

"How did you know?" The witch stopped pacing and stared out over Asphodel, as if Chad's words might summon the godsdamned thing. "Did you see it? Where is it now?"

"I didn't see it in person," he said. "Listen, I just made contact with the Dread Lord of IT. I'm still working out the kinks on the comms program, but it's really him."

"He's in on it too, Chad." She stared up at the heavy gray clouds, watching as fat snowflakes began to fall. "Carcosa told me—"

"Ichagno just sent me a video file," Chad said. "It's drone footage of a Spectral Forces convoy escorting a truck."

Well, *that* was a blow to her rock-solid conviction. If Ichagno was the Evil Angel, he wouldn't torpedo his plan by sending video evidence to Chad.

"Where'd they go?"

"That's just it. The footage doesn't make sense. I can't tell where it—"

"Bring me over," she said.

He sent her a meeting invitation with the location set to his office. The witch grabbed her broom and accepted the request. She ghosted through a quantum hellscape and resolidified with a nauseating swirl of suckitude.

Chad poked his head around a row of three monitors and beckoned for her to join him behind his desk. She dragged a chair over and sat down.

"Let's see this footage."

He rested his hand on the mouse and clicked play.

The video drone flew above the convoy, matching its speed. They watched as the flatbed drove across a snow-dusted field directly into the side of a hill. It didn't slow, didn't stop, didn't crash. It just disappeared.

"Could they have used the murder machine to make some kind of. . .of wormhole?" the witch asked.

"Not without electrical power."

Chad's BlackBerry buzzed. He shook his head and turned the device so she could see. A black chat box occupied the center of the screen. The neon-green text inside was a string of symbols that seemed to writhe and twist on the page.

"The Dread Lord of IT keeps trying to talk to me, but I can't read it."

"I can." The witch unzipped her backpack and pulled out her trusty pocket dictionary of barbarous tongues. "That's Archonic script. Give me a second." She glanced at the symbols to identify the root glyphs, then paged through the dictionary until she'd found the correct entries. "He says to look closer."

Chad cued up the video, enlarged the image and slowed it to a frame-by-frame walkthrough.

"Look at that!" He scrolled through the milliseconds before the flatbed disappeared. A glow of light—normal light, not the octarine netherlight of Archonic teleportation—gradually appeared at the hillside. It started at ground level and grew taller as the frames progressed. "I think it's something like a garage door. They opened it as they approached, and what we're seeing there is light from inside a—"

"Tunnel," the witch said. "At a General Session a few weeks ago, Y'ggarlos was bitching about unauthorized tunneling that caused a sinkhole."

"Where?"

"Near Dunwich Park."

He cued up the video and played it again. He leaned closer and squinted at the screen. "Is that the sacrificial softball field?"

"I'm not really a sports fan, Chad."

He ran the footage again, freezing it when the convoy was twenty feet from the hill.

"It is." Chad pointed to the lower left corner of the screen. "That's the third-base altar." He stood and tapped a map of Asphodel mounted on the wall above his desk. "This green wedge is Dunwich Park." He slid his finger to the other side of the circle and drew a box. "There's the town square, and right in the center of it is—"

"The Fathomless Abyss," the witch said. "The solstice is tonight, and Heather's throwing a party on the bridge over the Abyss." She stood and shouldered her backpack. "Za'gathoth created the Archons' nest in there because it's already a dimensional thin spot. I'm betting that tunnel leads straight to the Abyss. They'll set up the QT underground and trigger it tonight."

Chad frowned. "That makes sense, but then. . .why would Heather throw this party? Why invite all the Archons to be there, ready to meet the little white men when they come through?"

"So the Swarm can hit them with spheres," the witch said. "Then the Archons will be off the board, and this world will be theirs for the taking." She stood and grabbed her broom. "I'm heading to the tunnel to destroy that device."

"Hold up, Witch," he said, grabbing her hand. "We don't know how the QT works. We shouldn't do anything until—"

"I don't need to know how the godsdamned thing works to break it."

Chad squeezed her hand. "Then I'm coming with you."

Like hell he was. Heather's Spectral Forces goons would be guarding the murder machine. Chad was a lot of things, but "battle-hardened warrior" wasn't one of them.

"You can't," the witch said, groping for a compelling reason. "You have to. . .to update the WTF. They need to know what's going on."

"I'll do it on the way."

"And you need to track down the Clerk. I've been trying to reach her since yesterday morning." The witch made herself release his hand. "Send her that video. Tell her you're in touch with the Dread Lord of IT. Oh, and see if she has any idea who the real Evil Angel might be."

"Witch, promise me you won't—"

"I'll be careful," she said. "Just get a hold of the WTF."

"I'm trying." Chad clicked his mouse, glaring at his monitor. "What the. . ." He looked up at her. "I'm locked out of my account."

The witch propped her broom against the wall, frowning. "You were just using it. Something must be wrong with your computer."

He picked up his BlackBerry and touched an icon. "Nope," he said. "It's the account. I can still unlock my BlackBerry, but everything linked to my County profile is disabled. Calendar, email, messaging, phone—all of it." He tapped the screen a few times. "I don't know what's. . .Hold on." He looked up at her. "The Dread Lord of IT's still here. Check this out."

Chad tossed her the BlackBerry. A new line of text had appeared in the chat box.

The witch translated it as quickly as she could. "He says the mayor has deactivated your account."

"Try yours," Chad said.

The witch huffed an impatient sigh, but she pulled out her BlackBerry and tapped the Mail icon.

Account suspended.

"Gods dammit." She returned the useless thing to her pocket. "If she did it to both of us, twenty bucks says she hit the whole team. But how would she know—"

"The scheduling software." Chad shook his head. "She's a system owner. She can see everything, even private meetings. Once she knew you were onto her, she must've checked your calendar. If she saw a series of private meetings with the same people. . ."

"She's trying to cut us off."

"And doing a good job of it." Chad raised his hands in a gesture of helplessness. "How can I get in touch with the WTF?"

"Get *him* to do it," the witch said, pointing at the chat box.

"He can't. My BlackBerry's cut off from the network, and he's in my BlackBerry."

"Use your landline."

"I don't know anyone's numbers, and I can't access the internet to look them up."

"Is there, like, an operator we can call or something?" She scowled at his desk phone. . .and there was the answer, sitting in its charging cradle.

Vera's godsdamned walkie-talkies.

Chad followed her eyes and grinned. "You're a genius."

"Guilty as charged."

"Can I keep your dictionary?" he asked. "I think I can write a translation program if I upload the base glyphs."

"Have at it." The witch tossed it on his desk. She shrugged out of her backpack, pulled out her radio, and turned it on. "Call me on this thing if you learn anything new. I'm heading over to the tunnel." She clipped the walkie-talkie to her waist, then grabbed her broom and straddled it.

"Be careful," Chad said.

"You too."

With a flick of her wrist, the wall phased to mist. She kicked off and soared out into the open air.

A burst of white noise crackled from her bag.

"Attention, WTF. This is Time Lord. We have a situation."

CHAPTER THIRTY-ONE

Silent but Deadly

The witch hovered six feet above first base at the Dunwich Park softball field. Muddy tire tracks cut brown gouges through the snowy grass to a steep hill, where they abruptly disappeared.

An illusion was at work here. It wasn't Archonic tomfoolery, nor was it tech-nomancy. This was magic. . .*her* magic. And the only illusion she'd made in recent months was for a certain Spectral Forces officer named Deputy Woods. He must've joined Heather's personal team after his Jonah-esque time in the belly of the Unseen Creeping Horror.

"Time Lord, this is Rambo," a voice squawked. "What's your twenty? Over."

The witch silenced her walkie-talkie. She couldn't afford to telegraph her location with the mayor's minions on the loose.

She squinted into the swirling snow, searching the field for a telltale lump. A boxy protuberance squatted on top of the pitcher's mound. She hopped off her broom and used the stick to smash the illusion generator to magically useless bits. The image of a grassy knoll shimmered and dissolved, revealing an oversize garage door built into the hillside.

The witch cued up a curse to blow the door into metal shrapnel, but she hesitated before pulling the proverbial trigger. No telling what lurked on the other side. She should probably wait for Chad and the others. . .but it was almost two o'clock. The mayor's Darkest Night celebration started at six, and the solstice would hit at 10:51. Time was running out. Waiting for backup wasn't an option, but the witch could operate in stealth mode. Rather than the explosive curse she'd planned, she'd use the entropic strike to clear her path.

Silent but deadly.

She shaped the sacred K and fired, and the door dissolved in a swirl of glitter. Looming before her was the opposite of a dark, creepy tunnel. Blinding white light flooded from the opening.

The witch charged up her auric engines and willed her broom to top speed. The second she crossed the tunnel's threshold, the broom dropped like a stone. She hit the floor at an angle, and the handle smacked the bridge of her nose with a staggering crack of pain. Blood poured over her lips and chin.

Son of a star-steed, that *hurt*.

She grabbed her broom and jogged back to the field. Her magic was useless in there, which meant her only weapons were sheer bloody-mindedness and a dangerously acerbic wit. Less than ideal.

As a burst of entropine reknitted the bones of her nose, she stowed her broom under a bench in the coach's box. She'd didn't waste her energy activating its protective forcefield. Who'd dare to come out here? Heather had told the whole damn town the field was infested with Shoggoths.

The witch walked back to the mouth of the tunnel. Stepping inside that white void felt like fingernails scraping along the chalkboard of her soul. The Tamagotchi buzzed with Keyser's distress. It took everything she had to stay upright as she descended. She kept her eyes glued to a gray smudge at the bottom of the hill—the dark at the end of the tunnel.

A flicker of motion snagged her attention. A group of white blurs with flailing tendrils streaked toward her, each carrying a weapon. The LWAs were moving too quickly for her to make out what they held, but she caught a flash of bright blue. The witch braced herself as they barreled toward her.

And around her.

She turned and watched as they raced to the mouth of the tunnel. Then she heard the *ksh ksh ksh* of a spray bottle as they used Windex to scrub away drops of blood and smears of dirt.

Order. They required perfect order.

She wiped her hand over her still-oozing nose and skidded down the steep slope, smacking her bloody palm against pristine walls every few feet.

More LWAs appeared, streaming around her to clean up the mess. With her entropine level in the shitter, they didn't even register her presence.

A metal grate, half-raised to admit the little white Archons, spanned the circumference of the passageway. The witch ducked under it. She pushed a large red button on the wall to close it behind her, trapping the LWAs on the other side.

The chamber beyond the tunnel was carved from solid rock. As she'd feared, the space opened onto the Fathomless Abyss. Carcosa's quantum tunneler sat at the edge of the chasm. The machine's body was a long cylinder formed of steel ribs interspersed with glass tubes. Bundles of cables as thick as her arm snaked from the device to a control panel. A gleaming rod protruded from one end of the cylinder into the vertical shaft of the Fathomless Abyss. A metal plate with five spherical cavities covered the other end. Familiar white spheres occupied two of the depressions, but the other three were empty.

The witch stumbled toward the murder machine, weak from entropine depletion and low blood sugar. All she'd eaten in the past twenty-four hours was one and a half sticky 'nuts. How freaking stupid would it be for the world to end because she hadn't packed a snack?

Except. . .Holy Chao, she *had*. Vera's magic cookies.

She fished the bag from her coat pocket, pulled one out, and took a huge bite, scanning the cavern as she chewed. A row of trailer-size machines lined one wall of the cavern. Folding tables on the opposite wall held thick binders and a few toolboxes. The witch walked to the closest table and opened a notebook. The pages were filled with incomprehensible equations and complex technical drawings. It would've been nice if there were an arrow pointing to a critical mechanism, helpfully labeled *Achilles' heel*, but alas. . .

When in doubt, go with a brute-force assault.

She stuffed the rest of the cookie into her mouth, feeling the pleasant hum of entropine in her blood. Now she had more than enough juice to—

The Tamagotchi buzzed with a triple burst of alarm. The witch spun to see a squirming wall of LWAs packed against the grate. Its metal bars groaned under the strain. It wouldn't be long before they broke through.

Time to get this show on the road.

As she drew closer to the QT, she felt more than heard the buzz of high-voltage electricity. The hairs on her arms stood on end. The godsdamned murder machine was *on*.

Gods, she hoped the WTF hadn't misjudged. If the Swarm didn't have to wait for the moment of the solstice, Earth was about to take one up the—

A deafening crash drew her eyes back to the tunnel as a Spectral Forces Hummer plowed through the grate. Behind the vehicle, the tunnel swarmed with LWAs frantically cleaning up tire tracks.

The witch was prepping a defensive spell when the driver's door flew open, and Deputy Eye Candy leaped out. Chad climbed out the passenger side, and the back seat disgorged Vera, Magnolia, and the Dread Lord of Human Resources. Hank yanked open the SUV's rear cargo hold, and Chad crawled in. The Dread Lord spotted the witch and bustled toward her at a furious waddle. The poor bastard couldn't haul ass in a bucket.

Just as a wave of relief washed over her, two more Hummers roared into the cavern and slammed to a halt with a shrill squeal of brakes. A three-man Spectral Forces team burst out of each one, then an officer helped Heather from one of the vehicles. Her team formed up in a semicircle around her, anti-entropic shields raised. The mayor had those poor schmucks under contract, which meant they'd fight to the death if she ordered it.

Muscles straining, Hank and Chad lowered a fat metal tube about three feet long to the stone floor. Beelzebub's tan banana. . .a ball lightning cannon! Spectral Forces used it to stun Archonic offenders. When Heather caught sight of the weapon, she broke and ran, shouting a command to her guards as she charged toward the QT. Chad lowered his end of the cannon to the ground and followed at a dead run.

LWAs poured in from the tunnel, but they didn't attack the witch. They formed up in two knots, clambering on top of each other to form two thick pillars of writhing little white Archons.

Not pillars. . .*legs.*

Before the witch could even begin to make a plan, they'd grown into a not-so-little white man at least fifteen feet tall. Only one LWA did not join the massive construction. Its tentacles lashed like whips as it scrambled toward the QT. Vera and Magnolia rushed to intercept it as the panting Dread Lord shuffled to a halt next to the witch.

"I will fight beside you," he said, loosening his tie.

After everything she'd done over the years, after two rains of fanged toads—

"Help me!" Heather screamed. "Get him off me!"

The Dread Lord's face rippled, and he lunged in Heather's direction. The witch grabbed his elbow and hauled him back. Heather's security squad was already responding to her cry. Anti-entropic shields clattered to the stone floor as the Spectral Forces team drew their conventional sidearms. Six ugly black Glocks were now aimed at Chad.

"No!" Heather shouted, waving her arms frantically. "Don't shoot!"

The witch threw up a spherical forcefield around Chad a split second before one of the men fired.

The floor shuddered, and she tore her eyes away to see an immense white body lumbering toward her.

"Megawhite," the Dread Lord whispered.

The witch spun to face him. "Last chance to run for it."

"There's nowhere left to run, Witch."

"Then let's see this badass battle form."

The Dread Lord shrugged out of his suit coat. "Ahem," he said. "In battle, I take on the form of what I fear most, so—"

"Just do it!"

Megawhite took another earth-shaking step toward them. The witch levitated and floated out in front of the Dread Lord to provide cover. She shaped the sacred K and fired a bolt of entropy.

The gargantuan creature trembled under the impact, its surface rippling as individual LWAs disintegrated.

"My baby!" Heather shrieked.

The witch whirled, but the mayor seemed to be in no immediate danger. Chad stood between her and the guns, and the Goon Squad wouldn't shoot if there was a chance of hitting her. A sparking ball of blue fire tumbled into the uniformed men, knocking them over like bowling pins. Score one for the ball lightning cannon.

Something shoved the witch hard, and she plummeted to the floor. Above her, a gust of wind whooshed past as Megawhite swiped the air where she'd hovered a split second earlier. She looked up and saw the Dread Lord's battle form in all its glory. At first, her mind couldn't process it. She squeezed her eyes shut and opened them again, just in time to see him hit Megawhite with the entropic strike. The Dread Lord's battle form was *her*.

Their eyes met, or she met her own eyes, or—

"Are you okay?" he asked.

"*I'm* what you most fear?"

Megawhite lunged toward them. The Dread Lord turned and fired, but not before an enormous fist struck him with a glancing blow.

Heather's shrieks continued in the background. "No! Let me *go*, Chad!"

The witch hit Megawhite again, drawing its attention as the Dread Lord got to his feet. She was burning through entropy at a devastating rate, and she couldn't exactly stop mid-battle to eat another cookie.

Megawhite opened its mouth and roared. It sounded the way the tunnel made her feel—a million nails scraping down a million chalkboards. The Dread Lord soared past her, casting a barrage of entropic strikes. Clouds of glitter flew as individual bodies vanished from the monster. A few LWAs dropped off and wriggled toward the safety of the tunnel, but the rest of the godsdamned things just kept coming.

It swung at her again, but the Dread Lord streaked in front of her. The punch connected and sent him flying. Tentacles burst from his—her?—back and cocooned his body, breaking his fall. He tumbled to a halt by Hank's Hummer, and his limbs uncurled to reveal his natural form, limp and still.

The witch screamed and fired on Megawhite. Its gaping maw yawned open.

Maw. *Mouth*. That thing had a mouth, and she had cookies with enough entropine to turn an accountants' convention into Burning Man. She slid her hand into her pocket and grabbed one. When the monster roared its defiance again, she tossed a Holy Chao snickerdoodle down its throat.

The monster lurched to a halt. It trembled, then swirling colored light blazed from its midsection as it dissolved into a swirl of sparkling smoke. LWAs ripped free of its extremities and streaked toward the tunnel like rat-things fleeing a sinking ship.

Heather escaped Chad's hold and sprinted across the cavern, screaming about her baby. Her Spectral Forces guards roused, yanked to consciousness by her stark terror. They staggered to their feet and raced after her. One of them caught her by the shoulders and dragged her toward one of their Hummers. The combat situation must've activated the mortal danger clause of their contract. They'd get her out of harm's way whether she liked it or not.

Heather strained toward the Dread Lord as they passed his inert body. He was already wounded, but the mayor seemed intent on finishing the job. Her mindless minions were stronger, though. She shouted commands as a pair of guards forced her into the back seat.

Tires screamed as Heather's Hummers peeled out of the cavern, leaving two of her team behind. One of them walked toward the Dread Lord, and the other headed for the QT. The witch hit the guy advancing on the Dread Lord with a concussive blast of air that sent him cartwheeling into the stone wall.

"Witch," Vera screamed, "we need help!"

A rogue LWA had its tentacles wound around her arms. Magnolia tugged at the knot of limbs, but she lost her grip and rolled backward. One of the thing's flailing tendrils stretched and strained toward the control panel.

It was trying to trigger the device *now*.

The witch had just enough juice left for one entropic strike. If she missed, that was it. Game over.

"Don't fire!" Magnolia's voice was shrill with panic.

Vera and the LWA lurched to one side, giving the witch a clear shot at the QT. She had to take it. But as she fired, the struggling pair stumbled and fell. A blinding glare blazed when the entropic strike hit home. When it dimmed, the witch cracked open her eyes.

The electric hum of the QT continued unabated. The murder machine was totally unharmed.

CHAPTER THIRTY-TWO

Juggling Balls

Impossible. The witch *had* to have hit that godsdamned machine. It should be nothing but a cloud of glittery dust.

The LWA must've fallen in the path of her strike and taken the brunt of its impact. But with that little shit out of the way, maybe Vera could. . .

Where the hell *was* that woman?

"Vera?"

The witch sprinted for the QT, but Chad tackled her before she'd covered even half the distance. Gunfire cracked as she slammed to the ground so hard she bounced. Her diaphragm cramped painfully, and she wheezed and struggled to breathe. After an endless moment of agony, she managed to suck in a trickle of air.

"Woods, don't shoot!" Hank shouted. "We just want to—"

The officer fired again.

Chad untangled his limbs from hers and patted her cheek. "Are you okay?"

"Is Hank. . ."

He glanced over his shoulder. "He's fine. I think it was a warning shot. Heather must've ordered that guy to protect the quantum tunneler."

"Vera. . ." Her voice was a rough whisper. "We have to. . .find her. . ."

Magnolia knelt next to Chad. Her face was dirty and streaked with tears. "She's gone."

"Gone where?"

Magnolia's eyes darted toward the mouth of the tunnel. "We need to get out of here."

"But they can still use the QT," the witch said. "We have to—"

Tires squealed on the stone floor as the Hummer shrieked to a halt less than ten feet from where the witch lay. Through the open driver's-side window, Hank shouted, "Get in! The LWAs are coming back!"

"But—"

"Witch, we don't have time for this," Chad said. "Heather's guard will let us leave, but if we try to go near that machine, he'll shoot to kill." He jerked his head toward the tunnel. "And neither you nor the Dread Lord are strong enough to fight what's coming."

"I'm fine." The witch tried to stand, but her legs collapsed under her. Between entropine depletion and momentary oxygen deprivation, she was as weak as a larval ghast.

"I've got you." Chad scooped her up and carried her to the far side of the Hummer. He eased her onto the bench seat next to Magnolia, then climbed in.

Hank stomped the accelerator, and the Hummer slewed. He spun the wheel hard to the left and sped toward the fallen Dread Lord.

"Hurry!" Magnolia yelled. "They're almost here."

The witch craned her neck to peer at the tunnel. It was crawling with LWAs.

Hank slammed on the brakes, nearly hurling her into the front seat. Chad jumped out and opened the back hatch, and Magnolia rushed to the heap of tentacles lying limp on the concrete. Chad and Magnolia got their arms around the bulging mass at the center of the pile and wrestled the Dread Lord into the Hummer's cargo hold.

Chad slammed the hatch. He and Magnolia dove into the backseat just as LWAs spewed into the cavern. Before they'd even closed their doors, Hank revved the engine, and they shot into the tunnel. White bodies bounced off the windshield as the Hummer roared up the steep incline. They caught air as he cleared the top. Then they were bumping and skidding across the field through driving snow.

"Sathach, are you all right?" Magnolia asked, her voice shaking. "Sathach?"

Oh, gods, the Dread Lord had saved the witch's life, and now he was—

"Just exhausted," he rasped, his voice thick and slurred.

"And the. . .Is your. . ." Magnolia sounded every bit as confused and incoherent as the witch felt. She pressed her lips together, then tried again. "Are you sure you're not hurt?"

"Not hurt. Have to. . .rest."

"Thank Discordia he's okay," the witch said.

"Okay?" Magnolia repeated. She barked a harsh laugh. "Absolutely nothing is okay." She glared at the witch. "Whose side are you on, anyway?"

The witch recoiled. "What did *I* do?"

But before she'd even finished speaking, the awful truth skewered her heart like a barbed tentacle.

She's gone.

Vera. Oh, great goddess. . .

She'd warned the witch when she introduced the entropic strike: *Keep in mind that it will always be drawn to the most syntropic target.*

What was more syntropic than an LWA? When she'd fired, one of the little white bastards had Vera tangled in its tendrils like the Sacred Meatball of the Flying Spaghetti Monster.

"Is Vera. . ." The witch closed her burning eyes. "Oh, gods, she's dead."

Magnolia's eyes widened. "That's not what I—"

"The LWA was going to trigger the QT," the witch said, hot tears spilling down her cheeks. "I couldn't just let it. . .I had to do something. I had to—"

"It was reaching for the emergency shutdown switch," Magnolia said.

"But. . .But why would it do that?"

"The Swarm can't teleport, Witch. The ones who are here are stuck, and their only way out is the quantum tunneler." Magnolia shook her head. "They wouldn't risk a failed attempt. That's why I said not to fire."

"Vera died for nothing?" the witch asked.

"We can't be sure she's—"

"I killed her for *nothing*?"

"It was a horrible accident, Witch," Chad said. "We all know that. You were aiming for the device, and Vera fell. There's nothing you could've done."

"I wasn't talking about what happened to Vera." Magnolia's voice had lost its brittle edge.

"Then what the hell are you talking about?"

"This whole time, you've been—"

Chad held up a hand. "Let me tell her," he said. "Please."

Magnolia wiped tears from her cheeks, then nodded and turned to look out the window.

"The Dread Lord of HR had an electronic copy of that dictionary you gave me," Chad said. "I used it to embed translation software in my chat program so we could talk to Ichagno." He paused, staring down at his hands. "Witch, he told us Dr. Carcosa is the one who brought the sphere to his office and activated it."

"What?" There had to be a mistake, a misunderstanding. "No way. Carcosa's been working with me."

"Ichagno told us that too," Chad said. "Before he got stuck in my BlackBerry, he had access to everyone's data—emails, calls, texts, all of it. He said—"

"He said you've been feeding information to Carcosa since the very beginning." Magnolia met her eyes with a challenging glare. "He was your expert, wasn't he? The one you consulted about the sphere from the landfill?"

"He's a physicist, and he already had a County clearance," the witch said, hating the defensive whine in her voice. "I thought I could trust him."

"Yeah? Well, I thought I could trust *you*." Magnolia's lips curled in a small, sad smile. "Looks like both of us were wrong."

"Carcosa's been using you for information," Chad said. "I know you don't want to believe it, but it's true. The Dread Lord of IT tried to warn me. That's why he's been showing me those transactions. Until I made the chat program, all he could do was point me toward Carcosa's trail."

The transactions. Transfers from the mayor's general fund to E&I and the university partnership. "Does this mean Heather and Carcosa were—"

"Yep," Chad said. "They've been working with the Swarm all along."

It just didn't make any godsdamned sense.

"But they attacked him yesterday," the witch said. "They hit him with a sphere, and now he's turning into a little white man."

Magnolia frowned. "That can't be—"

"Carcosa begged me not to say anything. He was afraid of what the Archons would do to him if they found out."

"That's not possible, Witch," Magnolia said. "Remember the vision where I saw a man juggling five balls?" She held up her hand, fingers spread wide. "The Unseen Creeping Horror"—she folded down her thumb—"Keyser Söze, the Dread Lord of IT, the Living Flood, and the Yellow King." She'd ticked off a digit for each incident, leaving a raised fist. "None left to use on Carcosa."

"Then your vision was wrong."

"My visions are never wrong," Magnolia said. "The day I saw the Tamagotchi, Vera told us she ran into Dr. Carcosa on her way in. And he was waiting outside the Clerk's office when I had the Frozen vision."

"But that doesn't mean—"

"Don't you see? I was picking up *his* desires, *his* immediate future."

"He's the County's liaison to Cat U, Magnolia. He's in and out of County offices all the time."

"I've been wondering what was going on with Dr. Carcosa," Hank said. "I was at a couple of his early progress meetings with the Clerk, way back when the QT project first started. He doesn't even look like the same guy."

Well, the witch could explain that. Heather had gotten her hooks into him and remodeled him from the ground up. Only. . .

Heather told her they'd started dating before the election, before the witch got drafted into High Lordship, but Carcosa had still looked like an Einsteinian mess at the witch's first General Session. It was only later that he'd changed.

What could've possibly happened to. . .

Oh no.

She'd happened. This had all started after the night she observed Carcosa's experiment.

"Hank," the witch said. "In those early meetings, did Carcosa know why the QT wasn't working?"

"He said it didn't have enough power to make a stable gateway," Hank said. "He could get it working for a split second, but then the portal collapsed."

The murder machine earned its name by racking up a long list of casualties. Eleven lab rats, two rabbits, and a custodian—all turned into "marble statues," according to Ronnie. What if the quantum tunneler was keyed to the Archons' home universe? The Swarm had drained it of entropy. If the QT had broken through for even an instant, it would've exposed the test subjects to the entropic equivalent of hard vacuum.

"I just never dreamed Heather was capable of something like this," Chad said.

Dreams.

Keyser had awful dreams before he was attacked. So did the Unseen Creeping Horror. And Carcosa said the idea for his device came to him in a dream. The Mindless Mother told her some humans could visit the Dreamlands while asleep. If the Swarm had invaded the Dreamlands, they could've used dreams to seed the idea for the QT in Carcosa's subconscious mind.

Gods, the witch had been so blind. She'd never stopped to wonder how the little white assholes terrorizing Tophet County had gotten here in the first place.

"Heather sent me to observe one of Carcosa's tests about a month ago, and I. . .I did something." The witch gripped the Tamagotchi as the full implications of her actions settled over her like a weighted blanket of shame. "I thought if I was syntropic, like a curse breaker, I could get out of my contract with the Archons. When Carcosa powered up the QT, I converted my entropine to syntropine. But the process started severing Keyser from me, so I pushed all that energy away and. . ."

"You think it stabilized the gate long enough for the little white men to come through," Chad said.

The witch bit her lip and nodded. "Hank's right," she said. "Carcosa has changed. The first time I saw him after the experiment, he looked like a different man. I thought it was because of his, um, relationship, but he was in the room with the QT that night."

"What relationship?" Magnolia asked.

Chad furrowed his eyebrows. "Witch, what are you saying?"

"I think one of those things got pulled into Carcosa. I think he's been a little white man all along." The witch forced herself to meet Chad's eyes. "I guess what I'm saying is it's all my fault."

CHAPTER THIRTY-THREE

The Community Repository of Torture Implements

The Hummer marinated in thick, uncomfortable silence as Hank pulled around behind a nondescript brick building surrounded by a chain-link fence. The gate that had once barred external entry had long ago been removed, and the guard station stood unmanned. A sign, faded by three decades of sun and weather, read *National Guard Armory*.

Whatever was in there, it damn sure wasn't weapons. Who needed armed forces when the world was ruled by a de facto tentaclarchy?

"What is this place?" Chad asked.

"It's the Community Repository of Torture Implements," Hank said. "The way I've heard it, when the Archons first, um. . ." His eyes darted toward the back of the Hummer, where the Dread Lord still lay unconscious. "When they liberated humanity, they thought we'd be a bunch of pain-worshipping sado-masochists based on what they'd seen of our culture. They created this place as a community resource, but it never really took off." He shrugged. "I figured we needed somewhere off the grid to hide out and come up with a—"

Chad's stomach growled loud enough to drown Hank out. "Sorry, man. I haven't eaten all day."

The witch, who was physically ill with guilt and shame, swallowed a surge of rising bile.

"I'll order food," Magnolia said, sliding her personal cell phone out of her pocket. "I'm going to head inside and crank up the heat."

Chad watched her walk across the parking lot, then turned to check on the mass of tentacles in the cargo hold. "Speaking of heat, we need to get the Dread Lord out of the cold."

"It'd be a lot easier to move him if we had a dolly or something," Hank said. "Let's go take a look, Chad."

The witch sat numbly in her seat, staring at the Tamagotchi where Keyser Söze was imprisoned. . .because of *her*.

"Are you coming?" Chad asked.

The witch shook her head.

He closed the door and left her without a backward glance.

Well, as much as they must hate her, she hated herself even more. She'd opened the door for the little white men. She'd given Carcosa a detailed explanation of exactly how she'd done it. She'd told him what Keyser was to her, that he was her. . .What had she said?

Oh, yes. Her magical battery.

Keyser gazed at her from his tiny screen.

"I'm sorry," she said, stroking his pixelated cheek. "I'm so sorry."

Yep, the witch had given Carcosa everything he needed to carry out the Swarm's grand plan. She'd shared her suspicions with him, and he'd manipulated her—kept her chasing after that godsdamned cult when the real villain was right in front of her.

No. The *real* villain was the face she saw in the mirror every morning.

She hadn't meant to. . .to hurt Vera, but intentions were worth fuck all when someone was dead. The world's last witch should know that better than anyone.

She watched as Chad held the door open and Hank wheeled out a large, flat utility cart. As they approached, the witch slid out of the back seat and closed the door. *Discordia,* please *let the Dread Lord be okay.*

"Go inside and get warm," Chad said. "Hank and I have got this."

But she stayed where she was. They rolled the cart around behind the Hummer, opened the cargo hatch, and eased the Dread Lord out. He moaned miserably as they wheeled him toward the building. He'd said he was just exhausted, but what if he was wrong? What if he was mortally wounded? She hadn't seen any obvious injuries, but what she didn't know about Archonic anatomy would fill the Fathomless Abyss.

Three months ago, she'd have sworn on the *Principia Discordia* that she'd do a victory dance if she saw the Dread Lord of Human Resources weak and helpless. But he'd risked his life for her when they were battling Megawhite. If the WTF hadn't shown up when they did, if he hadn't been willing to fight beside her, the LWAs would've overwhelmed her. She imagined dozens of little white tentacles winding around her neck, crushing the Tamagotchi to plastic shrapnel. Hell, they could've *killed* her.

The witch couldn't stop replaying a greatest-hits list of her bad behavior over the past couple months. Chad, shivering in a snow-filled office. Magnolia, worried and disappointed when she learned the witch had relinquished custody of the first sphere. Hank, bellowing an Irish drinking song as she dragged him to the Bridge of Sighs. The Dread Lord, assuming his battle form and placing himself between her and Megawhite. Vera, vanishing in a blaze of light.

She was nothing but a fuckup. A selfish, mean-spirited, incompetent fuckup.

The WTF would be better off without her. Maybe she should grab her broom and fly until she ran out of entropine—take herself off the playing field so she couldn't cause any more damage. She even whispered the words to summon it, but she was too weak.

Too weak to run.

Too weak to face the fallout of her failures.

She opened the Hummer's door and climbed into the back seat, then leaned her head back and closed her eyes. Maybe she'd freeze to death and save them all the trouble of—

The door opened, and the witch's eyes flew open. Chad slid in next to her and closed the door. He rubbed his hands together, his breath frosting the windows with white clouds.

"Is this a one-witch pity party, or can I come too?"

A flame of anger sparked in her chest, but the icy wind of self-loathing blew it out. She was too damn tired for this. "Just go, Chad."

"Nope."

"What do you mean 'nope'?"

"I'm not going inside without you."

"Then I guess you're not going inside." She huddled deeper in her coat and pulled the hood down over her face.

"So it's like that, huh?" His voice held a snap of anger. "You're just going to leave the rest of us to deal with this while you. . .what, take a nap?"

The witch sat up straighter and met his eyes. "You want me to come in there with you?" she asked. "You want me to help? Just look what my *help* has done so far. I'm a total piece of shit."

"You're not—"

"I've fucked things up in every possible way."

"Ain't that the truth."

"Yes, I. . ."

Oh. He'd agreed with her. Not what she'd been expecting or, to be perfectly honest, hoping for.

"Now it's your job to unfuck it." Chad shifted in the seat so he was facing her. "You messed up royally. You made shitty decisions. You kept secrets, and you couldn't bring yourself to trust the people you were supposed to lead."

"Is this your idea of a pep talk?"

"But you know what I've learned about you over the past couple of weeks?"

She fixed a sullen glare on the floor between her boots. Enough of this armchair-psychologist bullshit.

"You push people away because you're scared."

Rude, she could see. Even cruel, though she hated to admit it. But chickenshit? Never.

"Scared of who?" she asked. "The Clerk? Sure. The Sheriff? Yeah. That just proves I don't have a death wish. But the rest of you? Even on your *best* day, not one of you could—"

"You're scared of being rejected," he said. "Scared of being abandoned."

"Oh, please."

"You spent your childhood in total isolation, Witch. I saw it with my own eyes, and. . ."

Oh, gods help her, he was getting choked up.

"You never learned how to make friends, how to *be* a friend." Chad rested a hand on her shoulder. She made a half-hearted attempt to shrug it off, but it stayed. "You pull pranks on the people you like the most. You make mean jokes at their—our—expense." He shook his head. "I'll be honest. It hurt me for a long time."

The witch looked up and met his eyes, which shone with unshed tears. "I'm sorry," she whispered.

"I know," he said. "Know what I think?"

She gave her head a minute shake.

"I think it's your way of testing people, of feeling them out. Will they leave you if you don't behave? Will they walk away if you disappoint them? Or will they stay no matter what?" He squeezed her shoulder. "I'm here to stay, Witch. We all are."

Her throat tightened, and her eyes burned. "No, Magnolia hates me."

"She's hurt and angry, and she has every right to be, but she doesn't hate you."

"And Vera. . ."

"Vera was with us when the Dread Lord of IT told us who attacked him," Chad said. "She wasn't mad at you. She called Carcosa a lying cabrón and said she'd rain the wrath of Discordia upon his worthless ass." He shivered. "And for a minute there, Vera was. . .indescribably terrifying. Don't tell anybody I said this, but I might've peed my pants a little."

The witch snorted. Laughed. Collapsed into body-racking sobs.

"Aw, come on, now," Chad said, pulling her in for a hug. "Bring it in, asshole."

The witch stiffened automatically at the unexpected embrace, but it felt so good to be held. He'd seen her cry before, and he hadn't treated her any differently, hadn't lost respect for her. Some part of her knew it was safe to let go. She melted into his arms and wept.

"We're stronger together, Witch," he said when her tears had slowed. "Better together." He released her, pretending not to notice when she wiped her nose on his sweater. "You look like shit, by the way. What happened to your face?"

"Whacked my nose with a broomstick."

Chad shook his head. "You really are your own worst enemy."

Chad led the witch through the deserted building. Humming, motion-activated lights flicked on as they walked, marking their passage. He stopped in front of a door labeled *War Room* and opened it. She followed him inside.

"Holy shit," she breathed. "This place looks like it hasn't been touched since the Emergence."

"I don't think it has."

The WTF had set up shop in a military command center dating back to humanity's last great war. Chad drifted past her and walked along a row of workstations lined with dusty monitors, moldy coffee cups, and yellowing stacks of paper. Whiteboards covered the opposite wall, with what looked like battle plans and troop movements sketched out in dry-erase marker. Yarn-ball-looking blobs marked the positions of senior Archons, with rows of tiny *X*'s arrayed around them to represent human soldiers and little pointy hats for witches.

Hank stood in front of a large corkboard on a wooden stand, examining a maze of red string wound between ball-tipped pushpins—exactly the same setup as in her palace of memory. He turned and looked at them, a wide grin dimpling his cheeks. "It's like those boards detectives use to solve murders," he said. "There's a detailed map of Tophet County—maybe we could use it to plot things out." He started unwinding the string, muttering about hidden patterns.

The witch opened her mouth to point out that they already knew exactly where the problem was and what they needed to do. But she didn't have the heart; he was having so much fun. Instead, she searched the space for the Dread Lord. His tangled body rested on the cart, which was parked in a back corner of the room, where Magnolia hovered by his side. She shoved her folded coat under his. . .Well, under some part of his anatomy, then she stood, patted her pocket, and glanced at her iPhone.

"Food's here," Magnolia called.

Chad threw up a hand. "I'll grab it."

To her surprise, the thought of food made the witch's mouth water. But as she watched Magnolia tending to the Dread Lord, her hunger edged toward nausea again. She needed to get her ass over there and apologize, but she was. . .

Gods dammit, Chad was right. She was scared.

With a herculean effort of will, she forced herself to cross the room. Magnolia looked up at the sound of her footsteps.

"How's he doing?"

"He's very weak," Magnolia said. "He had no business fighting with his. . .medical condition."

"What *is* his condition?"

"It's not my place to say." She returned her gaze to the Dread Lord. "But I'm worried about him."

The witch bit her lip. Was there anything she could do?

The Tamagotchi vibrated, and she unclipped it from the carabiner and checked the screen. Keyser Söze pointed at his open mouth, then rubbed his belly. She pushed a button, and cookies appeared in his food bowl.

Gods, *cookies*. She still had a few of Vera's edible entropine bombs. Eating one had helped Magnolia after her fit. It was worth a shot. She unzipped her coat pocket and pulled out the bag.

The witch offered one of the remaining two cookies to Magnolia. "Can you get him to eat this?"

"Isn't that one of Vera's cookies?" Magnolia asked. The witch nodded. "And you want to give it to Sathach?" Her eyes filled with tears as she took the treat. "Witch, I—"

"Oh, for fuck's sake, just give it to him."

Magnolia took a step toward the Dread Lord, but she hesitated. "He's in a fight-or-flight state right now. There's no telling what he'll do when I wake him up. We need a way to. . ." Her voice trailed off as she looked around the room. "I'll be right back." Magnolia jogged to one of the wall-mounted whiteboards and removed something from the metal tray. As she walked back toward the witch, she flicked her wrist, extending a telescoping hand pointer. "This'll do."

Magnolia gestured for the witch to back up, then tapped the bulbous swell of the Dread Lord's body with the pointer. His fanged mouth stretched open, and he shrieked in fury. She tossed the cookie into his yawning gullet. His cry cut off as though she'd muted him. He collapsed back onto the cart, chewing contentedly.

"Do you think he'll be okay?" the witch asked.

"I do." Magnolia's emerald-green eyes met hers. "What about you? Are *you* okay?"

"After everything I've done, after Vera. . ." She shook her head. "Why do you still care? Aren't you furious with me?"

"I'm not *not* furious, but I know you didn't mean for any of this to happen." Magnolia shrugged. "You're my friend, Witch. Of course I care."

CHAPTER THIRTY-FOUR

Fake News

H eads up, Witch!"

A foil-wrapped package hurtled toward her face with the desperate force of a Hail Mary pass. She caught it, then sat down at a conference table and unwrapped her meal: Mile High Clubs' famous Reuben. Her favorite.

Why was a frigging sandwich making her tear up like a politician on a post-dick-pic apology tour?

An earsplitting squeal sounded from the corner where the Dread Lord was recovering. Magnolia left his side and sprinted toward the table.

"Pickles," she panted. "I need all the pickles!" She snatched the dill spear that lay next to the witch's Reuben.

"I wanted that!"

"Sorry," Magnolia said, circling the table to collect every crispy wedge. "Sathach needs them. He's still weak, and. . .and vinegar has a restorative effect on Archons."

Well, he *had* saved her life. That had to be worth a pickle or ten.

Magnolia carried the napkin-wrapped pickles back to the corner, stopping just out of tentacles' reach. The next time the Dread Lord opened his mouth to issue a scream of hanger, she tossed the parcel into his tooth-rimmed maw. His cries transitioned into the wet, snuffly sounds of feeding.

It was almost enough to put the witch off her meal. She gazed at her sandwich.

Scratch that. Nothing could stand between her and this work of art. From the way Hank and Chad were shoveling down food, she wasn't the only one who felt that way.

Once everyone had eaten, Hank circled the table with a trash can collecting garbage. "I'm heading to the Sheriff's office. He needs to know Heather's gone rogue. She's got a squad of Spectral Forces with access to weapons and supplies. We can't afford to have those guys running around Asphodel."

"Be careful," the witch said. "The Sheriff's dangerous."

"I've been on the force for twelve years. I'm pretty good at dealing with him by now." Hank flashed his best Ken-doll smile. "Otherwise, I'd be. . .unemployed." He tossed his keys in the air, tried to catch them, and accidentally kicked them across the room. "You guys stay safe."

"Good luck, man," Chad said.

The witch checked the time on her otherwise-useless BlackBerry. "We need to get back to the Abyss and shut down the QT."

"We will," Chad said, "but let's talk things through first. The Swarm only has one shot at opening a gate, and they have to wait for the solstice. You already took out a bunch of their. . .their soldiers, but they've still got a few dozen LWAs, Heather and her guards, and Carcosa. If we can draw some of their forces elsewhere—"

"Look, I'm all for making a plan," the witch said, though she emphatically wasn't. "But the whole godsdamned county's gathering on the bridge for Heather's stupid party. We don't want all those innocent people directly over the murder machine. We should. . ." Her voice trailed off as the final piece of Carcosa's plan clicked into place.

Carcosa had plugged two spheres' worth of Archonic entropy into the QT. She could only think of one reason for that. He was planning to convert all that entropy to syntropy, just as she'd done the night the LWM came through. While prepping for her own attempt, she'd learned the process could cause a massive energetic discharge—and those calculations had been based on her body's natural reserves. The spheres held exponentially more.

"We should what?" Magnolia asked.

"Clear the area around the Abyss," the witch said. "Carcosa's going to use the spheres to boost the QT's power. If shit goes sideways, Tophet County might be kissing its tentacled ass goodbye."

Magnolia drummed her fingers on the tabletop. "What about the emergency alert system?"

"The only people with access are the Dread Lord of Fire and Rescue, the Clerk, and the Sheriff," Chad said.

The Living Flood was currently an ice cube, the Clerk was unreachable, and the Sheriff drank people. (But hopefully not Hank.)

Magnolia's eyes widened. "Social media!" She pulled out her personal cell phone. "I'll post it on Facebook," she said. "Witch, you hit Nextdoor."

"I don't have either of those."

"Twitter? TikTok?"

"I have Tic *Tacs*."

"You don't have any social media at all?"

"Gods, no," the witch said. "I don't even have a personal phone."

"Chad?"

"Heather made me model her unisex leggings line on Instagram Live," he said. "The first thing I did when she filed for divorce was delete all my accounts."

"We'll use mine." Magnolia tapped an icon. "There's a Tophet County Facebook group. I'll start there." She tapped furiously at the screen, reading aloud as she typed. "Stay away. . .from the Fathomless Abyss. . .tonight. . ." She paused, eyebrows furrowed. "What reason should I give?"

Good question. The citizens of Tophet County were used to rolling with some pretty unbelievable shit, but telling them to skip a free party because little white men were threatening imminent dimensional gentrification might be a stretch.

Chad stroked his divorce beard. "Try this: 'An unstable energy source has been identified in the Abyss. County experts advise evacuating the area.'"

"Perfect." Magnolia typed the message and clicked post. Then she copied it and posted the same text on Nextdoor and Twitter. "That should do it."

Her iPhone chimed.

"What's that?" the witch asked.

"Someone commented on Nextdoor." Magnolia tapped an icon and read the message. "You've got to be kidding me. 'As the Supreme Maglite of the Tophet County Illuminati, I can confirm this is nothing more than a plot by the Reptilians to ruin the Darkest Night party. They ruin *everything*. And they eat babies.' What on earth is wrong with—"

Her phone chimed again.

"Another comment?"

She nodded. "Facebook this time. This one just says 'Fake news.'" Another chime. "'The storm is coming. Enjoy the show.' What does that even mean?"

"Anthony's wiener," the witch muttered. "What it means is people are so thickheaded, they can't distinguish between life-saving information and their own bullshit conspiracy theories."

"Back to the drawing board," Magnolia said. "Um. . .let's see. Chad, you said the Clerk is an authorized user on the emergency alert system, right?"

He nodded.

"I'll give her a call."

"Good luck with that," the witch said. "I haven't been able to reach her for days."

Magnolia held the phone to her ear. Her brow furrowed as she ended the call. "The Clerk knows the invasion is happening tonight. She'd answer no matter what." She shook her head. "Something's definitely not right."

"Nothing is right at all!"

The witch turned at the sound of the Dread Lord's voice. He wore a brand-new human suit that sported multiple piercings and a large facial tattoo. Instead of his usual Brooks Brothers wardrobe, this skin still wore what she could only guess was its previous occupant's attire. A psychedelic Stüssy T-shirt stretched over his rotund midsection, his lower half wore acid-washed skinny jeans with more slashes than denim.

"Gods below," the witch said. "You've been right here the whole. . .Where in the hell did you *get* that? You look like a middle-aged hypebeast."

"It's an Elder thing," he said primly. "You wouldn't understand. And I'll thank you not to comment on my appearance. Tophet County policy clearly states—"

"Speaking of appearances, you neglected to mention that your battle form was me."

"Yes. Well. . .Ahem. I didn't think it would ever come up."

"You're telling me that, of all these eldritch terrors, *I* am what you most fear?"

He shuffled his feet, avoiding her gaze. "You make such cutting remarks!"

The witch rushed him. He took a few wary steps backward, but he wasn't quick enough to escape the violent hug she hadn't known she was going to give him.

"You saved my life," she whispered. "I'm glad you're okay." She released him. "Asshole."

Cheeks flaming, the witch returned to her seat. If Chad or Magnolia said a godsdamned word. . .

They didn't.

"I'm not an asshole." The Dread Lord sat down, crossed his arms on the table, and rested his forehead on his wrists, sniffling morosely. "And I'm not okay at all."

"What's wrong?"

"You know." Magnolia arched her eyebrows in a knowing expression as she patted the Dread Lord's back.

The witch raised her hands in a *what the fuck are you talking about?* shrug.

Heather, Magnolia mouthed.

Ah. They'd been pretty tight, hadn't they?

She should try to comfort him, try to be a. . .a good friend.

"I, uh. . .I know you must be disappointed in Heather." The Dread Lord moaned at the sound of her name. "In my experience, all politicians are manipulative dickheads. I'm sure the next mayor will be—"

"But she betrayed our love," he wailed.

Chad's eyebrows shot up so high, they met his hairline. "Your *what*?" He turned to the witch. "But you said—"

"Hold up, you're saying you and Heather are. . .like, a thing?"

The Dread Lord lifted his head and frowned, tentacles writhing under the prodigiously inked skin of his face. "I thought you already knew. Heather said you confronted her about our relationship."

"I thought she was banging Carcosa."

He puffed up his chest—well, he tried, but it was his stomach that moved. "She most assuredly is not. We are in an exclusive relationship." He sniffled again. "Well, we *were*."

"Oh, man. . .I think I get it now," Chad said. "The Temple of the Evil Angel isn't about Archonic worship or world domination. It's for couples like you and. . .and Heather. You guys used voice changers so I wouldn't recognize you."

"But the cult's logo is a little white man throttling an Archon," the witch said.

Magnolia flashed a pointed glare at the Dread Lord. "I told you we should've used a professional graphic artist." She sighed. "It was *supposed* to be a human hugging an Archon."

"It's an interspecies dating cult." The Dread Lord lifted his chin and rested his hands on the bulge of his belly. "I'd thought Heather and I were the only ones, but then another employee disclosed an interspecies workplace relationship. As a Human Resources professional, it is my sacred duty to promote an inclusive environment. I founded this cult for those of us who dare to love outside the lines."

"An employee," the witch said. "What employee? Those of *us*?"

Magnolia's cheeks flamed pink. "My partner and I are members."

"It's Ellie, isn't it?" Chad asked. Magnolia nodded, a shy smile curving her lips. "I thought I was picking up a vibe."

The witch said, "So the four of you—"

"Six," Magnolia said. "There were originally three couples, but one of our members. . ." She shook her head and pressed her lips together.

"One of your members what?"

"Alas, poor Yi'danag," the Dread Lord said somberly.

"The Unseen Creeping Horror? But he's an invisible fog monster. How would he and a human even. . ." Actually, she'd prefer not to know. "Who was he dating?"

"Lorelei," Magnolia said. "Poor thing, she took what happened to him so hard."

Carcosa's assistant. Dr. C was good. The witch had to give him that. He'd played her like a freaking bone flute.

"It could've been a lot worse for her," the Dread Lord said, leaning toward Magnolia. "You know she was planning to break up with him, right?"

"No," Magnolia breathed. "Why?"

"He was very controlling."

"Isn't that just a side effect of the fog?"

For the love of Lovecraft, this was turning into a seventh-grade lunch table.

"Sorry to interrupt," the witch said, "but can we get back to saving the world?"

"One more thing." Chad met the Dread Lord's eyes. "You were the one Heather was seeing when we split up? She left me to be with you?"

"I never meant to. . ." The Dread Lord hung his head in shame. "You must understand, Chad—it was love at first sight. I knew from the moment she wrapped that gelatinous membrane around my thoracic sac that she was the only one for me."

"It Hurts! ™?" Chad asked. "The weight-loss wraps?"

"I went to one of her sales parties, and. . ." A thin tentacle waved in agitation from the Dread Lord's right ear. "I apologize for how this has impacted you. I assure you, I didn't set out to. . .to. . ." He burst into tears. They were a viscous grayish yellow, but they were tears all the same. "I'm so sorry. I broke up your happy home." He wiped his face, and his hand trailed glistening strands of lacrimatory goop. "Love truly *is* an evil angel!"

"Dude, chill," Chad said. "I just needed to know. I'm not—"

"And now I'm having her baby!"

CHAPTER THIRTY-FIVE

The Godsdamned Pickles

The bulging belly. The mysterious medical condition. The godsdamned pickles.

By all hell's devils, the Dread Lord was pregnant.

"But you. . .You're. . ." The witch gaped at him, entirely at a loss for words.

"You're a *man*, man," Chad said.

"In Archonic relationships, the more nurturing partner is the one who bears the offspring." The black widow tattooed across the Dread Lord's face danced as his skin rippled. "Can you imagine Heather tending young? Preposterous," he lisped.

Chad looked like he'd been concussed. "But. . .but how could you and Heather. . ."

"When two consenting adult beings love each other very much—"

The witch held up a hand. "Nope. Stop right there. Don't know, don't wanna know." She shook her head. "You two had me fooled. That act you put on when I added Heather to the ballot. . .You called her a she-devil, a"—she searched her memory for his exact words—"'a demoness who swathes her limbs in whimsical knitwear.' Why did you say all that shit if you were so in love with her?"

"Being the human mayor is dangerous," the Dread Lord said, wringing his hands. "The Sheriff ate the last one."

Chad frowned. "This doesn't make any sense."

"Love doesn't have to make sense," Magnolia said.

"That's not what I mean. If Heather loves the Dread Lord, if he's. . .if he's carrying her baby, why would she help the Swarm?"

"I don't know. Maybe she. . ." The Dread Lord sniffled, then emitted a pained wail. "I don't think she wants to be with me anymore. She told me it didn't matter that I was an Archon. She said our love was strong enough to overcome anything. And all along, she was working with the ancient enemy to eradicate my species." He fanned his tear-slimed face with one hand. "I need my candy bag."

"I'm on it." Magnolia unzipped her backpack and handed him a canvas tote.

As the witch watched him tear into a king-size Zero bar, her mind flashed back to her conversation with Heather at Dee's. "When I saw Heather this morning, she said—"

"I would've given up everything for her," the Dread Lord said around a mouthful of nougat. Magnolia handed him a tissue, which adhered to the sticky goop streaming down his face. "I created a cult for her. I kept secrets. I abused the powers of my position to get her a larger Spectral Forces detail." He plopped heavily into a chair, the tissue waving like a flag of surrender. "I've been such a fool."

The witch said, "I talked to her at Dee's, and she said—"

"She always brought me a half dozen sticky 'nuts every morning!"

"Would you shut the hell up for a minute?"

The Dread Lord's breath hitched, and he began to sob.

"Not cool, Witch," Chad said. "You shouldn't yell at an expectant. . .parent like that."

"Listen, Heather said she was doing this *for* you—not *to* you." The witch got up and moved to the seat across from the Dread Lord. After a moment's hesitation, she took his hand. His sobs slowed, and he looked up at her. "Carcosa told her the entropic strain of the Archons' presence would destroy our universe. He told her life on Earth was doomed, and the Swarm was coming to save us."

"But that's just not true," Magnolia said. "You can't destroy a part of the multiverse. You can change it, you can reshape it, but at a quantum level, it's eternal."

Chad whistled. "Damn, hooking up with a Nobel Prize nominee is rubbing off on you, Magnolia."

Rubbing off. Nope. Not the time.

The witch forced her attention back to the matter at hand. "It might not be true, but that's what Dr. C told Heather. He convinced her—"

"He convinced me our world was dying."

The Dread Lord stood when he heard Heather's voice, but the witch tugged him back down and positioned herself in front of him. The mayor wasn't alone. She'd brought five of her pet goons. The witch prepared to summon her magic and flatten the poor bastards, but then it hit her. . .They were unarmed.

No guns. No Tasers. No anti-entropic shields.

That was a good sign, but she couldn't let her guard down yet.

"Hands in the air," the witch said. At a nod from Heather, the Spectral Forces officers raised their hands. "Last time I saw you, Madam Mayor, you were sending one of these shitheads to stomp the Dread Lord."

"That's not what I was doing!" Heather took a step toward them, but she stopped when the witch threw a firebolt at her feet. "I asked two of my men to stay and protect Sathach. I wanted to stay myself, but the personal security contract. . .They were going to drag me out of there no matter what."

"Don't lie to us," the witch said. "You sent one of them to guard the QT and one to take out the Dread Lord."

"I didn't! I don't know why Deputy Woods didn't obey my order. He hasn't been quite right since that garbage chute ate him."

The witch had a theory about that. Woods probably got a heaping helping of little white bullshit inside the UCH—enough to give Carcosa and his buddies a mental foothold.

"I found these guys at the Sheriff's office." Hank edged around the traitorous crew. "The Sheriff wasn't there, but they were arguing with the chief deputy about—"

"We were there to demand the Clerk's release," Heather said.

The witch narrowed her eyes. "What do you mean, her release?"

"The Sheriff had her arrested." Hank removed his hat and ran a hand through his hair. "He's got her locked up in an Archonic detention cell. According to the chief deputy, he's planning to interrogate her tonight."

"Interrogate her about what?" the witch asked.

"The chief deputy didn't know."

"That's not possible," the Dread Lord said. "Micana'gos outranks the Sheriff, and she's far stronger than he is."

"It's my fault." Heather stepped forward, her eyes locked on his face. "Dr. Carcosa told me how to use an inert AEV to—"

"What's an AEV?" the witch asked.

Hank's white eyebrows furrowed. "What's inert?"

"An AEV is an anti-entropic vortex. It's a white ball about"—she held out her cupped hands—"this big."

The Dread Lord leaped to his feet. "You used a sphere on the Clerk?"

"I didn't do anything to her," Heather said. "Well, not directly. Carcosa told me an AEV can weaken Archons even after it's detonated. He'd planned to use a live one on the Clerk, but too many people saw him hanging around her office."

The WTF meeting. Carcosa had been waiting to meet with the Clerk. If they hadn't been there. . .

"He told me about your task force," Heather said, shifting her focus to the witch. "He said we needed the Clerk out of the way, so he gave me the AEV from the landfill."

That explained why only two spheres were attached to the QT when Carcosa had three.

"I gave it to the Sheriff and told him planting it in the Clerk's office would weaken her," Heather said. "Then he could come back a few days later to arrest her." Heather ran a hand through her hair, leaving it uncharacteristically mussed. "I. . .I didn't want her hurt. I just—"

"Didn't want her hurt?" the witch asked. "Gods, Heather. I've seen those two fight. If the Sheriff had the upper hand, what would stop him from eating her alive?"

"Micana'gos is a favorite of Za'gathoth's," the Dread Lord said. "Mother wouldn't like it if the Sheriff killed her." His face rippled with anxiety. "But how could you do that to her, Heather? I thought you looked up to the Clerk."

"I thought I was saving the world!"

"And. . .and Yi'danag—you *knew* him." The Dread Lord shook his head. "Lorelei is absolutely devastated."

"Carcosa didn't approach me until after he was defogged. I had nothing to do with that."

"You've never liked him," he said, crossing his arms above the bulge of his baby bump. "You made that very clear."

"He's a misogynistic asshole! He made fun of my leggings business." Heather narrowed her eyes. "He called it a pyramid scheme."

"Well, in his defense," the Dread Lord said, easing back into his chair, "the business model is rather. . .ahem, triangular."

"You want to know the real reason everyone makes fun of companies like mine?" Heather asked. "Because the people involved are female. 'Look at the little housewives playing businesswoman!'" She propped her hands on her hips and glared. "Do I have it about right?" The Dread Lord opened his mouth to reply, but Heather cut him off. "I came here to apologize, to fix things with you and right my wrongs." She walked to the table and sat down across from him. "Dr. Carcosa told me this universe would be torn apart if no one acted. He didn't ask for much at first. Funding for repairs. A hiding place for the little white men."

"That's what happened to the Executive Hearing Room, isn't it?" the witch asked.

Heather ignored her and reached for the Dread Lord's hands, but he pulled away. "I'd been having nightmares for weeks—horrible dreams about the world breaking into bits. I've been watching you and our baby die every night." She fixed the witch with a fierce glare. "By the way, you told me chicken. . .parts would help, but roosters don't even *have* a penis. They have this thing called a cloaca. I ate at least five of them, but the dreams never stopped."

The witch wasn't sure whether to laugh or retch. "Uh. . .Chicken Cock is Kentucky bourbon."

Heather's complexion picked up a faint but noticeable tinge of green.

"More dreams," Magnolia said. "Dreams planted the concept for the QT in Dr. Carcosa's brain, and nightmares got Heather's cooperation."

Heather got up, circled the table, and knelt by Sathach's side. She raised a tentative hand and stroked his face. The silver bar that pierced his septum quivered with barely suppressed emotion. "I thought I was saving you. In my dreams, if I helped Dr. Carcosa, you didn't die. You became human, but you *lived*."

"You want me to be human?"

"Sathach, I don't care what you are, as long as you're with me." Heather took his hands, blinking as tears fell down her pale cheeks. "Carcosa made his plan sound so good. He said we'd never have to worry about being judged. There's so much hate out there." She glanced at the witch. "*You* know. The day you confronted me about our relationship, you said people would pin a scarlet *A* to my chest."

"*A* for 'adultery,' Heather," the witch said. "Not *A* for 'Archon.' I thought Carcosa was cheating on his wife with you."

But Heather had a point. People would've judged them. Even now, even seeing how much they loved each other, part of her mind was stuck in a morbid curiosity spiral about how they could possibly. . .

None of her business.

And honestly, it bothered her way more when couples fed each other in restaurants or posed for soft-focus engagement photos.

What was it Chad said? People are people, gills or not.

"None of that matters anymore, Sathach," Heather said. "Now I see what we should do—what we should've done all along." She pulled the Dread Lord to his feet and looked into his eyes. "We won't hide. We won't change ourselves so the world will accept us. We'll change the world instead."

CHAPTER THIRTY-SIX

Send in the Threenagers

C ould I talk to you for a sec?"

The witch looked up at Hank gratefully. "Gods, yes."

Anything to get away from the Dread Lord and Heather's sobfest. Hank led her across the room to the Spectral Forces officers who'd arrived with the mayor. And she had a bone to pick with these boneheads.

"Which one of you shit-gibbons shot at Chad?"

Heads turned as the uniformed men exchanged glances, but no one spoke. She shot jets of blue flame from her fingertips. Four fingers pointed at the unlucky bastard in the middle of the row.

The witch stepped toward him. "You worthless son of a—"

"You know they're under contract, Witch," Hank said, stepping between her and the terrified man. "Heather could've told them to jump off the roof of City Hall, and they'd have done it."

She opened her mouth to tell Hank to shut the entire fuck up, but the pleading expression on his face stopped her.

Oh, *hell*.

Well, if anyone could understand what it was like to get thoroughly rogered by a contract, it was her.

"People are already gathering at the Abyss," Hank said. "About a dozen food trucks have set up on Aylesbury Place. There are bouncy castles for the kids, and the succubi have a kissing booth. It's a total circus. We need to—"

"Clear the area," the witch said. "Yeah, we were talking about that earlier. Any ideas?"

Hank crossed his arms, showcasing biceps worthy of a *Men's Health* cover. "I can try to reach the Sheriff. Now that Heather's on our side, she might be able to get him to deploy Spectral Forces."

"I suspect he won't take orders from a human female."

"True," he said. "I could try to convince him, but. . ."

"But you don't have a particular desire to experience life as a liquid."

"Not really." Hank lifted his chin toward the still-unfolding romantic reunion. "What about the Dread Lord of HR?"

"He's pregnant," the witch said. "We're not letting him near that maniac." She rubbed her hands together in gleeful anticipation of mischief managed. "We'll just have to bust her out of jail."

"Bust her out of. . ." Hank shook his head. "You can't be serious."

"I am as serious as a myocardial infarction. We need the Clerk. The Sheriff has her." The witch shrugged. "*You* do the math."

"But the Sheriff's probably already interrogating her. Even if he's not, the Dread Lord of Corrections would, um. . .object. Strenuously."

Zsthaor. Gods dammit, he was right. She shuddered, recalling his mismatched eyes and mouthful of metal teeth. But what choice did they have?

The witch walked to the head of the table. "All right, enough with the tears and apologies," she said. "We've got a universe to save, and just a few hours to do it."

The remaining members of the WTF found their seats. Heather stood behind the Dread Lord's chair, her hands resting on his shoulders, and Hank formed up in front of the mayor's personal guard.

"What's the plan?" Chad asked.

She planted her hands on the table. "I'm breaking the Clerk out of County lockup."

The Dread Lord shook his head, causing his stretched earlobes to wobble alarmingly. "You can't break into an Archonic detention cell. It's impossible."

"Don't give me that bullshit." The witch scoffed. "People say nothing is impossible, but I've been doing nothing every day for almost thirteen years. We just have to figure out how."

"Well, before you dream up a scheme to blast your way in there—"

She pressed pause on the mental movie in which she was, in fact, blasting her way in there.

"—I'd like to try talking to Zsthaor," the Dread Lord said. "He's a reasonable being. Mostly."

"No freaking way," the witch said. "Not with your. . ." She waved a hand at his baby bump.

Heather squeezed his shoulders. When he looked up at her, she said, "She's right, Sathach. It's too risky."

"Doing nothing is what's risky." He pasted on a reassuring smile, but the undulating skin of his face belied his apparent calm. "I'll be fine."

Heather skewered the witch with a glare pointed enough to part flesh. "He'd better be."

If the mayor had been blessed (or cursed, depending on who you asked) with magic, the witch would've lost more than her eyebrows. Heather's protective papa-bear mode was downright terrifying.

"I'll go with him," the witch said. "I'll keep him safe. You have my word."

After a moment's hesitation, Heather nodded.

"In the meantime," she continued, "we still need to clear the area around the Abyss."

"I can take these guys and walk the crowd," Hank said, "but there are only six of us—"

"Seven." Heather raised her hand. "I'll go too."

Seven people walking through a crowd of thousands. It was a shitty plan, but it was all they had. "Okay," the witch said. "Warn as many people as you can, and—"

"The tornado siren!" Magnolia's face lit with excitement. "We could set off the tornado siren. It's out of season, but people are used to taking cover when they hear it."

"That's not a bad idea," Chad said. "But we'd need the Dread Lord of Fire and Rescue, and he's. . ."

"He's a godsdamned ice cube." The witch turned a furious scowl on the Dread Lord. "Don't Archons make succession plans?"

"We live for eons," the Dread Lord said. "And, not to be rude, but we *are* the apex predators of this universe."

Chad rubbed his chin. "If it's a storm warning system, wouldn't it have manual controls in case of a power outage? I mean, even an emergency generator could get crushed by a fallen tree."

"He's right," Hank said. "We should be able to climb the carillon tower and crank it up." He turned to the rank of officers and braced his hands on his hips. "Let's roll. Drop Cooper and me at the carillon, and the rest of you go with the mayor and walk the crowd." He tossed a set of keys toward the witch. They landed on the floor four feet in front of her. "We'll take their Hummer. You keep mine in case you need to move."

"Good luck, Hank," the witch said.

He saluted and led his men out of the war room.

Heather leaned down, kissed the Dread Lord, and patted his baby bump. "I love you."

"I love you too, bae."

The witch barely suppressed a dry heave. A cross-species relationship was fine by her, but "bae"?

"We should go, Witch." The Dread Lord pushed back his chair and stood. "The sooner we free the Clerk, the sooner we can—"

"Pumpkin Spice to Heiress," a tinny voice said through bursts of static. "Come in, Heiress. Over." Magnolia reached into her bag and pulled out a walkie-talkie.

Heiress. *Vera.*

The witch's heart sank. The neighborhood watch didn't know. She held out her hand for the radio, and Magnolia passed it to her.

"This is the County Witch. Heiress is. . ." Her throat tightened, and she squeezed her eyes shut. "I'm sorry. Heiress is gone."

"Gone where?" the woman asked. "What happened?"

"I. . ." She couldn't make the words come, couldn't say what she'd done.

Chad gently took the walkie-talkie. "There was an accident," he said. "We lost her."

"You don't mean. . .Heiress can't be. . ."

Her voice cut off in a strangled sob, then the radio played only static.

Chad pressed the button to speak. "I'm so sorry," he said. "We all are, but we're running out of time. Were you calling to report in?"

Static.

"Hello?"

"I. . ." Pumpkin Spice took a deep breath. "Yes. We're at the Darkest Night party." Her voice was thick and strained but growing stronger. "We saw LWAs in Dunwich Park on our way here."

Chad and the witch exchanged a glance. "Can you get them away from there? Distract them?"

"We're here with our kids. We couldn't possibly—" A bloodcurdling shriek interrupted her voice. "Paisleigh, do not put chocolate syrup on the baby!"

A voice like a lion cub roared a defiant reply.

"Oh, God," Pumpkin Spice moaned. "What a mess!"

A mess.

The LWAs couldn't ignore a mess. They had to impose order, had to clean it up.

The witch grabbed the radio from Chad. "Hey, Karen—"

"You know that's not my actual name, right?"

"Whatever. Are you with the others?" She groped for their code names. "Uggs? Lululemon?"

"Yes, a bunch of us came to the Darkest Night party together. It's me, Doterra, Keto—"

"How many?"

"Hold on a sec."

Static hissed in the background. Chad caught her eye and mouthed, *What are you doing?* She held up a finger to shush him.

"Hey!" he said.

Oops. Wrong finger.

"Eight adults, fourteen kids."

"Can you get to the softball field?"

"There's a nest of Shoggoths—"

"The Shoggoths were a lie to keep people away," the witch said. "We need your kids to keep the LWAs occupied."

"You want me to bring a bunch of innocent three-year-olds around those things? There's no way I'm taking my babies to—" She broke off with a horrified gasp. "Paisleigh Amelia, that is not a toilet!"

"All you have to do is create a distraction. If you don't, the Swarm will invade in a few hours." The witch took a deep breath. "Your kids will be as safe on that field as anywhere else in this universe. The LWAs ignore humans, and they're out of weapons."

"I don't know. . ."

"Come on, these bastards got. . .They got Vera killed. And all the kids need to do is make a mess."

"A mess?"

"Yeah," the witch said. "You think they can do it?"

"Oh, if there's one thing they can do, it's make a mess. Hold on," she said. The witch heard a muffled discussion, punctuated by outraged shrieks. "We're a go to send in the threenagers. Over and out."

The witch passed the walkie-talkie back to Magnolia. "You two hang tight here—"

"To hell with that," Magnolia said. "We're going to disable the device."

"No! Deputy Woods is still guarding the QT, and he's armed. It's too gods-damned dangerous."

Chad and Magnolia exchanged a glance, then he nodded and said, "We'll take the Hummer and wait for you on the field."

"Can you bring my candy bag, Magnolia? You know I get moody when my blood sugar drops."

The witch rolled her eyes, but it reminded her to check her coat pocket for the last Holy Chao cookie. She didn't have much faith in the Dread Lord's ability to talk Zsthaor into releasing the Clerk. The entropic strike wouldn't do shit to an Archon, but she could use her magic to prevent grievous mummification. Hopefully.

"I don't love the idea of you guys butting heads with two senior Archons." Chad's face was tight with worry. "Just play it cool, Witch. Be safe."

"I will. You too, okay?"

"Always."

The witch watched him follow Magnolia out of the room, then she turned to the Dread Lord. "Think you can teleport both of us to Zsthaor's office?"

His face rippled in confusion. "Of course I can. Why do you ask?"

"We had to lube you up with Vaseline a few weeks ago."

"I hadn't realized I was teleporting for two," he said stiffly. "Now that I know, the opening will be of sufficient girth."

She shook her head. Too easy.

"One thing before we go," the Dread Lord said. "Zsthaor is a bit. . .conservative in his views of Archon-human relations. I suggest you not speak unless he directly addresses you. He is of the opinion that humans are to be seen and not heard."

"Oh, is he now?"

"Witch. . ."

She held out her hand. "Shall we?"

CHAPTER THIRTY-SEVEN

This Time, It's Personnel

S athach, what an. . .interesting human skin."

Zsthaor sat behind his pathologically neat desk wearing a bland smile and an argyle sweater vest. His folded hands rested on the desktop, displaying nails filed to razored hooks.

"Between advances in mortal medicine and our Medicare for All plan, human suits are in short supply, I'm afraid." The Dread Lord of Human Resources leaned toward him and lowered his voice to a confidential whisper. "But, you know, the quality has really deteriorated. The last three I had split right down the middle."

Zsthaor stared at his rounded midsection. "Shocking." His mismatched eyes flicked back to the Dread Lord's face. "And to what do I owe the unexpected pleasure of this visit?"

"Two things, actually," the Dread Lord said. "First, I wanted to share my wonderful news." He patted his spherical belly. "I'm going to be a parent."

Zsthaor pushed his glasses up the bridge of his nose and bared wickedly pointed metal teeth in what the witch could only assume was meant to be a smile. "Delightful."

He didn't look all that delighted.

"This will be the first Archonic birth since the Emergence."

"A wondrous miracle," he said drily.

The Dread Lord's face fell.

The witch glared at Zsthaor, who hadn't appeared to register her presence. She could understand a lack of enthusiasm about someone else's stupid offspring, but he didn't need to be a dick about it.

"And the second thing?" Zsthaor asked.

"Well, as you can see, I'm here with the High Lord of Public Works."

The swirling black eye shifted to her, while the blue one maintained eye contact with the Dread Lord of Human Resources.

"I noticed."

"We're here to speak to you about the Clerk," the Dread Lord said. "We understand she's in custody."

Zsthaor rocked back in his chair and steepled his hands in front of his chest. "Indeed, she is. In fact, the Sheriff is interrogating her at this very moment."

Gods dammit, that wasn't good. The Clerk had been in a weakened state when she was arrested. In other circumstances, she could've called on the Archons' mutual aid contract to restore herself, but the detention rooms in Zsthaor's lair prevented it. If the Sheriff got the upper hand. . .

The witch opened her mouth to protest, but the Dread Lord cut her off. "I claim the right to defend her."

"Defend her?" Zsthaor's blond eyebrows rose. "In your condition?"

"The Sheriff arrested her under false pretenses, and he poses a grave threat to her. . .structural integrity. I therefore—"

"As you wish," Zsthaor said, raising a hand to silence the Dread Lord. He stood, smoothing the pleats of his charcoal dress pants. "Follow me."

After leading them through a winding maze of corridors that echoed with sounds disturbing enough to test her sphincter control, Zsthaor stopped in front of a nondescript door marked *Interrogation Room #3*. A chorus of bone-chilling shrieks and ground-shaking thuds emanated from the room.

"Since one of you is in the family way," Zsthaor said, "and the other is a frail mortal, it is perhaps best if I'm the one to. . .interrupt."

No argument here.

He cracked the door and slipped inside. The cacophony in the room came to a screeching halt.

Literally, *loads* of screeching.

The door opened, and Zsthaor burst out. He slammed it behind him, closed his eyes, and sagged against the doorframe, gasping for breath.

The witch stiffened. "Is the Clerk—"

"I am outraged," the Dread Lord boomed. "Micana'gos has the right to due process, and you have allowed the Sheriff to beat a false confession out of her."

Zsthaor wiped a spatter of mucilaginous fluid from one cheek. "I assure you, he was not beating anything out of her." He shook the slime from his hand. "In fact, with her most enthusiastic participation, he was putting something in."

"Putting something. . ." The Dread Lord gasped. "You can't mean they were. . ."

"Vigorously."

* * *

After an awkward conference between the Sheriff (entirely unapologetic), the Clerk (rigidly formal), and Zsthaor (utterly mortified), the Clerk was released. From the way the Sheriff tried to sneak a tentacle under the Clerk's shroud, the witch suspected she'd be cleared of all charges. While the Sheriff and Zsthaor finalized the paperwork, the Dread Lord did his reverse mind-flaying trick to get the Clerk up to speed on what they'd learned.

"You started an interspecies dating cult?" The Clerk's eyestalks stiffened with surprise. The Dread Lord lifted his chin and nodded, clearly expecting a rebuke. Something shoulder-like lifted under the shroud, and her half dozen eyes softened. "Love is in the air in Tophet County."

"You're not disgusted?" The legs of his spider tattoo twitched as his face rippled with anxiety. "Repulsed?"

"Oh, I am," the Clerk said, "but *all* sexual congress is disgusting. A fanged orifice here, a forked phallus there. . ."

Gods, no wonder there'd been so much screaming.

"It's a wonder anyone ever does it at all." A wave of blinks stuttered across her eyes, which swiveled to focus on the Dread Lord's swollen abdomen. "And you're expecting?" He smiled and nodded, cradling his belly. "That's wonderful, Sathach. How far along—"

"Hate to interrupt," the witch said. "But the Swarm is invading in less than two hours."

"You're right," the Clerk said. "What's our next move?"

"We've got one team distracting the LWAs and another trying to get people away from the Abyss."

The Dread Lord's eyes flicked from the Clerk to the Sheriff. "We were hoping you could convince Lomelzar to deploy Spectral Forces teams to clear the area. The two of you seem to be on, ahem, good terms."

"Quite." The shroud rustled self-consciously. "Witch, return to the cavern and disable the device. Lomelzar and I will disperse the crowd." The Clerk's waving eyestalks swiveled to the Dread Lord's belly. "And *you* should go somewhere safe for the duration."

"But—"

"Agreed," the witch said. "Can you drop me at the cavern on your way? Teleporting will be quicker than the broom."

He closed his mouth and nodded.

"May Azathoth be with you." The Clerk turned and oozed away.

The witch took the Dread Lord's proffered hand. A spark of netherlight appeared, flickered, and went out. "Are you out of juice again?" She patted her pocket. "I have one more—"

"It's not that," he said, frowning. "This is mortifying. I've never had performance issues before."

"I bet that godsdamned tunnel is blocking you from dropping me straight into the cavern. Can you get us to the softball field?"

"I'll try."

They staggered out of the quantum underbelly into the midst of a heated battle. The field swarmed with LWAs and echoed with squeals of outrage. A blond threenager streaked with camo-patterned fingerpaint blinked open-mouthed at their sudden appearance three feet in front of her. In one hand, she held a bedraggled stuffed otter; in the other, a red plastic gun.

The Dread Lord of Human Resources bent down to the girl's eye level. "Where's your mommy, sweetie?"

"Not sweetie," she yelled, delivering a vicious kick to his shin. "My name is Paisleigh!"

With a defiant scream, she raised the gun and fired. A cloud of confetti rained on them. Little white Archons swarmed from all directions, frantically picking up the tiny shreds of paper. Paisleigh planted a rain-booted foot on the tentacled white hindquarters of an LWA and kicked it. When it tried to get up, she shot it in the head and disappeared into the melee.

That kid was a godsdamned Valkyrie.

A harried woman in the winter uniform of a suburban mom (leggings, long-sleeved shirt, puffer vest, and tall boots) sprinted across the field after her. "I saw that, Paisleigh Amelia Martin!" she shouted. "We don't shoot faces!"

"You should get out of here." The witch found the Dread Lord's eyes in the black blotch of his face-spanning spider tattoo. "This could get ugly." She turned toward the mouth of the tunnel, but the Dread Lord caught her elbow.

"I'm coming with you."

"It's too dangerous!"

The witch sensed more than saw something hurtling down at them from above. She yanked the Dread Lord to the side just before Paisleigh pulled the witch's broom out of a near-suicidal dive.

Hastur's hanging hacky sack. The kid was a *wielder*.

"It's dangerous out here too," he said, with a wary glance at the overcast sky. "And until we shut down the QT, it's dangerous everywhere."

"But—"

"If we fail, Witch, that"—he straightened and pointed at an LWA methodically picking up confetti—"is my baby's future. I'm coming with you."

She stared at him, reading the ripples of his face, then nodded. "Let's go."

They sprinted across the field toward the mouth of the tunnel.

Well, she sprinted. The Dread Lord moved in a frenzied waddle, but he still made decent time.

A trio of armed threenagers guarded the mouth of the tunnel, supervised by a harried mom. The woman flashed a hand sign to the defensive line, and they parted to admit the Dread Lord and the witch.

"Ahem," the Dread Lord panted, cradling his belly as they jogged down the slope. "Are all human offspring so ferocious?"

"You're asking the wrong witch."

When they left the misery of the tunnel and emerged into the cavern, what she saw stopped her in her tracks.

"Ah, Witch, I have been expecting you."

What remained of Christian Carcosa paced in front of the QT. He still had a head of brown hair, neatly combed and precisely parted, but the face underneath had only rudimentary features. A gray silk tie hung around his neck, but he'd discarded the suit. He now stood only a few inches taller than the LWAs who held Chad and Magnolia wrapped in their whipcord tentacles. Deputy Woods stood blank-faced in front of the device, his hand resting on the butt of his Glock.

"I must admit, your security guards are quite fierce," Carcosa said. "They lured my forces outside, then blocked the door. They do have a weakness, though." Carcosa held up a tote bag emblazoned with the legend *Human Resources: This Time, It's Personnel.*

The Dread Lord's candy bag.

"I'm sorry," Magnolia said. "We thought the cavern was empty, and we could shut down the QT. Then one of the LWAs grabbed the bag, and—"

A tentacle snaked up to cover her mouth.

"All it took was a handful of treats scattered on the field, and your guards deserted their post."

The witch eased her hand into her coat pocket and pulled out the sandwich bag containing the last Holy Chao cookie. "I have a sweet tooth myself." She unwrapped the cookie and took a huge bite, grinning as she chewed.

Carcosa's rudimentary face clenched in a frown. "What are you eating? That is most. . .unpleasant."

She swallowed another bite, already feeling the buzz of entropine in her blood. "So, what's your evil plan?" The witch shoved the rest of the cookie into her mouth and choked it down. "Kick open the door and invite all your friends over?"

"Perhaps we will. But first, we need to—"

The witch pointed at Deputy Woods and whispered the Ouranian-Barbaric command for sleep. He dropped like a stone, and the gun clattered to the floor.

One asshole down. . .

Carcosa shook his bulbous head. "Good help is so hard to find."

She grinned. "You were saying?"

"First, we need to clean up the place," he said.

"Clean up the place?"

"I do not know how you endure it." Carcosa let go of the candy bag and shuddered. "The disorder here is so great that it bleeds out of this layer of the Sheaf. You have infected our home with your. . .dissonance. So many different species, different genders, different races—"

"I have an excellent training you should attend," the Dread Lord said. "It's called Celebrating Diversity in a Cross-Species Workforce."

"Silence!" Carcosa's paper-white face contorted in a cartoon grimace. "We thought we had eradicated the Archons eons ago, but no, you had to—"

"Witch!" Chad shouted. "We were wrong! He's got a—"

A snowy appendage blocked his mouth, muffling his voice.

"I believe your friend is trying to warn you that I have one remaining sphere." Carcosa raised his other hand, which cradled a white ball. "Stay back, or I shall use it."

Magnolia thrashed in her bonds. The witch didn't need to hear her to understand.

The initial wave of LWM had only brought five spheres. That meant this one had already been detonated.

Carcosa shifted his grip, revealing a mustard-yellow blotch marring its glossy surface. It was the sphere from the landfill, the one used on the Unseen Creeping Horror. And *that* sphere's activation mechanism had been damaged in the pre-conjugal battle between the Sheriff and the Clerk.

This little white shit stain was lying like a rug.

"I don't think so." The witch smiled and raised her hands, forming her fingers into the sacred K. "You can't activate that thing, so you might as well drop it."

"You could be wrong," Carcosa said. "Are you willing to take that risk?"

"I'm not wrong. The yellow stain is from the Sheriff."

He hissed in frustration, frowning as he turned the sphere in his hands.

"Can't you see it?"

"Little white men are colorblind," he snapped.

"That's not as woke as you think it is."

"Use the strike!" Chad had torn the tentacle from his face and held the writhing thing at arm's length.

"Are you sure that is the best course of action? Heterogeneity is the root cause of all your world's conflicts," Carcosa said. "Your wars, your crusades, your genocides. . .Every one of your greatest evils grows from the same seed." He lowered the sphere and met her eyes. "Difference."

The witch's childhood history lessons loomed in the forefront of her mind. So much death. So much hatred. If everyone were the same, would there still be violence? Would there still be war?

"His way isn't the answer, Witch." The Dread Lord's voice was gentle. "Yes, we've done horrible things—all of us, Archons and humans—but wiping away everything that makes us unique is monstrous. The solution is not assimilation." He rested a hand on her shoulder. "It's acceptance."

The Tamagotchi buzzed at her waist. The Dread Lord heard the vibration and reached toward it. He paused and raised pierced eyebrows, asking her permission. When she nodded, he unclipped Keyser from the witch's belt loop and held him up so she could see the screen. Keyser bared his teeth in Carcosa's direction and raised the middle finger on his single front paw.

The message was clear.

The witch fired everything she had at Carcosa, burning through her entropine in a single blaze of glory. But at the last moment, he raised the sphere like a talisman. Her strike lanced into it, drawn to the most syntropic target.

Oh, gods. . .what had she done? First Vera, and now—

The white shell split with a sharp crack, and a multicolored field of energy engulfed Carcosa. The LWAs holding Chad and the others scattered, fleeing for the relative safety of the tunnel. When the glare faded, a human Carcosa—wearing nothing but a necktie and a unibrow—stood swaying next to a little white man, which shrieked a psychic wail and fled.

Dr. Carcosa staggered and collapsed on the cavern floor. He wasn't the only one unsteady on his feet. The witch sagged against the Dread Lord, weak with entropine depletion. He pressed Keyser Söze's plastic shell into her hand and wound an arm around her waist. Chad rushed to her side and helped the Dread Lord walk her to a chair near the QT.

Carcosa groaned and tried to sit up. He squinted blearily at Magnolia, who knelt beside him. "Who are you?"

"My name's Magnolia," she said. "Do you remember what happened?"

Dr. Carcosa shook his head and looked up at the gleaming cylinder of the device. "That's my quantum tunneler, but this isn't my lab. Where am I?" He looked at this naked body and blanched, shifting to cover his crotch. "And where are my clothes?"

The witch stared at his groin, her mouth hanging open.

"Come on, now," Chad said. "That's rude."

"It's not that, it's. . ." She pointed at Carcosa's arms, one of which now ended in a suckered tentacle. "There must've been a little too much entropy in that sphere."

Dr. Carcosa's eyebrows drew together. "What are you—"

He gaped at his transformed appendage.

Magnolia caught him just before his head hit the stone floor.

"The past few months feel like a dream."

Dr. Carcosa was no longer naked, but the witch wasn't sure this particular clothing was an improvement. The only wardrobe option they'd had was the spare outfit Magnolia kept in her bag for impromptu overnights at Ellie's. According to Magnolia, Dr. C currently wore the Marissa asymmetric tunic in Shake Your Moneymaker green over cheetah-print leggings.

"I'm starting to remember some of what happened while that thing was in control, but it's patchy. I don't. . ." His eyes widened. "Is Mitsuki all right?"

"She's fine," the witch said. "Look, I know you've been through hell, but we need you. The little white men are coming." She gestured toward Chad and the Dread Lord, who huddled over a stack of technical binders. "We're trying to figure out how to turn that thing off, but we're running out of time."

"Is there anything you can tell us about their plan?" Magnolia asked. "Anything that might help us?"

"It started with the dreams." He closed his eyes and rubbed his forehead. "They had to build the QT here instead of in their world."

"Why?" the witch asked. "They came up with the damned thing. Why didn't they just—"

"'Invention, it must be humbly admitted,'" Magnolia said, "'does not consist in creating out of void, but out of chaos.'"

Dr. Carcosa smiled. "Just so. Mary Shelley, if I'm not mistaken?" Magnolia nodded. "They showed me the end product they wanted," he said. "But to get from idea to execution, they needed our world. The night you, um. . ." He trailed off and looked at the witch.

"I know," she said. "I screwed up."

"That night, the gateway held long enough for them to send through an advance team. They had five spheres left from their war with the Archons, which they used to target the most entropic—"

"We know," the witch said. "They needed to reduce the local background entropy."

"That was their initial plan, but after they learned you converted entropine to syntropine, their strategy evolved." Carcosa ran his human hand across the chest of his tunic. "I just have to say it. This is the most comfortable thing I've ever worn."

"I know!" Magnolia's face lit up. "We have a men's line if you're—"

"Could we not?" the witch snapped. "Keep talking, Doc."

"Once my. . .passenger learned about the thin spot in the Abyss and the effects of the solstice on our dimensional membrane, he realized he could convert the contents of the spheres and use that energy to create a *permanent* gateway."

"And a horde of little white assholes will invade." She looked from Carcosa to the device. "Where's the power button?"

"I'm not so sure they plan to invade."

"What else would they do?"

"My passenger wanted to 'make this world suitable,' but I don't know what that—"

"Don't know, don't care." The witch grabbed Carcosa's elbow and dragged him toward the device's control panel. Chad and the Dread Lord looked up from the table and followed them. "Turn the godsdamned thing off." She tapped a large black dial. "Will this do it?"

"No. That's the field modulator—"

"What about that one?" she asked, pointing at an orange switch.

"That cuts the power to the—"

"Perfect." She reached for it.

"No!" Carcosa's suckered tentacle wound around her wrist and yanked her hand away. "The QT is powered up and locked onto a set of dimensional coordinates. They've already extracted the entropy from three spheres—"

"How?" the witch asked. "Ellie said the quantum hypersphere thing would. . .would make a big boom." Dammit, she sounded like a total threenager.

"Just as you have an affinity for the entropic, the Swarm can safely manipulate the stasis bubble. The important bit is that, if you cut the power, massive quantities of energy will—"

"Boom?" the witch asked.

"Yes."

"Why didn't *you* explode when I blasted that sphere? Shouldn't that have disrupted the quantum whatsit?"

"Were you *trying* to blow me up?"

"You weren't you at the time." The witch shrugged. "I wasn't *not* trying to."

Carcosa's annoyance faded in the presence of a scientific mystery. "That, I can't explain," he said. "My best guess is that your entropic magic neutralized the inherently syntropic stasis bubble. Then the entropy in the crystal flowed to the most syntropic target, which was my. . .uninvited guest."

Gods, she'd done it. She'd reversed the effects of the sphere, which meant she could do the same for Keyser. She just needed—

"Witch, we're running out of time," Magnolia said.

Time. Right. Keyser would have to wait. *Hang in there, buddy.*

The witch glared at the QT's control panel. "We've got to kill the power to this thing. Why in the hell would you build a machine that can't be turned off?"

"I didn't," Carcosa said defensively. "I told you, they've modified it. There's an emergency shutdown protocol, but I can only execute it from a computer."

Chad's BlackBerry buzzed. "The Dread Lord of IT says we can connect him to the control panel with a cable. Then he can execute the emergency shutdown."

The witch looked from Chad to Dr. Carcosa. "What do you think?"

Carcosa nodded. "Let's do it."

CHAPTER THIRTY-EIGHT

The Great and Terrible Bearded Clam

The Tamagotchi vibrated so hard, the witch's hand went numb. She glanced at the screen. Keyser Söze scrabbled at the left-hand edge of the tiny square. She followed the trajectory of his path to a shadowed recess of the cavern, where a flash of white caught her eye.

A little white man crawled over a pile of rubble and stood, its body clearly illuminated under the fluorescent lights. The ends of its stumpy arms were fingerlike tentacles. One set of those tiny appendages held a Spectral Forces Glock, which it raised and aimed at the witch. The Dread Lord of Human Resources squealed and gripped her elbow.

"Get behind me," she whispered.

"But it's got a gun!"

"Exactly! I'm drained dry," she said. "I can't shield you." The witch pushed him behind her, which was a bit of a challenge since he wouldn't let go of her arm.

"What do you want?" Dr. Carcosa's voice trembled as he faced the creature who'd once ridden shotgun in his body. He shook his head violently. "I won't let you in again. I'd rather die!"

He dropped the loop of cable he'd been holding and sprinted toward the mouth of the tunnel. The little white man never flinched; it kept the witch dead in its sights. She reflexively tried to juice up her shields, but it was no use. The creature stepped out of the shadows and swung the gun toward Chad and Magnolia.

"Move away from the device."

Fingers weren't the only design upgrade. Unlike the other little white miscreants, Carcosa's former possessor could *talk*.

Chad lifted his hands away from the QT's control panel. His eyes flicked from the LWM to the witch. She arched an eyebrow in question, and he shook his head.

Shit. The Dread Lord of IT hadn't finished uploading.

"I said move away from the device," the thing yelled.

Magnolia backed away from the QT, but Chad didn't move. He was monitoring the upload. The witch had to buy him some time.

"You don't have to do this," she said. "The Sheaf is endless. There's plenty of room for everyone."

"You will thank us in the end." The LWM's head turned toward her, but the gun never shifted away from Chad. "We will civilize this universe, and you will join the Swarm. Being inside one of you, stuck in that rotting meat suit. . ." It shuddered. "It altered me, separated me from my brethren, but that is about to change. And once we have taken your world, we will move on to the next layer of the Sheaf, and the next."

The witch risked a glance at Chad. His eyes were glued to his BlackBerry, which was connected to the control panel by a long black cable. His head jerked up, and he met the witch's eyes and nodded. Mission accomplished.

"You're too late," the witch said. "We're shutting this godsdamned thing down. It's all over."

"You are right." The little white man's slash of a mouth curved in a smiley-face grin. It raised its free hand and pointed at the large wall clock. The witch looked up just in time to see the second hand cross twelve. The moment of the solstice had arrived. "It *is* over."

A prismatic starburst appeared in the center of the Abyss. It opened like a blossom and emitted a bubble of white light that shivered and grew.

They'd failed.

She had failed.

As the glowing ball of light expanded, the Tamagotchi vibrated in a series of finger-tingling pulses. The witch looked at Keyser, who was waving his front paw. This was probably the last time she'd ever set eyes on him. It sucked donkey balls that he had to say goodbye as a digital pet.

Magnolia cried out, and the witch's eyes snapped to the QT. The white bubble had lost its perfect spherical form. It surged and billowed like a cloud, flowing over and around the device. And Chad was already inside it. His body shifted and shrank as he transformed.

"No!" The witch lunged toward him, but the Dread Lord still clutched her arm. "Let go of me!" She struggled to free herself, but he only clung tighter. As the field continued to grow, the Tamagotchi's vibrations intensified. Keyser clawed at the screen as if he could dig his way free.

"Magnolia!" the Dread Lord cried.

The plastic egg buzzed again. On the tiny screen, Keyser jabbed a finger at her waist.

No, he was pointing at the carabiner clipped to her belt loop, where she'd hung Vera's bolo tie.

Even when it seems all hope is lost, She is only a prayer away.

The witch clasped the golden apple, closed her eyes, and poured her rage and grief and pain into a wordless, desperate plea to her goddess.

The electrical hum of the QT ceased, and the Dread Lord of Human Resources squeezed her arm.

"Witch, what did you *do?*"

Her eyes flew open. The Dread Lord released her and walked toward the QT. The white cloud hung motionless in the air with her transformed friends stuck inside like fruit in a Jell-O mold.

The Dread Lord turned and looked at her, his pierced eyebrows raised. "What is. . ." His eyes darted to something behind her. "Someone else is here!"

The witch whirled, expecting to find. . .Well, she wasn't sure who or what she'd been expecting, but it certainly wasn't a spinning office chair. She saw a flash of bright blue as the seat's occupant dragged a toe along the ground to slow her rotation.

Vera fucking Vásquez.

The witch fell to her knees. *Thank you, Discordia.*

"It's so damn good to see you," she said. "We thought you were—"

"Oh, Azathoth, Cold One who sleeps at the center of the multiverse, forgive us for waking thee from thy eternal slumber!" The Dread Lord knelt beside her, covering the tattooed face of his human suit with his hands.

"What are you going on about?" The witch looked from Vera, who was smoothing the fabric of her *QAnon Is for Qlueless Qrackpots* T-shirt, to the cowering Dread Lord.

He whimpered, shaking his head. "Spare my life, mighty Azathoth, for I am with child!"

"No, that's not. . ." She stood and tugged him to his feet. "That's *Vera.*"

"I assure you, Witch," he said, lowering his hands to glare at her, "I recognize my god when I see him. Behold, the bivalve shell on manifold legs, the tentacular protuberances, the fearsome face." His voice dropped to a trembling whisper. "The loathsome beard."

"That's me," Vera said. "The Great and Terrible Bearded Clam." She kicked off for another spin.

When Vera finally drifted to a stop, the witch focused on her and opened her third eye. Vera smiled and waved. Then her image shifted, and the witch saw. . .

Mother of dragons, she saw a godsdamned enormous hairy mollusk. The image twisted again, and she saw a man in a suit. Another shift, and she saw Nanny's marble goat head. And behind it all was a swirling, glittering ocean of light. Its colors ran circles around Roy G. Biv, dancing into impossible hues the witch had never seen before.

She closed her third eye. The blasted thing must be shorting out.

The Dread Lord frowned and peered at Vera. "Now that you mention it, I do detect a hint of Vásquez."

Vera waved a hand. "Oh, see whatever you like. You people always do anyway." She stood and straightened her pencil skirt. Bizarrely, she wore a men's dress sock—just one, not a pair. It was bright blue with a white phone booth emblazoned on the shin.

The witch froze. She recognized that sockrifice.

"Sometimes, just for fun," Vera said, "I even introduce myself as Eris."

Eris. *Heiress.*

The witch was in the presence of Discordia, who was also apparently the thrice-cursed Idiot God of the Archons. Vera had been Discordia's avatar all along—guiding the witch, manipulating her, *using* her. She'd recommended the witch's services to Mitsuki. She'd been Heather's suspiciously effective campaign manager. And She'd left so many clues along the way, dropped so many puzzle pieces into the witch's lap.

But why the hell would Discordia want to get Heather elected? Heather had betrayed them, sold them out to Carcosa.

"To tell the truth, I just really liked her vibe," Vera said.

Of course she could read minds.

"I have a soft spot for strong women. Besides, I knew she'd come around."

The Dread Lord looked from Vera to the witch. "Whose vibe? Who'd come around?"

The witch shook her head. "Doesn't matter." She scowled at the goddess. "Your timing is shit. The device has already been triggered. Once time starts up again, we're screwed."

"Not necessarily." Vera held her hands up, making finger guns, and shot the control panel. A stunned swarm of titanium insects appeared.

"Ichagno," the Dread Lord of Human Resources breathed.

The witch rolled her eyes and crossed her arms. "If you can do that, why don't you just frigging fix this?"

"That's not how it works, mija." Vera blew on the ends of her smoking index fingers and holstered them at her waist. "If you want to be saved, you've got to do it yourself. I've tried it the other way. Never ends well." She sat down in the office chair and looked up at the witch. "But I might be persuaded to help." She kicked off and set the chair spinning.

The witch waited, seething, for the chair to drift to a halt. She hooked a thumb toward the Dread Lord of IT. "Is that the help?" she asked. "Please tell me you're not just giving us metal bugs and pissing off to. . .to wherever the hell it is you usually lurk."

"I stopped time for you, didn't I?" Vera said, gearing up for another spin. "And that'll hold until the sand runs out."

"What sand?"

Vera pointed at the witch's formerly empty left hand, which now held a small hourglass.

"Can you at least bring Keyser back?" the witch asked.

"Keyser Söze never left you."

She ground her teeth. To the seven hells with Discordianism. If she made it out of this, she was signing up with the Pastafarians. They grew excellent weed, and their potlucks were legendary.

"I'll tell you three things before I go. One," Vera said, raising her index finger, "this machine makes doors. All you do is enter the coordinates for where you want to go, and abracadabra! Doors work both ways, but this one only locks from one side."

She raised her middle finger. The witch seriously considered raising hers as well.

"Two, you're stronger together."

"Who's stronger together?" asked the Dread Lord of Human Resources.

Vera's ring finger joined the other two. "And three. . ." The ghostly image of Nanny's hircine face appeared, superimposed over Vera's features. "Re-meh-eh-eh-ember my lessons," she brayed. Then she dug her heel into the cavern floor and pushed off. The chair spun faster and faster until Vera was nothing but a blur.

And then just nothing.

The empty chair drifted to a halt. In the eerie stillness of her wake, the Dread Lord raised his hand. "Ahem. I'm not quite sure what Azathoth wants us to do."

"I told you," she snapped. "That was Vera Vásquez."

Who was also Discordia.

Who was also Nanny.

Who was also, apparently, the Idiot God.

Bloody hell.

"And I don't know either." The witch chewed her bottom lip. Discordia had given them three cosmic revelations. What did they mean? The irritating buzz of Ichagno's insect horde rasped at her attention like a cheese grater. "Well, she unfroze Mr. Personality over there. He's got to be part of the plan."

But what was so special about the Dread Lord of IT? All he did was force cybersecurity training down everyone's throats and screw around with the scheduling software.

Her eyes widened. The scheduling software.

The Swarm had used dreams to seed Carcosa's brain with the concept for the QT. He'd used the device to punch through to their layer and bring over an expeditionary HOA of little white men. That meant the coordinates for their universe were *already in the machine.*

If they could come here, she could go there, because doors work both ways. But she'd have to lock the door from the other side.

"I think I know what we have to do." The witch turned to Ichagno. Where was she supposed to focus? She picked a bug and met its faceted eyes. "The QT is linked to the Swarm's world. Can you pull those coordinates and use them in the scheduling software to send me there?"

The swarm rippled and flowed, ribbons of silver insects moving as one. The Dread Lord of HR looked at her expectantly.

"That was his answer?" The witch fought the urge to growl like Keyser Söze facing down the UPS guy. Sand seemed to slip through the hourglass faster by the second. "What did he say?"

"He says as long as the quantum tunnel is open, he can send you through. Archons can freely enter this layer, but he needs the tunnel to get you out."

She nodded to the metal bugs. "Let's do it." Some of Ichagno's. . .parts alit on the control panel, buzzing furiously.

"What will you do once you get there?" The Dread Lord of Human Resources wrung his hands. "Won't being in their realm turn you into one of those?" He gestured toward the LWM, frozen in time with one fist raised in triumph.

"Not if I destroy the tunnel right after time restarts."

"But. . ." His eyes filled with slimy tears. "But how will we get you back?"

Good question. Ichagno's connection would only hold while the door was open, and the reason she was going through was to close it.

Wasn't that a kick in the babymaker?

The witch pushed the thought away. If she let herself dwell on it, she might penis out. "We'll cross that bridge when we come to it." What else had Vera said? *Remember my lessons.* Well, Vera was the one who'd taught her the entropic strike. That must be how she could lock the Swarm's door. "Once I'm there, I'll blast the tunnel, and—"

"With what?"

"With the entropic strike, dumbass."

"There's no need to call names."

"I don't have time to coddle your delicate—"

"But you said you didn't have enough entropine to shield us from the gun."

By the weeping eye of Polyphemus, he was right. And she'd eaten the last of Vera's Holy Chao cookies. Maybe the Dread Lord of Human Resources could destroy the tunnel. She looked from his face, earnest under the black blotch of the spider tattoo, to his basketball belly.

No way.

"Can the Dread Lord of IT do it?"

"I think he's too. . .diffused. Besides, he can't send and be sent at the same time." Gelatinous tears oozed down his cheeks. "It's over, Witch. They've won."

Why would Discordia have bothered showing up if there was no way to win? They had to be missing something.

You're stronger together.

The world's witches had been no match for the Archons when they burst forth from the Fathomless Abyss. Witches were individualists, anarchists, rebellious to a fault. According to witch lore, covens were just for dancing naked and getting shitfaced. When it came to magic, "cooperation" was a four-letter word. But the Archons were different—they were all bound to a mutual aid contract. When they needed power, they could simply draw from the reserves of the collective.

The witch cleared her throat. "What's the time frame on your Archonic mutual aid contract?"

"What?" The Dread Lord blinked in surprise. "Eternity."

Of fucking course.

"And does it work across layers of the Sheaf?"

"It originated in our home universe, and it's just as binding here as it was there. The contract is linked to each Archon, not to a specific location." His eyes grew as round as dinner plates. "You don't mean—"

"It's the only way," she said. "The Dread Lord of IT can send me over. Once time starts up again, I'll pull entropy through the contract to destroy the tunnel."

The Dread Lord sniffled. "We'll be. . .like brother. . .and sister. It's just. . .It's so—"

"Gods dammit, will you just do it before I change my mind?"

He wiped his face, stretching strands of slime from his cheeks to his fingers. The witch gagged. Brother and sister.

"Ahem. I'll, um. . .I'll need your true name, Witch."

She shook her head. "Like hell you will."

"I can't create the bond without your birth name," he said. "I'll use a pseudonym in the public astral copy. Just please not"—he lowered his voice to a whisper—"Connie Lingus."

Was she really going to do this? To become, for all intents and purposes, an Archon?

It was that or spend eternity as a little white man.

"Fine." She leaned toward him to whisper her name, but she hesitated when Ichagno's buzz ceased. That nosy shit was eavesdropping. "What about. . ." She jerked her head toward the titanium swarm.

The Dread Lord snapped his fingers, and a shimmering conical force field formed around them. "The cone of silence," he said with solemn reverence.

"I didn't know you could—"

"I learned it from watching you." He turned his ear toward her. A tiny tentacle waved merrily from the canal.

She pushed it back in with her thumb, put her lips to his ear, and whispered her name. It was the first time she'd spoken it aloud in. . .well, ever. As he drew up the contract, their minds opened to each other.

Here in the cone of silence, he knew her deepest secrets, and she knew his.

The witch raised her eyebrows. "You stole *The Get-It-On-Onomicon*?"

"Interspecies mating is complicated!"

That saucy little devil.

He furrowed his pierced eyebrows, annoyance shifting to anxiety. "You won't tell Ellie, will you?"

"I'll take it to my grave."

Which might happen sooner than she'd hoped.

An astral copy of the contract appeared in her mind's eye. She read the printed pseudonym under the line awaiting her signature.

"That's the public name you chose?"

"Is it okay?" he asked.

"It's freaking perfect."

The witch signed, and that was that. It was done. She felt into the bounds of the contract, sensing the immense reservoir of power pooled at the edges of her awareness.

Oh, this would do. This would do just fine.

The Dread Lord dropped the cone of silence and turned to Ichagno. "Ready?"

The titanium swarm shifted, and the witch's BlackBerry vibrated with an incoming calendar invitation. Once she accepted, that was it. She'd be gone, and even with the power of all Archonkind at her fingertips, she didn't know if she could return. She slid her BlackBerry out of her pocket and opened the invitation. Her thumb hovered over the screen.

"If I pull this off," she said, "what will happen to Chad and Magnolia? Will they be stuck like—"

"*Zzzee energetic backwazzzh from zzzee devizzze should rebound and rezzztore zzzem*," Ichagno said.

Huh. She really *was* an Archon now.

The Dread Lord of Human Resources wrapped his arms around her and squeezed, heedless of the hard bulge of his belly. "May it serve you right, you foul-mouthed turd blossom."

She blinked back tears. Damn dusty-ass cavern.

The witch touched the screen of her BlackBerry and clicked accept.

CHAPTER THIRTY-NINE

The Equal Suckitude Principle

The witch staggered. She'd thought teleportation was bad, but travel between universes was more nauseating than watching the Clerk consume the Sheriff's glowing organs. She swallowed hard against a flood of saliva. Her eyelids fluttered open, but she immediately squeezed them shut again. Gods, it was bright. As she watched the dancing spots on her eyelids, the soft hush of static filled her ears. White noise. She took a deep breath and opened her eyes.

The witch stood alone in a featureless void—an alabaster sea extending out to infinity. Where were all the little white men? Her eyes watered as she squinted into the milky distance, turning to examine the endless plain.

There.

A rippling circle of netherlight shimmered in midair. Its nimbus painted a faceted mountain with an octarine glow.

The netherlight emanated from the quantum tunnel opened by Carcosa's device. Now that she saw it, the full weight of her mission dragged her spirits down like a Deep One who'd snagged a Girl Scout. There was no way around it. This had been a one-way trip. She could save herself, or she could save Magnolia and the Dread Lord of Human Resources and. . .

And Chad.

Not much of a decision after all.

The witch glanced at the hourglass, which was emptying faster than her Friday-night bottle of Chicken Cock. She sprinted toward the tunnel, trying not to jostle the hourglass. She stopped at the foot of the towering crystalline mountain, just a few yards from the door that led home. Her fingers formed the sacred K. All she could do now was wait for the sand to run out.

The familiar sound of footsteps echoing on a tile floor shattered her concentration. She spun to find a man walking toward her. Not a little white man. . .a human—specifically, the suited man she'd seen when she looked at Vera with her Sight. His black business suit and red tie stood out against the snowy background like an undercover cop at a warehouse rave. Wire-rimmed glasses topped his weak-chinned face, and his gray hair was streaked with white. He stopped six feet away from her and offered a bland politician's smile, the kind that doesn't reach the eyes.

"Welcome to utopia," he drawled.

"This empty hellhole is your idea of utopia?"

"Oh, it won't be empty for long," he said. "That deity of yours is playing with time again, but it'll start up soon. And when it does, my syntropium crystal will provide me with billions of followers."

Oh, *balls*.

The mountain looming over her was pure syntropium—tons and tons of it. That's why Chad and Magnolia had been transformed when the tunnel opened. That's what Carcosa's passenger meant when he said they'd "make this world suitable." And that's why there were no little white men in sight. Whether they'd volunteered or been forced, the poor bastards had been crystallized. Probably no great loss for a hive mind, but still. . .

"Who the hell are you?" the witch asked. "A little white man?"

"Ma'am, I'm not *a* little white man," he said. "I'm *the* little white man: the Great White. This"—he swept a hand over his face and body—"is just to put you at ease."

Discordia must've shown her this guy for a reason. The Archons worshipped Azathoth, so this douchebag must be the Swarm's deity. Was there a chance she could negotiate with him? A chance she didn't have to stay here and die alone? The sand was getting low, but she had a little time left. It was worth a shot.

"Wiping out a universe makes me very freaking uneasy."

"You just can't see the big picture." He tapped his temple with one forefinger. "Small mind. I'll try to put in terms you can understand."

That mansplaining piece of—

"This is all part of an endless tournament between the forces of order—that's me, the good guy—and the forces of disorder." He waggled his fingers. "Your tentacled friends. I won the last match, and little lady, I intend to win this one as well."

"Little lady?" The witch bared her teeth. "Listen, you patriarchal asshat, if you want to have it out with Azathoth, take your dick-measuring contest away from here and leave us out of it."

"Who precisely is 'us'?"

She opened her mouth to say *humanity*, but that wasn't the whole truth, was it? The Archons needed saving too.

"'Us' is everyone," the witch said. "Everyone but you and Azathoth. You two can go battle it out somewhere else."

"You don't understand the rules of the game. The Idiot God and I cannot directly impact each other. We wage war through our followers. Until now, my only game pieces have been the little white men. The Idiot God has his messy, stringy nightmares." He took a step toward her, rubbing his hands together. "But now there's a new set of toys."

"Toys?" The witch checked the hourglass. Not much longer now. "Well, playtime's over, asshole."

"I'll end it myself," he said. "Decisively. Azathoth lets his creations run rampant without a never-you-mind. He won't even show up for the war. He just lays around dreaming." The man lifted his chin and straightened his lapels. "It's time for a leader who will lead. Besides, those monsters are a constant irritant. I can feel them through the dimensional membrane."

"You'd wipe out billions of sentient creatures because you're irritated?" The witch shook her head. "I don't know how you sleep at night."

"I generally sleep well," he said. "And if I ever do have trouble, I don't have to count sheep. I count all the layers of the Sheaf I plan to absorb. When we battled those monsters, I realized we didn't have to coexist with them. There was another way. A *better* way."

"Oh yeah?" the witch said. "Enlighten me."

"Assimilation." His blue eyes sparkled in the netherlight. "Don't you see? Everyone will be the same. No predators or prey, no class, no gender, no race, no religion. It's the way things *should* be. All I want," he said, "is true equality."

"Bullshit." The witch looked at him, not even trying to hide her disdain. "All you want is for people to be like *you*."

"Difference is a nuisance," he hissed. "A pestilence. A plague. You just don't understand, Witch. You're getting stuck on principles."

Principles.

The witch froze. When she'd looked at Vera with her Sight, she'd seen the Idiot God. And she'd seen the Great White. But she'd also seen Nanny, and the last thing Vera said before she vanished was *Remember my lessons*. She'd thought Vera meant the entropic strike, but Nanny had also given her lessons on the principles of Discordianism.

"When I'm done with the Sheaf, everyone will be the same," he said. "We'll all be little white men. We'll want the same things, be on the same team. Just imagine what we could accomplish if we—"

The witch tuned out his Bond-villain speech. She had to think.

In the space of a heartbeat, she was in her palace of memory.

The witch flopped on her beanbag, panting with exertion. "I thought using magic to clean my room would be easier."

Nanny shook her head with the sound of grinding stone. "It's just another kind of hard, little witch."

She stepped up onto her pedestal, and the witch rolled her eyes. Nanny was about to enter lecture mode.

"It's the Equal Suckitude principle of magic," she said. "If the mundane performance of a task sucks ass, the magical performance of that task must suck an equal amount of ass."

"Then what good is—"

"Speaking of principles, please recite the three key principles of Discordianism."

The witch stared at her fingernails, avoiding eye contact. "I didn't do the reading."

"We only have a year and a deh-eh-eh-ay," Nanny brayed. "You're wasting my time."

"You said rebellion is my sacred Discordian duty."

"Touché-eh-eh-eh." Nanny's face wrinkled in what the witch thought was a smile. (Marble goat faces were tough to read.) "Listen well, witchling. . .Discordianism teaches three key principles. The Aneristic principle is that of apparent order. The Eh-eh-eh-ristic principle is that of apparent disorder." She arched an eyebrow. "Any guesses about the third?"

The witch shrugged. Didn't know. Didn't care.

"The third is the principle that the first two are hogwash," Nanny said. "There is no distinction between order and disorder. They're artificial divisions of the true nature of reality. Only by rejeh-eh-eh-ecting the first two principles and embracing the third can you see reality for what it is."

The witch tried to wait her out, but statues are long on patience. "What is it?"

Nanny grinned, baring her protruding teeth. "Pure chaos."

Reality was chaos, a constant dance between order and disorder. Pure order wasn't natural. This white husk of a world yearned to be restored.

When the Dread Lord saw Vera/Discordia as the Idiot God, the witch thought that meant they were versions of the same deity, and the final battle would pit disorder against order in a death match for ultimate supremacy. But that wasn't it at all.

The Idiot God and the Great White were two kids trying to claim the high end of a seesaw. No one got to stay on top for long. . .and Discordia was the whole-ass playground.

"—and you'll see that my plan serves the best interests of everyone."

"Sure," the witch said absently. "Sounds good."

But what did this revelation mean? What should she *do*? She could close the quantum tunnel and seal off her world, but nothing would stop the Great White from trying again. He'd just target a new puppet to carry out his little white scheme, and now he knew their weaknesses.

"I'm so glad you agree." He offered her his hand with a slight bow. "Shall we shake on it?" His face wore a sly grin of triumph.

The witch took his hand, wincing at the electric buzz of his touch. "You're planning to whiten me, aren't you?"

He tugged her toward him. "Needs must when the devil drives, my dear."

The devil was driving this megalomaniac to eradicate everything that wasn't like him.

Wasn't like *him*. . .

Gods below, she knew what she had to do.

"Yeah? Now *I'm* taking the wheel."

The witch glanced at the hourglass. Only a smudge of sand remained. She dropped it and formed the sacred K with both hands, curling her fingers against the Great White's palm. As the last grain of sand fell, she fired an entropic strike at the quantum tunnel with her left hand. With her right, she opened a channel to the vast sea of Archonic energy pooled in the astral shell of her contract. The Great White tried to jerk his hand away as he sensed the cresting tsunami of entropy.

"You. . .you linked yourself to the Archons," he said. "My operative said they're your sworn enemies."

"They were." This time, it was the witch who pulled him closer. "The best way to vanquish your enemies is to turn them into friends."

The tunnel shivered and collapsed, resealing the dimensional membrane. She opened herself to the Great White, and the pure order of his syntropy met the pure disorder of the Archons' entropy in a swirling vortex of chaos. The Great White's eyes widened as realization dawned. He roared in outrage, draining entropine from her faster than even the gushing Archonic flow could replenish. Her hand pulled free of his as she collapsed, but he was too late to stop her. The damage was done.

As the witch's depleted body succumbed to the irresistible tide of unconsciousness, she saw a ribbon of blue flame streak skyward from the horizon. The vast syntropium crystal exploded into billions of sparkling motes of light.

The Great White was gone. Within seconds, so was the witch.

CHAPTER FORTY

Coming Home

Witch?" A cool hand caressed her cheek. "Come on, wake up."
She cracked an eyelid open. "Chad?"

"Welcome back." He took her hand and pulled her up. "Are you okay?"

Her head was pounding, and her mouth was as dry as a sand demon's dung, but considering she'd expected her jaunt to be a one-way trip, she was fan-frigging-tastic.

"I think so," she said. "What happened?"

"All I remember is uploading the Dread Lord of IT to the QT's control panel. Then there was a flash of white light. After that. . ." He shook his head and shrugged. "How'd you stop it?"

She propped her elbows on her knees and massaged her throbbing temples. What to say. . .

I spoke to an avatar of the Creatrix, sold my soul to the Archons, and defeated the quintessential little white man.

Nah. Best to keep it simple.

"I closed the tunnel from the other side and flooded the Swarm's universe with entropy."

"That's genius!" Chad gave her a fierce hug. "Entropy in a closed system can only increase."

"I definitely knew that."

The witch stood, swaying as a wave of dizziness washed over her. A flash of sparks drew her attention to the QT, which was now a smoking ruin. The spheres that had powered it were now melted white puddles. Dr. Carcosa buzzed around the wreckage like an agitated wasp.

"How did you get me back?" the witch asked. "I destroyed the tunnel, and the Archons can't teleport out of this layer without punching a hole. I figured the same would be true for the scheduling software."

"They can't teleport *out*, Witch, but the Dread Lord of IT had no problem bringing you *in*." Chad cocked his head, eyebrows drawing together. "What I don't get is how he latched on to you over there? Wouldn't you have to be—"

"One of them?" The witch sighed and nodded. "You're looking at the newest signatory to their master contract. I didn't have enough juice to get the job done without them." She lifted a shoulder. "It was the only way."

"So, you're. . .like, basically an Archon?"

"Yep."

"For how long?"

"Forever."

"I'm sorry, Witch," he said. "I know you—"

"Keyser Söze!" If Chad was back to normal, her familiar should be too. She looked around the cavern, searching for the furred mask of his face. "Have you seen Keyser?"

Chad rested one hand on her shoulder. "I'm sorry. . ."

Her hand found the plastic egg dangling from her belt. She unclipped it and looked at the screen. Keyser stared back at her. He rocked back on his haunches and pressed his paw against the display. She covered it with her fingertip.

After everything she'd done, everything she'd given up. . .

It wasn't fucking *fair*.

"You and Keyser must've been between worlds when. . ."

He didn't need to finish his sentence. She held the bitter truth in the palm of her hand.

A metallic jangle echoed through the space. Dr. Carcosa had picked up a warped and smoking fragment of his device, burning the suckers of his new appendage. He was probably stuck that way. The sphere had released too much entropy when—

Oh, gods—the sphere!

When the witch hit it with an entropic strike, the surge of entropy had restored Dr. Carcosa to his old self. She could do the same for Keyser. The sphere used on him was still sitting in a cooler in the basement of her building. With the whole impending end-of-the-world thing, she'd never gotten around to giving it to Carcosa for safekeeping. The witch pulled entropine from her new contract and snapped her fingers. The cooler appeared in front of her. She took off the lid, and there it was—Keyser's salvation.

Hang on, buddy.

"Chad, I can use this to bring Keyser back," she said. "All I need to do is—"

A cry of grief tore through the cavern. The witch spun and saw Magnolia lying on the ground, her head resting in Sathach's lap. Her pale green melon quivered with the force of her sobs, and the Dread Lord's face was slimed with viscous tears. The sudden sprouting of several dozen tentacles had torn her leggings to shreds as the entropic backwash recovered her original form.

"It'll be okay," the Dread Lord said, stroking her seafoam skin. "Everything will be okay."

The Tamagotchi vibrated in the witch's hand. She looked down to see Keyser pointing at Magnolia. The witch closed her eyes and squeezed the plastic egg of his prison so hard, he vibrated in protest.

No. It was too much for him to ask of her, even for a friend.

Keyser buzzed again. Pointed again.

Her memory showed her Magnolia at the fire station, shivering so hard her teeth chattered but grinning like a godsdamned idiot.

Being in this body feels like. . .like coming home.

The witch took a shuddering breath, opened her eyes, and grabbed Chad's arm. "Give this to Magnolia," she said, pushing the cooler toward him with her foot.

He cocked his head and frowned. "Why?"

"Ellie said if we pressed the button again, it would suck up more entropy."

"Yeah," he said. "And then—*boom*."

A metal bug hit the witch squarely between the eyes. The rest of the Dread Lord of IT surrounded her in a humming cloud. *"If zzzhee zzztandzzz at the edge of the Abyzzzzzz, zzzhee can drop the zzzphere after zzzhee triggerzzz it."*

Grief squeezed her guts like Zsthaor's clawed fist. The sphere would be gone after that. *Gone g*one.

"Tell her to stand at the edge of the Abyss, activate the sphere, and throw it in right after it goes off."

His eyes widened. "That should work! But *you* should be the one to—"

"She won't do it if she has time to think about what it means for. . .for. . ." The witch looked at Keyser, who held her gaze and nodded. "Just take it, asshole!"

Chad lifted the sphere from the cooler and walked across the cavern to Magnolia, trailed by Ichagno's host of titanium wasps. He crouched, handed her the sphere, and relayed the witch's instructions. Then he helped the Dread Lord of HR to his feet and escorted him well clear of the detonation zone.

The witch closed her eyes, but she heard the soft plastic snick as Magnolia pushed the button, as her hopes for Keyser's return died. A few seconds later, a brilliant flare of white light blazed. She heard a cry of joy from Magnolia, tearful congratulations from the Dread Lord.

It worked.

Good. That was. . .good.

Keyser vibrated in her hand, and she glanced at the Tamagotchi's screen. A blinking question mark hovered over his head. She nodded, and he did a little happy dance. Her eyes filled with tears.

"Witch!"

She looked up to see Chad jogging toward her and turned away to wipe her face on her sleeve.

"Hey, Chad, do you think we could get out of—"

Her voice cut off in a strangled gasp as he wrapped her in a bone-crushing hug. "I told you you're not a total piece of shit." He released her and stepped back, grinning.

"I try." The witch swallowed against the tightness in her throat. "Hey, um. . .do you think we could build one of those spheres?"

The grin faded. "We can try, Witch, but Ellie couldn't even tell what it's made of. The materials aren't from *here*." When her face fell, he said, "We'll keep at it, though. Ellie and I won't stop trying until we find a—"

"Greetings, Witch."

She turned at the sound of the Clerk's voice. Micana'gos oozed toward her, flanked by Hank and his Spectral Forces comrades. Heather had arrived too, but she had eyes only for Sathach. If she hugged him any harder, she was gonna pop that baby right out.

"The entire world owes you a debt of—"

Magnolia practically clotheslined the Clerk on her mad dash to reach the witch.

"You gave up the last sphere so I could become human again," Magnolia said, "knowing it meant that Keyser would. . .would be. . ." She wrapped her arms around the witch and squeezed.

The Clerk's half dozen eyes were burning holes in Magnolia's back. In fact, the whole frigging cavern was watching them. Gods, this was awkward. Maybe the witch could melt a hole in the rock to escape.

"Remember what you said at Larry's?" Magnolia asked, releasing her. The witch shook her head. "You told me it would be a cold day in hell before you'd sacrifice yourself for an Archon."

"I never actually *said* Archon."

But they both knew she'd been thinking it.

"Not only did you risk your life for all of us, you. . .you gave up. . ."

"I suppose it must be snowing in Hades," the Clerk said. "I was going to offer my sincere thanks, but it appears you've been subjected to all the gratitude you can endure. So, I shall offer you something else."

A shimmering spark of netherlight appeared in front of the Clerk. Her shroud rustled as she raised a dripping tentacle. It snaked through the portal, and a few of her eyes squinted in concentration. "I know I saw it right. . .over. . .here. . ."

"What are you—"

"Aha!" the Clerk crowed. She reeled in the tentacle and allowed the portal to collapse. "Magnolia was wrong. You did not give up the *last* sphere." The ropy limb lowered to the floor and its coils fell away, revealing a slime-covered white ball. "I'm quite sure Mother won't mind."

The witch stared at it. She could get Keyser back. . .*right now.*

She met a pair of the Clerk's eyes and nodded. "Thank you." As soon as her fingers brushed the sphere, it zapped the shit out of her, and she yanked her hand away.

"I've got it," Chad said, but then the residue of Clerkian slime burned *him.*

One quick healing spell and a swipe of the Clerk's anti-corrosive shroud later, they were ready.

"Make some room!" the witch yelled. She set the Tamagotchi on the cavern floor and motioned for Chad to put the sphere next to him.

"*Zzztop!*" Ichagno's bugs formed a wall between Chad and Keyser. "*Take the zzzphere zzzomewhere with high background entropy. Little brother muzzzt have the lowezzzt entropy in the detonation zzzone.*"

Little brother?

Well, if the witch was now an Archon, she supposed Keyser was one too.

"What did the Dread Lord say?" Chad asked.

"Take him to the softball field," the Clerk said. "It's saturated with the relentless chaos of the threenage army."

A spark of netherlight appeared and grew into a human-sized portal. The witch picked up the Tamagotchi, gripped Chad's hand, and stepped through. The full moon illuminated a field littered with confetti, Goldfish crackers, and candy wrappers. She could almost hear Paisleigh's bloodcurdling shrieks of defiance.

Yep, this should do.

She knelt and set the Tamagotchi on a drift of confetti. The golden apple slide of Vera's bolo tie glinted in the moonlight. *Don't you dare screw me over*, she prayed. *You owe me, gods dammit.*

The witch nodded to Chad, unable to speak, and he set the sphere next to the Tamagotchi. They jogged back to a safe distance. She drew entropy from the Archonic pool, formed the sacred K, and fired. The white shell cracked like an egg, and a prismatic energy field billowed out and swallowed Keyser whole. The witch squeezed her eyes shut. She couldn't bear to look.

Twenty-one pounds of raccoon hit her chest like a furry bowling ball. Tears streamed down her cheeks as she wrapped her arms around Keyser and held him as tightly as she dared. He rubbed his muzzle against her neck, almost purring. Then he bit her shoulder, pissed down the front of her shirt, and wriggled free. Eyes watering now with pain as much as emotion, she watched the little shit waddle through the field, hunting for uneaten candy.

Magnolia was right.

It felt like coming home.

CHAPTER FORTY-ONE

Magna Innominanda

T hree weeks later

The witch of Tophet County slipped into the Read at Your Own Risk room. She glanced over her shoulder and locked eyes with Lululemon, who gave a brisk nod. A chime sounded from the intercom system.

"Attention, patrons," gargled the Dread Librarian. "We invite you to join us in the children's section for story time."

A shrill cry shrieked from the walkie talkie in her bag. Pumpkin Spice was broadcasting live so the witch would know if Chlogha was heading her way. She adjusted the volume to a tolerable level.

"Paisleigh, we do not bite our friends!"

Excellent. The threenagers were in place.

"Spit that out right now!"

Judging by the bloodcurdling screams, Paisleigh had just taken an ear in combat. She was a fierce little thing. Good negotiator, too. When the witch showed up to claim her broom, Paisleigh held out for twenty bucks and an inexhaustible supply of Dum-Dums.

The witch eased the door closed and slid the lock bar into its socket. She deposited her squirming backpack on the table and unzipped it, then she scanned the bookshelves and whispered a spell of summoning. A thick book burst from the shelves and flew into her palms with a satisfying *thwack*.

The witch smiled. At long last, she was going to give the Dread Lord of Human Resources exactly what he deserved. When their minds joined, she'd seen his soul laid bare. She knew his secrets, including how he'd stolen *The*

Get-It-On-Onomicon. She'd been expecting a complicated illusion or a subdimensional secret passage, but his method was painfully simple. All it required was an X-Acto knife and a roll of tape. Of course, she could've just asked the Dread Librarian for what she wanted, but it was the principle of the thing. If Sathach could steal a Nomicon, then by Discordia, so could she.

A rustling flutter drew her attention back to the shelves. A familiar freckled volume lurked at the end of a row. Lovecraft. That spying, sneaking douchebag.

The witch had come prepared. She unclasped her black velvet cloak, spread it out on the table, and clapped her hands. *The Necronomicon* lurched into the air and landed on the table with a *thud.* She bundled the fabric around the struggling book. Keyser Söze nosed his way out of the bag, sniffed the cloak, and plopped on top of it for an impromptu nap.

"Paisleigh, put your pants back on!"

Gods, that kid had the soul of a Discordian. She'd make one hell of a witch if she had a smidge more entropine.

The witch's BlackBerry vibrated. She glanced at the screen and saw a text from Chad.

It starts at eleven. Don't be late.

It was already ten past nine. No time to waste.

The witch sliced away a square of cellophane around the barcode sticker on the back of *The Lazy Gourmand's Calamari Cookbook.* It seemed an appropriate choice for this task. Now came the tricky part. The Nomicons didn't have book jackets, so she had to wiggle the knife under the barcode sticker without wrinkling or tearing it. After a few minutes and a few creative curse words, she swapped the barcodes, taped them in place, and inserted the cookbook into the gap on the shelves.

After she'd returned *The Necronomicon* to its spot and incinerated her cloak (no amount of washing would remove the psychic taint of Lovecraft's ass cheek), she left the RAYOR room with Keyser riding shotgun in her backpack. The lobby rang with the shouts of exasperated parents and the battle cries of recalcitrant preschoolers as the witch headed for the self-service kiosk. Her heart pounded as she scanned the bar code. But the computer obediently printed a receipt, and she was on her way. She glanced at the checkout slip as she pushed through the lobby doors, her eyes tracing the letters of the pseudonym Sathach chose for her.

Magna Innominanda. Roughly translated, the Great Not-to-Be-Named.

She couldn't resist a cackle of triumph as she kicked her broom into the air and streaked out of downtown Asphodel.

Welcome, Tophet County Employees, to the Mountains of Madness Casino and Convention Center! The first annual team-building retreat will begin at eleven with icebreakers in the Cthulhu Room, followed by a light luncheon.

The witch shuddered as she crumpled the agenda and threw it over her shoulder.

"Witch!"

Chad glared at the paper with his hands propped on his hips. "Come on, now," he said. "Somebody has to pick that up."

She snapped her fingers, and the paper curled and blackened, burning away to a smudge of ash. "Happy, Mr. Clean? You—"

Her voice cut off with a squeak as he wrapped her in a fierce hug.

"Man, it's great to see you," Chad said. "How was your vacation?"

The Dread Lord of Human Resources had insisted she take a few weeks off. As a signatory to the master contract of the Archons, her travels were no longer limited to Tophet County. She and Keyser had fulfilled a lifelong dream and spent eighteen glorious days in Key West. He'd come home with sand fleas and battle wounds from fighting a gang of six-toed cats, but gods dammit, they'd seen the ocean.

"Incredible. Did you have a good. . .whichever holiday you celebrate?"

"Christmas," he said. "Yeah, it was nice."

"I'm glad." The witch glanced at the large wall clock, which read 9:41. "Which way?"

He pointed at a door labeled *Employees Only*. "Need any help?"

"No." The word popped out automatically, the product of years of stubborn self-reliance. But as Chad turned to go, the witch reconsidered. "On second thought, I wouldn't mind a hand."

He broke into a wide grin—gods, what a smile—and gestured toward the door with a gallant bow. "After you."

The witch wound through a labyrinth of service hallways until she arrived at her destination. She pushed through a metal swinging door and looked around the large room. It was antiseptically clean and filled with arcane tools she'd never seen, much less used. This would be a true test of her skills, both magical and mundane.

She freed Keyser from her backpack and set out a bowl of water and a dish of trail mix. By the time she walked back to the stainless steel counter where Chad waited with the book, Keyser was face down in his food bowl.

"*The NomNomicon: Tasty Treats for Any Occasion*," Chad read. "So how do we do this?"

"We tell it what we need, and it'll create the recipe." She whispered to the pages, and the book shivered and fluttered open.

Chad whistled. "That looks complicated. Think we can pull it off in time?"

She arched an eyebrow. "I'm the County Witch. Of course we can." But damn if it wouldn't be tight. "Let's get the ingredients."

"Sure thing." Chad propped his elbows on the counter, his shoulder pressed against hers, and started reading. He pointed to a line of text and frowned. "'Personal foci from both parties.' What does that—"

"Heather already gave that to me."

"'Miscellaneous pupae'?" His eyes widened. "What kind of recipe *is* this?"

"I'll take care of the magical elements." She tapped a column of more conventional items. "You grab this stuff."

Even with both of them working at top speed and the witch burning through entropine to speed up the baking process, they didn't finish until six past noon. Heather was probably shitting bricks. They eased the bulky creation onto a wheeled cart and hauled ass toward the Cthulhu Room. The witch left Chad guarding the cart—more accurately, protecting its cargo from Keyser, who sat on Chad's shoulder and eyed it with naked hunger—and crept through the open door.

The Dread Lord of Human Resources stood in the center of a circle of employees. One hand rested on the swell of his abdomen, which was emphasized by a paternity-cut business suit. An eager smile animated his tattooed face. "Now that we've made our introductions, let's dive right into team-building with a round of trust falls. Who'd like to begin?"

The room was silent, save for the shuffling of feet and the psychic buzz of mental pleas for death's sweet release.

"I'll start," called the witch.

Magnolia beamed and stepped aside, opening the circle so she could enter.

"I'm so glad you're here, Witch," Sathach said. "You're technically still on vacation. You didn't have to—"

"How do we do this?"

"Choose your partner," he said. "It's best to select someone of a similar—"

"You." She walked toward him, stopping an arm's length away. "I choose you."

The bar in his pierced septum glinted in the fluorescent light. "Me?"

"You heard me."

"But. . .but I'm. . ." He gestured vaguely to his midsection. "I can't—"

"Do you trust me?"

The Dread Lord met her eyes. Well, one eye did. The other was rolling around like a pig in shit.

She closed the distance between them and took his hands, then repeated her question in a whisper. "Do you trust me?"

"I. . ." He looked from their clasped hands to her face. "I do."

"Excellent." The witch gripped his shoulders and spun him to face away from the door. She searched the circle, found Heather, and nodded to her. "All right, cross your arms and close your eyes."

Ellie flashed her a thumbs-up, confirming that Sathach had followed her directions. The witch waved a hand to dispel the illusion she'd had Hank set up in the room. The projection faded, revealing a large banner on one wall. It displayed a soft-focus portrait of a shirtless Sathach with Heather embracing him from behind, her hands cradling his baby bump. On the opposite wall, garlands of streamers and balloons framed a table loaded with gifts.

"I'm heavier than I look," he said. "Are you sure you can—"

"I'm sure." The witch glanced over her shoulder. Hank and Chad wheeled the cake into the circle behind her. Hank looked at Sathach and raised his eyebrows in question. She nodded for him to join her on the business end of the trust fall. "On the count of three," she said. "One. . .two. . .three!"

The Dread Lord toppled backward. Hank and the witch staggered under his weight as they caught him and heaved him upright. He turned to face them, sporting a wide grin.

"That was—" His voice broke off as he took in the transformed room. Heather joined him in the center of the circle and took his hand. He looked from her to the witch, his eyes shimmering. "Is this—"

"It's a baby shower." Heather stood on tiptoes and kissed his cheek. "*Our* baby shower."

"And the cake," he said. "That's for us, too?"

The witch shook her head. "No." His face rippled in distress. She hurriedly added, "The cake's just for *you*."

"And it's not just any cake," Chad said.

The Dread Lord stepped closer and examined the confection, which looked like a giant rubber ducky. One wing held a sign that read *What the duck is it?*

"It's a species-reveal cake!" He looked at Heather. "I thought you didn't want to find out."

"The witch talked me into it," she said. "Besides, I knew it was important to you."

"Can I. . ." He gestured toward the giant duck.

"Hell yeah," Chad said. "The suspense is killing me."

Sathach picked up a knife and carved a piece of cake. He lifted it onto a plate and examined it. "I don't understand. . .It's just plain chocolate."

"Look!" Heather pointed to the gap where he'd removed the slice.

The missing wedge revealed an empty cavity in the center of the cake. A flash of motion inside startled the Dread Lord, who stepped back in alarm. A butterfly fluttered its way into the air, prompting a chorus of oohs and aahs. Its wings shimmered with a riot of color. Instead of the expected slender, segmented body, the wings of this butterfly were attached to a writhing knot of tiny tentacles.

"It's an Archon!" Heather cried. "Oh, Sathach, I'm so—"

"There's another," Magnolia said.

A second butterfly emerged from the center of the cake. Its wings were black, and it had a tiny human face. As it flew, sparks of white light spewed from its wings.

"We've got a human, too," Heather said.

"Not just any human." Sathach met the witch's eyes. "That's a witchling."

"A witchling?" Heather asked with a faint smile. "That's. . .that's just. . ."

She dropped like a stone.

The witch stepped out onto the patio and slid the glass door closed behind her. She set her backpack down on the flagstones, unzipped it, and released Keyser Söze to do his business. Truth be told, she'd needed the break as much as he did. All this happy friendship shit was wonderful, but it was a big change.

Gods, *so* much had changed.

Sathach and Heather were married, the first interspecies couple in Tophet County to take the plunge. (She'd kept Chad's last name. Her maiden name was Poots, and pronouncing Sathach's surname caused human tongues to fork.) Heather was still the mayor, but she'd relinquished the helm of her leggings empire to Pumpkin Spice and shuttered the It Hurts!™ weight-loss-wrap business. Her new side hustle was selling vegan human suits and multi-species sex toys (or, as she called them, "intimacy enhancers").

Magnolia and Ellie were still dating, but they weren't rushing to the altar. In fact, Ellie was gearing up to take a leave of absence in the fall to finish up her PhD in dimensional physics under Dr. Carcosa. He and Mitsuki hadn't been able to make it today. They were off on a couples' yoga retreat to work on their marriage. (When the witch passed their regrets on to Heather, she winked and said that, given the size of Mitsuki's order from Toys in Us, their relationship would be just fine.)

Pretty much everyone else from work had come. . .Ronnie, the Clerk, most of the High Lords and Dread Lords. The Unseen Creeping Horror and the Living Flood couldn't attend due to logistical challenges, but they'd sent gifts, as had the Dread Lord of Corrections. The witch had seen to that.

Of course, Vera wasn't here either. The black butterfly flitted in front of the witch, trailing streamers of glittering sparks.

Then again, maybe she was.

The witch watched the butterfly land on the tightly closed bud of a potted chrysanthemum, which promptly opened into full bloom. Her life felt totally different but also the same. She was still the County Witch, but she was also, for all intents and purposes, an Archon. She still had Keyser, but she also had. . .friends.

A choked sob interrupted her train of thought. She looked around and spotted a tangle of black locs sprouting from the slanted back of an Adirondack chair positioned between two patio heaters.

"Chad?"

He leaped to his feet, wiping his cheeks with the sleeve of his sweater. "Uh, hey, Witch," he said, trying for nonchalance and failing miserably.

"What's wrong?"

He flashed a wry smile and held up a book. The cover depicted a woman in a black dress and a white bonnet gazing up into the eyes of a strapping young farmhand sporting a round-brimmed straw hat. *The Thrill of the Chaste.*

The witch's stomach plummeted to her toes, but she plastered her game face on. "What in the seven hells are you reading?"

He frowned. "Seriously?" At her uncomprehending stare, he said, "Don't you remember? You wouldn't shut up about this series that night we went to Asenath's."

She most certainly did *not* recall that conversation. Her cheeks burned.

"You were right," Chad said. "It's a great love story. I just preordered the last book."

"Oh. Um. . .cool." Desperate for a distraction, the witch snapped her fingers and a lit Swisher Sweet appeared in her hand.

Chad sighed and shook his head.

"It's a free country."

"Sure, you can smoke all you want," he said. "I just. . .It's not good for you." He shrugged. "I worry."

"You do?"

Now it was *his* turn to blush. "I do."

She bent down and stubbed the cigarillo out on the ground, then tossed it into a trash can. "Better?"

"Much."

The patio door opened, and Heather leaned out. "Get in here," she called. "We're about to open gifts!" She disappeared inside but left the door standing open—a not-so-subtle hint.

The witch whistled for Keyser. He trundled out of the bushes and flopped down in a sunny spot on the pavement, shamelessly seeking a belly rub. She knelt and stroked his silky fur.

"What do you think will happen?" Chad asked.

"Raising a witchling won't be easy, but they'll figure it out." She gave Keyser's belly a final pat and stood. "And I'll be around if they need help."

"Not that." He raised the book. "I meant Amos and Sarah's breakup. We've got a few months to wait for *Chaste Makes Waste.*"

"Hmm. I'm not sure."

"You know what I think?" Chad said, stepping closer to her.

The butterflies from Sathach's cake seemed to have taken up residence in her abdomen. "What's that?"

He slid his arms around her waist and rested his forehead against hers. "It's been a long time coming, but I think they'll wind up together."

The witch looked up and met his deep brown eyes. A wave of liquid heat rolled from her chest to a more southerly location. "I think so too."

Chad flashed that sunbeam smile of his. "I was hoping you'd say that."

About the Author

J. H. Schiller writes satirical stories about tentacled eldritch monsters and the horrors of bureaucracy. In an earlier incarnation, she earned a graduate degree in international affairs and spent more than a decade working for the federal government in Washington, DC. She has since escaped to Ohio, where she writes full-time.

DISCOVER
STORIES UNBOUND

PodiumAudio.com

www.ingramcontent.com/pod-product-compliance
Lightning Source LLC
Jackson TN
JSHW080156141224
75386JS00029B/871